ALSO BY LAURA HANKIN

Happy & You Know It
A Special Place for Women
The Daydreams

One-Star Romance

LAURA HANKIN

BERKLEY

New York

BERKLEY
An imprint of Penguin Random House LLC
penguinrandomhouse.com

Copyright © 2024 by Laura Hankin
Penguin Random House supports copyright. Copyright fuels creativity, encourages diverse
voices, promotes free speech, and creates a vibrant culture. Thank you for buying an authorized
edition of this book and for complying with copyright laws by not reproducing, scanning, or
distributing any part of it in any form without permission. You are supporting writers and
allowing Penguin Random House to continue to publish books for every reader.

BERKLEY and the BERKLEY & B colophon are registered trademarks of
Penguin Random House LLC.

Library of Congress Cataloging-in-Publication Data

Names: Hankin, Laura, author.
Title: One-star romance / Laura Hankin.
Description: First edition. | New York : Berkley, 2024.
Identifiers: LCCN 2023035706 (print) | LCCN 2023035707 (ebook) |
ISBN 9780593438213 (trade paperback) | ISBN 9780593438237 (ebook)
Subjects: LCGFT: Romance fiction. | Novels.
Classification: LCC PS3608.A71483 O54 2024 (print) |
LCC PS3608.A71483 (ebook) | DDC 813/.6—dc23/eng/20230815
LC record available at https://lccn.loc.gov/2023035706
LC ebook record available at https://lccn.loc.gov/2023035707

First Edition: June 2024

Printed in the United States of America
1st Printing

Book design by Daniel Brount

To Dave and Rosie,
who showed me new meanings of love

Perhaps if I make myself write I shall find out what is wrong with me.

—Dodie Smith, *I Capture the Castle*

One-Star Romance

★☆☆☆☆

Part One

MAY 2013

FROM: AngusStoatTheThird@gmail.com
TO: NatalieShapiro5@gmail.com, RobertKapinsky
@gmail.com, and 72 others
SUBJECT: A Very Gabby Party

Greetings, fellow appreciators of Gabriella Alvarez!

I am parachuting into your inboxes to inform you that Friday is your lucky night. My beautiful girlfriend is turning twenty-five and has agreed to let us celebrate her. I've reserved the bar area at The Pig, the Duck & the Farmer on 33rd Street starting at 7:30 p.m. We shall gather for general merriment, food and drink, and maybe even a serenade if enough members of my business school a capella group can make it. (Fellow members of the Large Scale Business Boys, let me know!)

Wear your finest party clothes. It's going to be a night to remember!

1

★☆☆☆☆

Natalie Shapiro was twenty-four years old, walking down a city street that smelled like hot garbage and possibility.

A couple of friends with whom she'd gone to college had moved out to the suburbs—already!—and she imagined they spent their time breathing in freshly mown grass. (And drinking wine? Waving to nosy neighbors? Power walking while wearing visors? Natalie didn't really know anything about the suburbs.) Others had been picked off by consulting firms that sent them across the country each week, and the smell of an airplane was more familiar to them than that of their own bedsheets.

But to Natalie, that hot garbage stench was magic. Not that she wanted to stand right over the trash bag to her left and take a deep breath, but it was nice to know it was there. Because things weren't supposed to be perfect and manicured at this age, not when you were bravely pursuing what you loved despite the difficulty of it.

Natalie loved writing. And sure, if the city's most high-powered literary agent appeared in front of her, leaping over the trash bag in her high heels to scream, *You! I could sense the power of your imagination from across the street, and I've already gotten you a six-figure book deal!*, Natalie would have taken that in a heartbeat. (Well, she might've had some questions: Was this agent in her right mind? Also, how did she jump in heels without breaking an ankle? Assuming it all checked out, though, Natalie would've signed right on the dotted line.)

But despite the occasional daydream, she knew it didn't work that way. Becoming a writer was tough, competitive. Anyone pursuing it was supposed to struggle and get discouraged for a little while. In fact, the struggle and the discouragement were what made a writer *good*. If everything came too easily to someone, whatever art she made would probably be shallow, doomed to be forgotten as soon as the reader turned away. So, while a writer figured out what lit her soul on fire and how to express that to the world, she worked a job she didn't care about, or maybe a handful of jobs she didn't care about cobbled together. At the moment, Natalie had four part-time gigs: dog-walker, personal assistant to a psychiatrist on the Upper West Side, caterer, and freelance writer for a website that paid her fifteen dollars an hour to regurgitate the latest celebrity gossip. She lived in a sixth-floor walk-up in a bedroom so tiny that she'd had to buy a bed with drawers built in underneath the mattress because there was no room for a bed *and* a dresser. To put on her clothes every morning, she had to climb on her bed to make space to open the drawers.

But as she juggled jobs and crouched on the bed, the real work was happening, the work of becoming a person with something to say. It was just like all those stairs Natalie had to walk up each day—the climb was annoying, but it did wonders for her health (and ass).

Besides, it didn't matter if Natalie's bedroom was tiny, because on the other side of the wall, her best friend lived in a slightly bigger bedroom. Natalie walked down those garbage-strewn streets toward the promise of a night stretching luxuriously ahead of her, a night when she might have the most fun she'd ever had or might end up weeping on a street corner at two a.m. And while she'd certainly prefer the fun version, at least the two a.m. weeping session could be dissected over coffee the next morning with said best friend, huddling, hungover, on their couch, listening to Stevie Nicks or Jenny Lewis or some other woman who understood their pain.

So Natalie charged ahead, stopping only to link arms with her roommate beside her. "Have I told you how absolutely smoking hot you look tonight?"

"Hm," Gabby said, tilting her head up, a smile cracking across her face. "At least twice."

"It's your birthday. You deserve a continuous stream of compliments."

"Then, please, continue."

"You look absolutely smoking hot."

"It's not too booby, is it?" Gabby gestured at the floral-patterned dress she was wearing, which was, in fact, rather boob-forward.

"You look amazing," Natalie said. "And besides, why not let the girls see the sights?"

Gabby cackled, Natalie's favorite laugh in the world. "You make it sound like they're my sheltered daughters, finally getting to leave the bunker." She pulled her top up a bit. "I don't know, Angus was being so unhelpful about how fancy this party was going to be. Like, I assumed it was a fun night out at a bar, but he just texted me, 'Do your parents prefer a man who wears a tie or a bow tie?' Which, first of all, is something that I do not think my parents have any opinion about, but, secondly, made me think that maybe he invited my *parents* to this?" Natalie pulled a face. Gabby's parents were wonderful, but they had given Gabby a curfew of 9:30 p.m. throughout high school and clearly wished they could still enforce it. "I love them, but I'm not looking to spend the whole night sipping a drink demurely while telling them about my progress at work."

"Right, it's your twenty-fifth birthday party. You're supposed to do something wild and crazy."

"I was thinking," Gabby said, "maybe tonight is the night that I finally dance on a table."

"Whoa, tiger."

"Okay, shut up. My cousin did it once and fell off and broke her rib. Also, I'm afraid of heights. So there's a lot to consider here."

"We can find you a low table," Natalie said. "Like, a coffee table."

Gabby nodded seriously. "You know how I get into it when I'm dancing, so please spot me. But if I'm falling off at the wrong angle, get out of my path. No sense in us both getting concussions." She smoothed down her thick wavy hair. "Of course, this whole conversation is moot if Angus *did* invite my parents."

"That does seem like something Angus would do," Natalie said, her tone snarkier than she'd intended. Gabby raised an eyebrow, and Natalie rushed on. "He's a great guy! But maybe he doesn't always think things all the way through?"

In other words, Angus was an absolute moron. Despite being in his midtwenties, Gabby's latest boyfriend was somehow an unholy amalgam of a sturdy middle-aged man (complete with beer belly and dad jokes) and a toddler who threw himself into all sorts of ridiculous situations because he hadn't yet learned anything about the world. Angus had managed to cling on to Natalie's gorgeous, ambitious, going-places best friend for a full year now, and Nat was not quite sure how. The most persuasive theory she'd hit upon was that Gabby and Angus shared a highly specific kink, and Gabby wanted to milk that for a while before settling down with a man who deserved her.

Sure, in the moments when Natalie really stopped and looked at herself in the mirror (pert face; dark brown hair that never quite did what she wanted it to do; big smile full of big teeth, resembling a cartoon mouse that some fairy godmother had turned human), she could admit that part of her disdain for Angus came from his trying to take her spot at Gabby's side.

Gabby and Nat had lived together ever since freshman year of college, when some administrator in the housing office had decided that Natalie Shapiro from Philadelphia and Gabriella Alvarez from Long Island would do just fine as roommates. Who was this administrator? She had probably picked their names at random, yet Natalie wanted to send her a large basket of expensive nuts.

Because Natalie didn't believe in love at first sight. Well, not anymore. She had for a brief window at age fourteen after watching the Claire Danes and Leonardo DiCaprio version of *Romeo + Juliet* while on vacation with her mom at the beach. For the whole rest of their stay, she'd walked by teenage boys on the boardwalk, intensely trying to catch their eyes in hopes of activating a soulmate connection. Only one boy really looked back, though he'd turned out to be less interested in true love than in the possibility of a hand job behind the funnel cake stand.

But she *had* experienced that feeling of locking eyes with another person and knowing immediately that your world had changed. It hit her when she was lugging a box of books into her dorm room, on the verge of dropping them all. A girl sitting on a neatly made bed rushed up to help. Nat caught a glimpse of the dorm room before she saw the girl's face. Somehow, this small room, with its two extra-long twin beds, already felt cozy, lived-in—a vase of fresh flowers on the desk, pretty yellow curtains, a framed poster of Paris on the wall (every college girl was required to love Paris) next to a painting of a nature scene that Nat had never seen before.

"If you don't like any of this stuff," the girl said, noticing Nat's gaze, "I can totally take it down!"

"No," Nat began. "It's amazing. You did all this already? Weren't we only allowed to get into the dorm rooms, like, three hours ago?"

"Yeah, but I didn't want to wait to make it feel like a home." Their eyes finally met. They grinned at each other. And there was no rational explanation, but still, Natalie knew in that moment: Gabriella Alvarez was going to be a love of her life.

Now, Gabby and Natalie had lived together long enough to be considered common-law married in the eyes of New York State, a milestone they celebrated by referring to each other as "my beauuuuutiful wife" in increasingly ridiculous voices while trying not to crack up. Gabby had made their New York apartment feel even homier than the dorm room, though it was practically the same size. She painted patterns of blooming hydrangeas and roses on the walls. (That pretty nature scene she'd hung up in their dorm room had been one of her own creations! Art was just a hobby, she claimed, though Nat cherished a hope that, someday, Gabby would chuck her advertising job and make a go of the artist's path with her. Gabby sometimes approached life like it was one giant checklist, but she was never more relaxed, never looser, than when she was painting.) She pushed their couch into a nicely centered position and somehow knew the correct number of pillows to put on it so that you always had back support but weren't overwhelmed, which Nat considered a real talent. She organized their spice rack, hung their pots and pans from the ceiling, and breathed life and air into the tight space. Natalie knew how to arrange words on the page, but Gabby knew how to arrange their life together.

Yet Angus had wormed his way in, lingering around their apartment at unexpected times so that Natalie actually had to close the door when she went to the bathroom (a thing she and Gabby never bothered to do when it was just them), which of course was silly and small and a sacrifice she'd be more than happy to make for Gabby to spend time with a man who was worthy of her. But instead, Angus was a guy who told unfunny jokes and had spent his life failing upward with the security of family money. He had swooped in to tell Nat that she should not plan anything for Gabby's birthday because he was on top of it and then had planned a party at some bar in MIDTOWN, of all places, a stretch of New York City that she and Gabby did their best to avoid.

"You might want to fix your face before we go inside," Gabby said.

"Huh?"

Gabby laughed, reaching out a finger to poke at the space between Natalie's eyebrows. "You've got an angry crease right here. What's wrong? Are you getting upset again about how Emily Dickinson was never fully appreciated in her lifetime?"

"Yes," Nat said, "but I suppose I can let that go for one evening."

She clasped Gabby's hand in hers, and together, they walked into the night that would upend their lives.

2

★☆☆☆☆

As the party swelled around her, Natalie could admit that Angus had not done a terrible job. The inside of the bar felt less soulless than the other restaurants Nat had been to in this area. People milled around in party dresses and nice pants—some of Gabby's coworkers, their friends from college, Angus's business school classmates. No parents in sight, thank God, although there was Gabby's sister, Melinda, who was always difficult to pin down, the flighty older daughter to Gabby's steady younger. Kudos to Angus for getting her to show up. The lighting was dim but not dark, the soundtrack of Justin Timberlake and Miley Cyrus thumped pleasantly underneath everyone's conversations, and, in a nice change from the establishments Natalie tended to frequent, the floor wasn't sticky.

Natalie nudged Gabby and pointed to a low table over in the corner. "That little guy is calling your name."

Angus came running over, skidding to a stop in front of them. "Milady," he said to Gabby, doffing an imaginary hat for some reason, then throwing out his arm to indicate the rest of the room. "Your party awaits!"

"Baby, this is incredible," she said, and he put his arms around her, her stiletto heels making the two of them the same height (five feet six inches).

"You look . . . wow, you're stunning," he said, going moony at the sight of her boobs but even moonier at the sight of her face. Then he blinked and registered Natalie's presence. "Oh, hi!"

Already, people in the crowd were angling for Gabby's attention. Angus gave her a little push forward. "Go and greet your adoring public!"

Angus and Natalie both looked after Gabby as she disappeared into the throng, then turned to each other. Angus had an uncharacteristically nervous strain to his smile as he cast about for a conversation topic, his hair a messy mass of dark blond curls. *Ah, screw it.* Natalie could make an effort.

"How's life?" she asked.

"Busy. I've been advising my father on growth strategy, on top of all the responsibilities of business school." Natalie had heard that the biggest responsibility of business school was getting drunk at networking events, but she gave Angus a serious nod anyway. Angus went on. "I don't know if I've mentioned it, but my father owns a furniture empire." (He'd mentioned it every time they'd hung out.)

"I've seen the billboards," Natalie said. "'The Futon King of New Jersey,' right?"

"That's him!"

When Natalie had first heard Angus's name (Angus Stoat the *Third*!), she'd imagined that he was stuffy old money, the kind of guy who'd grown up in a country club, a golf ball in one hand. But when she met him, he felt more like someone who was trying to sneak into the club, pretending he belonged. Gabby had told her the story of his upbringing: his father's family *was* old money, but Angus's dad had fallen hard for a woman who could've been an extra on *Jersey Shore*. The senior Stoats disapproved and cut Angus II out of both the family banking business and the will, assuming that would send this gold-digging harlot away. But the marriage had gone on to be remarkably successful, and to spite his family, Angus's father had founded a furniture chain that was now *the* place to go for all your futon needs.

"You angling to wear the futon crown yourself someday?" Natalie asked.

"Oh, no, no. The boardroom is more for me than the furniture floor. Not that I'm insulting the family business! There are no better futons around, anyone would be lucky to—"

Then Angus turned his head and caught sight of someone. His sentence cut off abruptly, turning into an actual squeal of glee. "You're here!" he called as a tall man with a lock of dark hair falling over his forehead approached.

Most guys their age were firmly *guys* to Natalie. She and her friends were in a strange liminal moment: not boys and girls anymore, not yet men and women. But something about this person—the serious set of his thick eyebrows, maybe, or his clean-shaven face, or the black-frame glasses he wore along with a navy button-down and khakis—screamed "GROWN-UP!" A sort of old-fashioned grown-up too, from a time when men still combed their hair.

"I wasn't sure, with your flight home," Angus was saying, pounding the man on his chest, attempting to put him into a headlock, which the man accepted with patience and a hint of a smile even as Angus ruffled his neat hair into a mess. "I know how you love to get to the airport three hours early."

"For this," the man said, "I decided to risk cutting it a little closer."

Angus let out a happy bellow, then squatted down, wrapped

his arms around the man's waist, and attempted to lift him up like a pro wrestler. "All right," the man said, ducking his head so that Angus did not accidentally thrust him through the ceiling.

With a big huff of breath, Angus released the man, who stood back up to a bit of a slouch. "Natalie, meet Rob Kapinsky. Current linguistics PhD student, future professor, heartbreaker of the West Coast—"

"That part is not true," Rob Kapinsky said.

"Well, that's only because you're spending too much time in the basement of the library, and the ladies don't know that you exist!" Angus stepped back, narrowing his eyes at Rob. "*Have* you been getting out of the library? You're a little . . . what's that word for when you're all pale and weak-looking?"

"Wan," Natalie offered. "Feeble. Anemic."

"Yes!" Angus pointed triumphant finger guns in her direction.

"I am none of those things," Rob said. "I see the sun for at least fifteen minutes each day."

"Anyways," Angus said, "this man is also my best friend in the entire world." Rob reached out a hand and politely shook Natalie's as Angus continued, "Except for Gabby."

"Have I been replaced already?" Rob asked, his eyebrow arching up, his voice pleasantly rough. Distracted by Angus, he'd looked away from Nat but forgotten to let go of her hand. They were stuck in something that was part handshake, part hand-holding for a moment, until Natalie loosened her grip (even though Rob's grasp was warm), and he looked down in surprise and perhaps a bit of embarrassment.

"Buddy." Angus reached up to take Rob by the shoulders. "Never." He shot a glance at Gabby in the crowd. "Well, maybe. She is much prettier than you are, I'm afraid."

"Ouch," Rob said.

"You could compete," Nat said to Rob, "if only you weren't so anemic."

He half laughed in surprise, his serious face momentarily transforming.

"Oh, they're here! I should . . ." Angus began, catching sight of someone across the room. "Nat, entertain him while I'm gone?" Angus bustled off into the crowd, leaving the two of them alone by the bar, suddenly responsible for each other.

"A drink?" Nat asked after a beat of awkward silence, and Rob nodded. They turned to the bar and ordered.

As they waited, he cleared his throat. "Angus gave my entire biography, but I'm sorry, who are you?"

"I'm Gabby's Rob. Her best friend."

"Ah. I always thought my doppelganger would be taller."

"I'm still holding out hope for a growth spurt. Drinking lots of milk, stretching, but there's only so much a person can do."

"We'll have to settle for being doppelgangers in every aspect except height."

"And that I could never live on the West Coast. East Coaster through and through."

"But at least you're also studying to be a linguistics professor," he said, deadpan.

"I have to admit that I don't quite understand what linguistics is."

"Well," he said, "have you heard of words?"

She smiled. "Yes, I know it's something about the science of them. But that makes me picture you in a lab coat peering at a petri dish containing a long and complicated word, and that can't be correct."

"No, that's exactly what I do all day." He squinted his eyes and did a winding motion with one hand while making a circle with the other. "That's a word, all right. Next dish."

She copied his motion. "What is this? You are . . . using a magnifying glass while also going fishing?"

"It's a microscope."

"Of course. How could I not see it?"

"I thought it was very clear." He shook his head. "Actually, linguistics was my second choice for a career path."

"Oh?" she asked sympathetically as she took a sip of her drink.

His expression was solemn. "Sadly, the mime academy wouldn't take me."

At that, she snorted so hard that the whiskey in her mouth shot up somewhere into her brain. He did not seem, at first glance, like a man who could be particularly silly, more like a man who devoted himself to thinking about important problems in the world. She looked more closely at him. The corner of his mouth had turned up, as if he were pleased and almost surprised at how fully he'd made her laugh. Then he cleared his throat and went on.

"But to your question, linguistics is the study of how we form speech, where different words come from, et cetera. Language is fundamental to our social interactions, and those interactions can seem mysterious or unpredictable, but linguistics reveals that they all follow a pattern. There's an order to everything—" He caught himself. "And now I will stop, since normal people do not need to spend hours discussing words."

"Yeah, I could take them or leave them," she said, then flashed him a grin. "I'm a writer, by the way. Or, well, learning how to be one."

His spine straightened. "Which MFA program are you in?"

"I'm not."

"Ah." For a brief second, a doubtful look flashed across his face before he turned back to the bar and took a sip of his whiskey soda.

"What?" Natalie asked.

"Nothing." He looked down at his drink, turning the liquid around in the glass. "What kind of writing—"

"Try not to let your head explode, but I'm not planning to attend a graduate program."

A huff of breath escaped him—was that . . . a *scoff*?—before he said, neutrally, "To each their own."

Natalie folded her arms across her chest, thrusting her head up. "Go ahead, say it. Tell me why I'm making a big mistake."

"I don't necessarily think you are."

"Yes, you do. So, go on."

His expression darkened. "If you insist. Academia helps other people take you seriously, but it also helps you take yourself seriously."

"Did you get that from an admissions pamphlet?"

"No, my father. He's a professor." He shook his head, then went on. "Grad school proves that you want to do the rigorous work of your future profession."

"Sure, maybe I'm lazy," Nat said, a fire starting up behind her eyes even as she kept her tone level. "Or maybe I decided that I couldn't take on more student loans for a program that wouldn't guarantee me a steady job at the end." He began to say something, but she continued, unable to stop now even if she'd wanted to. "So instead of being 'rigorous,' I'm just juggling four part-time jobs while working my way through every book on writing that I can find at the library, attempting to befriend other writers so we can trade pages, submitting to literary journals, and attending every free author talk that I can cram into my schedule."

She stopped and caught her breath. Around them, people laughed and flirted. Rob looked at her with a steady expression. She didn't normally let herself get so worked up. That, or people didn't normally stay to hear it.

"Anything else?" he asked.

"Yes, actually," she said, throwing her shoulders back. "Sometimes these author talks have free wine, so I'm saving on my liquor budget."

The tension stretched out between them, brittle and tight. And then he said, "I hardly ever get free wine in my PhD program."

"Whew." Nat shook her head. "Did I get overly defensive?"

There was a small smile on his face now. "Only as much as I got overly didactic." He stopped for a moment, as if trying to articulate something in his mind. "Sometimes when you're in the middle of it, it's easy to forget that academia is not the center of the universe."

"Same thing with writing! It requires so much of you that you have to convince yourself it's the only thing you could love in order to keep going."

"I don't know that I have to *convince* myself," he began.

"You came out of the womb loving academia and have never wavered since?"

"Hm," he said, a look of concentration on his face. Natalie couldn't help leaning forward as she waited to hear what he'd say next. Brushing her hair back behind her ears, she realized that her palms were clammy for some reason. "The womb bit is not entirely inaccurate."

At parties, Natalie often found it difficult to stay put in a conversation. She didn't like this aspect of herself. But there was always somebody else to talk to, someone who could end up changing the course of your life. Another guy to flirt with when you were single, or somebody who could have a connection in the literary world. So she flitted away the moment a conversation got awkward, a master of the excuse. *(I'm just going to get another drink! I have to pee! I think I see my long-lost friend in the shadows!)* Somehow, though, talking to this strange, reserved man, with his dry wit and serious eyes, she wanted to stick around and figure out how he worked. He gave as good as he got, all without breaking into a sweat or a smile (mostly). She could tell he was an academic—he had that look, as if he was working out a problem in his mind. Studying her. Truly taking in her words instead of just thinking of the next thing to say to make himself seem impressive, like so many other men did. (And like she did herself so much of the time.) A voice in the back of her mind told her that she *should* flit away, but she ignored it. Because something about the way he was studying her made her want to give him all the relevant information. It was only fair.

"I did apply to Iowa," she admitted. "My senior year of college. It's the Holy Grail, so I figured, why not at least try?"

"Ah. But I take it . . . ?"

"Rejected. Which sucked, of course. You must have felt a similar way with the mime academy." Now it was his turn to choke on his drink, and the corners of her own mouth turned up in satisfaction. "Rejection can happen to anyone, though. Iowa is incredibly competitive. But maybe . . ." She leaned forward. She didn't often say this part when people asked her about grad school. "Maybe part of me worried that, if I applied more widely, I still wouldn't get in anywhere. That my work would be too girly, not serious enough, not the kind of writing that an MFA program would be looking for. I can dismiss one rejection. But ten? If that happened, I don't know if I'd be able to make myself pursue it anyway. I'd feel . . . like an idiot."

"Well, I haven't read your writing. So I can't tell you that *they'd* be the idiots for not accepting you."

Natalie waited a beat. "That's it? There's not a more encouraging end to the sentence?"

"Er, no."

She couldn't help herself. A laugh bubbled out.

"But—" He scratched at his temple. "Why do you want to write?"

She thought a moment, because the answer to that seemed too big to distill. A swirling tornado of reason upon reason, sweeping up everything in its path. "I think it has to do with recognition," she finally said.

"Prizes and such?" He looked a little disappointed.

"No, not that," she said quickly, though of course she wanted prizes and such. "I mean . . . there have been moments when I've read something in a book that feels like it was written just for me. Like the author reached inside my brain, took all the thoughts I didn't know how to express, and put them into a perfect paragraph. And in those moments, I've felt so utterly connected to a person I didn't know that it made me think, 'Yes, the world can be hard, and people can be awful to each other. But there is also such beauty in the fact that we can recognize each other like that.'" She fiddled with her straw. "I want to be able to give that feeling to other people."

"Well then," he said. "Screw any MFA program that wouldn't want to give you the chance."

In the dim lighting of the bar, she thought she could see a flush on his cheeks. So many people, when she told them she was a writer, fell into one of two categories. They talked down to her—*You? Little girl, you think you have things to say?*—or they blew smoke up her ass, telling her they were sure she was *incredible* without having read a lick of her work. Rob, though . . . He might have looked like a snob, but he took her as she was.

Rob opened his mouth to go on, and her heart began to thump, like she was nervous to hear what he was going to say, though that was ridiculous. She barely knew him. He wasn't an expert in her field. Still, her heartbeat grew louder in her ears.

But suddenly Angus was pushing through the center of the crowd, a drink in his hand, banging a knife against the glass. "Attention! Attention, all!" The ding of cutlery on glass turned to a shattering sound, Angus accidentally cleaving the top of the cup off onto the ground, where the glass splintered. "Oops, would somebody mind—?" A waiter bustled forward and began cleaning as Angus took a step to the side. Typical Angus, a privileged bull in a china shop. "Would Gabby come on up here?" Gabby waved at everyone from the sidelines. "No, no, come up!"

Gabby raised an eyebrow but acquiesced. "Hey, everyone, thanks for coming out tonight," she said as Angus gazed at her with a slightly dazed expression, a bead of sweat rolling down his forehead. She leaned into him with a nervous smile. "I'm not supposed to give a speech, am I?"

"No, don't worry. But I want to say a few words to the crowd." Angus cleared his throat. "For those who don't know, I met Gabby a year ago, when I convinced my dad to take a meeting at the ad agency where she works. Not that our commercials weren't already great—" Nat had seen a few of them. They starred Angus's father, speaking to the camera from the furniture floor while Angus's mother "relaxed" on a futon in a leopard-print dress. Angus's parents were not exactly thespians.

"But now that I'm an NYU business school man, I thought it was time to shake things up," Angus went on. "Gabby's junior at her agency, but they gave her a piece of the pitch anyway. And as soon as she delivered it, it was obvious why. She was so prepared, a go-getter who made everyone around her better." Angus turned to Gabby. "I don't know if you know this, but that night, I told my parents I'd met the woman of my dreams."

"You did not," Gabby said, putting her hand over her heart.

Meanwhile, Gabby had told Natalie that she'd "give him a chance" even though he was "a bit of an odd duck." Gabby had always liked odd ducks, though, and ugly dogs and mean old cats. When they went hiking once, she'd become fascinated by a bulbous toad in their path and spent a full five minutes trying to coax it onto her hand. Nat had once joked that Gabby would probably try to befriend a subway rat someday, and Gabby had shaken her head. "That's a bridge too far even for me." Then she had paused. "Then again, *Ratatouille*."

Now, Angus wiped his forehead and turned back to the crowd.

"We're here to celebrate your birthday tonight, Gabby, and I'm sorry to hog the spotlight. But there was just one thing I wanted to do."

The a capella performance. Natalie looked around for Angus's fellow business bros, bursting through the crowd to start step-touching while a white man beatboxed, as threatened in Angus's email invite.

But instead, Angus reached into his pocket and pulled out a small box, and Gabby's mouth dropped right along with Nat's stomach.

3

★☆☆☆☆

Natalie watched in disbelief as Angus sank down to one knee. "Gabriella Alvarez," he said, "I love you more than anyone in the world. No offense, Mom and Dad!" Nat glanced around and saw Angus's parents, the Futon King and Queen themselves, emerging from a corner of the crowd, right next to Gabby's parents, all with anticipatory looks on their faces. Angus opened the box to reveal a ring, and Gabby wobbled in her heels with shock. "From the moment I met you, I knew you'd be my future wife. Well, if you want to be! Do you want to be?"

Gabby's hands flew up to her mouth. Natalie's cheeks burned in secondhand embarrassment for her friend. Oh God. She must be feeling *mortified*. She was a planner—when she and Nat went on vacation together, Gabby always drew up an itinerary and spent hours researching. A surprise proposal was probably one of her greatest fears (along with heights). She would've wanted to pick out the ring. She would definitely think that the pinkish diamond in Angus's hand was ugly as fuck. Also, they'd only been dating for a year! They didn't even live together. What the hell was Angus thinking?

"Yes," Gabby blurted, and people erupted in cheers.

Natalie could barely hear for the ringing in her ears. Amid her disbelief, a theory presented itself. Despite being strong-willed, Gabby had a people-pleasing streak, never wanting to create fuss or drama. Angus had to know that just as well as Natalie did. So he'd ambushed her in front of all her nearest and dearest. Natalie worried that Gabby didn't want to let anyone down. And in trying not to make a scene, she was making a Jupiter-sized mistake.

If Gabby truly wanted to marry Angus, Natalie would support her. Of course she would. But she knew what Gabby looked like when she was besotted. She'd seen it with Gabby's college boyfriend, Tony. Anytime someone said the name "Tony," Gabby would burst out into an idiotic grin, which was a bit problematic during the weeks that their English class read *Beloved*. She'd developed a severe case of mentionitis. *(Oh, you were just on the phone with your mom? Tony called his mom the other day!)* She'd let out great, heaving sobs when he'd broken her heart. Gabby had displayed none of these signs about Angus.

Natalie turned to Rob, who looked surprised, though not stunned. "Did you know? That he was going to do this?"

"No." He pursed his lips. "Well, he has been referring to her as his 'future wife' for a while now. And he's mentioned proposing, though never with a specific timeline. And he *was* strangely insistent on me coming tonight. But I assumed he just wanted me to finally meet her."

So, Natalie was the only one to be truly blindsided. Not that she expected Angus to have asked for her blessing. Still, it was normal to give someone's best friend in the whole world a little heads-up, consult them about ring styles or proposal preferences, wasn't it?

"Sometimes when Angus gets an idea, he likes to run with it," Rob was continuing, and the only thing Natalie could think, all-caps in her mind, was *RED FLAG, RED FLAG, RED FLAG.*

Gabby finally emerged from the hug pile made up of her and Angus's families, her eyes finding Natalie's across the room, and Natalie felt grateful that even in this moment of insanity, they looked for each other. Gabby jerked her head in the direction of the bathroom, and Natalie nodded.

They met outside the women's room, a single-person rest-room with a drunk girl staggering out of it. Gabby pulled Nat inside, where it smelled vaguely of shit, despite the hibiscus-scented candle working overtime on the ledge above the sink.

The door swung closed behind them. Stunned silence for a moment, then Gabby hit Natalie's arm. "Why did you let me wear such a low-cut dress?"

"I didn't have any idea that this was happening."

"Oh my God," Gabby said, gawking at the ring on her finger. "I'm engaged. I'm an engaged woman. This is insane. Is it insane?"

"It's . . . well, it's definitely unexpected."

"If I'd known he was going to do a surprise proposal, I would've told him absolutely not to," Gabby continued, dazed, and finally Natalie felt like she was standing on solid ground. She'd *known* that Gabby didn't want this.

"Okay." She took Gabby by the shoulders. "You can just play along for tonight, and then talk to him tomorrow. Everyone will understand if you change your mind after sleeping on it . . ."

Gabby blinked. "What?"

"I mean, if he took you by surprise."

"He did. And definitely for the first few seconds, I was like, 'Oh, hell no!' But then I looked over at that table in the corner that you were saying I was gonna dance on, and I realized . . . I'm not a person who gets wild and crazy. I want to settle down! Even if the ring is absolutely hideous. We can fix that."

"Are you sure? You haven't even had a chance to live together. What if he has some weird habit that he does in the privacy of his own home, like cutting his toenails in the kitchen sink—"

"He cuts them over a trash can, I've seen it."

"That's just one of many examples."

"My parents would never want me to live with someone before getting engaged. You know how Catholic they are. I think it's really thoughtful of him to remember me saying that and to not be freaked out by it. A lot of guys wouldn't be so respectful."

"Oh. Right. That's . . . great."

Gabby stared at Natalie. Natalie stared back. "So"—Gabby smiled, a bit uncertain—"are you going to congratulate me or what?"

This was happening all wrong. Your best friend was supposed to meet the man of her dreams, and you were supposed to be so happy that you cried tears of joy. But the tears threatening Natalie's composure now were decidedly NOT of the joy variety.

It was too soon. She and Gabby hadn't yet had enough time to be the most important people in each other's lives. Would Gabby start referring to Angus as her best friend now? Would he always be there whenever the two of them tried to hang out, redirecting the conversation in his exhausting way, offering Natalie terrible, unsolicited advice on her love life and career?

Now Gabby would talk to Angus first about everything. The moments when she came home from the office buzzing with fury about how a senior advertising partner had treated her or alight with excitement over a successful pitch and needed to talk it all through, the moments when Gabby figured out the solution, the sheer force of her talent so exciting that Natalie would get goose bumps, those moments would go to Angus. Gabby would still tell Nat about them, but they'd be the leftovers, the reheated version. She and Natalie would always be catching up instead of figuring things out together.

Nat's brain was frozen and fuzzy for one more second. Then she exhaled. "Oh, duh, congratulations! This is—whew!—so exciting!"

"Thank you!" Gabby threw her arms around Natalie, and they held each other tight. "You'll be my maid of honor, of course."

"Of course."

"My sister might be mad, so watch your back in case she tries to push you down the stairs, but you know she'd be a disaster. And I promise I'll be a chill bride."

A pause, then they both cackled, because if Gabby got this neurotic about dancing on a table, Natalie could not imagine how she would survive wedding planning without having an aneurysm. "Okay," Gabby continued. "I'll do my best to be as chill as possible." She straightened her shoulders, pulled her dress up to a more respectable level, and opened the door. "Now back out there to my *fiancé*!"

Natalie beelined straight to the bar and ordered a shot of tequila. Rob was still there, sipping on a whiskey, his face furrowed in concentration.

They let the alcohol burn their throats for a moment. Then Natalie asked, "So, what do you think of all this?"

"If she's actually as amazing as he says—"

"She is."

"Then I think it's good. As long as he's happy."

"Mm." They sipped their drinks in silence for a moment, until Natalie couldn't stop herself. "It's just so quick, right? You should be ending your twenty-fifth birthday puking on the subway, not getting engaged."

He gave her a sideways glance. "I'm not sure you should aspire to puke on the subway."

"I'm obviously not *aspiring*."

"Sounds unpleasant, not to mention inconsiderate to the MTA workers—"

Natalie swatted his arm. "Bad example, okay?" Rob looked down at where she'd touched. Had she hit him harder than intended? "I just mean that now's the time to be trying things, figuring out what we want."

In the center of the room, Angus was picking Gabby up and squeezing as Gabby wiggled, tugging the hem of her dress down so she didn't expose herself to the roomful of well-wishers. As Natalie watched, a partygoer jostled past, unintentionally pushing her into Rob. She collided with his chest, and he startled, his arms coming up to steady her, gripping her shoulders. Their area of the bar had grown crowded, everyone grabbing another round of drinks to celebrate, and for a moment, Natalie didn't have the space to move backward, the two of them thrown together, suddenly still in the midst of chaos. The shouting and laughing and Daft Punk's new single blasting on the speakers for the third time already that evening, it all seemed to blur around her. The only thing she could focus on was the weight of Rob's hands on her shoulders.

"Sorry," she said, her voice faint.

"That's all right," Rob replied, his dark eyes intense. "To what you were saying, though . . ." His voice caught, and he cleared his throat, eyes still locked on hers. Still gripping her, steadying her in a way that made her feel entirely off-balance. "Maybe some people get lucky. They find someone early on and don't need to figure anything out because there's no doubt at all."

Amid all the turmoil inside her at the turn the night had taken, something sparked in Natalie's chest. Fluttered. And then a twinge of guilt. Dammit, she should have mentioned Conor by now. The space behind her had cleared. There was no excuse for her to keep touching Rob.

"I'm probably having trouble wrapping my mind around it because marriage feels so far away for me." She stepped back, leaned against the bar, and looked over at the crowd, away from Rob's gaze. "I mean, I get hives when my boyfriend wants to sleep over two nights in a row."

Rob blinked, then nodded. "Ah. Is your boyfriend here?"

"No, he's out of town doing an artist's residency."

"An artist, huh?"

"A writer. You'd approve of him; *he* did an MFA." Rob rolled his eyes and she went on. "He writes these experimental short stories. They're brilliant."

At least, Conor received enough accolades that the stories *had* to be brilliant. If Natalie didn't understand them, she probably wasn't smart enough. Conor liked to give her drafts, then insisted on watching as she read. Whenever this happened, half of her mind paid attention to the story. The other half silently freaked out, struggling to find something intellectual to say.

"The wounded rabbit. So . . . melancholy. I couldn't help thinking of the lost innocence of childhood," she'd said the last time they'd performed this strange ritual.

He'd furrowed his brow, as if disappointed in both her and himself. "I was actually hoping to convey the crushing weight of capitalism."

"Yes, I was about to say that I felt that too!"

Conor took her to literary salons with his friends from his writing program. Natalie tried to network. But Conor's friends were terrifying. If they found someone, particularly a writer, lacking, they immediately knew the perfect, devastating sentence to expose that person's deeply uncool core.

God, there were so many ways to like all the wrong things in this world, weren't there? Was there anything more pathetic than having bad taste? When she was younger, Natalie had just wanted to write things that made people feel, things that people understood. She'd fantasized about a version of herself wearing a flouncy, indulgent nightgown and drinking champagne while typing away. But Conor's friends made her feel like the only way to write well was to smoke a cigarette and burn it on her arm, and then catalog the pain she felt. *Everything* made her feel that way, actually, from book reviews in papers of note to the writing classes she'd taken in college, and when she looked at the novel she was currently writing, she wanted to despair—it had no animating fury, no *bite*. Conor's friends would snark about it for hours. She had to toughen up and dig deeper if she wanted to write anything of value in this world.

"I've personally never gotten into experimental short stories," Rob said, "but he sounds impressive."

"Oh yes, he's very fancy," Nat said, and forced a grin. "Not sure why he bothers with me."

Rob's eyebrows knitted together. "Don't say that."

Her breath caught in her throat. Because suddenly Natalie knew that she was playacting with Conor, keeping up a facade of being cooler and artsier than she actually was so that he wouldn't get bored. Somehow, she'd shown more of her true self to Rob in the past hour than she had to Conor in the entirety of their three-month relationship.

But she didn't want to be the kind of person who clung on to something that wasn't real just so that she didn't have to be alone. She'd seen where that had gotten her mother. After her father had left (five days after Nat's bat mitzvah), Nat's mom had dated a string of men who had broken her heart, and Nat's too by extension. Throughout it all, Nat had picked up the pieces, and her mom had been fine eventually, because it was the two of them against the world. But when Nat had gone off to college, her mother had been unable to stand the silence and loneliness of her empty house.

Soon enough, she was engaged to Greg, a man Natalie barely knew, a man Natalie's mom didn't even seem to like all that much. She was just so far out of Greg's league that she knew he'd never leave her. She tolerated him, and Nat couldn't think of anything more depressing. (Well, she could. Climate change, etc.) Now, her funny, lovely, bubbly mother spoke through gritted teeth, always annoyed, wishing for the solitude of which she'd been so afraid.

A chill ran through Natalie. God, she hoped Gabby hadn't just consigned herself to the same fate.

"All right, doppelganger," Rob said, breaking through her reverie. "Tell me what I need to know about Gabby." Natalie turned back to him, and Rob shrugged. "I've got to do my research, because Angus asked me to be his best man."

4

★☆☆☆☆

Robert Kapinsky liked arriving early at the airport. Frantic, last-minute runs to catch a flight made his heart pound in a way he did not appreciate.

Angus told him that, for efficiency's sake, you should always be the last person boarding the plane. His consultant friends at business school had apparently done the math. Even if you missed every fifth flight, you still saved yourself time on balance by arriving as late as possible.

Rob thought that was the stupidest thing he'd ever heard.

Life was already stressful enough. Why create more situations of anxiety? Instead, you could arrive early, factor in any unexpected delays in the security line, and then sit at an airport Chili's and do work. You could also order yourself a sugary margarita that you'd otherwise never drink because you knew it was bad for you. A small indulgence. At an airport, you were allowed those.

Now, he found his gate and sat down on the ground to wait. The airport Chili's was closed at this hour of the night, but he supposed he didn't need a margarita anyway, not after the two drinks he'd had with Natalie. Plus, there'd been that shot of tequila with Angus when he had pulled him aside and asked Rob to be his best man with tears in his eyes. Rob understood the importance of this. Angus had—how best to put it?—a singular spirit that not everyone could appreciate. When they were younger, he had borne his fair share of teasing and rejection while remaining unfailingly kind. He deserved people who loved him for all that he was, people who were proud to stand beside him.

"I'll . . ." Rob had begun in response to Angus's question, then had to clear his throat. "It would be an honor."

The scratchy airport carpet prickled at his legs, even through his pants. His phone buzzed in his pocket, and he took it out to see a message from his newest contact.

NATALIE: Thanks for giving me your number! It's important to keep the chain of communication open between the maid of honor and best man.

ROB: Agreed. The success of this wedding depends on us.

For a moment, he felt a strange urge to send a winky face, a heretofore unfamiliar compulsion. He did not act upon it.

NATALIE: You get to the airport okay? I hope I didn't make you late with my incessant yammering.

ROB: I'm here in plenty of time. And not incessant. I got at least three words in.

NATALIE: Well you can't mention Nabokov and not expect me to have opinions!! Okay, I'm going to

bed, but see you at the wedding, whenever that
may be!

He slipped his phone into his pocket. Then, balling up his
jacket into a makeshift pillow, Rob leaned back against it and
tried to get comfortable. His flight wasn't for another four hours,
the first one out in the morning.

He'd missed the one he was supposed to take. His shuttle to
Newark Liberty International Airport had left Midtown while he
was still back at The Pig, the Duck & the Farmer ordering one
more round with Natalie. The shuttle after that had gone too.
The flight attendants on his plane had been demonstrating how
to put on an oxygen mask, the passenger in 34B sprawling out
into the empty seat next to her, not believing her luck. Rob had
checked his watch, known that he should leave. But Natalie had
been saying something interesting, and he had wanted to hear it.

Part Two

MAY 2015

Two Years Later

Together with their families,
Gabriella Alvarez and Angus Stoat III
request the honor of your presence at their wedding,
to be held at the Larchmont Inn in New Jersey,
Saturday, May 23. Ceremony at 4:30 in the afternoon.

Formal attire requested.

Dinner and dancing to follow.

5

★☆☆☆☆

Being maid of honor required the organizational skills of a professional scheduler, the enthusiasm of a cheerleader, and the patience of a kindergarten teacher. Natalie had never been particularly into pep, patience, or spreadsheets, but when you loved someone, you did what they needed you to do. So here she was at an Italian restaurant in New Jersey, attempting to explain to the rest of Gabby's bridesmaids that they needed to keep their rehearsal dinner toasts to under five minutes, please.

"And how much time are you giving *yourself* tomorrow night?" Gabby's sister, Melinda, asked. Her glare threatened to freeze Nat's blood in her veins. A wild child who could also hold a grudge like no one's business, Melinda had spent the wedding planning process alternating between semi-terrifying jokes (*I'm like the maid of honor understudy. In case you break your neck before the wedding.*), insistences that she didn't even want the responsibility because she was VERY busy with her latest business idea (*I make jewelry into which I'll carve the names of your lovers or enemies.*), and the current moment's flat-out hostility.

"I am also limiting myself to five minutes," Nat said, "as Gabby and Angus requested."

Melinda huffed. "I'll believe it when I see it."

Their college friend Shay jumped in. "A wedding toast from a professional writer! I can't wait. But also . . ." She indicated Becks, their other friend from school. "Since there are two of us, we assumed it meant five minutes per person."

"No, it's a joint toast. So the joint time should be five minutes."

"Oh no," Becks said. "Oh, oh no. That's going to be tough." Becks had a tendency to catastrophize.

"I guess we could take out the story about her hooking up with that bartender in New Orleans on spring break?" Shay said.

"Yes," Natalie said. "What? Why would you tell that story in front of her parents?"

Shay blinked. "Because it's funny."

Gabby and Angus weren't the first of their friends to get married—that honor belonged to a dormmate who had married her high school boyfriend when they were all twenty-two, when the idea of going to a wedding of your peers still seemed utterly unfathomable. But now, Gabby and Angus were leading the new guard, blazing the trail for all their marriage-curious friends. None of them knew what they were doing, where the limits were. Did they actually need to buy a gift off the registry if they'd already spent money on train fare AND a hotel? Wasn't their presence a present?

At the rehearsal dinner, Natalie could sense half of her coupled-up friends taking notes in their heads. The other half wore a look of a dawning awareness—they could not imagine following Gabby and Angus's path with the person currently on their arm. Natalie was calling it now: this weekend would set breakups and engagements in motion.

As a kid, Natalie had told herself that she'd be married by age twenty-seven, and though that birthday loomed a few months away, Natalie did not even have a boyfriend about whom to brag, having parted ways with Conor of the inscrutable short stories only a month after Gabby and Angus got engaged. She'd dared to offer some constructive criticism on his latest work (*Perhaps it's a bit too opaque?*), he'd reacted poorly, the rest of the night had been awkward, and she'd broken up with him the next morning before he could do it first.

But she had something better than a boyfriend. She had a book. A slim paperback novel that had come from her very own brain and determination. All those nights that newly engaged Gabby had been off with Angus, Nat had poured herself into her manuscript in an almost manic state of inspiration, and the result had been published a little more than two weeks ago. Two hundred and eighty-eight pages of Nat's quivering heart offered up for the world to see.

How exciting it had been at this dinner to be able to mention it when people asked what she did and watch them reevaluate her. Twenty-six and already a published novelist. She was *not* a fool for trying. All this time, while maybe some people thought she'd been delaying the start to her real life, she'd actually been brave, following a guiding light that only she could see.

Sure, publishing a book did not solve every problem in her life, at least not when it was a small printing with a $5,000 advance. It did not clear her skin or help her move to a nicer apartment without a roommate, or at least a nicer apartment with a roommate who did not hide cheese in his room. (In most ways, Daryl—who had taken over Gabby's room after she left—was fine. But the bottle of Parmesan was always going missing from the fridge, and whenever Natalie made pasta and wanted to use it, Daryl would retreat to his room and pull it out from under his bed. Did he eat handfuls of it at two a.m.? Also, it was the cheap kind of cheese with a ton of preservatives, but still, you probably weren't supposed to leave it out overnight, right? No matter how many times she asked him to please return it to the fridge, he never did. Natalie half expected to die of food poisoning any day now. But it wasn't like she was going to stop eating cheese on her pasta.) Publishing did not allow her to quit *all* of her part-time jobs, only the one she hated most—goodbye to personal assisting for that psychiatrist who would watch porn in his office while she sat in his waiting room!

But her novel was *real*. She'd found it in a bookstore on her publication day and burst into noisy tears, startling the elderly woman browsing next to her. It had a Goodreads page with fifty-three ratings and/or reviews, and all of them were either four or five stars except for a few pesky three stars from people she didn't know, all of which were just the rating except for one, which said, "Reads sort of like the author's diary. Fitfully amusing." But she'd gone to that person's profile, and they had also given three stars to *Le Petit Prince*, for God's sake, so she was in good company. And okay, yes, a lot of the gushing reviews on there were from friends and family to whom she'd sent a big mass email, asking them to please remember to write kind things if they enjoyed the novel and to please forget to rate it if they did not. But still, the reviews were specific and kind and thoughtful. She was "capturing the millennial perspective on life and love in an honest, biting way I've never read before," her writing style "nuanced yet page-turning."

Not that she spent a lot of time reading compliments about her work. Yes, she went on the Goodreads page sometimes when she was feeling bored or low or even happy. Or hungry. But it wasn't like she was OBSESSED.

(Were the reviews slowing down, though? Did it matter? No,

surely she'd reach a tipping point soon, and the word of mouth would spread, and the book would sell as well as she'd hoped.)

"Angus told me you just published a novel," one of Angus's cousins said to her now as Natalie grabbed a glass of champagne from the bar.

"That's kind of Angus to let people know," Nat replied. He and Gabby had come to her book launch and sat in the front row, whooping. As far as Nat could tell, though, neither one of them had gotten a chance to read the book yet. Gabby had started it—she'd texted Nat after the first page that she was madly in love with it already. But then she'd fallen off. Well, she'd had a wedding to plan. Maybe she was saving the book for her honeymoon. Natalie was learning that you couldn't force anyone to read your novel. The people you thought would be the first to read might drag their feet, while your mother's friend's aunt who you'd met once would email you a week after it came out with a detailed recap of her thoughts.

"What's it about?" the cousin continued.

Nat could recite the pitch in her sleep at this point. "*Apartment 2F* follows a young woman living in New York during the after-effects of the recession, wondering if the future dangled in front of her generation—the promise that we could somehow find true love, a fulfilling career, and financial stability—was a lie."

The cousin held up a glass to clink with Nat's. "Sounds thrilling."

"Are you talking about Natalie's book? It's *so* good," Shay said, walking by and inserting herself. "You have to buy it!"

Angus's cousin smiled. "I will. Good for you!"

"Thanks so much," Nat said, beaming.

The book might not have moved the needle much on her finances, but it had moved the needle on respect, something Nat felt like she'd been struggling for ever since she learned to be self-conscious. For much of her teenage years, she didn't respect herself. She thought her mind had nothing to offer, at least not in comparison to the boys around her who moved through the world with such ease. Those boys seemed to have better taste in everything and were always so confident in it.

And when she finally did start to take her own ideas more seriously, no one else seemed to. Was it that she was too small or too quick with her uncontrollable smile? Too apt to wear sundresses, too frazzled from running around to all her jobs? When she said that she was trying to be an author, people actually said, "Really? You?" That, or they'd ask, "What genre? Young adult? Chick lit?" And there was nothing wrong with young adult fiction or chick lit—though Nat preferred the term "women's fiction," and actually just preferred the word "fiction" since there was no genre called "men's fiction"—but it drove Nat nuts that people were so quick to put her in a box. Now, though, she could literally point them to a bookstore, to her novel with its arty, moody cover, a painting of a young woman's face in shadow. *That serious enough for you, assholes?*

There had been one person she'd met who gave her respect in their very first interaction. Who neither blew smoke up her ass so that he could get in her pants, nor wrote her off as frivolous. And now, she scanned the room for him.

The restaurant was classic old-school Italian: checked tablecloths with red candles flickering and melting all over their holders. The kind of place used to holding parties for big Italian Jersey families, clearly picked out by Angus's mother, who had spoken maybe six sentences to Natalie so far, yet had used two of them to proudly declare that she was Sicilian.

There he was in an opposite corner, wrangling Angus's

groomsmen, who didn't seem to be giving him nearly as much trouble as the bridesmaids. Rob Kapinsky.

Since their meeting two years ago, he'd flitted across her mind every once in a while. She'd wondered, sometimes, what might have happened between them that night if she'd been free or, once she *was* free, what might've happened if they lived in the same city instead of on opposite coasts. And every once in a while, a text would pop up:

ROB: Angus told me that he might like to try backpacking for his bachelor party, despite never having spent a night in the woods. How angry would Gabby be if I lost him in a forest?

NATALIE: Angry enough that you should also disappear into the trees forever.

ROB: Never mind, he has retracted the backpacking idea after taking a long walk.

ROB: Thank God.

NATALIE: Luckily Gabby just wants to rent a house on the beach. But she has requested games that I have to coordinate.

ROB: Settlers of Catan

NATALIE: Ew, no.

ROB: Excuse me. That's a great game.

NATALIE: I think she means more like "everyone takes a quiz on how well they know me, and the prize is a penis hat"

ROB: I assume you'll win the hat, and I assume you'll
wear it to the wedding.

NATALIE: But of course.

He'd proven remarkably difficult to stalk online. No social media, no old embarrassing YouTube videos. A few articles in academic journals that she'd have to subscribe to read, which felt like a bridge too far.

She'd spotted him ten minutes earlier, loping in, shoulders slightly hunched, in a button-down shirt and dark pants, face furrowed in concentration, a man with a *task*. (He would be a man who completed his tasks. She could not imagine him missing a deadline or being willing to disappoint. She admired that kind of follow-through in a person, she thought with a little shiver.) Her efforts to catch his eye had proven futile so far. But they had the whole weekend.

Earlier in the week, as she and Gabby were getting their nails done, Natalie had very casually asked, "So, Rob. What's his deal? Is he single?"

"As far as I know. You trying to get sloppy with him on the dance floor?"

"I only met him once, but I have a hard time picturing him getting sloppy in public."

Gabby raised an eyebrow.

"But, yes, I wouldn't be opposed to getting sloppy with him," Natalie went on.

"Okay. Not my type, but I could see it."

"A brooding academic might make a nice change from brooding artists."

"I don't know if 'brooding' is right," Gabby said. "We've only hung out a couple times, so I've yet to break through the ice with him. But he struck me as less moody, more serious. Maybe a little shy."

"I can work with shy and serious. At least for a weekend."

"Okay, just fair warning from what I've heard from Angus: Rob isn't really a for-a-weekend kind of guy. He is on a *track*. I'm surprised he doesn't yet have some impressive academic wife-to-be."

"Sure, but what guy doesn't like the occasional no-strings fling?"

Gabby shook her head. "Well, good luck to you. I'm just saying, don't be surprised if he makes you discuss your futures as a prereq to falling into bed."

Now, as Rob finished giving the groomsmen their marching orders and sent them on their way, Natalie crossed the room to his side. Her heart pulsed in a strange sped-up rhythm. Was she nervous? Natalie knew she wasn't for all markets, but she'd generally done okay with men. The trick was in identifying the types that would be interested in her, avoiding frat boys and football stars who wanted blond bombshells. She could not imagine Rob going after blond bombshells.

He was staring out at the room, over to where Angus and Gabby were greeting an endless stream of aunts and uncles, seemingly oblivious to her approach, so she threw her shoulders back and leaned over to him. "What wild surprise do we think Angus has in store for us tonight?"

He did not startle or turn to her, which made her think that maybe he had seen her approach after all. Only a slight downward curl of his lip indicated that he'd even heard her. After an excruciating beat of silence, he finally spoke. "What do you mean?"

"Just . . . the last time we were together, he pulled a proposal out of his back pocket. I wouldn't be shocked if, tonight, he announces that we'll all be hopping on a plane to Vegas so that he and Gabby can get married by an Elvis impersonator."

"Angus hates Vegas," Rob said, continuing to stare straight ahead.

Well, this was destabilizing. Was he distracted? She scrambled to regain her footing. "Really? He seems like the up-for-anything type."

"He thinks casinos take advantage of people. But if he must partake, he would obviously go to Atlantic City, because he is loyal to his home state." Rob's voice was growing strained. God, he still wouldn't look at her. She felt like someone had promised her dessert, then hit her in the face with a pie.

What had changed? Had Rob also thought more about their previous meeting over the years and decided that she'd been a tease or had talked too much without managing to be interesting? Maybe Gabby had been wrong, and he was dating someone after all, and he found Nat SO attractive that he couldn't even look at her, or he'd do something he'd regret. (No, she couldn't flatter herself that much.) He could be overwhelmed by his best man duties. She understood that—thinking about her to-do list for the next day sent a chill down her spine. Still, this was no way to deal with stress. This strange unpleasantness, whatever the cause, made the idea of getting sloppy together on the dance floor seem extremely unlikely.

He cleared his throat and said stiffly, "Excuse me, I think I am needed at the meatball bar." And then that asshole walked away.

6

★☆☆☆☆

That night, Natalie returned to her room at the bed-and-breakfast where the wedding would be held. She was sharing with Melinda to keep costs low, despite her fear that Melinda might smother her with a pillow in her sleep.

Though Natalie wanted her friends to keep finding love and getting married, she worried about what it would do to her bank account. If they could all hold off for a few more years—she had started working on another book that she felt in her bones was even better than *Apartment 2F*. So she'd bring it to her editor when it was done and get a larger advance, and then she could afford to buy people things on their registry that they actually wanted instead of a random twenty-five-dollar lemon squeezer.

The rehearsal dinner had gone well. Sure, the speeches were far too long. And Melinda's toast had included at least three passive-aggressive jokes about how Gabby was their parents' favorite. But Gabby had thanked Nat profusely at the end of the night.

Still, she was unsettled. While Melinda quickly fell asleep—Melinda was the kind of person who seemed to be able to do everything at the drop of a hat, from falling in love to quitting her job to accessing REM cycles—Natalie fixed her eyes on the ceiling, mind racing. Why had Rob been cold? Had she done everything she needed to do for tomorrow? Would Gabby be happy? What was Rob's deal?

Screw it, she decided, pushing the covers back and grabbing her laptop, going to sit in the chair by the window as Melinda lightly snored. Time to self-soothe with some kind reviews. There was so much in life she couldn't control, but at least she'd made something that people enjoyed. That had a 4.3 star rating average, and—

She squinted as the page loaded. Wait. Her star rating had dipped precipitously. When had that happened? She'd gotten one more rating since she'd last checked two days ago, but how could a single review do this, unless it was a . . .

She scrolled down and found it. One star. No text. No explanation. Submitted an hour ago. She gasped out loud, then clapped her hand over her mouth. In the bed, Melinda stirred, flopping onto her stomach.

Natalie held her breath for a moment, then turned back to her computer screen, that solitary star seeming to grow larger and larger in her field of vision.

Her eyes flitted over to the name. Addison K. No profile picture. Did Natalie know an Addison? She'd been friends with a girl named Addie in middle school, but her last name was Schilling. So One-Starrer was a stranger.

Maybe this stranger didn't understand star ratings. Natalie had heard of people getting confused and giving a book one star as a reminder to themselves that they wanted to read it. Natalie clicked on Addison's profile, holding her breath.

But no, this Addie person had marked *Apartment 2F* as "Want to Read" a couple of months ago. (The proper way to do it.) And while she hadn't rated many books, she'd generally given the ones she kept track of somewhere between three and five stars.

Okay. People were entitled to their opinions. It was impossible to make something that everyone loved. Plenty of books that Natalie treasured had far lower ratings than this. It was fine! She'd once read a one-star review of one of her favorite novels, where the reader didn't like that the main character was named Jake because that was her ex-husband's name. Perhaps something unknowable like that was behind this rating. Some stranger hated her book. That was fine! Everything was so INCREDIBLY FINE that she didn't realize she was lightly whimpering until Melinda flicked on her bedside light.

"What's wrong with you?" Melinda snapped, her voice a sleepy growl.

"Sorry!" Natalie said. "Nothing."

Melinda sat straight up, her hair a mess, glaring. "If you're going to wake me up, you have to at least tell me."

"It's so stupid." Melinda's glare intensified, so Natalie threw her hands in the air. "Someone just gave my book a terrible rating."

"Oh. That *is* stupid."

"I know. Like, obviously it was bound to happen at some point. I think . . . you can prepare yourself intellectually for this, but it feels different when it actually happens. I'm sure you felt this way the first time someone said something mean about your jewelry line."

"No one has ever said anything mean about my jewelry line."

Natalie bit her lip. "Mm. Got it."

Melinda flopped back down onto her pillow. "Maybe this person just has terrible taste."

"Yeah! I'm sure that's it." Nat scanned Addie's other ratings again. Shit, she did not have terrible taste. Addie's taste was actually pretty perfect, insofar as "perfect" meant that it aligned with Natalie's. Addison K also felt that the sophomore effort by Young Male Intellectual was wildly overrated, despite all the breathless reviews in newspapers of note. Addison K also loved the book from their childhood about a female knight in disguise that most people Nat knew had never read (which was ridiculous, because it was a masterpiece, full of adventure and romance). So, if someone whose taste matched her own hated the thing she had written, did this mean that Natalie's novel was . . . bad? That this unbiased stranger had been able to see something rotten in it that Natalie hadn't?

"No book appeals to everyone. I just need to focus on all the positive reviews," Nat said. "I know plenty of people who told me they really, truly enjoyed it."

"Right, those people are the ones who count," Melinda said. "Unless they're all just being nice." And with that, she turned off the light, leaving Natalie stunned, the self-confidence she'd cloaked herself in rapidly evaporating.

7

★☆☆☆☆

Th](hese dark circles, no good," the woman doing makeup for Gabby's bridal party said the next morning as Natalie plopped into her chair. "Were you up all night?"

It's hard to fall asleep when you're tossing about in a sea of self-doubt, Natalie considered saying back.

But Gabby, in the midst of getting her hair curled, turned to her. Her forehead wrinkled. Stress radiated out of all her pores. "Could you not sleep? Are you okay? What's wrong?" Her pitch grew successively higher with each question.

Under normal circumstances, Natalie would have told Gabby about the one-star review immediately. *Well, screw them!* Gabby would have said, or maybe, *They were probably just jealous that they didn't write your book themselves.* She would've let Nat throw herself a pity party, then talked her out of it, and then Nat would have been able to shake this uncertainty off. But today wasn't about Natalie.

"I was just so excited," Nat said as the makeup woman liberally dabbed concealer under her eyes. "But I've got an extra-large coffee, and I am totally fine."

"Ooh, coffee," Angus's mother said, over the *Us Weekly* she was reading. "I think I accidentally drank a decaf this morning. So distracted, thinking about my baby . . ." She teared up for a moment, then turned to Natalie. "Would you mind going to get me a cup? I don't know how I'll make it through the day without."

"Um," Nat said as the makeup artist poked an eyeliner pencil far too close to her cornea.

"Lisa," Gabby began in a tight voice. "Maybe you could get your own since you're already done with hair and makeup—"

Lisa thrust her magazine down. "But I don't know where the coffee bar is—"

"It's fine!" Nat said. "I'll go after this is finished."

"As long as you're going," Gabby said, "will you take a peek at the ceremony setup and let me know if everything looks okay?"

So, once she'd been appropriately primped, Natalie went to get a coffee from the clearly marked station in the lobby, by which Lisa had passed multiple times. Then she headed outside.

The bed-and-breakfast Gabby had chosen for the wedding had an absolutely charming garden area, bordered by a forest in the back. A pond stretched along one side of the property, its smooth cerulean surface dotted with lily pads. Gabby had designed many of the decorations herself, and the whole scene looked like one of her paintings come to life. White wooden chairs sat in rows over soft, green grass. The sky was clear, the only clouds dotting it so fluffy Natalie longed to reach out and run her fingers through them. It looked like the platonic ideal of a pastoral scene.

And it felt like being stuffed inside a furnace. Though it wasn't even afternoon yet, the temperature had climbed to the nineties. Natalie cast around for the right word. The heat was stultifying. Not at all the adjective you'd like people to use when describing your wedding.

Sweat already beginning to bead at her brow, Natalie looked for the person in charge. One of Angus's groomsmen was fiddling with a tree at the edge of the forest, putting up some sort of platform. Perhaps for the photographer to get a better angle?

Her eyes landed on the flowers being set up at the altar—hydrangeas, lush and blue. Her mother had those at her second wedding. That had been a much smaller affair than this—second weddings generally were. Natalie had walked her mother down the aisle to Greg, then stood off to the side as her mother recited her lines. Because that was what it had all felt like—a play, an unconvincing leading actress delivering a monologue about love and commitment with no feeling behind it.

Maybe the majority of the guests hadn't picked up on the false sentiment in her mother's words. But they hadn't seen Nat's mom the night before.

Ellen had asked Natalie if the two of them could spend her last unmarried night together. No bridesmaids (Ellen felt it undignified to have bridesmaids this time around), just a mother and daughter splurging on a fancy hotel suite, some quality time to harken back to the days when it had been the two of them against the world. Natalie was newly twenty-one, so they drank pretentious cocktails in the hotel bar and then opened a bottle of wine in their room to share.

Up until that point, Natalie hadn't spent that much time with Greg. Just some dinners here and there, at which her mother had been almost frantically cheerful. Greg had an annoying habit of giving Natalie life advice that she had not requested. But whatever, her mother loved him. She deserved to be happy, especially since Natalie's asshole father had moved on almost immediately after the divorce went through.

Tipsy in their hotel room, wrapped in a white bathrobe so

plush and comfortable she would have liked to someday be buried in it, Natalie had held up her wineglass. "This might be unorthodox, but a toast to Dad."

Her mother frowned, surprised, so Nat went on. "He's a total asshole, but cheers to him for getting out of the way so you could find someone better for you."

"Oh. Sure, to your father." They clinked glasses. Then her mom looked down into her wine, face suddenly tired. "It's funny. If you'd asked me what was going to happen the night before your father and I got married, I'd have told you we were going to end up like the couple in that *Notebook* movie. I never thought I'd be doing it all again with someone else."

"Well, I think it's nice," Nat said, alcohol turning her sentimental. "That you can go through heartbreak, but things work out the way they're supposed to, and the love of your life will be waiting on the other side."

Her mother snorted.

"What?" Nat asked.

"Nothing." Ellen took another long swallow of her wine.

"Am I getting too sloppy and sappy?"

"No. It's just . . ." She let out a sigh. "You don't need to romanticize. Sometimes you can call things what they are."

Natalie sat up, suddenly alert. Ellen waved a hand through the air. Alcohol had turned Nat sentimental, but for her mother, it had done the opposite, removing her filter. "Oh, I know. You want a shiny love. Like me when I was young. But let me save you some time and heartbreak. Shiny men, like your father, they'll get bored of you eventually."

Natalie tried to smile. "As my mom, aren't you required to think that I'm endlessly wonderful?"

"Well, of course I do."

"Okay, because it sounded like you were saying that anyone interesting and worthwhile is going to eventually dump me for someone better."

In the months after her father left, Natalie's mom had assured a weeping Natalie over and over again that she *was* lovable. That her father's abandonment had nothing to do with a lack in her, just a lack in him. That the sun shone out of Natalie's freaking ass.

But now, drunk in a hotel suite, her mother was admitting the truth Natalie had always feared—that, maybe, Natalie wasn't enough.

"I'm just saying that someone like you . . ." Ellen went on. "You want a Greg. A man who thinks you're the best thing that ever happened to him."

"Someone like me?"

"Well, you're trusting. You're soft."

"I'm not *soft*," Nat said, scowling in her hotel bathrobe. "After all those guys you brought home, I hardened myself up a long time ago."

Ellen frowned, her voice sharp. "I'm your mother. I know. You want to see the world as better than it is, people as better than they are. It's all over your writing too. And that's admirable, in a way. But don't fall in love with a man whom you've put up on some pedestal."

"Better to settle for a man who puts you on a pedestal instead?" Nat shot back, and her mother shrugged. She tried to calm her heart, her voice. "But . . . but you love Greg. Right?"

"Sure," Ellen said in the least convincing tone Natalie had ever heard.

Natalie slammed her glass down on the nearby side table so sharply, she nearly broke it. "Oh my God, Mom. Don't marry him if you feel this way!"

"Honey, you're twenty-one. You don't understand anything about this yet."

"I hope I never *understand* these things the way you do. Because this is the most depressing shit I've ever heard."

They glowered at each other, then retreated to separate corners of the suite. The next morning, Natalie gritted her teeth and got through that wedding. But things had never fully been the same with her mom since.

Now, anytime the two of them hung out, Ellen invited Greg along as if to underline how much she loved spending time with him, unable to admit that maybe she'd made a mistake. But Greg's presence annoyed both her and Natalie, so they stopped hanging out as much, and the distance grew and grew.

Even now, sometimes, Natalie would hear her mother's voice when she was with one of the many artists who enthralled and intimidated her, even when they were gazing into her eyes with total fascination: *They'll get bored of you eventually.* They'd realize that she wasn't enough and leave for someone who was.

Determined, Natalie put on a show for them, hiding any flaws or weaknesses until she didn't recognize herself. But then she ran into a new problem. How could she love anyone who couldn't see the real her?

At least she had her book. *Apartment 2F* proved that she had talent, things to say, even if Addison K—no, she was going to put all thoughts of Addison K aside for the rest of this wedding.

Right. The wedding. Natalie pulled herself back to the task at hand as she spotted a middle-aged woman in a severe black dress supervising the setup while chugging from a water bottle.

Nat hustled over as quickly as possible in the heat. "Hi," she said, and pointed to herself. "Maid of honor here. This looks amazing. But I was just wondering, is there any way to get some shade to help cool things off?"

The woman sucked her teeth. "We do have a canopy we bring out sometimes for situations like this."

"Oh, perfect!"

"But unfortunately, the bride and groom didn't choose to rent our canopy package, so we lent it out to someone else."

"Got it. Okay. That's fine. We'll just take a page out of your book and keep everyone hydrated."

"Exactly. We have this water dispenser right here." The woman indicated a beautiful canister on a nearby table, patterned glass catching the light, set on a wrought iron base. Natalie looked closer. The dispenser contained maybe twenty glasses of water. And Gabby and Angus had two hundred guests on their list.

"This . . . this is the only dispenser?"

"The bride and groom picked our smallest water package."

"And you can't add another?"

"No, because they didn't pay for that option." God, this place had the face of a sweet, family-run inn and the soul of Spirit Airlines.

"Okay, what if *I* pay you for it? How much to add, say, four more of these?"

"Three hundred and twenty dollars, plus tax."

Buying anything for a wedding was like going to a foreign nation with a terrible exchange rate, where your dollar was suddenly worth far less than normal. "You know what? Thank you so much, and never mind."

Natalie ducked back indoors, delivered Angus's mom's coffee, then returned to Gabby's side.

"How does it feel out there?" Gabby asked, worrying at her bracelet as her hairstylist spritzed her dark curls.

"It's . . . a bit toasty."

"I don't know why this is happening!" Gabby said. "It's fourteen degrees higher than the average temperature for this time of year." Weather.com had become her top visited website over the past month.

"Global warming," Becks said. She was extremely pretty and extremely gloomy. "You think it's bad now. Just wait until your children want to get married. They'll have to do it in the dead of winter." She fluffed her shining blond curls, regarding her reflection with woe. "If we even *have* winters anymore."

Nat checked the clock. Still plenty of time before the ceremony. "I'm sure we're not too far from a big-box store. I can run out and buy some umbrellas for people to use for shade, plus some extra bottled water."

"Bottled water is part of the reason we're running into this issue in the first place," Becks continued. "Too many single-use plastics." Shay nodded sympathetically. The rest of them ignored her.

"Yeah?" Gabby asked. "You don't mind?"

"Not at all." This was great! A mission. Something she could easily complete in a five-star way.

Gabby nodded, pulling out her phone to tap a message. "I'll have Rob meet you out front to drive you."

"No!" After their rehearsal dinner interaction, the last thing Nat wanted to do was spend quality time with Rob. Gabby gave her a strange look. Natalie scrambled. "I just mean, you probably need him to help out here. I can borrow a car and drive myself."

"I know how nervous you get on the highway. And the New Jersey Turnpike is no joke." Technically, Natalie had her driver's license. She had passed her test by one point, almost gotten into an accident her first week on the road, and then proceeded to live only in cities with excellent public transportation. Calling her "rusty" was an understatement. Gabby's fingers flew over her phone, texting away as she continued, "I do not want you dying in a fiery wreck on my wedding day!" She heard herself and took a breath. "I'm sorry. Obviously, I would be devastated if you died in a fiery wreck on any day."

"I get it, though. Today would be particularly bad."

Gabby's phone dinged and she looked down. "Great news, Rob is driving you."

8

★☆☆☆☆

Nat met Rob in the driveway of the bed-and-breakfast wearing the ratty sweatpants and T-shirt she'd put on for hair and makeup. He walked out the door already in his dark blue suit pants and button-down shirt, and she couldn't stop herself from doing a double take at the way the pants hugged his lean frame. What right did he have to look so good? Impeccable tailoring, that was all this was. A good tailor could make anyone look dapper.

For a moment, the sun seemed to get in his eyes, blocking his view of the driveway. He squinted into the glare, rubbing the back of his neck, the expression on his face deeply unhappy. Then his eyes landed on her.

She waved, flashing him her most incandescent smile. She was determined to be extremely pleasant.

"Thank you so much for driving!" she chirped.

His unhappy expression remained unchanged. "We should hurry up," he muttered, unlocking his car and cranking the air-conditioning. His sound system automatically began to play the last thing he'd been listening to: Fiona Apple. He quickly reached out and turned the music off.

They set off in silence, Rob checking his mirrors and backing up carefully.

As they pulled onto the highway, she cleared her throat. "So, what have you been up to for the last two years?"

"Finishing up my PhD."

Normally, she'd ask a man one question, and he'd talk about himself for the rest of the night. In any other circumstance, she might find this change refreshing. "Thrilling. What's the topic?"

"It's linguistics."

"Yes, I remember. But what area?"

"Specifically, neologisms. How new words enter the mainstream and become, quote unquote, 'real.'"

"Wow, congratulations! And how has the whole process been?"

"A lot of work." His jaw clenched. In fact, his whole body seemed to be clenched, from jaw to butthole.

Unfortunately, he smelled nice. An overwhelming attractive scent of soap and pine. She cracked her window. The incoming wind threatened to turn her blowout into a rat's nest. She rolled the window up again. She could live with the smell.

Despite their time constraints, Rob was only driving one mile per hour over the speed limit. Cars flew past them. "Maybe we should go a little faster," she said. "We do have a wedding to get back to."

"I grew up in Jersey." His voice was edged with irritation. "It's near the end of the month. The traffic cops have their quotas to fill."

"They're not going to pull someone over for going ten over the speed limit."

"You never know. And the time lost if we get pulled over will add up to much more than the time we'd save by speeding."

Nat could feel her hands balling into fists. *Patience.* She was doing this for Gabby. She thought of the owls. Once, years ago, she'd mentioned to Gabby that she thought owls were majestic creatures. And ever since, Gabby had bought her owl trinkets whenever she stumbled upon one—mugs and dish towels and nonfiction books about the hunt for a particularly elusive species. Sometimes, even though they lived in the same city, Nat would get a package in the mail and open it up to find some necklace with an owl charm on it and a note from Gabby: *Saw this and thought of you!!* At one point, years into the owl gifts, Nat had mentioned to Gabby that it was so thoughtful of her, and she absolutely did not want to seem ungrateful, but she had to come clean: she didn't actually care about owls *that* much. Gabby had nodded, but there had been a wicked gleam in her eyes, and a few weeks later, Nat had opened her door to a delivery of a five-foot-tall painting of Natalie surrounded by owls that Gabby had made for her.

For this woman, Nat could sit in a car with a silent, scowling man. For this woman, Nat could do a lot of things. Gabby was getting married today, and marriage could make a friend disappear into a little world of two. But if Nat helped the wedding go off as well as it could, Gabby would remember that. And maybe she would have a harder time leaving Natalie behind.

At the store, Nat and Rob loaded pallets of bottled water into a cart with silent efficiency. "I'll look for umbrellas," Nat said, terse.

"I'll find fans," Rob said with a grunt.

On her way to meet back up with Rob, having cleaned out the umbrella section, Natalie passed the books aisle. She couldn't stop herself. A siren song called her to check for her own. It wouldn't be here—this was a small selection, made up mostly of bestsellers and mass-market paperbacks—but still, there was a chance, and how nice and validating that would feel. Clutching her armful of umbrellas, she scanned the shelves, looking past what felt like a million copies of *The Girl on the Train*, *All the Light We Cannot See*, and *Refractions*, that sophomore effort from Young Male Intellectual that had gotten breathless reviews in every newspaper of note, that nobody except Nat and fucking Addison K seemed to think was overrated. But not a single copy of *Apartment 2F*. Of course not. Because it was a one-star book. She felt her chest deflating. She'd put her whole self into this novel, all the most interesting thoughts she'd ever had, and if that wasn't enough . . .

Stop that! she told herself. *Don't let this random stranger destroy your sense of self.* Then, *But maybe strangers are the only ones whose opinions you* should *trust—*

Rob wheeled the cart up to her, now crammed with boxes of battery-operated fans. "We should get going," he said.

"Right." She shook herself out of her funk. His eyes briefly landed on the *Refractions* display, and he made that scoff-like noise that seemed more natural to him than laughter.

"What?"

"Nothing," he said. Then, after a brief pause, "That's one of the most pretentious books I've ever read."

"Yes, thank you! I could barely get through it. And whenever I hear anyone else talk about it, I feel like I'm living in an alternate reality!"

He shrugged, a flush coming over his face, then turned the cart toward checkout.

As Rob began to bag up their items and the cashier told them their total, Natalie pulled out her wallet. "Okay, can we put the eighty dollars on the debit card here, then the remainder on this credit card? Oh, but if the remainder is over a hundred, actually, I should put the last bit on a different card instead." She fumbled around in the mass of cards and receipts. "Hold on, I have it in here somewhere."

"Stop," Rob said. "Just put it on mine." He took his wallet from his back pocket, pulled out a card, and handed it to her as he continued to bag their umbrellas.

She glanced down at the card as she passed it over to the cashier. Simple, black, with his name printed on it: Robert Addison Kapinsky.

ROBERT. ADDISON. KAPINSKY. She froze with the card still in her hand, the cashier reaching out to give it a tug. She was barely aware of letting go; her mind began to spin.

Addison was not the most common name in the world. That opinion about *Refractions* was not the most common opinion. And not that many strangers had heard of her book. It made sense that Rob would use his middle name and no profile picture for something like a Goodreads account—he was a private person who didn't even have social media. It was him. It had to be.

She thought back to the timing. He'd submitted the rating shortly after their strange encounter at the rehearsal dinner.

She looked at him as he continued to bag, a great rage rising up in her.

What the actual hell? This was a mistake. It had to be. Right? Because people were allowed to rate books any way they wanted. Of course they were! But polite society dictated that you didn't savage a book by someone you *knew*. Unless you knew them because they were your nemesis or your high school bully or had stolen your dog.

But when you were maid of honor and best man at a wedding together? When you would literally have to walk down an aisle arm in arm while people watched and took pictures? It was the height of incivility! ("The height of incivility"? Who did she think she was, a Jane Austen heroine?) Fine then, rude. Not only rude but idiotic, showing a startling ignorance of how people should treat one another.

But then again, this man hadn't shown himself to be a model of social grace up until this point.

She followed him back to the car in stunned silence.

Maybe this was why he'd been so brusque with her at the dinner. Her work had been so bad, had created such offense to his taste, that he didn't even want to look her in the eyes.

No. She refused to let this man steal her pride in all that she'd done. What had *he* ever done? (Most of a PhD, apparently. But that was different!) Cold, pretentious Robert Kapinsky did not get to decide her value as a person.

The Fiona Apple album started up again automatically when he turned the car on. So, Rob thought that *some* women were allowed to express their feelings in art. What would he rate this album? He left it on this time, apparently thinking that they wouldn't have much to say to each other, but she pressed pause.

Being extremely pleasant wasn't enough anymore. She would kill him with kindness. Yes, she would absolutely murder him. She made her smile so full and enthusiastic that she could feel crow's feet forming as a result.

"Robert," she said, "you didn't ask me what *I've* been up to for the past two years."

A moment of silence, then he forced the words out. "What have you been up to?"

"Oh." She waved a casual hand through the air, her tone light. "I published a novel."

"Your DIY graduate school worked out for you, then."

"Thank you, yes. I'm proud of the book." She beamed at him, even if the beam didn't reach her eyes. "And it's doing well. By and large, people *really* seem to love it. Especially the people whose opinions I respect, so that's nice, you know?"

The more she talked about it, the tighter his hands clenched on the steering wheel. If she kept talking, perhaps he'd leave dents in the leather. That, or his knuckles would explode. The prospect held a certain appeal.

It was almost fun, almost delicious, to see the discomfort she was causing him. Almost.

He pressed down on the gas, finally going that ten miles per hour over the speed limit that she'd been wanting. "Well, congratulations," he said, then turned the music up as they sped back to the wedding.

Natalie sat back, staring straight ahead.

Let him give her life's work one star. She couldn't care less. He could have whatever opinion about her book that he wanted and share that opinion with whomever. For instance, he could tell his mother. He could tell strangers on the street. He could even tell Satan, because Robert Kapinsky could go to hell.

9

★☆☆☆☆

Any other day, Natalie would've told Gabby about Rob's review immediately upon seeing her again. *That fucker*, Gabby would've said, drawing up a ten-point plan for how to ruin his life. Gabby held her grudges as tightly as a dog's leash at a busy intersection.

But instead, Nat plastered on what she hoped was an *everything's great here* smile as she walked back into the bridal suite. "Okay, bottled water, umbrellas, and fans acquired! People will make it through the ceremony fine and then come inside for the reception—" Dimly, she registered that the room had become even warmer than the outdoors. Then, less dimly, she registered Gabby's face, a mask of despair.

"What happened to the air-conditioning?" she asked slowly.

"Broken," Gabby whispered. She seemed frozen, etched in marble, a classical sculpture of a tragic goddess in a silky pink bathrobe. Then, all at once, she came to life and grabbed Natalie's hand. "Please accompany me to the bathroom!"

Gabby dragged Natalie down the hallway, shut the door, then turned on the water in the sink. "Everything is going wrong," she said. "And you know I don't believe in signs." She paused. "But is this a sign?"

"Of what?"

"That . . . we rushed things! That we're too young, we're not ready."

Nat kept her face carefully neutral. But in some ways, this was everything she had been wanting to hear. She still didn't understand this relationship. And, more than that, her favorite person was going to stand up in front of everyone and declare that *her* favorite person was somebody else. It felt selfish to grieve. That was just the way life was. Your friends were the most important people to you until you found your partner. (*But why?* she wondered. *Why did everyone accept that it had to be that way?*)

Over the past months, as Gabby had been consumed by wedding planning, a new depth of feeling had begun to separate the two of them. For so long, they'd experienced life together. Now, Gabby was embarking on an adventure that still seemed fuzzy to Nat.

"Adventure." That was the word that people kept throwing around in the lead-up to this wedding. (Since Nat had signed up for online dating, it was also the word she'd seen most frequently in profiles, except for maybe "cocktails" or "tacos." Every man in New York City wanted to "go on adventures with you" or find their "adventure partner.") "Adventure" conjured excitement, thrills, an expansion of opportunity. But when Nat imagined tying her life to any of the men she'd dated so far so that she could get some nice matching towels, she felt her throat constrict. Rather than opening new doors, marriage seemed to shut them. You always had to consider another person's wants and needs right alongside your own. If you were offered your dream job in a new state, would your partner be willing to move there too?

What if you needed total silence to sleep, but your partner snored? Would you just never get a good night's sleep again? So many people talked about weddings with excitement ("The best day of your life!") but then spoke about marriage itself as a slog. Weren't sitcoms always making jokes about nagging wives or how boring it got to have sex with the same person for the rest of your life? To jump into something like that seemed inconceivable, and Natalie had never met anyone who'd made her reconsider.

So even now, on the day of Gabby's wedding, Natalie couldn't quite stop herself from believing that Gabby was exaggerating her feelings in service of checking off an achievement. Because the alternative—that Gabby had accessed a level of love Natalie could not imagine or ascended to a level of maturity still far beyond Nat's reach—indicated a terrifying gulf between them. Like they'd been looking at one of those optical illusion pictures together for years, agreeing that it was a vase. And then Gabby had blinked one day and said, *Wait, it's also a couple, kissing.* Nat could not make herself see the second image no matter how hard she focused, and now it was the first thing Gabby saw.

"Well," Natalie said as Gabby paced back and forth, "do you feel like you rushed into this?"

"I don't know. I didn't before today, but now I'm freaking out!" Gabby said. "And I am trying *really* hard not to cry because it's going to mess up my makeup, and that'll be one more thing going wrong."

"If this is just about the heat, it's not that bad!"

"It's not just the heat. Everyone has so many opinions—the mothers are driving me up a wall, and it's impossible to please them both, and I know you're supposed to just say, 'Screw it!' at a certain point and accept that whatever happens is outside of your control. Literally. I read it in this wedding prep book. You find a moment where you say, 'Screw it, things will go wrong but they're not my problem anymore,' and then you focus on enjoying your special day. But I'm so in my head that I can't! I just can't!"

"What if we said it right now, together? Ready? Screw it!"

Gabby blinked. "Screw it," she said half-heartedly, then shook her head. "That didn't work." She rubbed her temples, her voice going all high and tremulous. "And I haven't even told you . . . Angus wanted it to be a surprise for everyone . . ."

Natalie steeled herself. The way Gabby was talking, it sounded like Angus was planning to pick one wedding guest to be a human sacrifice.

Instead, Gabby whispered in horror, "He's going to zip-line into the ceremony."

Nat blinked. "I'm sorry. What?" Gabby bit her lip. "I think I misheard you. Did you say 'zip-line'? Like, the thing where you hang on to handles and glide around?"

"His friend Teddy is starting a new extreme sports business, and I guess last week he mentioned that it would be fun if Angus zip-lined in, and it would also help him get some content for his website. And you know how openhearted Angus is. He was like, 'Sure thing, buddy!'"

"So, he's going to steal all your thunder."

"No, he's not . . . I don't love when people look at me anyway, so I don't care about that. But it's turned into this whole complicated thing about where his friend is going to run the zip line and how they need to arrange the chairs, and it's just one more stressful variable, and also, is it ridiculous? Zip-lining into a wedding ceremony? Am I marrying a ridiculous human?"

Yes, Natalie thought. Instead, she took Gabby by the shoulders.

"Look. If you think you've made a mistake and this is more than the normal cold feet, we can leave. I'll drive the getaway car."

Gabby let out a watery laugh. "No, *I'll* drive the getaway car."

"Fair. I'll handle music and navigation. We can get new identities and move to a farming town in Iowa so you never have to face the embarrassment of people you know asking why you didn't show up to the ceremony."

Gabby sniffed. "What would our new identities be?"

"Half sisters who own a lot of cats."

"Oh, owning cats with you would be so nice." She had a faraway look on her face, and for a moment, Nat thought she was actually considering it. Then, in a quiet voice, she said, "I'm just scared that everything will change."

"With you and Angus?"

"That. And with you and me."

"Well," Nat said, a lump in her throat, "it will change. That's true. But I'll still be here for you. That won't change. We can still have movie nights and call each other up to talk for hours." Gabby nodded, her eyes locked on Nat's. "And, hey, if you decide you really hate this life . . . there's always divorce."

Gabby smacked her arm. "How dare you mention that word today!"

"I'm just saying! Nothing in life is a permanent commitment except having kids. And I don't think you've taken that step yet, unless there's something you need to tell me?"

"No," Gabby said. Then she leaned forward, urgent. "Wait, how about this? When I get pregnant, I promise you'll be the first to know."

In this moment, with their hands clasped together, Natalie wished that friends could stand up in front of a crowd and make vows to each other too. Vows to love each other even when things got hard, vows to be there in sickness and in health, vows to not let the little complications of life tear them apart. She held Gabby's hand tighter. This would have to do. "Really? But Angus . . ."

"I'll tell him immediately afterward. But that way, you'll be a big part of it too. I want you to be part of it." Gabby shook her head. "Why am I talking about future babies? I should focus on my actual wedding."

Natalie folded her into a hug. "You keep looking for that 'screw it' moment, okay? I'll make sure everything else is under control."

After changing into her dress—a flattering pale blue silk sheath with a slit up the skirt, Gabby had been kind— Natalie power walked to the groomsmen's suite. The door was open a crack, so she peered in, not wanting to disturb any rituals or add to Angus's stress.

But the atmosphere in the groom's room was worlds away from that of the bridal suite. A wedding photographer snapped pictures of Angus putting on his cuff links. He looked the nicest that Nat had ever seen him—handsome, for those who went for his whole vibe, with a neat suit and a small white blossom pinned in its buttonhole. Most of all, though, he wore the bright, anticipatory look of a boy on Christmas morning.

This was only the third wedding she'd attended as an adult, but already she'd gotten a good whiff of some patriarchal double standards bullshit. Brides were expected to show up at seven a.m. to begin their beautification. The groom combed his hair and shrugged on a jacket. Everyone asked the bride about napkins and the schedule as if the groom had no stake in the day at all. *Let brides be lazy!* she wanted to shout.

Despite the heat, Angus's groomsmen sipped from beer bottles and cracked jokes, suit jackets slung on the couch behind them. All except Rob, who sat in a chair, spine straight, peering at a video of some sort on his phone, headphones in and brow furrowed in concentration like he was watching a documentary. Infuriating! Here she was, running around in three-inch heels, and he was futzing on YouTube? Maybe if he didn't expend his energy giving one-star reviews to people he knew, he'd be able to make himself useful.

"Robert," she spat from the doorway. He didn't hear, too wrapped up in his screen. A nearby groomsman took pity on her and tapped Rob on the shoulder. He pulled his headphones out, an eyebrow cocked, then swiveled his head to where the groomsman pointed. For a moment, as he registered her appearance, he seemed startled. Thrown off-balance, his eyes traveling over her dress. She looked down—did she have a stain or something? No, everything seemed fine.

"What is it?" he asked.

"A word."

Reluctantly, he put his phone down and followed her out into the hallway.

"I'm a little busy—" he began.

"What is with this ridiculous zip-line idea? Gabby is stressing out. Just get Angus to walk down the aisle like a normal human."

"Oh," he said, the tension in his shoulders releasing like he'd *also* been harboring doubts. "Gabby doesn't want him to do it?"

"Clearly not."

"Okay. I can try talking to him."

"Good, I think that will make Gabby feel better."

He paused. "Wait. Did she ask you to stop him?"

"Well, not exactly."

He gave her a sharp look. "So, it's merely your personal opinion that my friend shouldn't be allowed to do what he wants at his own wedding?"

"Come on. I hardly think I'm the only person here who knows that this is a terrible idea."

"Last I checked, the maid of honor does not get to overrule the groom."

"Oh, is that in the official wedding bylaws?"

"It's common sense."

She threw her hands up in the air, her patience running out. "Fine! Obviously, there's no reasoning with you. But let the record show that if this all blows up and Gabby has no choice but to become a runaway bride, I tried to stop it."

She turned on her heel and went back to the bridal suite. And then it was a stress-filled whirl: Final touch-ups. Zipping Gabby into her dress. Taking photographs where they got down on the ground and fluffed Gabby's enormous skirt while looking up at her like ladies-in-waiting. Natalie and Gabby running to the bathroom, where Natalie held up said enormous skirt so that Gabby could pee. Walking over to the entryway where the bridal party was assembling for the procession. (They'd walk outside and into the garden, then Angus would do his horrible zip line from a different location, and finally Gabby's father would escort her to the altar.)

Gabby had tucked Kleenex under her armpits to catch the sweat—a combination of anxiety and heat. She was taking deep breaths in through her nose, out through her mouth, as if following some instructional meditation video only she could see. She paused in the middle of a breath. "Shit, my bouquet!"

"Back inside?" Nat asked. Gabby gave a frantic nod. "On it."

Natalie took off, nearly colliding with Rob as he exited the dining room. Running late to the processional lineup, adding even more stress to Gabby's heavy load!

She spotted the bouquet on a nearby table and grabbed it, registering as her hand closed around the stems that for the first time in a long while, she felt pleasantly cool. "Hallelujah," she said, turning to one of the inn's staff. "You guys got the AC working again? Thank you!"

"Don't thank me," the woman said. "Thank the tall guy in the bridal party. You know, the one who's handsome in a sort of scowling way?"

"He found a repairman?"

"No, I guess he watched a video about common problems with this particular unit and figured it out. The hero of the day, huh?"

Nat stood there with her mouth open. Her mind was blank. A stretch of barren sand. One tumbleweed blowing across the great expanse, carried by wind that whistled, *Rob saved the day*.

Then she remembered that a wedding was waiting on her to begin, and she ran back, bouquet clutched tightly in hand.

Nat pressed the flowers into Gabby's hands, then found her own spot in line next to Rob. Was that a small smirk at the corner of his mouth?

"Link arms, everyone!" the wedding planner called.

Reluctantly, Nat lifted her arm up to thread it through Rob's right as he lifted his own, and the strange angle caused their hands to momentarily collide. His hand was hot. Their bare skin touching was a shock to her system. She snatched her hand away, unable to stop herself from looking at him. A flash of something crossed his face, then he turned his head straight ahead, his jaw set. He cleared his throat, glued his arm to his side, and crooked his elbow an inch. "Here."

They stood still, arms entangled, for an uncomfortably long time as the pairs ahead of them slowly processed. Nat cursed the event planner who had told them to link up so early. The pressure of his arm on hers made her feel slightly off-balance. Her attraction to him was an inconvenient fact. But as of this moment, she was no longer interested in trying to impress men who thought she was beneath them. Her own worth did not depend on whether she could make an asshole like her. There were far better ways to use her time.

"I hear you saved the day with the air-conditioning," she said, her sweet tone turning acidic despite her best efforts.

"Just wanted to make myself useful," he said stiffly. She detested him.

Finally, the coordinator gave them the nod to go ahead. Natalie plastered a smile onto her face and began to walk.

Immediately, the problem presented itself: Rob's legs were much longer than hers, meaning that each stride he took required her to take two. So while he walked at a normal pace for himself, she had to practically skip down the aisle. She jabbed her elbow into his side. "Slow down," she said out of the corner of her mouth, her smile still wide. His arm tightened, an involuntary flex, as he slowed. His bicep was rangy, not ostentatious but firm. She wasn't trying to feel it. Her hand just fell naturally on that part of his arm.

Now, Nat walked at a normal speed. But next to her, Rob was stuck in a strange sort of slow motion, taking his normal-sized step, then pausing a beat before moving again. "Can't you speed up?" he whispered, voice tight.

She gritted her teeth. "Just take smaller steps!"

After some more halting, herky-jerky motions, they finally found their stride and walked like normal people for the remaining three feet of aisle. At the altar, she withdrew her arm from his with a breath of relief, the two of them separating to their allotted sides of the officiant.

The string quartet in the corner paused their rendition of "God Only Knows" and switched to a new theme for Angus's entrance: the music from *Indiana Jones*. People in the chairs craned their heads, awareness sweeping over them as Angus appeared on the platform in the trees. He waved to everyone, then grabbed on to the contraption.

Nat had never zip-lined before. Not because she was opposed to it in its proper time and place. But so far in her adult life, she'd never had the disposable income to take the kind of vacation where one might do it. She didn't know much about the mechanics, but weren't you supposed to wear a harness?

Angus simply clung on to the handles. His friend had strung the cable from a particularly tall oak tree on the edges of the forest and over the property's small pond, ending at another tree behind the altar where Angus would apparently let go.

He kicked off from the platform with a smile on his face. The crowd turned, murmuring. And though Natalie had thought that everyone would cover their faces in secondhand embarrassment, people seemed amused, poking one another in appreciation or indulgence. The kids in attendance oohed and aahed as Angus began to glide.

And as he flew through the air, Nat had to admit that . . . she did not hate this. She still thought he was bonkers for doing it.

But this whole day had been so serious, so stressful. Weddings were supposed to be about two people expressing themselves and their love, right? Instead, Gabby had gotten swept up in concern about *Will the guests be too hot? Will everything go as it is supposed to? Will other people have a good time?* By doing this ridiculous entrance, Angus had chosen to inject some fun into the proceedings, to say, *Look, love makes us into fools, so here I am showing you just how much of a fool I am,* and maybe that was admirable in its own misguided way. It certainly wasn't anything like her mother's sad second wedding. Nat smiled, in spite of herself, as Angus achieved both liftoff and a strange kind of beauty.

Then, with Angus halfway across the pond, the slider jammed, caught on some sort of knot. Angus juddered to a halt and dangled. His nice dress shoes nearly skimmed the pond's surface. The smile drained from his face, replaced by a look of terror.

Natalie's side of the altar was closer to the pond, and Rob had stepped forward, without her noticing, standing to her right. The two of them stared in shock as the crowd gasped.

One of Angus's hands began to slide down the handle, then grasped for purchase. And seemingly without thinking, Rob shot his own hand out and grabbed on to Natalie's. She was so caught up in watching Angus that she didn't register anything besides *Warm, comforting, strong.*

"Hold tight, buddy!" his friend Teddy called as the string quartet stopped playing in confusion. He gave the line a tug, as if to dislodge the jam. But instead, he dislodged Angus.

And letting out a strangled cry, Angus plummeted straight into the water below.

Nat squeezed Rob's hand tighter, but he wrenched it from her grasp. Tearing off his jacket, he ran to the edge of the pond and

waded in. Did he think he was a lifeguard? This pond was maybe
five feet deep in the center. Already, Angus had come up for air,
paddling and sputtering, wiping water out of his eyes as he found
footing on the murky bottom. Rob dove under the water and,
with steady strokes, made his way to Angus's side. Coming up,
hair plastered to the side of his face, he said something to Angus
in a low voice, but Natalie couldn't make it out among the whispering of the guests, all craning their necks, holding back laughter or dismay, a mix of concern and embarrassment for him and,
in a few cases (the children), wild entertainment.

Angus nodded, and together the two of them paddled toward
shore, Rob matching Angus's slower pace. (So he *could* go at
someone else's speed! Just apparently not hers!) They scrambled
up the bank, mud and algae on their pants. Waterlogged. Rob's
white dress shirt had gone see-through, clinging to his chest underneath. She could see practically everything: a whorl of chest
hair; abs that, like his biceps, were firm without being ostentatious. Annoying, for a chest like that to be wasted on an asshole.
He caught her staring and narrowed his eyes in confusion, then
looked down to follow her gaze. Realizing how exposed he was,
his eyes flitted to the rest of the gathered crowd, his jaw working.
He picked up his jacket from the bank, awkwardly held it in front
of himself for a moment, then proceeded to put it on over his wet
shirt, which could not have been comfortable.

Then he turned his attention to Angus, who was wringing out
the sleeves of his own jacket. Natalie hadn't known if it was possible for Angus to get embarrassed—he seemed to move through
life with so little awareness—but now, his mortification was
clear. Rob gave Angus a fortifying pat on the back, then picked a
trail of green algae off Angus's shoulder. "You okay?" he asked in
a low voice. Angus nodded. "Let's get you married, then."

Angus turned to the crowd and gave a little wave and a bow, an attempt to break the tension. It half worked: his extended family clapped, a couple of older uncles whistled. But plenty of other people shifted in their seats.

Natalie stepped aside to let Angus pass her and take his place next to the minister, whose face was frozen in shock. This man was old. He'd performed many a wedding in his day, so if this had discomfited *him* this much, Natalie could only imagine how Gabby—

Oh God, Gabby. Secreted in the entryway, out of sight. What had been conveyed to her? Did she know the scene that she was about to walk into? Surely the wedding coordinator in charge of cueing her had told her something, but what? Natalie picked up her skirt, ready to run back and talk Gabby through exactly what to expect out here, but Angus had already given a shaky nod to the string quartet, and they'd begun to eke out Pachelbel's Canon.

So Gabby emerged from the door on her father's arm and began to walk down the aisle. She'd affixed a beatific smile to her face and seemed to shimmer: the sun gleaming off her full dark curls, the skirt of her dress swishing around her feet.

Then she took in the scene, and it was clear that the wedding coordinator had *not* told her the full extent of what had gone down. Her expression changed in slow motion. The beatific smile wilted (though now that Gabby was closer, Nat could see the strain and stress in it). Her mouth began to drop in incredulity, her eyes going deer-in-headlights as they landed on her waterlogged fiancé.

And now, as she walked, she was veering.

She.

Was.

Veering.

Extricating her arm from her father's. Turning from her path down the aisle toward a break in the chairs. Starting to cut a circular route that would take her back up to the double doors she'd emerged from.

Oh God. She was going to pull a runaway bride after all.

Natalie readied herself to run after her—to be a comfort, an accomplice, whatever Gabby needed—and though she was freaking out over the messiness and heartbreak of it all, a little part of her also thought, *She is coming back to me.*

Nat and Rob locked eyes for a moment, the horror written on his face. She'd warned him. He'd done nothing.

Everyone watched, frozen, as Gabby kept walking, almost as if her feet were taking her somewhere beyond her control. She headed to the path by the pond, where she'd turn back to the house.

Except she didn't turn. Natalie kept waiting for the moment when the path would change, but somehow, Gabby just kept going down the bank, toward the water's edge. In her poofy white gown, the most expensive thing she owned, she walked straight into the pond up to her thighs, her expression stoic. Then she turned and locked eyes with Angus. Natalie held her breath.

"Screw it," Gabby said, and plopped down into the water.

And in that moment, as the guests gasped, as Gabby resurfaced with her mouth open in laughter, as Angus ran down to the pond, whooping, to help Gabby out, Natalie knew: her best friend was not rushing into marriage simply to check a box. Strange and inconceivable as it seemed, Gabriella Alvarez wanted to marry Angus Stoat the Third.

And in a gown bejeweled with algae, she did.

10

★☆☆☆☆

The vows had been made, the hors d'oeuvres passed, and Rob Kapinsky was hiding in a corridor, practicing his speech one final time.

Rob had not, for one moment, entertained the thought of saying no when Angus asked him to be best man. He could stand up straight in a suit, plan a bachelor trip, and handle any last-minute crises without collapsing under pressure. He understood that to be a best man was to put the groom's needs before your own, so he would not be annoyed if he was taken away from the party to run errands. (In fact, his introverted heart might enjoy the momentary break from socialization.)

But one part of being best man had caused him significant anxiety ever since the wedding planning began: giving the toast.

One might think that an aspiring academic would relish an opportunity for public speaking. But Rob's ultimate career goal involved research and seminars over lecturing to packed auditoriums. He'd chosen his specialty carefully: students were not lining up around the block for Linguistics 101.

The way that people could hold a microphone with ease seemed entirely foreign to him. Were they not always worried that it was too close to their mouth, creating an unpleasant plosive sound that caused the listeners auditory discomfort? That or too far away so that no one in the audience could *quite* hear, and everyone wanted to say, *Bring it closer!* but did not because of the social awkwardness that interrupting would entail?

But for Angus, Rob was determined to give a speech that meant something. He'd signed up for an online public speaking course and taken notes through the lectures. He'd practiced in his bathroom mirror. He'd scoured various websites for wedding toast advice. Then he'd written three drafts, performing it once for his roommate to get feedback, even though he hated asking for favors. The resulting toast was a tight four minutes and twenty seconds when Rob read it straight through, enough time built in for laughter and other delays so that it would stay under the requested five-minute limit.

In the privacy of the hallway, he recited it under his breath, pacing, tugging at his collar. The back of his neck itched from the way his shirt had dried, stiff and crusted, after his unplanned swim. His fingers landed on a fragment of leaf that had gotten stuck right above his shoulder blade, and he pulled it out, placing it in his pocket when he didn't see a trash can readily available.

Despite what Natalie probably believed, he had considered talking Angus out of the zip-line plan, going so far as to bring it up at the bachelor party earlier that week. But the moment that Rob said the word "zip-line," Angus had lit up.

"It's perfect, isn't it? Gabby's nervous about walking down the aisle. Can you imagine being that beautiful and yet not liking it when people look at you?" Angus shook his head in disbelief. "I can't." Then he stared off into the middle distance, smiling dopily as if seeing Gabby there.

"And how does zip-lining play into this?" Rob prompted.

"Ah, right! If I come in that way, it takes the pressure off! It'll loosen people up, make it so that Gabby doesn't have to get all in her head about her walk down the aisle."

After that, Rob didn't have the heart to pour cold water on the plan. Angus knew his relationship with Gabby better than Rob did. Better than Natalie did too, though clearly she thought otherwise—

The door to the bathroom opened, and Natalie emerged, stopping short at the sight of Rob. She also held a piece of paper in her hands, and her eyes flitted down to his.

"Practicing your toast?" she asked. "Me too."

He cleared his throat. "Just want to do well for Angus and Gabby."

"Of course. It's not a competition," she said in that irritating voice she'd been using with him all day, honeyed and insincere, a voice that didn't seem like her at all. But then again, he didn't really know her. The past couple of weeks had made that all too clear.

Beyond the toast, another part of being best man had begun to cause him anxiety in the time leading up to the wedding. This anxiety was different, though. Anticipatory. Almost pleasant. The anxiety of seeing Natalie again. Sometimes, without meaning to, he'd think of the way her big smile turned her face . . . well, the only word that seemed to fit was "luminous."

Angus kept Rob apprised of the latest in Natalie's life, though Rob had never asked outright for information. Angus was a gossip, in the nicest sense of the word. He spread not secrets or judgment but updates. The people he knew, even barely, were fascinating to him, and he wanted to broadcast their achievements to all. Someday, he'd be the kind of father who knew exactly what was going on in the lives of all his children's school friends. Rob and Natalie had met one time; therefore, in Angus's mind, Rob would surely appreciate any pertinent updates in her life until he was on his deathbed. Even after that, perhaps, Angus would come visit his gravestone bearing flowers and an update on how Natalie had won last week's bingo night at the nursing home.

So Angus told Rob all about Natalie's book deal, beaming with pride as if he'd written the book himself. He had not written it, nor in fact read it. Angus's literary tastes veered more toward business books and *Dune*. But Rob liked literature of all kinds. Or he had. In recent years, his PhD program had sucked the joy out of reading for pleasure. He read for research. Oh, how much he read for research. He walked out of the library and stood motionless in the sun for five minutes and then went back down and read for research some more. And when the research was done, he had no energy left for complicated text. (He unwound with nature documentaries instead.)

But he'd taken note of Natalie's release date, then bought the book as soon as it was available at his local bookstore. She had actually done it—what she'd said she was going to do.

And as he'd begun the book, for the first time in a long time, reading had not felt like work. Natalie had a clever, engaging voice. Perhaps it was more cynical than he'd expected from how she'd talked about the magic of writing when they'd met, perhaps he could feel the writing striving to impress, but still, he'd read eagerly about the travails of a twentysomething woman in New York City. Then he'd reached page 28.

"Right," he said to her now, staring down at the speech in her hand. "Not a competition." He turned and walked back into the dining room, determined to win.

He had time for one more sip of his whiskey and a bite of

salad before the DJ called his name. Steeling himself, he approached the microphone stand, an unpleasant ticking in his ears—his heartbeat.

Looking over the assembled guests, his eyes fell upon his parents. Angus had invited them—after all, he'd spent many afternoons at their house, gone on family vacations with them, listened to Rob's father regale them all. Now, Professor Kapinsky held court at table seven, telling some anecdote to Angus's second cousins, Rob's mother fading into the background beside him. This was how it always was. His mother deferred—well, except during that strange, chaotic three-month period when Rob was young that they never talked about, that had been erased so fully from their family history that Rob sometimes wondered if it had all been an exceptionally vivid dream.

His parents' dynamic had been set up from the beginning of their relationship, when his mother secured a highly sought-after position as his father's graduate student. Only a few months after starting in his office, she became pregnant with Rob, an event that broke up his father's first marriage and instilled a lifelong enmity in Rob's two older half siblings, who were determined to hate this invading baby forever. *Who hates a baby?* Rob sometimes wanted to ask them whenever awkward family functions forced them together, but it was a lost cause.

Rob's father was brilliant. Rob's father was a cliché.

Now, Rob's mother gave his father a diffident pat on the shoulder to indicate that he should stop talking and pay attention to his son. Rob grasped the microphone. He couldn't stop himself from looking at Natalie, who was leaning back in her chair, arms folded across her chest, an eyebrow raised. He yanked his eyes from her, cleared his throat, and began.

"Hello, everyone." Irritatingly, his mouth was dry, despite the recent whiskey sip. He forced a swallow, then went on. "I met Angus in the spring of eighth grade, when I transferred schools. Now, being a boy with pimples and a changing voice, coming into a group of ruthless middle schoolers who have known each other for years . . ." He paused for effect, just as he'd practiced. "This may surprise you, but it's not the optimal way to make new friends."

A murmur of laughter from the audience, and Rob's shoulders loosened a smidge.

The key to a good toast was understanding what to leave out. The strangers in this ballroom did not need to know where the story really began, the confluence of factors, the decisions small and large, that led to Rob's transfer in the first place.

But if he *were* to tell the whole story, he'd begin with the fact that his father was a legend. Professor Stuart Kapinsky, Princeton University's preeminent constitutional scholar. Admired, feared, and sucked up to in equal measure. If you wanted to see a perfect public speaker, all you had to do was attend one of his classes—if you could get in.

Rob loved academia as a child. How could he not? His father brought him into class once or twice a semester, where college students doted on him. Professor Kapinsky would have Rob come up to the front to help illustrate a point, and all these al-most grown-ups would laugh and coo and beg to babysit. Some-times, at night, he and his parents would get ice cream from one of the many shops dotting the small downtown and wander the campus, stopping off in an archway to listen to a concert by one of the student a capella groups, and as they sang some Paul Si-mon song in perfect harmony, Rob would think he'd never heard a more beautiful sound. Everywhere, great minds discussed great topics. Someone could be solving some heretofore unprovable mathematical theorem, and you'd never know it because they'd be sitting in the student center wearing baggy sweatpants, unwashed and ripe, like any other student, clutching a Red Bull in one hand and scribbling furiously with the other.

It all made his own education feel a little boring. After you'd sat in on your father's special seminar—hundreds of students applied for it, and his father only picked fifteen!—junior high history classes paled in comparison.

But when Rob was in eighth grade, a teacher came in and shook everything up. Ms. Lindsay was twenty-four. She wore flared jeans and drove a car with a bumper sticker that read THIS IS WHAT A FEMINIST LOOKS LIKE years before corporate America decided feminism was something to splash all over tote bags and coffee mugs. For their first lesson in American history, she held up a copy of the pocket Constitution.

"This document governs how we live our lives. A bunch of brilliant men wrote it hundreds of years ago, and there's so much good in it," she declared to the class in a raspy, thrilling voice, a voice that indicated that she'd spent time smoking cigarettes or maybe even marijuana. "But we've got some bright minds in here too." Then she ripped the pages in half. "And I think we could do better."

In that moment, thirteen-year-old Rob fell in love for the first time.

Their assignment was to write an essay proposing what they'd put into a new Constitution, a document to govern the country *now* if they were starting from scratch. They'd all present their ideas and use them to make a Classroom Constitution. "After all," Ms. Lindsay said, "so much has changed since these old dead men wrote the rules. They didn't even consider Black people and women to be full citizens with rights!"

Rob went home, put his head down, and worked harder than

he ever had before. He was determined to impress Ms. Lindsay. And more than that, he liked the assignment, which made him think differently about something he'd always taken for granted. That night over dinner, he presented what he had to his father, knowing that he'd have excellent notes. Rob imagined burnishing his arguments, presenting them in front of everyone, Ms. Lindsay trying to collect herself when he was done. She would put her pen down, take a deep breath, and say, "Well, class, I think we've found our Thomas Jefferson."

But instead, when Rob stopped talking, his father frowned for a long moment. Then he sat back, folded his hands together, and said, "The entire premise of this assignment is flawed. Of course the Constitution is an imperfect document. That's why the founders gave us the ability to write amendments. But to suggest we toss the whole thing out is, frankly, ridiculous."

"But don't you think that the world has changed a lot since they wrote it?"

"Sure it has. So the fact that the core tenets hold up so well only confirms the brilliance of the founders."

Arguing with his father was like being tossed around in an angry ocean. Professor Kapinsky was relentless, letting you catch your breath for a moment only to knock you off your feet again before you could formulate a full response. (No wonder all the other professors in his department seemed to fear him.) And he was *not* pleased that Ms. Lindsay had ripped up a sacred document in what he dismissed as some "pandering display of theatrics." By the time he was done, it was hard for Rob to remember what he'd liked about the assignment in the first place.

So, the next day in class, when it was Rob's turn to present his ideas, he stood and said, "I disagree with the premise. I don't think we should throw out the Constitution."

Ms. Lindsay smiled. "Dissent! I like it. But you do still need to do the assignment. I'll come back to you tomorrow."

But the next day, Rob refused again, egged on by his father, who told him that he was standing up for his principles, just like the founders did. Ms. Lindsay admired that Rob had a strong point of view. But he simply didn't do the work, so he left her no choice. She gave him a D.

It was the worst grade he'd ever gotten, and his father was incensed. Not at him. At Ms. Lindsay. Professor Kapinsky rode his high horse all the way to the principal's office for a meeting in which he railed about the curriculum. What were Ms. Lindsay's credentials, anyway? Also, she had a public profile on this new Myspace website, on which someone had posted a picture of her drinking in a bikini—was that not incredibly inappropriate for a teacher of children?

Rob was one of the quieter kids in class, but he wasn't unpopular. They'd all grown up together, and the friendships he'd formed in the sandbox had mostly stuck. But as the news of his father's war against Ms. Lindsay spread, Rob got caught in the crosshairs. Everyone liked Ms. Lindsay, who started coming into class dampened and sad, holding on to her job but on a sort of probation that made her scared to do anything but teach straight from the textbook. Many of Rob's classmates stopped speaking to him or called him "Daddy's little prince" or worse. Rob's father wasn't overly concerned with harming someone's career—he'd done it before to up-and-coming colleagues who threatened his position or when it helped his own advancement. That was simply what you needed to do to succeed in this world, and didn't Rob want to succeed? Didn't he want the things that his father had? But if Rob couldn't deal with the fallout, if his son was too *sensitive* . . . well, then Rob's father would pull him out of that school and send him to a private academy half an hour away, a cliquey, competitive school where Rob seemed doomed to have even fewer friends than he already did.

"The first day of my new school, no one spoke to me," Rob said now to the wedding guests. "I found out later that the most popular kid in class had made a rule that no one was supposed to talk to new kids for at least the first week, and nobody was brave enough to defy him. So I ate lunch in the bathroom, which was very unhygienic. I resigned myself to going through the rest of the year unhappy. But things changed the second day. Because on my first day of school, one kid from my class had been absent. And that kid was Angus."

A knowing murmur from the crowd. Rob took another deep breath, feeling more and more in control.

"Day two, I was sitting at my desk, and this kid with a startling amount of headgear takes the chair next to me. Despite having been informed about the new-kid rule, he leans over and offers me a Capri-Sun. For some reason, his backpack was full of them. I later found out that he carried them around to offer to people whenever they were thirsty. And he says, 'Hey, buddy! Where did you come from?'

"And from that moment on, I wasn't alone. Let me tell you what it's like to go through the world with Angus at your side. He cheers you up. He makes life into an adventure." Rob was feeling so good, he decided to go for an ad-lib, of all things! "For example, he might decide to zip-line into a wedding." The crowd laughed again. Oh, Rob was riding high. Perhaps public speaking was not so terrible after all, when you felt strongly about your topic. He continued, not even needing to glance at his written copy. "And then along comes Gabby, a smart, hardworking woman who embraces Angus's irrepressible spirit but also grounds him in a way that has been really heartening to see. And, Gabby, though we don't know each other as well as we'd like to yet, I get the sense that the reverse is true for you. That Angus loves you for your drive and focus while also encouraging you to, every once in a while, walk into a pond in your wedding dress." Gabby laughed and nodded, and Rob squared his shoulders to deliver his final lines. "So, Angus and Gabby, I know you'll approach your journey through the world together with the same curiosity and kindness that Angus had even as a headgear-wearing eighth grader. And the world will be all the better for it."

Gabby put her hand over her heart. Angus mouthed a *Thank you*, his eyes red. And Rob held up his glass, prompting the ballroom to raise their own in a cheers to the happy couple. Rob sat back down amid a hearty round of clapping, resisting his urge to shoot a triumphant glance at Natalie. His speech was good, and his speech was done. The groomsman sitting next to him clapped him on the back. "Nice job, man!"

Then, at the next table over, Natalie rose to her feet.

"Let's give our best man one more round of applause," she said, baring her teeth in his direction. A tendril of hair had unwound from her updo over the course of the day's exertions, and now it clung to the soft curve of her neck, the same way her blue dress clung to the curves of her body. "A beautiful speech and a tough act to follow." She paused. Collected herself. "But I'll do my best." Then she shot the crowd a smile of such confidence and ease that Rob knew he was screwed.

"I'm Natalie, Gabby's maid of honor, and I met her in college, so at that point, she was past the 'unfortunate orthodontics' phase." There it was, the first chuckle from the audience, and with an ad-lib too. Natalie held the microphone steady in her hands as she went on.

"Gabby has an amazing way of making you feel at home. So it made perfect sense that, our senior year, she became a resident adviser. Which was great for me, because as her roommate, I got to live in a sweet dorm room without having to do any of the work of comforting homesick freshmen. No surprise, Gabby thrived as an RA. You should have seen this girl lead icebreakers. Those freshmen in our dorm were the luckiest kids in the world—Gabby kept them in a constant supply of snacks. She made sure they were all getting 4.0s and held their hair back when necessary. There was a line out our door of kids who claimed they were having a hard time adjusting, but really, they just wanted an excuse to hang out with her.

"She was so good at it that she got nominated for an award: the Spirit of the School, meant for students who demonstrated exceptional commitment and compassion. Gabby hadn't been trying to get nominated, but once she was, she set her heart on winning. I mean, you got a certificate AND a small cash prize? I'm not sure if you know this about our girl, but under the surface, she's incredibly ambitious. She schmoozed, she committed, she was on track to win it all.

"And then, the morning of her final interview with the nominating board, I woke up in excruciating pain. See, the day before, I'd gone to the campus gym with this cute guy who wanted to show me his weight-lifting routine, and, in trying to appear more badass than I was, I worked out harder than I ever had in my life. The things we do for men with six-packs, huh?" she said, as if every single person in that ballroom was her best friend, grabbing a drink after work with her. In response, they leaned forward. Rob even felt himself leaning too, before he pulled back. Because if anyone else but her had been delivering this speech, he would have been just as charmed. This toast was good, but more than the words, it was the way she delivered it, totally at ease, taking the perfect pauses. She was a natural and she knew it.

"But," Natalie went on, "I ended up getting this rare complication of overexercise called rhabdomyolysis, which involves muscle breakdown and other gross things I will not mention, because I know you're all trying to eat your individual portions of cod. Gabby found me crying in bed. She rushed me to the medical center and sat with me for hours, holding my hand, refusing to leave my side, no matter that it meant losing out on the award she'd tried so hard for. She never once made fun of me for being an idiot, though I probably would have deserved it. I always thought that she demonstrated the spirit of the award better than anything she might have done in her interview, but still, the college gave it to Emily Weinbacher instead, which was a gigantic mistake." Nat paused. "Oh hey, Emily!" The ballroom gasped, and she burst into a grin. "No, she's not here, can you imagine? And look, I'm sure Emily is a great person. But she's no Gabby."

Amid all the laughter, Natalie's face softened with true affection. "Because Gabby is a once-in-a-lifetime woman. And I know she and Angus will have a once-in-a-lifetime marriage. Angus, I bet all those freshmen kids in our dorm are steaming with jealousy that you get Gabby to be your resident adviser through life."

And that would have been a solid enough closing, but she wasn't done. "And because I continue to feel terrible about making Gabby miss out on that award, I called up the university's alumni office last month. They agreed that you deserved some sort of recognition after I made a very persuasive argument, aka promised to donate to them every year for the rest of my life. But joke's on them, because they did not specify the donation amount, so until I pay off my loans, they will annually be receiving five dollars. Anyways!"

She was reaching down to the paper she'd been carrying earlier, which he'd assumed was a printed-out copy of her speech. Had she brought a prop? Natalie held the paper out for the ballroom to see—fancy-looking, with their college crest on it. "I'd like to present to you the certificate you should've gotten all those years ago. Please ignore the asterisk on here where the school stipulates that it's not an official award."

"Stop!" Gabby said, tearing up, and the rest of the guests clapped, full of the satisfaction that arrived when a story came back around to a surprising yet inevitable conclusion.

Natalie began to read the honor aloud. "'The university recognizes the exceptional compassion and commitment that Gabriella Alvarez'"—she paused—"'and Angus Stoat the Third'"—here, Angus let out a bellow of surprise and delight—"'have shown to each other and to the people they love. They truly demonstrate the Spirit of the School, even though Mr. Stoat the Third did not go here.'"

Natalie handed the certificate to Gabby, who had happy tears streaming down her cheeks now. "May your marriage be full of compassion and commitment for all the years to come. It's the two of you, so I have no doubt it will be."

With that, she thrust her glass of champagne into the air, and the ballroom burst into applause. The toast was a triumph. Rob would've admired her, maybe even asked her for tips, in any other situation. She was radiant, a gladiator emerging from the arena with a lion's pelt on her arm. He would not be receiving any more compliments for the rest of the night. Her toast had eviscerated the memory of his. And when she shot him a look, he knew with absolute certainty something that he'd suspected over the course of the day.

She knew about the rating he'd given her book.

The night he read the novel, finishing it at four a.m., he'd logged on to his Goodreads, skimmed all of her gushing reviews, and typed out one of his own, along with one star. He'd let his finger hover over the submit button for one tantalizing moment. Then he'd deleted it all, determined not to stoop to her level.

Until he saw her again at the rehearsal dinner, looking infuriatingly pleased with herself and pretty in her red dress, accepting compliments on her book left and right, then coming over to him to make a crack about Angus flying them all to Vegas. The moment he returned to his computer, fuming, a whiskey running through him, he pulled up the website and clicked submit on one star before he could talk himself out of it. It was justice. Let the world know that not everyone worshipped at the altar of Natalie Shapiro.

The whole ballroom seemed to be worshipping her now, though. After the dinner portion, Rob's parents found him at his table. Rob's father clapped him on the shoulder. "That maid of honor really blew your toast out of the water, huh?"

Rob's mother gave him a gentle push. "Now, be nice." She turned to Rob. "Yours was lovely too." Somehow that faint praise felt even worse.

"Thanks," he said. Then, desperate to get away, "I should see if Angus needs anything."

He made his way over to the dance floor, where Angus and Gabby were sweating up a storm in a throng of friends and family.

"Hey, buddy," he called into Angus's ear. "Can I do anything for you?"

"Yes!" Angus turned to him and clasped his arms. "You can dance!"

Rob laughed, giving a small shake of his head.

"Come on, Robert," Angus bellowed. "What is life for, if not dancing?"

Rob had no illusions about it: he was an unfortunate dancer. But then so was Angus. The pond water had caused his curls to dry into a blond halo of frizz, and he wiggled his body like one of those tubular inflatable creatures outside a car dealership. Gabby laughed at the sight, but not in a cruel way, not the kind of laughter that Rob had seen directed at Angus at times over the years. Then Gabby began to shake herself in a similar ridiculous wiggle. A veil of formality still hung between her and Rob, their conversation stilted whenever Angus left the two of them alone. But now, Rob could not stop himself from grinning because Angus had done it. His odd, enthusiastic, openhearted best friend— who had saved Rob from the bullies despite knowing it would make him even more of a target himself—had found a woman who understood him, who saw the full picture of who he was and wanted to walk alongside him through life, to the point where she would follow him into a pond in her wedding dress. And what was more beautiful than that? One had to celebrate. Even if one moved with the range and stiffness of a Lego figurine, one had to dance.

So Rob threw his arms in the air as "Don't Stop Believin'" played, and for the length of one glorious eighties rock song, he lost himself in joy. Then, as the DJ transitioned into "Dream a Little Dream of Me," he turned to find himself face-to-face with Natalie.

Her cheeks were flushed. A challenging look came onto her face, her jaw set. "I wanted to ask you . . ." she began, the edges of her words slightly fuzzy with alcohol.

"Oh, yes, Rob, dance with her!" Angus said, jumping in, making assumptions, and Rob and Natalie both gave him a startled look. "A dance for the two people who helped this wedding go so smoothly!"

"Would we say *smoothly*?" Gabby asked with an affectionate nudge.

"No," Angus said. "But we couldn't have done this without you both."

"Thanks," Natalie began, "but we don't need—"

Angus turned to the people in their immediate vicinity as Mama Cass's lush, hypnotic voice unspooled from the speakers. "Clear some room for our superstars!"

"Superstars!" Gabby shouted, a little drunk herself, leading a round of applause.

Rob and Natalie stared at each other. No way to back out without making a scene. So, as the drums kicked in, Rob extended an arm, and Natalie stepped forward. He clasped her hand in his and pulled her in, making sure to maintain a careful distance between their bodies. Slowly, background vocalists oohing, the music lush and full, the two of them began to sway.

At first, she pointedly looked anywhere but at him, smiling instead at various people in the crowd as if all was fine. Two could play at that game. He turned his own head.

As he gripped her waist, the heat of her skin burned through the thin fabric of her dress. His hand tightened around her in spite of himself, and she let out a sharp exhale. Briefly, their eyes met before they both looked away again. For a moment she stopped swaying while he kept going, so that their bodies accidentally drew closer, too close, brushing against each other. At that unexpected touch, she stumbled a little. He tightened his grip even more to steady her, a reflex.

But that had the effect of bringing her in even closer, her chest now pressed against his, her head nearly on his shoulder.

As Mama Cass sang of longing, the smell of Natalie's hair lingered in his nose, making him momentarily dizzy. Slowly, as if against her will, she tilted her head up so that her eyes locked on his, and somehow he could not tear his gaze away. He willed himself to release her, to step back. He would. Any moment now.

And then, Angus's voice sounded faintly, telling the people around them to join back in the dance for the final choruses.

As the others began to move, Rob cleared his throat. "What were you going to ask me?"

"Oh." For just a second, her expression was unguarded. And then that challenging look came back onto her face. "I wanted to ask how many stars you'd give my speech."

Rob nearly choked on his own spit.

She went on. "After careful consideration, I'd rate yours four stars. So, what's mine? Don't be shy, I know you have opinions."

His jaw clenched. "You know very well that yours was better. There's no need to be cruel." He spun her out and then back again. "Although I guess that comes naturally to you."

She sputtered. "*I'm* cruel? What are you even talking about? And what about you?"

Around them, people started to shoot furtive glances at their argument. Thank God the song was ending. The moment it faded into the "Cha-Cha Slide" (an odd transition from the DJ), Rob made his way off the dance floor and into the hallway. She followed, blazing after him.

"It isn't cruel to give one star to someone you *know*?" The door shut behind them, turning the thumping dance floor music faint.

"I had issues with the book, and I expressed that," he said, more calmly than he felt.

"Oh, okay. And that's perfectly normal? How would you feel if I eviscerated you on Rate My Professors?"

"I'm not a professor yet, so you couldn't."

"Well, *someday*."

"In this scenario, have you taken my class?"

"No. You couldn't pay me enough—"

"Then I'd be angry that you were misrepresenting yourself. But if you did take my class and had legitimate grievances with it, I'd feel that it was within your rights."

"There are plenty of things within our rights that we don't do. I'd be perfectly within my rights to go back into that reception, pick up the microphone, and announce to the crowd that you're an insufferable asshole." She moved closer to him in righteous fury, the pupils of her eyes expanding, black holes that wanted to suck him into oblivion. "But I would never do that because of common human decency!"

"It also shows a real lack of common human decency to—"

At that moment, the door swung open, and Angus's grandfather hobbled out into the hallway.

"Oh hello, you two," he said.

"Hello," Natalie said pleasantly. "Having a nice evening?"

"The most wonderful."

"A joyful occasion," Rob forced out.

"I'm off to bed. Can't keep up like I used to."

"Sleep well," Natalie said, waving him off, and they watched him as he slowly moved down the hallway to the main entrance. He stopped to check his pockets. Satisfied he hadn't forgotten anything, he opened the front door and disappeared, after what felt like eons, into a taxi waiting outside.

The moment he was gone, Nat and Rob turned back to each other.

"Please," she said, "continue telling me about my lack of decency. I'd *love* to hear it."

"You want to know why I didn't like the book?" he asked. "Because you used your talents to be petty and mean."

"What are you even talking about?"

"The character of Dennis? It's the most uncharitable reading of Angus that I can imagine."

She stared at him for a long moment, her big eyes blinking rapidly, chest heaving up and down, her full lips slightly parted. Then she let out a scornful laugh. "Dennis isn't Angus."

"Sure. He's a man with no basis in reality who happens to be intent on carrying the protagonist's vibrant best friend off to the land of suffocating matrimony. A totally random vehicle for your biting commentary on . . . what was it you wrote? 'Boys who fail upward, who approach the world as if entitled to everything on offer. Boys who would, unlike the rest of us, receive all that they'd been promised, though not because of any talent beyond sheer unearned confidence'?"

"For someone who hates the book so much, you sure can quote a lot of it from memory," she said with a smirk, folding her arms across her chest. It had the unsettling effect of drawing his attention to said chest, which was especially distracting in this dress.

"Anger has a way of burning things into my brain," he retorted.

She took a deep breath and said, in a calm, patronizing voice, "The book is a work of fiction."

"In the loosest sense of the word."

"I like Angus!" Her tone was unconvincing. "You want me to list all the differences?" She held up a hand and began ticking them off on her fingers. "Dennis is tall, Dennis is *Southern*, Dennis is—"

"A bumbling fop modeled after my best friend."

"Okay, the vast majority of fiction pulls some inspiration from real life. Did I use some of Angus's qualities as a jumping-off point? Maybe. But then I spun them out into something different. Are you saying that an author can never use anything they encounter in the world as inspiration?"

"No, but—"

"Because if so, say goodbye to almost every book you've ever read. Tear up *The Bell Jar*, burn *The Great Gatsby*—"

"There's a way to be inspired by the things around you without being so blatantly obvious and uncharitable! And the hypocrisy of you giving that wedding toast just now, when in your epilogue, you imply that Dennis and Victoria's marriage is unsatisfying, that she's *trapped*, but our heroine holds out hope that, maybe someday, her friend will find the strength to initiate a divorce—"

Natalie moved even closer to him now, her finger poking into his chest, her head thrust up so she could look him in the eyes. He could feel the heat coming off her, smell the scent of her lotion, or maybe her deodorant, or maybe just her sweat: a faint, enticing blend of cucumbers and jasmine. Her fury made her buzz, as if her outline were electric. She was the angriest and most alive person for miles. He leaned forward, or maybe she pressed against his chest harder, with *all* her fingers now, as she went on, "Calling Dennis a simple stand-in is a willful misreading, showing both a lack of imagination on your end and an assumption that I share that lack of imagination. You're as good as saying that I can't do anything but plagiarize what I see in front of me. And honestly, it's a bit insulting to Angus from *your* end to say that you don't see him as anything more than the character in the book."

"Oh please." *She* was the one who didn't see Angus, or had

chosen to see him only in the most unflattering light in order to give herself something to write about. And someone who was so lazy and cruel, that wasn't somebody he wanted in his life. "You know he's my closest friend in the world—"

"Well, nobody else has expressed this concern to me, so maybe this is more of a you issue. And I think you know that, or else you would have said something to my face instead of posting it anonymously like some basement-dwelling internet troll."

The pressure built up inside him, from her hand on his chest, from the inescapable fullness of her around him, the way her body in that dress curved toward him, the slit in the fabric up her thigh, from her words and words and more words, pretty and biting and infuriatingly superior, the kinds of words you could get swept away in if you weren't careful. He wanted to stop her mouth, and for a wild, out-of-nowhere moment, the best way to do that seemed to be by pressing his own mouth against it. But he swatted that impulse away.

She would not win this battle too. He'd read all the other reviews on her page and had noticed a conspicuous absence. So he dealt the fatal blow. "If it's not a problem, then why can't Gabby bring herself to finish it?"

Immediately, the fury drained from her face, replaced by a deep pain. In seeking to reflect her cruelty to her, he'd become cruel himself, touched a deeper nerve than he'd meant to. Her eyes reddened, and she stepped back.

"Natalie." He reached out a hand toward her, but she pulled her arm away.

"Screw you," she said, her voice barely above a whisper. She turned toward the stairway that led up to the bedrooms. "If Gabby asks, tell her I got drunk and went to bed."

At the top of the staircase, right before she disappeared from view, she whirled back around. He stood there, unable to move. In a cold, clear tone, she said, "I hope we never see each other again."

But of course, they did.

Part Three

SEPTEMBER 2016

A Year and a Half Later

FROM: GabriellaAlvarez88@gmail.com
SUBJECT: A Break at the Lake

Hi!

We all know how supportive and encouraging Angus can be. But now it's *his* turn to be showered with love and praise, because our guy has landed his dream job at Insight Capital! For those who don't know, it's an incredibly well-respected financial firm, and this position is a huge step up. He'll be starting soon, but before he gets sucked into the world of Wall Street, we'd like to invite you all to a weekend of fun with us. We've rented a luxury vacation cabin on a lake in Pennsylvania for a long weekend. Our treat! Think lots of wine, swimming, relaxing, and quality time. Let us know if you can make it. I've attached an itinerary, suggested packing list, the weather report for the weekend, and a map with detailed directions to the property, since I'm told that phone service can get a little wonky. If you have any other questions, I'm here!

11

★☆☆☆☆

Natalie was standing in her kitchen, eyes fixed on the broken burner on her stove—the one that her landlord had been promising and failing to fix for months—when Gabby rang the bell.

In a normal kitchen, one broken burner wouldn't be that big of a deal. How often did you use all four at the same time? But Natalie still lived in the same crappy apartment she'd moved into right after college, an apartment in which everything was a little too small. That included the stovetop: a two-burner unit on top of a half-sized oven. Two burners were fine when you were twenty-two and subsisting on ramen packets, a person without standards. But somehow the years had passed, and her apartment had stayed small and her life had too.

Now, she opened the door to Gabby, who smiled and held out a bottle of wine. "Hey! Sorry I'm late, the trains were so backed up." She walked in and hung her jacket carefully in the small closet by the door, just as she'd done when she lived here.

"Thanks for coming. I was thinking maybe we do a fun one-pot meal? Rice and beans?"

"Sure," Gabby said, bending down to rummage in her bag. "I also brought some veggies I can start sautéing."

"Great. Um, we'll just have to do it in stages," Nat said, her cheeks flushing. "Because one of the burners isn't working."

Gabby straightened up and squinted at the stove. Her eyes flitted around the rest of the living room / kitchen, as if she'd forgotten just how small and shabby it was. Or maybe she hadn't registered the size and shabbiness before because she'd been used to it, but now that she and Angus lived in a two-bedroom in a luxury apartment building (with a roof deck and a gym!), she couldn't see anything else. Natalie and Gabby had tried, ever since the wedding, to have a good long talk at least once a week, either in person or over the phone. Mostly, Natalie came to Gabby, or they met at a restaurant in the middle, but this week she'd felt too sad and broke to go anywhere else, so Gabby had invited herself over. Here she was, a local girl made good returning to her shitty hometown, feeling utterly relieved she'd gotten out.

Natalie couldn't help seeing the place through Gabby's eyes: The tiny rickety table. The peeling paint up by the ceiling. A pipe in the corner began to clank, as it liked to do at random intervals, including in the middle of the night.

"No need for the veggies," Gabby said, settling herself down at the table and opening up the wine bottle. "A one-pot meal sounds wonderful."

Natalie began to chop an especially large onion with a dull knife, wincing as she tried to cut the whole thing in half. She paused and rubbed her wrist. A few weeks ago, she'd tripped up the apartment steps on her way home from a late-night catering event (she was exhausted, not drunk, at least not that night). She'd used her wrist to break her fall, and it hadn't felt right ever since. But she was off her mother's health insurance now that she was twenty-eight, and since none of her part-time jobs gave her benefits, the only plan she could afford was a basic emergency version. It would come in handy if, say, she was run over by a taxi, but made less-urgent care seem out of reach. A doctor's visit would probably cost her a few hundred dollars, only for them to give her the same recommendations she could get from WebMD—wrap it in an Ace bandage, take some Tylenol, try to be gentle with it.

She recommended onion-chopping more gingerly, glancing over at Gabby to see if she'd noticed. She had not.

Natalie could feel the walls of this place closing in on her. She needed to get out. But moving was expensive. Once she got this new book deal and the first chunk of her advance came through, then she could get on StreetEasy and make some changes. As Natalie sautéed the onions and Gabby began to chat about the latest annoying stunt that her work nemesis had pulled, Natalie reached over to her phone on the counter and checked her email. Still no word from her agent.

"Hello?" Gabby asked.

"Sorry, I am listening, I promise."

"No offense, my love, but you look like a zombie. What's going on?"

Nat sighed. "It's just been a stressful few weeks, waiting around for these editors to get back to me about the new book."

"Mm," Gabby said, her tone sympathetic. "I'm sure someone will come through soon."

"Yeah. They have to. I mean, I got a deal for *Apartment 2F*, and I know this one is better." She shot a look at Gabby. "You're welcome to read it, if you want."

Gabby made a noncommittal noise, a little door inside of her seeming to slam shut. Rob's face, during the wedding reception, flashed into Natalie's mind, a familiar and annoying intrusion.

In the year and change since that night, Natalie had tried a few times to delicately feel Gabby out on the subject of *Apartment 2F*, and each time, Gabby had closed herself off. Maybe Rob's horrible barb had been true. Or maybe Gabby just felt embarrassed that she hadn't gotten back to reading, and *that* was why she was so weird about it! If the latter, Natalie certainly didn't want to start apologizing and bring up a whole unnecessary mess.

Because, yes, she could admit to herself that Angus had provided her with a certain inspiration. How could he not have? In the thick of her writing process, he was always either sweeping Gabby away for another celebratory engagement dinner (At what point did you stop celebrating? He was really milking it.) or joining them in the apartment ("Girl talk time!" he'd say, settling himself on the sofa like he belonged there). Her resentment of him was top of mind, along with her sadness that Gabby was abandoning her, leaving up searches for luxury apartments on her computer screen as if each one wasn't a dagger in Natalie's heart.

Natalie had channeled it all. And the writing had swept her up so fully that she'd never stopped to think about other people actually *reading* it. She'd thrown in details to disguise the portrayal, but during the revision process, it felt impossible to make bigger changes to Dennis without doing fundamental damage to the whole book itself. Besides, it wasn't *that* obvious, was it? And people understood the nature of fiction!

"The new one is super different from *Apartment 2F*," Natalie said to Gabby now. "I think writing about a woman during the suffrage movement allowed me to get outside my own head and experiences, you know? Think about bigger issues?"

Again, Gabby made that noncommittal noise. Back in college, she and Natalie would occasionally proclaim their dorm room an "artists' den." They'd turn off their phones for a whole afternoon, light some candles, and Gabby would paint while Natalie wrote. To-do lists melted away. Hours flew by. And when they finally yanked themselves back to the real world, Gabby always demanded to read whatever Natalie had been working on. She declared to all their friends that Nat was her favorite author. Was she not going to read any of Natalie's work going forward, slowly but surely unraveling another one of the ties that bound them to each other?

Tonight, her wrist aching and her anxiety spiking, Natalie couldn't move on like she had every other time this had happened. She put down the spatula and braced herself.

"Speaking of *Apartment 2F*," Natalie began, and Gabby started concentrating very hard on pouring them both glasses of wine. "You do know that it's all fiction, right? I hope you don't feel strange about it."

Gabby sighed, setting the bottle down on the table a little too hard. "Look, I started reading and it was good. Really good. But it did hit a little close to home, so I put it down. I talked to my therapist about it, actually. We agreed that maybe it's best for our relationship if I cheer you on but don't finish reading, at least not for a while. Is that okay?"

Natalie forced a smile, even as her heart cracked at the knowledge that Rob had been right. "Of course. You should do what you need to do."

If your best friend was a doctor, you didn't need to watch her perform an open-heart surgery in order to love her. Nat didn't attend Gabby's marketing pitches, so why should Gabby have to read her books?

And yet. She couldn't stop herself from feeling like her writing was more than a career to her. That it was like she'd invited Gabby to her wedding, and Gabby had sent a gift but not bothered to attend the ceremony. But she knew that was childish, so she turned and reflexively checked her email again. Still nothing.

"How many times have you checked that today?" Gabby asked.

"Five hundred and twenty-two. Roughly."

"Oh, Nat. Things are really hard right now, huh?"

Gabby looked at her with such concern, her face so familiar and comforting that Natalie couldn't stop herself from leaning forward and grabbing her best friend's hands, a hope seizing her.

"Maybe we could go away, just the two of us. Nothing fancy. Take the train out to your parents' house for a couple nights and explore the beaches of Long Island. Or, I don't know, borrow a tent from someone and camp?" Time together, quality time, could help fix everything: Nat's current anxiety, this weirdness between them over *Apartment 2F*. She needed her best friend.

Gabby looked down at their hands, frowning. Nat wasn't so much grabbing as holding on for dear life. "Work has been nuts, and I already took off for Angus's weekend away, so I don't know if . . ."

"Right. Just a thought." Natalie let go and stepped back, turning toward the stovetop, unable to stop her shoulders from slumping.

Behind her, Gabby let out a soft sigh, then said in a bright voice, "You should come to the cabin with us this weekend."

Natalie paused. "For Angus's special trip? I can't intrude like that."

Gabby waved a hand through the air. "You know him. The

more the merrier. He wants other people to come. That's why he rented such a nice place. Well, that, and I think he wanted to celebrate by throwing around some of his signing bonus, which, when I saw the amount, I was like 'This is obscene,' but I guess that's the finance world for you."

Don't be jealous, Natalie told herself, biting down on the envy that rose up in her throat. *You don't want to work in finance.* The money would not be worth the misery. She'd have to develop some extremely expensive hobby to make her life worth living—tasting thousand-dollar bottles of Scotch, getting into sailing—but now, she worked on her life's purpose / career in every hour outside of her money jobs, and she had no time for expensive hobbies, so maybe the finances all evened out anyway. *And you certainly don't want to be married to a finance bro, especially not one like Angus.*

"Anyways, it's already all paid for, so you could come for free," Gabby said. "You just might have to share a bed with my sister."

"Melinda and I are old pros at room-sharing. I didn't realize that she and Angus had gotten close."

"They haven't, particularly. But she invited herself along as soon as she heard about it."

"Of course she did." Natalie laughed. It felt unfamiliar as it came out. Had it really been that long since she'd laughed that the act of it felt foreign to her? All the anxious waiting lately had sucked the joy, the color, out of her life. She was living a sepia-toned existence. Maybe this wouldn't be the uninterrupted alone time with Gabby that she craved, but it would be far, far better than sitting here in her apartment. "Okay, yes, I'm in. Thank you so much."

"Yay! This will be fun." Gabby began to type furiously into her phone. "I'm telling Angus that you're coming too." She sent the text and, almost immediately, the phone dinged with a response. "He says, 'Excellent,' with five exclamation points."

"That's kind of him."

"Forwarding you the email with all the details now. You can hitch a ride with us."

As Gabby kept chatting about how much fun they were going to have, Natalie pulled up the email, her mind whirring ahead to visions of herself rejuvenating, revitalizing. Emerging from a swim in the lake dripping with water and newfound peace. Serenely sipping a glass of wine as the sun set. Having a heart-to-heart with Gabby. Making a group dinner on a stove with more than one fucking burner. Not even thinking about the fate of her new book for a brief shining weekend.

Gabby, as per usual, had loaded up the email with details. Nat began to skim them, then stopped, her eyes skipping back up to the email's recipients. Angus. Melinda. And Rob Kapinsky. She strove to keep her face blank as her mind whirred.

No. Shit. No. Natalie still hadn't told Gabby that Rob was her sworn enemy, because that would require explaining exactly *why*. She had a feeling that Rob had never told Angus either (which she supposed was decent of him—he was loyal but not a tattletale). Their best friends were blissfully unaware of the roiling hatred between their former best man and maid of honor, and it was probably best to keep it that way.

So she should tell Gabby that she'd just checked her calendar and had some unmovable conflict. Anything to avoid being stuck in a house with Rob, especially after her most recent contact with him.

Now, a month after that late night at her computer, she couldn't believe that she had given him the upper hand. How idiotic, how impulsive of her.

She'd finished revising her second book, burnishing and polishing until it shone so bright she thought that anyone who saw it would want it. She'd written with a fire under her ass: the sooner she finished this book, the sooner she could move to the next stage of her life. She'd researched the suffrage movement for untold numbers of hours. She'd turned down a promotion to management at her catering company because it would have interfered. She'd given up offers of vacations with Shay and Becks, passed on parties and events, even at one point fasted for a day to understand the hunger pangs her protagonist experienced in jail. (She was Method Writing.) And yet when her agent had sent it out to the editor with whom she'd worked on *Apartment 2F*, they'd waited and waited only to get a rejection email—not even the decency of a phone call!—about how they were so sorry, but due to budget cuts and the fact that her first novel had underperformed, they could not take this one on.

She'd gone out with a couple of friends and gotten stupendously drunk. And when she came back and stumbled up the stairs to her apartment, Rob's name had flashed in her mind. Because Rob was the turning point on her first novel. Everything had been hope and possibility until he'd made her ashamed of her book, hadn't it? He'd given her that one-star rating, and then others had started to trickle in, reviews delighting in their own cruelty, perhaps feeling like Rob's one star lit their way, encouraging a race to the bottom, and then the reviews had largely stopped. Rob's face kept appearing in her mind when she doubted her talents now, all her negative self-talk taking the form of one annoyingly handsome man who smirked in satisfaction that she'd gotten what she deserved.

It struck her then that she should write him an email. So she copied his address from a group message that Angus had sent and started a new one, attaching her latest draft.

What's your opinion of this one, oh arbiter of great
literature and all that is morally right in the world?
I dare you to tell me that it's not a step forward!

(To be completely honest, the actual email included many
more typos.) Before she could think better of it, she clicked send.

Then she went and fell asleep on the living room floor. Forty-
five minutes later she jolted awake, filled with a sense of nameless
unease, like a heroine in a horror movie investigating a strange
sound in her basement.

Cursing under her breath, she sprinted to her computer, ig-
noring her pounding head, and read her email again. Oh, it was
bad. So bad that she wished she *could* go investigate a murder
basement, because being chainsawed to death seemed more ap-
pealing than the idea of Rob opening her message.

Okay, how could she undo this? Was there any world in
which Angus might know Rob's Gmail password, and Nat could
use it to log in and delete her message before he saw it? Maybe
Angus and Rob shared a Netflix account, and Rob was one of
those people who used the same password for everything.

No, no way Rob was one of those people. He probably had a
unique and hacker-proof password for every website he'd ever
visited.

Shit. She gaped at the email, her face burning and her brain
exploding, then quickly typed, Whoops, meant to send this to
someone else, please delete!

Only after sending that did she realize that her excuse didn't
make any sense, and perhaps made the entire thing even more
embarrassing. (Who else would she have been sending that
email to? How would she accidentally send it to Rob when she
had never before emailed him in her life?)

Mercifully, he had never responded. But the act of pretending that her emails had never happened would be much more difficult if they went on vacation together.

Speaking of emails, she clicked back to her inbox and refreshed it. Still nothing from her agent, Iman. Of course not. It was eight p.m. and Iman had a life. Nat and Iman had put together a list of other editors at other companies. Maybe this rejection was a blessing in disguise, Iman had said, an opportunity for Nat to find a new home that would cherish and support her more. And yet, slowly but steadily, the rejections from all those potential new homes had rolled in. *Not the right fit* or *My list is too full, and I can only take on the rare projects that I absolutely love.*

But still, Natalie was waiting on three. Three editors who were potentially interested and just needed some time to think it over or bring it to their higher-ups for approval. Three editors who had promised to get back to Nat and Iman very soon.

Natalie refreshed her inbox again. Fuck. She *needed* this weekend. How often did she get offered an all-expenses-paid trip to the Poconos with her best friend? Never. Nat hadn't really had a vacation in years.

"So, we'll pick you up at four?" Gabby asked.

Screw it. She could stay out of Rob's way, right? Awkwardness be damned, she was going to dip herself in a lake.

"Can't wait," Natalie said.

12

★☆☆☆☆

Rob was sitting in his parents' living room when he learned that Natalie would be attending the cabin weekend, thus destroying all his plans for a calm escape.

He'd looked forward to this East Coast retreat for a month now. Every day as he trudged from his apartment to his office under the blazing Arizona sun, he called up the lake in his mind. Its smooth, untroubled surface. Its fringe of firs and other trees that wouldn't grow where he currently resided. Rob longed to hold a pine cone in his hand.

He'd spent the past year of his life doing a postdoc at the University of Arizona. And while there was much to be said for the school—interesting coworkers, a fine institution—and the state—wildlife, canyons, burritos—the arid climate was not for him. The constant heat prickled the back of his neck, caused him to burn in the sun like a lobster. Rob was made for changing seasons, for temperatures that dipped below freezing. Maybe he could get some relief from the pressure-cooker environment, from the nagging feeling that something was off, if he could occasionally go outside and take a deep breath of chilly air. But the academic job market was not what it had been when his father was starting out (a fact his father could not seem to grasp). Rob went where the openings were. Now he was waiting to hear if Arizona wanted to offer him a more permanent position. A tenure-track job had unexpectedly opened up for January—a professor leaving for a career opportunity in New Zealand—and of course Rob would accept if he were lucky enough to get it. He was good at what he did, but he was in no position to look a gift horse in the mouth.

His mother had gone into the kitchen to refresh their mugs of tea. His father was sitting in an armchair across from Rob on the phone with a colleague asking him for advice. Giving advice, Professor Kapinsky was in his element. At least, when he was giving advice to someone who posed no threat to him. He stretched his left leg over his right knee and sat back, genially ribbing his young colleague. Rob took his phone out of his pocket and checked his email. He was limiting himself to five checks a day during this waiting period. Still nothing from the university. But Angus had sent him a message about the inflatable kayak he'd bought for the cabin.

PS did I tell you Natalie is coming too? Sounds like she's going through a bit of a rough patch and Gabs wants to cheer her up, which means we've been ordered to have even more of a good time than we'd planned to previously. I BELIEVE WE CAN DELIVER!

Rob inhaled sharply. Perhaps it would be better for him to stay here with his parents for the long weekend. It had been a while since they'd partaken in some quality family time. Natalie would inject all sorts of chaos into the lake getaway. Not like here, where Rob knew what to expect: his father bloviating, his mother taking care of them all. A hum of competitive unease, sure, but *predictable* competitive unease.

Right on cue, his mother handed him a steaming mug. "Here, sweets." She smiled at him from behind her tortoiseshell glasses, not a hair out of place on her head. He hadn't seen a hair out of place since he was seven years old, when she'd decreed that she wanted to be her "own person" for reasons he didn't quite understand. She'd taken Rob off with her to a shabby one-bedroom apartment in NYC, where they'd remained for a full summer, an apartment so infested with cockroaches that Rob had ended up killing a few with his bare hand out of desperation. His mother had worked the lunch shift at a diner while she waited to hear from the jobs she actually wanted. And yet somehow those jobs never came through, and she picked up dinner shifts too while Rob sat in an empty booth and read his way through the Laura Ingalls Wilder books. The day they'd had to put back half the groceries in their cart because her card was declined, he truly understood what it was to feel ashamed, of both their circumstances and the fact that he couldn't stop crying in front of the cashier. That night, his mother had called his father. Professor Kapinsky showed up the next morning, magnanimous, to help them pack, then drove them all back to New Jersey, and they'd never talked about it again. Failure was not their family way.

"Thanks, Mom," Rob said. Briefly, she touched his cheek.

"Right," his father said into the phone. "Well, you just remember that you can dance rhetorical circles around them. You *can*. I don't take just anyone under my wing! All right, now go enjoy the weekend. You're welcome, of course. Bye, now." He hung up and looked at Rob, indicating the phone. "I should introduce you to Keith. He's a real killer. When he was on the job market, you know how many places were competing for him?"

"How many?" Rob asked, voice dull.

"Six! But he knew that Princeton was the place to be." He shook his head. "I still don't understand why you couldn't choose a department in which Princeton had more of a concentration. I could have been more helpful to you that way. But ah well. Any word from Arizona?"

"Not yet." Rob gritted his teeth, then offered up, "They said by the end of the weekend, hopefully. But I did hear that they've been passing my dissertation around more broadly within the department, which seems like a good sign."

Professor Kapinsky nodded sagely. "Ah. And when are you going to let *us* read, then?"

Rob's mother shot his father a glance. Because Rob had sent it over to them months ago, a bound copy with the title *Understanding How Neologisms Spread: The S-Curve Model and Morphological Innovation* (he could fully admit that it sounded boring and pretentious), and his parents had called him up to compliment him on it a week later.

"Honey, we did read it," his mother said quietly.

"Oh," his father said, shaking his head. "Of course." He readjusted himself in his seat, then snapped and leaned forward. "Neologisms, yes. It was very good, I thought."

Perhaps Professor Kapinsky had skimmed it, and it had meant so little that he'd pushed it out of his mind. It had only been a substandard piece of work from his substandard son, who had entered the same profession but would never reach the same heights. (Though Rob wondered: How would his father have reacted if Rob had surpassed him? The one thing Professor Kapinsky might have had a harder time forgiving than his son's failure was his son's success.)

But Rob suspected something else: his father had never even

read it at all. He'd looked at a page or two and let Rob's mom summarize the rest. "What was your opinion on the ultimate conclusion?" Rob asked, folding his arms, fury blooming in him. He'd spent months, no, *years* of his life working on this, and his father couldn't even be bothered to pay attention. Briefly, Natalie flashed into his mind, the hurt in her eyes when Rob had thrown it in her face that Gabby wouldn't read her book. Somehow, this made Rob feel even worse than he already did.

His father seemed legitimately flummoxed, and so Rob's mother jumped in. "I remember you saying how you enjoyed the way Rob compared the spread of new language to a highly contagious disease."

Professor Kapinsky brightened. "Yes, that's right. An interesting intellectual connection."

Not good enough. "What did you find so interesting about it?"

Rob and his father regarded each other, his father's eyebrows knitting together, and Rob could tell that it was one of those rare occasions in life when Professor Kapinsky had nothing to say. For a moment, Rob thought he might actually get his father to admit defeat for the first time, and amid his triumph, he wasn't entirely sure he *wanted* that. But then, his father leaned back in his chair, a wry smile on his face.

"Well, to be completely honest, Robert, your writing was a bit impenetrable for anyone outside the field. This is what separates the good from the great. A good academic speaks to his fellow experts. A great academic speaks to everyone. Something for you to work on."

There it was, his father twisting things around on him like always, unable to allow Rob a true win. Desperate, Rob played the closest thing he had to a trump card, forcing a smile through his gritted teeth. "Funny, Zuri didn't have any trouble, even though she's over in postcolonial art."

"Well," his father said, "she must be an extraordinarily smart one."

"She is," Rob said, keeping his tone even. "She just had an excellent paper published in *Art Journal*. I'll send it to you. I think you'll find that it speaks to everyone." Here it was, Rob's consolation. His father might be an untouchable academic, but at the end of the day, he hadn't been able to face a partnership of equals. Rob, on the other hand, didn't have to maintain his own self-worth by only going after graduate students whom he could keep eternally in his thrall. (No offense to his mother.)

"She's reading your dissertation!" his mother said, beaming. "Things must be getting serious. Can we start officially using the word 'girlfriend'?"

Zuri was not his girlfriend yet. But things had been going well since they'd met at a university lecture one and a half months ago.

His father raised an eyebrow, dubious. And before Rob could second-guess himself, he replied, "Yes." Close enough to the truth. He'd make it official with Zuri as soon as he returned.

"Well, good for you," Rob's father said. "We look forward to meeting her."

Rob's mother smiled. "Now, are you sure you can't stay longer? I bought fresh corn at the farmers' market."

Rob found it hard to look at either one of his parents. Even being around Natalie would be better than this. "No," he said. "I should get to the lake."

13

★☆☆☆☆

The "luxury cabin" Angus was renting had seen better days. Natalie surveyed the living room. Clearly the photos in the listing had been taken years earlier, before a parade of guests had overrun the place with their pets and kids and parties. The large couch across from the fireplace had gone from invitingly squishy to an injury lawsuit waiting to happen. Angus plopped down on it, then got up, wincing and rubbing his butt.

"They really should replace this," he said. "I'll leave them a card for Stoat and Sons."

The decor was Cabin Americana: a sculpture of a fish, mouth splayed open in a howl of pain, pinned to an oval-shaped slab of wood. An odd triptych of signs that read, WHO SAYS YOU CAN'T HAVE WINE WITH BREAKFAST? then IF YOU WANT OTHERS TO BE HAPPY, PRACTICE COMPASSION. IF YOU WANT TO BE HAPPY, PRACTICE COMPASSION—THE DALAI LAMA, then I'M NOT TOO DRUNK, YOU'RE TOO SOBER! But, oh, the windows. A whole wall of them lined one side of the cabin, looking out onto trees and, beyond that, the promised lake.

Natalie threw open the sliding doors and inhaled. A stone-step path led down to the water. There was a large dock made of planks of sun-bleached wood with a tied-up rowboat rocking gently in the water. On the dock sat two Adirondack chairs, inviting relaxation in their low-slung seats.

"Should we change into our bathing suits and jump in?" Gabby asked, bumping Nat's hip with her own.

"Absolutely." Nat's fingers itched. She would just check her email before they did so. But when she pulled her phone out, she had no service. "What's the Wi-Fi here?"

"The owner said it had been on the fritz, but she was going to send someone out to repair it, and in the meantime, we should just use data."

"I don't have any signal."

"Huh, me neither. That's weird," Gabby said. "Well, work has been exhausting lately, and what with all the stressful election news, I think it could be nice to unplug!"

No. Not nice at all. Natalie could have an email sitting in her inbox RIGHT NOW telling her that an editor was offering her a book deal. She'd read it and shriek with joy, and everyone would rush over to ask what had happened. And then how much nicer this weekend would be. (How much better she'd feel about seeing Rob too, with that armor to put around herself.)

"Come on, bathing suits," Gabby said, dragging her back into the house. "Before the sun sets and it gets too cold!"

But as they went to grab their suitcases by the front door, a car came squealing into the driveway, dirt and dust rising around it. "That sounds like Melinda," Gabby said.

Gabby, Nat, and Angus traipsed out to the front porch, the welcoming committee. Melinda threw open the door to the car as an unfamiliar man unfolded himself from the passenger seat. "Everyone, this is Dante. My lover." Dante had a shaved head and the build of a wrestler, but Natalie didn't have time to register much else about him, because after a speed round of introductions and a quick tour of the cabin, Melinda and Dante ran off to the bedroom into which Nat had been planning to lug her suitcase, slamming the door behind them.

Angus, Gabby, and Natalie gawked at the closed door.

"I thought I was sharing a room with Melinda," Nat said.

"I thought so too," Gabby said. A grunting began from the bedroom, and the three of them backed away into the front hallway. "I've never heard Melinda mention a Dante before in my life."

"Well," Angus began, "I guess you'll have to get cozy with—"

From outside, the sounds of crunching gravel, then a car door slam. "Rob!" Angus shouted, and flung himself out the door.

Natalie's stomach plummeted. No. She was not about to live a romance novel trope. Couldn't Gabby just sleep with her and Rob with Angus? But that was the thing about married friends—they didn't see it that way anymore. Of course Gabby and Angus would share a bed, and of course they'd get the biggest one. Their marriage conferred legitimacy on them, made them the senior statespeople of their group. The true grown-ups.

Gabby nudged her and said under her breath, "You used to think he was kinda cute, right? Maybe you could have a little hanky-panky before you and Jeff go official. Live a little!"

"I think I already have lived a little."

She'd lived a lot, actually, over the past few years. Since Conor, she'd had one other boyfriend, but it hadn't lasted more than four months, at which point he'd revealed that his ultimate goal was to move to Alaska and have lots of children who ran around the wilderness, a life that did not appeal to her at all. (She wasn't sure if she wanted children, but if she did, she certainly didn't want to set them loose to roam with grizzly bears.) And somehow, without noticing it, she'd moved beyond the point where she was willing to keep dating someone if it didn't seem like they had a future.

She'd gone out with plenty of people. There was the Christmas tree salesman who'd invited her back to his "place," aka the van he was living out of for the month, the one in which he'd driven down all his trees. She'd found pine needles in her hair for weeks afterward. The second time they'd hooked up, he'd asked to come back to hers, and she'd realized he was more excited by her shower than by her.

Then there was the woman with whom Natalie had a glorious six-hour date, pouring out their hearts to each other. By the end of the night, Natalie had been convinced she'd met her true love, but Lily had declined Natalie's overture for a second date after finding out that Natalie had never been in a relationship with a woman before, only had the occasional hookup. Lily couldn't "teach another baby queer how to do everything," and also, was Natalie actually looking for a romantic relationship with her, or did she just want someone to replace the best friend who had clearly given her some abandonment issues?

There had been the married couple Nat had gone home with, in a brief moment in which she was trying to believe she was more adventurous than she actually was. The vibes had gotten worse the moment Nat had stepped inside their apartment. It became clear that she was either going to save their marriage or ruin it, and either way, they'd hate her afterward, so when they offered her ecstasy so that they could all "loosen up a little," she declined and slipped back out the door.

And in between, there'd been so many others: men she kissed at bars without even knowing their names, men she went on two dates with but couldn't bring herself to kiss at all, crushes on unavailable men, people she stopped contacting, people who stopped contacting her.

"Besides," Nat continued to Gabby, "I thought you said at the wedding that Rob didn't do one-night stands."

"Look, he still seems a bit formal and rigid to me. But I'd find it *very* entertaining if you could loosen him up."

Nat suppressed a sigh. She was not dating for Gabby's entertainment, even if Gabby sometimes made her feel like it.

The last time Nat had gone over to Gabby and Angus's for dinner, they'd taken her phone and swiped through one of her dating apps for, she swore, a full half hour. They were just "so curious" to see what was out there, because they'd never had to go on the apps themselves. Gabby pronounced all her judgment on the people who popped up, swiping them away before Nat even had a chance to decide for herself.

After she'd left their apartment, they'd probably turned and held each other tightly, murmuring, "Thank God for you," all little arguments about loading the dishwasher melting away in their gratitude.

Being the dating jester had grown exhausting. She was tired of opening every coffee with her coupled-up friends by reciting the gory details of her love life. She hated checking for a wedding ring every time she met a man, was exhausted from forcing herself to go to parties when she'd rather not just in case the love of her life might be in attendance.

And then Natalie met Jeff, who had the healthy glow of a camp counselor. (Because he *had* been a camp counselor for many years!) He was extremely competent, full of plans, nodding in fascination at everything she said. When setting their first date, he sent her three options of well-reviewed places at which he'd already made reservations. At the end of the night, he smiled at her with such pure happiness before leaning in to kiss her, and it was very sweet, even if part of her was calculating how much longer she'd be able to kiss him and still make her subway train.

They'd only been on three dates so far, but if things kept going the way they were—easy, nice, promising—a "define the relationship" talk was on the horizon. And if he wanted to go exclusive, to put a label on things, she would. Happily. She imagined that being able to say she had a boyfriend would feel like finally getting a good night's sleep, something that no longer seemed like it was in store for her this weekend.

Rob and Angus walked in the front door, Angus keeping up a steady monologue while Rob carried a small rolling suitcase. He wore a short-sleeve button-down. Weren't lakes for T-shirts? (Though, to be fair, she'd packed her cutest sundresses in anticipation of this trip. She'd lost the power by sending him those embarrassing emails, but she could at least look good.)

"Rob," Gabby said, and walked over to give him a polite hug, the hug of two people who respected each other but weren't particularly close.

"Thank you for having me," he said.

And then Gabby and Angus looked at Rob and Natalie, and there was simply nothing else for them to do but acknowledge each other.

"Hi!" Nat said, far too loudly. "Wow, long time!"

"Ages," he said.

Natalie hugged him while endeavoring to keep as much of her body from touching him as possible. As he gave her back a stiff pat—the kind of back pat an emotionally constipated father gave his son after a strong showing in his Little League game—she wanted to open up the lid of the nearby trash can and crawl inside. How much was he thinking about her email?

Her head had fallen into the crook of his neck. His pulse beat against her cheek, quick and hot. A low moan of pleasure rose up from behind the door of Dante and Melinda's room, and Natalie startled.

Rob extricated himself, looking in the direction of the noises.

"I worry that we may be hearing a lot of that this weekend," Gabby said.

Outside, the sun was slipping beneath the horizon, the day's warmth fading away with it. So much for that relaxing swim.

"Where should I put my things?" Rob asked.

"Well, I believe Melinda and Dante have already . . . claimed this one." Gabby led them all down the hallway and opened another door, right off the living room. "So if you and Natalie don't mind sharing, this is the room that's left."

Rob looked into the room, which featured a double bed crammed against the wall, then back at Natalie, then at the couch. "Natalie can have the bedroom," he said. "I'll sleep out here."

The next morning, Natalie woke to the steady plink of rain.

She tiptoed into the hallway to use the bathroom. The couples were still cocooned in their bedrooms. Rob sat up on the couch, rubbing his neck with a grimace, his face creased from sleep.

They locked eyes and froze, as if maybe the other person wouldn't notice them if they stayed stock-still. Outside, a birdcall cut through the rain.

"I never told Gabby or Angus about what happened at the wedding," Natalie said, her voice barely above a whisper.

"I didn't either." His voice was rough in that just-woke-up, pre-coffee way.

"So it's best if we're . . . civil to each other this weekend."

"Yes."

"And we can try to stay out of each other's way."

"Agreed." He rubbed his neck again.

"What's wrong with you?"

"It's nothing." She stared him down until he threw his hands in the air, scowling. "This couch is a torture device."

"Poor Rob," she said. "You require a bed of down?"

"No."

"Twenty mattresses, but you can still feel one pea underneath. This couch is just too tough on your weary, ancient bones—"

"I am one year older than you are."

"I'll sleep on it tonight and you can take the bed."

"No."

"It's no big deal. I'm not fussy."

"I'm not fussy either!" He glared, thrusting his head up high, but the effect was ruined by the wince of pain he gave.

"I know you think I'm a selfish asshole, but I'm taking the couch. It's settled. Now I'll get out of your way."

But the rain didn't let up. Not through the pancakes Gabby made for them all or through playing an old game of Trivial Pursuit they found in a dresser, with its questions from the eighties and its outdated answers about the Soviet Union. Not through the hour after lunch when they retreated into their reading material—fluffy magazines for Gabby and Natalie, a self-help business manual for Angus, Rob tearing through a Kazuo Ishiguro book. "Since when did you start reading so much again?" Angus asked him, and Rob shrugged. On the other side of the sliding doors, the awning groaned in the wind and the rain fell in steady sheets. Natalie tried not to be too grumpy about Rob enjoying a novel.

Avoiding him when she couldn't go outside and also wanted to stay as far away as possible from Dante and Melinda's bedroom (they'd only emerged to grab some pancakes and water, then returned to their bed) proved too challenging. Natalie gave up sometime around early afternoon, when Gabby declared that they should all watch a movie. Her choice was either to share a small love seat with Rob or sit on the floor, which did not seem to have been vacuumed in the last decade. She settled for the love seat, looking out the wall of windows at the dreary scene outside.

The television was old-school, with a VCR and DVD player. "Hm, no Netflix or anything," Angus said, so Rob got up and looked at the movie collection in the TV console, frowning. "What are you seeing there, buddy?" Angus turned to her and Gabby. "Rob here is a bit of a film buff."

Of course he was. "What's wrong? Not enough Jean-Luc Godard in the lake house collection?" Natalie asked. "Or are you more of a Tarantino guy?"

"I'm a good movie guy," Rob said. "I'm just trying to decide." He held up two options: *The Portal Makers* and *Cruel Intentions*.

"Yes!" Gabby yelled, bouncing up to grab both options out of his hand with the most energy that Natalie had seen from her on this trip. She'd been taking the "relaxation" part of this relaxing weekend away seriously, lounging up a storm, even neglecting the watercolor supplies she'd brought in hopes of taking some time to "get back to her art." Now she looked back and forth. "Oh, I'm so torn. I have this memory of Tyler Yeo being the world's best and cutest actor in *Portal Makers* and am worried that seeing it again would ruin that."

"*Cruel Intentions* it is, then," Rob said.

"You want to watch *Cruel Intentions*?" Natalie asked Rob. "Are you aware of what it is?"

"I want to *rewatch Cruel Intentions*. It's a great film. Does exactly what it sets out to do."

And that was how Natalie ended up watching a teen sex movie inches away from her mortal enemy.

Competing voices clamored in her mind. Part of her devotedly watched Ryan Phillippe woo a virginal Reese Witherspoon. But another part of her kept shouting about Rob's proximity: *Aren't you bothered?* And then there was the part that she'd barely been able to turn off all weekend. The part that kept intruding even when she was nodding along with conversation or watching Sarah Michelle Gellar teach Selma Blair how to kiss. The part waiting on something potentially life-changing. Like a song stuck in her head, it ran on a loop: *Is there something in your inbox? The delay is good, right? It means that hope is still alive!* She wished she could skip time forward just to know. Intellectually, she told herself to prepare for rejection. But her heart couldn't quite believe that rejection would come. Things HAD to work out. After all she'd poured into this book, all she'd given up?

Somewhere in the midst of all this mind clamor, the movie ended, and it was still raining, and they made spaghetti for dinner, cracking open a bottle of wine to share, pulling on cozy sweaters as the temperature dropped.

During Natalie's second glass of wine, the lightbulb above the kitchen table burned out with a faint pop. "I've got it," Rob said, and hunted around the cabin for a new bulb. When he found it, they all cleared their sauce-stained plates, and he climbed onto the table. He stretched his arms up to unscrew the fixture, the sleeves of his shirt falling, revealing a hint of shoulder, a small spray of freckles. He caught his bottom lip between his teeth in concentration. Natalie had never noticed before quite how full that bottom lip was.

A beep emanated from Rob's pocket, startling Natalie.

"What was that?" she asked.

"A notification."

"You've got service?"

"I didn't until now. There must be a patch of it up here," he said. Still standing on the table, he took his phone out and pressed a button, his face unreadable.

"Oh damn," Gabby said. "I kind of liked being off the grid. It was very calming."

"Mm, yes, so zen," Natalie said. At the prospect of checking her email again, her heart started beating so fast she thought she might faint.

"Well, tell us," Angus said, "what's the news from the outside world? Has there been an apocalypse without us knowing?"

"Not seeing anything about the apocalypse." Rob shoved his phone back in his pocket.

"But something happened," Angus said. "I know that forehead wrinkle. Spit it out."

"I got the job at Arizona. Assistant professor."

"Buddy! Yes!" Angus said, throwing his arms up in the air as Gabby clapped her hands. "This calls for champagne!"

"No," Rob said. "That bottle is to celebrate *your* new job."

"Pshaw, that's old news at this point! I insist." Angus practically ran to the fridge, pulling out a cold bottle.

"Angus," Rob said sternly, crossing his arms over his chest.

"Not listening," Angus said, banging open the cabinets in search of fresh glasses.

"Congratulations," Natalie said to Rob through gritted teeth, and he gave her a stiff nod. Casually, as he climbed down to the floor, Natalie climbed up onto the table. "Just going to make sure I didn't miss anything important real quick," she said in response to Gabby's questioning glance. "And then I'm ready to celebrate!" Sure enough, her phone began to buzz. It took maybe five seconds for her email to load, though it felt like years, and during this interminable wait, Natalie strove to appear like the lake to the others, lovely and calm on the surface, even if all sorts of murky flotsam tangled underneath.

Her agent's name appeared, twice. Natalie couldn't catch her breath. She clicked the first email. A forwarded rejection: So sorry to say this . . . Then the second, a paragraph of praise followed by Unfortunately . . .

She swallowed hard. She would not cry, as much as she wanted to throw herself down and wail right here on the dinner table. She zeroed in on a message from Iman, sent as a follow-up to this second rejection.

Still waiting to hear back from Leslie Wickham at Penguin, and she seemed quite passionate about this. She's been passing around the manuscript at her imprint to generate excitement. I'll follow up with her now. Remember, it only takes one yes!

Only one yes. She'd focus on that. Besides, Leslie was the dreamiest of her dream editors, the one who'd edited a couple of Natalie's favorite books over the past few years. If Leslie said yes, these other rejections wouldn't matter at all, and someday Natalie wouldn't even remember the sting. She'd look back and say it was fate, that everything had led exactly where it was supposed to.

Natalie looked up and caught Rob staring at her in a level, searching way. She shrugged and stuffed her phone back in her pocket, then grinned with what she hoped looked like joie de vivre. "Let's have that toast!"

Angus popped the cork of the champagne, sending it flying off somewhere into the living room. "To Rob!"

"And to Angus," Rob said.

It only takes one yes, Natalie repeated to herself.

"To us all," Angus said. "Making moves, making dreams come true!"

14

★☆☆☆☆

The next day, the sky finally cleared after lunch, the temperature warming into the midseventies. "We are going swimming!" Gabby declared as they washed their plates. "Well, we have to wait half an hour since we just ate. I'll set a timer. But go put on those bathing suits!"

Everyone suited and sunblocked up, then traipsed outside. But Natalie hung back. It was a Saturday, so any news from her agent was highly unlikely. But just to be safe, she'd check her email one more time. Making sure that everyone was gone, she clambered up onto the table, letting out a grunt of pain. Oh God, her neck. She'd never admit it to him, but Rob had been correct: that couch was not meant for people to sleep on, or perhaps not meant for people to go within ten feet of.

She paused to stretch her neck out, then held her phone up to the ceiling. A text from Iman dinged:

> IMAN: Sorry to contact you on a weekend, but figured you'd want the update. Leslie apologized profusely for the delay. She had a family

emergency this week and is just plugging back in
now. Said she'd aim to get me a definitive answer
today. I'll send over as soon as I get it. Fingers
crossed!

A knot of anxiety and anticipation lodged itself in her throat, threatening to cut off her air supply. She would find out today. At any moment, maybe.

Nothing would change if she saw the email immediately versus a couple hours after it was sent. She would not lose an opportunity if she didn't respond right away. It was the freaking weekend. Natalie would get down from the table and go in the water and then come back and check later.

But she could not move.

Not that she was stuck physically, though it would take a bit of effort to heave her aching body back down after the night spent tossing and turning on the torture couch.

She just could not make herself leave that patch of service. So, okay, she'd refresh her email one more time, then go.

She refreshed one more time. Nothing. She stayed.

Again and again, she refreshed, each time telling herself it would be the last, each time growing more frantic. She felt . . . addicted, like when, as a thirteen-year-old, she'd gotten really into playing this online game called Bubble Trouble. Each time she lost, she was convinced that the *next* time, she'd get to the next level, so she couldn't turn it off. Eventually, her mom had to block the website on their computer. Now Natalie was waiting for proof that she'd get to the next level too—the next level of financial and career stability. The next level of being an adult.

How much could she have accomplished with all the hours she spent checking her email for news that would change her life?

She probably could have learned Mandarin or gone to med school.

She climbed off the table, went to the bathroom, reapplied sunscreen, made it all the way to the door. Then she ran back to the table again for just one more check.

An unknown period of time slipped by, punctuated by false alarm emails: a sale on Old Navy's flip-flops. A political candidate asking for "a chance to explain" why he needed her time and money, as if he were a deadbeat ex-boyfriend. And then she refreshed again, and the phone chimed with a notification she felt in her belly. Because Iman's name had appeared on the screen.

Blood roaring in her ears, she read the email, Iman's quick Looks like we've reached the end of the road with this one. Let's regroup and find a time to talk, over a forwarded message from Leslie at Penguin. And then she pushed herself off the table, tripping out the back door of the house into the sun.

Gabby. She needed to find Gabby, to crumple into her arms, but she didn't want any of the others to see. She couldn't bear Angus's loud sympathy, Melinda's bluntness, Dante's . . . whatever Dante's deal was. She especially couldn't face Rob and his infuriating superiority.

They were all on the main dock, Melinda and Dante playing music from a speaker, drinking beer, and shoving their tongues down each other's throats. Rob was doing laps, Angus floated on an inflatable alligator, and Gabby was napping in an Adirondack chair, an open magazine splayed over her chest. Gabby looked so calm, a woman who had her life all figured out. Natalie crept closer, taking a side path, weaving around tree roots and low-hanging branches instead of walking down the main steps.

"Gabriella! Come in here and fight me with a pool noodle!" Angus yelled.

Gabby opened one eye. "I'm relaxing."

Angus shrugged and jumped off his floatie. Melinda and Dante were wrapped up in each other. Now was the moment to beckon Gabby over. But Nat found that she couldn't do it.

Because whatever Gabby said to comfort Natalie now would be hollow, half-hearted. Any of her platitudes about how the publishing world didn't know what it was missing were sure to ring false. How could she know when she hadn't read Nat's work in years?

Nat had plenty of other people who wanted to know everything. Her mother. Her endlessly supportive writing group. The friends who had read and loved *Apartment 2F* (or who claimed to love it—Natalie now had trouble believing that anyone had really meant the positive things they told her), who kept asking when they could expect a new Shapiro novel for their shelves. But none of them were here.

So she turned away from Gabby and stumbled down the path along the side of the house, over tree roots and patches of moss, to the smaller, more hidden dock around the bend, little more than a place to tie up an extra rowboat. She would deal with this alone.

To be devastated in a place like this felt wrong. The ferns and rushes rustled in the breeze, the afternoon sun casting a great golden beam across the water, the surface of the lake a glimmering soft blue. Goddammit, here came a loon, gliding by her with its low call. The beauty of it all seemed to say, *How can you look at me and feel anything besides awestruck?*

And yet Natalie was miserable. The water shimmered in front of her, yes, but so did the future she'd pictured for herself. That future grew fainter, then was carried off by the wind, to be given to someone else instead. What was she doing? She was twenty-eight years old. Everyone else had been laying the groundwork for the rest of their lives while she'd fixated on this book being her purpose, convincing herself that she didn't need to worry about backup plans. So much time had slipped by while she'd let herself be dazzled by the illusion that she was special. Now, not only was she not special, she was unprepared for everything else.

Why had she thrown herself into a career with so much heartbreak involved? She could have been . . . an accountant and not cared too much and had BENEFITS and saved her energy for other things instead of basing her entire self-worth on whether some people she'd never met decided that her book was worth publishing.

She glanced down once more at the email on her phone, reading the message from Leslie at Penguin, a paragraph of praise followed by:

> Unfortunately, after consulting with the team here, we don't have a vision for how to publish this book in a big way, so I'm going to have to step aside. I'm sure someone else who loves it will snatch it up!

But there was no one else who loved it. Natalie, apparently, was the only one. She loved it with a passion so deep it hurt. With a certainty that this was the best thing she'd ever done. The best she *could* do. She'd dug inside herself, then dug even more, tunneling into her core until there was simply nowhere else to go, and this book was what she'd returned with, dirt-stained and exhausted and triumphant. And the response had been a collective *Sorry, but not good enough.*

A noise startled her, and she whirled around. Rob appeared

in his bathing suit, neat navy shorts, a few remaining droplets of water clinging to his skin. He approached hesitantly, a man stumbling upon some wounded animal in the woods, feeling it was his duty to investigate. Dammit, he was the last person she wanted to see her like this.

"What are you doing here?" she asked.

"I thought I saw you over by the other dock, peering through the bushes, looking all shifty and morose."

"I'm not morose!" she said. Then she burst into tears.

He took a step forward, reaching out a tentative hand before thinking better of it and gluing it back to his side. "What's wrong?"

Water sloshed against the dock. Hot tears stained her cheeks. She tried to wipe them away, but they kept coming, uncontrollable. "I . . ." She sniffled. "I've got great news for you. I won't get to publish another book."

"Ah," he said.

"Yup. Go ahead and gloat."

"Why would I do that?"

"Because you wanted to burn *Apartment 2F* at the stake."

"Because of Dennis." He scratched at his ear. "And the new one doesn't have a Dennis type."

"You don't know that."

"I do."

She stared at him in disbelief. "You read it? I told you to erase that email from your inbox and your memory!"

"Well"—he cleared his throat—"I was curious."

"And what did you think?" She cut herself off, shaking her head, furiously scrubbing her face. "No, I don't want to know."

He shoved his hands in his pockets. "Okay."

She paced the length of the dock back and forth, wiped the snot from her nose, then said, "Fine, tell me."

He hesitated. "I thought it was good."

"Wow. Stop before my ego explodes from the torrent of praise."

"You're a talented writer."

She bit her thumbnail. "So, what? Two stars this time?"

"Five," he said, avoiding her eyes.

"You are a terrible liar." Still, silence, as he gazed out over the water. "*Robert.* How many stars?"

"Fine. Three point five."

She let out a disbelieving laugh. "Thank you for your generosity."

"Three point five is good. Four is amazing. Five is one of my favorite books ever."

"My God, you don't have to have such rigid standards for everything." She paused. "So, why only three point five?"

"I liked it. I thought the main character was compelling, and the setting was well researched."

"Harder for people to assume I'm writing about them—or their best friend—if it's historical fiction."

He scratched at the back of his neck, making a noncommittal noise.

"What's the complaint, then?"

"Nothing." She glared at him until he relented. "It just seemed clear to me that, in *Apartment 2F*, even with its cynical, unforgiving bent, you were having more fun."

She sat down onto the sun-stained slats then, her legs practically collapsing under her. "I can't win. When I'm having fun, my writing isn't serious. When my writing is serious, I'm not having enough fun."

He sat down next to her. Insane to be confiding in him of all people, to be giving him the power to wound her more deeply than he already had. She turned off everything she knew of him outside this moment, outside this expression on his face like he wanted to keep listening, and went on, her voice small. "I just feel like I've lost my way. And all the rest of you are doing so well. I've gotten turned around while you guys have been happily hiking forward, and now I'm on the edge of the parking lot while Gabby is reaching the summit of the mountain. And you, you're going to be a professor. You're not even thirty!"

He shrugged, an uncomfortable expression on his face. "Well, assistant professor. And I'm a legacy. And it's in Arizona, which is far too hot for me. And comparison is the thief of joy."

"Or does comparison just get you off your ass so you stop wasting your life?"

"I'm not sure about that."

"Me neither." She shook her head and said softly, as the wind rushed through the pine boughs, "This book is the best thing I'll ever do."

"That's not true."

"I worked so hard. I don't know how to dig any deeper. I have nothing more interesting than that to say."

"Well, maybe not now." He pushed himself to his feet. "Olympic gymnasts do their best work when they're young. But maybe for writers, it goes the other way. Don't you think? You live more life, get more perspective."

"So . . . what? I'm just supposed to wait?" She stood up too, pacing again. "I'm impatient! I want . . ." Without realizing it, she'd paced very close to him. She turned, and he was right there, still only in his bathing suit, his shoulders glowing in the sun. "I want things now," she finished, slightly out of breath.

He swallowed, his chest moving up and down. Slowly, softly, he said, "It's not the best thing you'll ever do."

She stepped back. "Thank you for listening to me be a whiny little brat."

"I think you're allowed to whine about this. It's a big deal."

"Yeah." She let out a bitter laugh. "I've been so distracted by this the whole weekend that I haven't even gone into the water." She held up her phone. "I just kept checking this godforsaken thing."

Rob looked at her, his eyes gentler than she was used to seeing them. He reached out, indicating her phone. "May I?" Confused, she gave a half nod, and, carefully, he took her phone from her hand, as if to make sure that she couldn't keep rereading her rejection email. He laid it down on the bleached slats of the dock, far from the edge. Then he moved toward her. For one strange moment, she thought, *Is he going to kiss me?* And, strangest of all, she wanted him to. He brought his arms up toward her, as if to pull her to him. Then he gave her a swift push off the dock.

She crashed into the water, still in her sundress, her shriek cut off as lake sloshed into her mouth. The cold shocked her system, and she came up sputtering. "What the hell!"

He'd folded his arms on the dock, his mouth quirking up slightly in amusement. "Now you've gone in." She splashed as much water as she could in his general direction, spraying his legs. "Refreshing, thank you," he said, then did a shallow dive in to join her. Excellent form. Was he good at everything except for being a kind person? (Well, besides in this particular moment.)

The wake from a motorboat some yards out rippled toward them, pushing her one way and then another. She could float, or she could swim against it. She'd been swimming so hard for such a long time.

He emerged beside her, droplets in his hair, rivulets streaming down his back, and she watched the passage of those rivulets as they slid down, down, until she caught herself and averted her eyes, focusing instead on the vast sky above.

"The water is nice. Thank you for the . . . encouragement."

"You don't have to keep thanking me for being a decent human being."

"It's out of surprise. I didn't know you had it in you."

He rolled his eyes. "Okay." Then he sent a great wave of water her way. She yelped in surprise and went to smack his shoulder in retaliation, but he grabbed her wrist (thankfully her good one) before she could.

They froze in that position, the lake thrumming around them, his fingers firm and strong and warm as they encircled her skin, her pulse beating against his thumb.

"Reflexes," she said, her voice faint.

"What?" His dark eyes were clouded, his pupils huge.

"You have good reflexes."

"Thank you."

A moment more, in which the only sound was the quiet push and pull of the water, the shiver of wind through the trees, Natalie's heartbeat in her ears, Rob's ragged exhale. His thumb traced the soft, thin skin of her wrist, then moved, so slow it made her ache, up her palm, pressing the tender center of it. Her fingers curled onto his, doing so of their own volition, traitorous. Her whole body was being a traitor to her now, humming and buzzing and full of want.

"I should let you go," he said, his voice strained.

She swallowed. "Don't."

Later, she couldn't identify which one of them leaned forward and closed that final sliver of distance between their bodies.

Maybe it was both of them at the same time, racing to press their mouths against each other before they remembered themselves. His hands were in her hair, rough in the best way, her arms around his neck. Every part of her that was touching him burned, and every part that wasn't pressed against him felt cold, too cold, wanted to be touching him too. She was dizzy, unsteady, maybe from the current around her (but she didn't think that was it), and so she clung to him, because if she let go, she might just slip under the surface and never reemerge.

Her first kisses with people before had been sweet and shy, or drunk and messy, awkward or nice. This, though, was entirely different. There should be a new word for something so fiery, voracious, so full of need and feeling. He was the linguist. She could ask him: How did one go about inventing a new word? But to ask would involve removing her mouth from his, something she did not want to do.

His bare chest was separated from her only by her thin white sundress, now completely see-through. His hands slid down her back, pulling her even closer, until she could barely breathe. She grasped him harder too, an unspoken competition between them even now to hold more tightly, kiss more fiercely, destroy the other more completely. Hatred and passion shared such a fine line. And she hated him, this man who had made her doubt herself and had never apologized for it, who still thought that he was in the right.

With that, she remembered all the reasons she should not keep pushing into him and turned her head away, gasping. He loosened his hold on her. They untangled themselves and stared at each other in disbelief. He seemed to be having trouble catching his breath, looking at her with such ferocious intensity that she knew she should look away.

"Dammit," he muttered under his breath, and moved forward again. In the second before he could take her in his arms, she realized this man was dangerous to her. Somehow, he saw her more fully than the other men she'd known and wasn't afraid to let her know what he thought. He'd already judged her once and found her lacking. Could she bear to let that happen again?

"I'm starting to date someone," she blurted right before their bodies collided.

"I . . ." Before he could control himself, his face fell, and she felt a spark of triumph. Then he stepped back and ran his fingers through his hair, leaving it sticking up. When he spoke again, his voice was professional. "I am too. I think it's going to get serious."

"Same. So we can write this off as a moment of weakness. Or . . . or like we had to let that out, and now we can stop being so weird and just be civil to each other."

"Yes," he said, angling his lower body toward the dock so that she wouldn't notice what was happening down there. (But it was too late. She had noticed, all right.) "This will definitely stop everything from being weird."

"Your sarcasm is not appreciated right now!" She tossed her head, then winced from the sudden movement. The kiss had erased, momentarily, the crick in her neck from the previous night. It was like being drunk, the way you'd go around bumping into things and hurting your feet in high heels, and not feeling it until the next morning. Kissing him had intoxicated her. But now the pain was setting back in.

He registered the expression on her face. "The kiss was that bad, huh?"

"No, it's just . . ."

"What?"

"My neck . . . from the couch."

"Mine too," he said, and slowly, they both started laughing.

"You were right. It is a torture device."

"Vindication," he said. "I am not a delicate flower."

Not delicate at all, she thought, an aftershock rippling through her at the way his body had felt against hers, so lean and strong.

"I'll take the couch again tonight," he said.

"That's not fair." Then he'd get to be the decent one, suffering twice as much as her. The kiss was still making her brain slow, allowing her to stumble into dangerous territory. "We can share the bed tonight." He arched an eyebrow, and she continued, quickly, "No funny business! Just so we can both get a decent night of sleep."

"You sure?" She was having trouble telling whether his expression was disbelieving or smug, like he was goading her to admit how much she'd enjoyed what had just happened. God, why had she made this suggestion? But she couldn't back out now, couldn't just say, *You know, on second thought, this might be dangerous, because that kiss was far more thrilling than I ever imagined it would be. Not that I spent a lot of time imagining kissing you! It just flitted across my mind every once in a while, mostly before I got to know you better. But anyways, it was very good, and while I intellectually don't want to do it again, physically a night in bed with you is going to be uncomfortable as hell.*

They stood in an unspoken standoff.

"I think I'll be able to control myself if you can," she said, her tone entirely dry.

"I have excellent self-control," he said, and an unwanted tingle ran up her spine.

"Good. Because I don't know about you, but I'd prefer for neither of us to leave this weekend in a neck brace."

He gave her a serious nod. "For the sake of our necks."

15

★☆☆☆☆

That night, Rob and Natalie lay next to each other in the bed, light off, their bodies stiff, Rob extremely aware of the six inches between them. Natalie turned over, her arm brushing against his.

"Sorry!" she said.

"No, I'm sorry." He scooted closer to the edge of the bed.

They'd performed their nighttime routines in silence. At one point, he'd caught sight of her in the bathroom as he passed by in the hallway. She was flossing her teeth aggressively and scowling at her reflection in the mirror, as if to say that while she might not have a book deal, she would at least have strong and healthy gums.

The house creaked around them, the wind outside rustling through the branches. Rob normally only slept in his boxers. Maybe a thin T-shirt on top in the dead of winter. But tonight, he'd felt it prudent to keep as many layers between him and Natalie as possible, wearing a long-sleeved shirt and shorts on top of his boxers. He was far too warm underneath the blankets, but removing any clothes now could only lead to chaos.

She lay still beside him as his own body jittered with adrenaline. Had she managed to fall asleep, despite everything? Perhaps she had been telling the truth in the lake—it had been a momentary urge for her, meaning nothing. She did have an impulsive streak. He didn't want to disturb her, so, quietly, he tried to wriggle out from underneath the covers, turning first one way and then the other, and when he turned briefly toward the side of the bed where she'd been curled into a ball, she was turning his way too.

Despite the darkness, he could just make out the features of her face, scrubbed free of any makeup. Her lake-soaked hair had dried into wild curls in the sun and the wind. His heart began to thud.

"Having trouble falling asleep?" she whispered, mint toothpaste on her breath.

"It appears so."

"Me too." She sighed, a low, sad sound, and he felt an almost irresistible urge to comfort her, just like earlier in the day.

"Are you still feeling bad about the book?"

"Strangely enough, it might take me longer than half a day to get over the dashing of my dreams." He was silent, and after a moment, she began, "Do you think—" She cut herself off.

"What?"

"Could you hold me, for just a minute?"

Rob hesitated. The feeling of her body tangled up with his in the water came flooding back to him. It had been hard enough to pull himself away from her the first time.

She turned her face up to the ceiling. "Never mind. Sorry, I just thought it might help—"

"No, that's . . . Sure." Rob moved closer to her, and she turned over, facing away. Leaving a few inches between their bodies, he tentatively wrapped an arm around her. For a moment, she did not seem to breathe, and Rob realized that he was holding his own breath too, fighting an urge to pull her fully against him. She reached her hand up and clasped his forearm, and they stayed like that for a minute, a minute of agony that bordered on sublime.

Then she turned around to face him again.

This did not make any sense. Back across the country, he had a smart, attractive woman with whom he'd gone on five dates. Zuri was kind and interesting, a high achiever who knew how to handle any social situation with aplomb. He could get to her place with a simple six-minute walk instead of a six-hour flight. They got on swimmingly, never argued. She even had the same dietary restrictions as him—they were both pescatarians— which, looking into the future, would make life together much easier. The last time they were supposed to see each other, he'd come down with a terrible cold. She'd canceled their date, which was very sensible—she was on an important deadline and could not afford to get sick herself. But she'd made him soup, *excellent* soup, and homemade bread (!), and dropped it off outside his door. (In contrast, Rob was willing to bet that Natalie was the kind of person who'd insist on seeing a sick partner anyway, insist on kissing him, only to get horribly sick herself, thus requiring that partner to take care of *her.*) After eating Zuri's bread, he'd almost called her up right then and there to ask her to be his girlfriend, but he'd held off—perhaps it had felt strange to do something so important over the phone. But she *felt* like his girlfriend, right? He'd already told his parents that she was.

So why in the world was he six inches away from frustrating, messy, stubborn Natalie, fixating on her bottom lip, aching to lean forward and kiss her again?

The voice boomed in his head: *What's the argument for this?*

Defend it. His father across the dinner table, barking at him whenever Rob said something that didn't quite make sense. *Go on, back up your position.* And to this indefensible position in which Rob currently found himself, Rob had nothing to say besides *Well, because I want to. Very, very much.*

On the other hand, he could make a million arguments for why he should immediately get out of bed and return to the torture couch. Beyond the Zuri of it all and the fact that Natalie was chaos incarnate, she had been awful to his best friend. And she'd done nothing to make up for it, as far as Rob could tell. Even here on this weekend, which Angus had gifted them all, Natalie seemed simply to tolerate him, showing no particular interest in his life. After how she'd treated him in her novel, she should— Rob didn't know—be bringing Angus breakfast in bed! Picking him flowers from the bushes outside! How could Rob date someone who would be cruel to somebody like Angus simply for her own advancement? (He already had one person in his life who put his own success over everyone else's feelings, and that was plenty.) And how hurt would Angus be if he realized what Natalie's book contained, how wounded if he learned that Rob had known and decided to be with Natalie anyway? Angus was the kind of guy who would defend the people he loved until his dying breath, and he deserved the same.

"Maybe we could . . ." Natalie began in a low, throaty voice. He pulled his arm away from her, drawing back, trying to maintain an iota of control. Natalie bit her lip.

"What?" he asked. Was she going to ask for more? Despite his better judgment, he could feel with startling clarity how easy it would be to wrap himself around her, taste her, touch her. He couldn't. He shouldn't. But as their eyes met again, the million arguments in his head grew fuzzy, impossible to grasp. He leaned closer. Despite Zuri and Angus and Natalie herself, he could. He would.

Natalie opened her mouth. Closed it. Then, in a rush, she said, "We could hate-fuck."

For a moment, his ability to speak deserted him. Her words reverberated in his head. A hate-fuck, as if he were nothing more than a piece of meat. In the face of his silence, she went on.

"I know we're both starting things with other people. But we haven't defined anything yet, right?" Her voice had lost its throaty edge. The more his own face closed off, the more casual Natalie's tone seemed to become. "And clearly we're attracted to each other. So, for just this one night, this one time, we get it out of our systems. And then we don't have to think about it again."

Her hair was falling in her face, her chest rising and lowering, her lips slightly parted. What an idiot he was, considering going against all his principles for something meaningless. She craved a quick distraction, and he was the guy available in her moment of need.

His voice was hoarse when it came out. "No."

Sure, the physical temptation remained. But this was for the best. Because doing something you wanted to do just one time didn't always work. You didn't get it out of your system. You opened the floodgates. There were days that Rob didn't feel like showing up to guest-lecture his classes. He wanted to call in sick, get in his car, and drive. But that wouldn't cure him or make him appreciate his job more. The likelier scenario was that he would just keep driving into a whole different life, disappointing every-one who had worked so hard for him to be where he was, the advisers who'd advocated for him, the journals that had given him space, his family. (And where would he even go? What was he meant for if not academia?)

Besides, in grad school, he'd tried having sex with two women he was dating at the same time, nonexclusively, just to see where things went. He simply did not have the bandwidth. It didn't make him feel adventurous, just insincere. He grew stressed, miserable, second-guessing his feelings at every turn. It was the tyranny of choice, the same way he didn't like going to restaurants with more than one page of options on their menu. If he had sex with Natalie right now, he'd clench up the next time he saw Zuri. Not to mention that he and Zuri had discussed STI testing before having sex without a condom the first time, affirming that they hadn't been intimate with anyone else since getting a clean bill of health. He'd have to go back to her and say that the circumstances had changed. And relationships at the beginning were so tenuous, so fragile. Zuri might draw back, and this one night of giving in to what he wanted would ruin their bright future. (He could not believe that his mind was even processing these thoughts now with Natalie so close to him, her eyes so big.)

"No?" Natalie asked, the word wobbling as it came out, and for a moment he thought that maybe she hadn't viewed him as a piece of meat after all.

"It's not a good idea."

She lay back, focusing on the ceiling again, her breath speeding up. Then she rose in one rapid movement, threw the covers back, and walked out of the room.

He sat up too, awake as if he'd downed a pitcher of cold brew. Should he go after her? Offer to sleep on the couch? Maybe she just needed some space. He'd found a strange pleasure in comforting Natalie earlier on the dock, but lest he forget, she was dangerous, with a talent for tearing down that she could wield like a sword.

Dammit. He'd go talk to her anyway. He swung his feet out

of bed. But as he rose to standing, Angus stumbled in, half-asleep, almost knocking over a lamp in his disorientation.

"Scoot over, buddy. Natalie took my spot, so we're bunking up," he mumbled, then immediately splayed out over two-thirds of the bed's surface and began to snore.

The next morning, with the hours before they'd have to leave rapidly dwindling, Angus poked Rob awake, bouncing in excitement. "We have to try the inflatable kayak! I'm not leaving before we do."

Angus did not drink coffee. Rob downed at least four cups a day—he used to only drink one, but grad school changed him—and yet he'd never artificially gotten himself even close to Angus's natural energy.

Out onto the water they went, heading toward a small island with a rocky beach. Angus was not an amazing paddler—he'd get caught up in telling a story, and begin to gesticulate, and somebody had to keep the boat sloshing through the water. Rob charted a steady course as Angus chattered away about the new directions the Futon King was thinking of taking with the store. ("I suggested he expand into futons for pets, and he's looking into it!")

"And are you feeling ready to start the new job?" Rob asked.

"At Insight? Oh yeah. All the normal first-day jitters, of course. But it really changes things for me, you know? Proves my success so far wasn't a fluke."

"Did you think it was a fluke before? You've worked so hard."

"I know, I know. But this is a whole new level of respect, not to mention of money. I can shower Gabby in . . ." Angus furrowed his face.

"Fur coats," Rob grunted, muscles aching as he steered them closer to their destination.

"With how much she loves animals? If I gave her a fur coat, she'd probably divorce me. Designer bags, maybe. Is that something women care about?"

"Don't ask me," Rob asked, giving a final paddle and taking them to shore.

They lay back on the sand, turning their faces to the sun. "But speaking of new jobs," Angus said, "how excited was Arizona when you told them yes?"

Rob held a hand over his face to block the light. "I haven't responded to them yet."

"Really?" Angus sat up. "What are you waiting for?"

"Oh, I don't know. They told me that I have until the middle of next week to make the decision. So I thought I should sit with it."

"I didn't realize it *was* a decision," Angus said.

Rob sat up too. "It's not, really. Sure, lately the work has been"—*Unrelenting? A bit boring? Somehow extremely stressful while seeming meaningless in terms of practical application?*—"a lot. But it would be ridiculous to say no. I'm lucky to have gotten this offer." He dug a stick into the ground, scratching a line into the damp sand. "Even if it's partially nepotism."

"Stop that! *You* got this. You're brilliant."

"Yes, but there are lots of brilliant people in academia, and most of them can't get a job."

"Hey, I know what it's like growing up with a big-deal dad. The Futon King casts a long shadow. That's why I wanted to carve my own path. So I get if you're having doubts."

Rob couldn't even think about doubts right now, not after everything else that had gone on this weekend. So he merely said, "I suppose you shouldn't run away from something just because a parent has already done it well."

"Hm." Angus peered at him. "You think?"

"Take Laura Dern."

"Oh, I *love* Laura Dern!"

"The world would be a worse place if she'd looked at her parents' successful careers and said, 'They've already conquered acting, I guess I should be a lawyer instead.'" Rob stopped scraping the dirt, letting the stick fall.

"Righto," Angus said. "No *Jurassic Park*."

"Well, they still would have made that movie. Just with a different actress. But it wouldn't have been as good. And think of how her absence would have affected *Blue Velvet, Citizen Ruth*—" Angus was still nodding along, but less assuredly now, and Rob caught himself. "You haven't seen any of those, have you?"

"No. But I do love *The Truman Show*."

"That's Laura Linney. Anyways. The metaphor has gotten away from me."

"Well, do you love academia like Laura Dern loves acting?" Rob hesitated, and Angus waggled his finger in warning. "Don't you dare say something like 'What is love anyway?'"

Rob swallowed, because that had been exactly what he was going to say. "I don't know what I was going to say. I didn't get much sleep last night."

"Yes, I wanted to talk to you about that." Angus put his hands on his hips, the picture of a stern father. "Natalie seemed pretty upset when she came into our room. Now, you know you're my best friend, so I take your side in things, but I have to ask: Were you mean to her? Because she's practically family now, so I have to stick up for her too."

Rob scoffed. "You ever stop to think that maybe Natalie could have been the mean one?"

"Natalie, mean? Never!" Angus chortled. "Well, unless you're one of those poor saps trying to date her. After hearing some of her stories . . ." He looked more closely at Rob. "Wait, *are* you trying to date her?" He lit up. "Ooh, you should!"

"Didn't you just call her suitors 'poor saps'?"

"But our children could be like cousins!" Rob narrowed his eyes, and Angus went on. "Besides, they're just poor saps because she's not excited about most of them. Except maybe this Jeff guy. He seems to be sticking around. So if you want to get in there, you've got to make an aggressive play now—"

"I'm not trying to 'get in there,'" Rob said. "I want to be with Zuri."

"Right, Zuri!" Angus clapped his hands together. "Well, Gabby and I will have to befriend her too. Because I'm into this kids-like-cousins idea now."

16

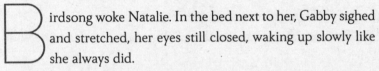

Birdsong woke Natalie. In the bed next to her, Gabby sighed and stretched, her eyes still closed, waking up slowly like she always did.

Natalie looked up at the ceiling, yesterday coming back to her. She'd already let Rob reject her mind, and then, like when she was younger and willing to sleep with jerks who thought they were so much smarter, she had offered up her body instead. But Rob wouldn't even take that.

Normally, the first time she had sex with someone, the potential intimacy of it overwhelmed her. She had to have a few drinks beforehand to cast a pleasant haze over the whole thing, to dull the anxiety of revealing herself so fully to another person. But last night with Rob, a strange and reckless feeling had come over her. She'd pulled back from him in the lake, terrified by the knowledge that he really saw her. But next to him in that bed, she'd suddenly *wanted* to reveal herself and to see him fully in return in a way she never had before. It had been so big and new and scary that she couldn't even ask him without pretending it didn't mean that much to her.

Now the hurt she was feeling cut much deeper than a regular rejection. She was furious with herself. No, fury required energy. She was just drained. A tear traced its way down her cheek, and she brushed it away.

"Oh, Nat," Gabby said in a foggy voice, reaching out to touch Natalie's wet cheek.

"God, I'm sorry."

"You don't have to apologize."

Natalie turned in to her best friend, who enfolded her, stroking her hair in silence for a few minutes. Last night, Gabby had opened the door to Natalie's choked "Can I sleep in here with you?" She hadn't asked any questions. She'd just pushed Angus out of bed and ordered him to go elsewhere, then spooned Nat until she fell asleep.

"Do you want to talk about it?" Gabby asked now, and Natalie pulled back. The two of them curled on their sides, facing each other, Gabby's eyes full of sympathy, their hair spread out messily on their pillows. Here they were, having a sleepover, as if they'd been transported back to when they were roommates, to the nights they'd accidentally fallen asleep in each other's beds because they hadn't wanted to stop talking.

"It's exhausting to want things," Natalie said, her voice barely above a whisper. "Things I have to fight for that no one wants to give me." Gabby nodded. "I can't . . . I can't keep feeling all this rejection. Maybe it's time to stop fighting and take the things that come to me instead."

"Maybe," Gabby said, touching Natalie's cheek again. "But I hope you don't do that forever."

Natalie squeezed Gabby's hand, then rubbed her eyes. "What time is it? We should get up."

Gabby groaned. "I could lounge all day. Work has really been taking it out of me. I thought I could catch up on rest this weekend, but I'm still pooped."

"Too much sun." Nat put her hand on Gabby's forehead. "Or are you sick?"

"No, I feel fine otherwise. Except, I guess my boobs are a little tender—"

She cut herself off, and they gaped at each other.

"Do you think it's . . . ?" Nat began.

"Could I be . . . ?"

"Have you and Angus been trying?"

"No! The plan is to wait a couple more years. And you know I am *rigorous* about taking my pill." Her eyes widened. "Except for when I got food poisoning this month—there were a couple days where I couldn't keep anything down and basically just slept all the time, and I may have skipped a pill then."

"Shit," Natalie said. "But there could be a million other explanations."

"Yeah." Gabby took a deep, calming breath in through her nose and let it slowly out of her mouth. Then, in a high, fast voice, she asked, "You wanna come to the pharmacy with me real quick?"

Nat jumped out of bed. "Let's go."

They ran to the car. As soon as Gabby turned the key, the *Hamilton* soundtrack that Angus had insisted on playing during the entire drive there began to blast from the speakers. Gabby turned it off with a sharp jab. "I love that Angus loves it," she said, "but after a full year, I simply can't listen anymore."

Gabby drove them carefully up the winding tree-lined road to the nearest CVS and bought a pregnancy test. Then, as she followed the GPS back to the house, she kept up a stressed, steady monologue.

"If I'm pregnant, and we should remember that it's far more likely that I am *not*, we could make it work with our finances. We've got that extra room in the apartment that we've been using as a home office slash art studio, but who needs a home office? It could be a nursery for now." She turned down the winding lane back to the lake.

"And we're near Prospect Park, which would be a good place to take walks so the baby could experience nature. I wonder if the Uppababy is really worth it. And sure, I sometimes look at momfluencer accounts, so I have a bit of a sense of what to expect. Not that you can ever really understand until you're in it."

Natalie stared at her friend. "What the hell is an Uppababy?"

"A stroller," Gabby said, as if it were common knowledge.

Angus and Rob were still out on the water when they returned, though Nat could just make out them paddling back (or rather, Rob paddling back) in the distance. Melinda's car was gone—she'd texted Gabby that she had gotten bored with Dante and decided to take them both back to the city. Gabby turned toward the cabin. "Let's go inside."

"Don't you want to wait for Angus?"

Gabby gave her a look. "Excuse me, no. Remember? If this is anything, you're the first one I tell."

Natalie's heart flooded with love for her friend. "Now come on," Gabby continued, "because I'm really anxious and need to know." They grabbed hands and ran into the house together.

After peeing on the stick, Gabby came out to sit with Natalie on the mattress in the bedroom where, just an hour ago, they hadn't realized how easily their lives could be upended.

Gabby's leg jiggled up and down. "My God, I never knew a few minutes could last so long."

"Do you need distraction?" Natalie asked.

"Yes, tell me something interesting."

"Um . . ."

"Anything. Please. I don't care what it is—"

It came out in a rush. "Rob and I made out in the lake."

Gabby shrieked. "I knew it! Well, not about the lake, but I thought I sensed a vibe—" She cut herself off. "Wait, did *he* make you cry? What did he do, and do I need to kill him? I like Rob fine, I don't want to hurt him, but I will."

"He and I are just . . . I don't know. He's a dick, but you should let him live."

"I want all the details—"

Natalie looked away as she tried to figure out how to even begin. Her eyes fell on the test between them. "Gabby," she said, and pointed.

A hushed moment as they took it in. Tears beaded in Gabby's eyes. "Holy shit. I'm having a baby."

"You're having a baby." They both spoke in whispers. Somehow the news felt so big that all they could do was whisper in the face of it. Like walking into a cathedral, reverent. Natalie squeezed Gabby tight, holding on to a body that was already changing in ways she couldn't comprehend. "I can't wait for there to be even more of you in the world for me to love."

"Aunt Natalie," Gabby said into her shoulder. Then she sat back. "Do you think . . . ? I'm not going to lose myself, am I?"

"No," Natalie said, though it was more of a hope than a certainty. Because as happy as she was now—practically full to bursting—the joy was bittersweet. Their friendship had survived marriage, but things were different than they had been, diminished. A baby, well . . . they'd soon be living in two different realities. Natalie literally could not imagine having a child right now. Even if things continued to go well with Jeff and they decided to take that step, it would be years away. And what was it that Gabby had said in the car at one point during her stressed-out monologue? *Not that you can ever really understand until you're in it.*

"I hope Angus isn't sad or disappointed," Gabby was saying now. "He's just starting this new job, we'd talked about taking all these trips—"

A clatter sounded outside the bedroom—the screen doors opening, someone tripping through them. "I think they're back," Natalie said, "and he'd better not be disappointed."

"Yeah. It's his swimmers that did this."

An unpleasant image of Angus's swimmers in her head, Natalie followed Gabby out into the living room, where Rob and Angus were finishing drying off. Rob caught Natalie's eye, then looked away, then looked back again as if trying to interpret her expression.

"Angus?" Gabby asked. "Could we talk for a minute?"

He was bending over and toweling off his hair, but he whipped back up to standing at those words. "What's wrong? Is everything okay?" Then he registered the pregnancy test, still in Gabby's hand. "What is . . . ?" he began, his mouth sagging open. He took in Gabby's hopeful, overwhelmed face. He blinked rapidly as he processed the situation. Then, "We're having a baby?" he asked, whispering just like Gabby and Natalie had.

Gabby nodded, and at that confirmation, Angus turned incandescent, beginning at once to grin and to sob. "Oh, wow!" he said through his happy tears. "Oh, *wow.*" He ran forward and swept Gabby into a kiss, then picked her up, spinning her around as the two of them began to laugh, an uncontrollable burst of feeling between them.

Suddenly Angus froze and set her down, his face full of terror. "Should I not have done that?"

"What, picked me up?"

"Yeah. Was it dangerous for the baby?"

"I don't think a bit of twirling is going to hurt it."

"Thank God," he said, tears streaming down his cheeks. "Whew, almost gave myself a heart attack there!" He kissed her again, then leaned down to her stomach. "I never want to hurt you, little buddy."

It was extremely corny, but Nat felt a tingle in her throat anyway. She started to back away, thinking that maybe the two of them needed a moment alone. Then Angus looked up, zeroing in on her and Rob. "Godparents!" he said.

Gabby laughed. "Honey, they're not Catholic."

"Oh right. Godparents in spirit, then." He stepped away from Gabby for a moment and caught both Natalie's and Rob's hands, pulling them in for a group hug, all four of them locked together.

The feeling of Rob's body smushed against hers was nearly unbearable. Her relationship with Gabby was about to change. But in that moment, despite everything that had happened that weekend and everything that was to come, Natalie looked at Rob and smiled. He swallowed, smiling back at her, and in unison, both of them wiped their eyes.

Part Four

APRIL 2018

A Year and a Half Later

Dear Friends and Family,

We'd like to joyfully invite you to celebrate a gift from heaven, our daughter, Christina Alvarez-Stoat. These first months with her have been a beautiful adventure. Now please join us at her christening ceremony at the Church of the Blessed Sacrament, where Gabby herself was christened. Details below.

17

★☆☆☆☆

The trees surrounding the church were just starting to bud with blossoms. Rob couldn't stop himself from slowing as he passed beneath them. Though the church itself was nothing special to look at—brown brick, chosen because it was where Gabby herself had been christened twenty-nine years ago and where her parents continued to attend services each Sunday—Rob wanted to stop and stare as if before a great work of art in a museum.

Beside him, Zuri raised a questioning eyebrow, so he gestured at the blossoms. "There's just nothing like an East Coast spring."

She cocked her head and took in the trees. Her face softened the same way it did when she came across a particularly beautiful painting in her research.

"It is lovely," she said. Then she waggled a finger at him. "But don't start getting wanderlust, not when you're on the tenure track."

"I suppose there's beauty in cacti too," he said, and began to move forward.

"Wait. If you want to keep looking, we are"—she checked her watch—"four minutes early."

"No, we've got the next few days to gawk at trees."

The travel here had been easy. But everything was easy with Zuri. They anticipated each other's needs, their priorities and interests almost all the same. Of course they would agree to get to the airport two and a half hours before their flight. They'd each made a list of podcast episodes they wanted to listen to on the car ride out to Long Island, and they laughed when they showed them to each other because those lists were almost identical. He loved her insights when they discussed the episodes afterward, the careful way she chose her words, wasting nothing. He even loved the way she challenged him when he was wrong—not taking offense, swiftly dismantling his argument and then moving on.

Moving in together had been easy too. They'd done it three months ago now. Together, they'd made list upon list—packing, tasks to do—and checked off all the boxes. And all the while, they'd been checking off boxes on another more subconscious list: the qualities they wanted in a partner. Cool under pressure? Check. Respectful to the movers? Check. Strong work ethic, ability to be a team player, a willingness to give each other personal space when necessary? Check, check, check.

Now, their apartment was starting to feel like home. Leaving paintings and pictures unhung would be an affront to Zuri's whole world order. Her willowy frame clad in overalls, her dark braids tied up in a head wrap and amber eyes narrowed in focus, she'd created a gallery wall in their living room, photos of them together and with their families, framed pictures of both her and Rob at their PhD ceremonies, plus some work from up-and-coming artists of color who could use the support. No surprise that an art history professor could turn a plain beige wall into a thing of beauty.

A few weeks ago, they were sitting at their dining room table, doing work, and Rob went to make them mugs of tea. When he put hers down on the table in front of her, she caught his hand. "Hey," she said, "we live together."

"We do."

"That's lovely, isn't it?" She pressed his hand to her lips. Zuri was not always touchy-feely, which made these moments of affection and intimacy all the more special. Rob blew on his mug, struck by gratitude that he had found someone he liked and admired so much. Their lives locked into each other like puzzle pieces. In that moment, as chamomile wafted up in front of them, the warmth of her full lips on his skin, he'd decided to make this trip as special as possible.

It was all too easy when he and Zuri were together to sink into quiet contentment, sitting side by side as they did their research or a crossword. Arms linked, the two of them had fast-forwarded straight into a comfortable middle age, despite only being thirty. That was perfectly fine with Rob. Even as a teenager, he'd felt that he had the soul of a forty-five-year-old.

But this long weekend out east, well, this would be something different. They'd be staying on Long Island, going up to the North Fork for a small vacation since they were out here anyway. Rob had researched inns and wineries, planning the most romantic itinerary he could. First stop, Christina's christening and the ensuing reception. A chance for Zuri to spend some more time with Angus and Gabby, and for Rob to meet his unofficial niece. Then, on to North Fork, and the rest of their lives.

Rob held the church door open for Zuri, then followed her inside. Immediately, piercing wails echoed off the walls. There, in the growing crowd of well-wishers, were Gabby and Angus and a small yowling human with a tuft of dark hair on her head.

Though Gabby had dressed up nicely, she looked exhausted, purplish half-moons under her eyes. Angus waved at Rob, beckoning him over with the energy of an average human, which meant that he was exhausted too. Rob and Zuri made their way through the church to say hello.

After a round of hugs, Gabby thrust the baby forward. "Meet Christina." Christina, clad in a puffy white dress, scrunched up her face, on the verge of bursting into more tears. "She's perfect, but she's a holy terror."

"We really do love her, though," Angus said.

"Yes, more than anything. We'd die for her. If she doesn't kill us first."

The two of them looked at each other and let out a sleep-deprived laugh that bordered on unhinged.

"So, are you back at work?" Zuri asked in her calm, steady manner, and Gabby nodded. "How is that?"

Gabby sighed. "I wouldn't say that maternity leave was a natural fit for me, so it's good to be getting out of the house again."

"The problem is that everyone is so grateful to have Gabby back," Angus said, "that they're loading her up with work and assuming it's the only priority in her life, like they don't remember the reason she had to take three months off in the first place."

"At least they gave me three months," Gabby said with a dark look.

"Ah yes." Angus grimaced. "I hate to say a bad word about my employers, but Insight Capital was not the most understanding about paternity leave."

"I'll say the bad word," Gabby cut in. "Those fuckers are such an old boys' club. You know what they said to him when the baby was coming?"

"What?" Zuri asked.

"They were like, 'Congratulations, we can be flexible and give you as much time as you need with your family.' And then how much time off do you think they offered him?" Rob opened his mouth to make a guess, but Gabby just kept going. "A week and a half."

"A week and a half," Angus echoed. "It was not good."

"His bosses think that's generous because they all have stay-at-home wives plus multiple nannies, and can barely remember their own children's names."

"Shh, some of them are here." At that, Angus turned around and waved at a cluster of men, all of them smooth, besuited, and bored-looking. As the men nodded back, Angus puffed his chest out in a way that seemed unnatural on him.

Gabby pursed her lips, steam practically coming out her ears. But then she noticed someone walking up behind Rob, and her scowl melted away, replaced by a relieved joy. Her shoulders loosened, her eyes brightened. *Natalie*, Rob thought, before he even turned around. That was the kind of look reserved for Natalie.

Sure enough, there she was, waving and smiling at Gabby. She wore a simple dark green dress made out of some sort of sweater-like material. Formfitting. She looked more put-together, somehow less wild, than the young woman she'd been the last time they'd been together, nail polish slightly chipped and dresses wrinkled, all impulse and need, untamed.

A broad-shouldered blond man followed a step behind her. All-American and hearty, a Boy Scout all grown up. Something about him communicated that he was *capable* and could easily build a fire in the woods. This must be the Jeff Angus had talked about. Not the kind of man Rob would have pictured Natalie with.

What kind of man *did* he picture her with? This question was difficult to answer. Her dress really was about as formfitting as it could be without veering into inappropriate, an impressive balance to strike.

Natalie's smile faltered just a moment when she saw Rob, and Zuri standing next to him. She and Rob caught each other's gazes. Color flooded into her cheeks. His own face felt hot. And then the two of them exchanged a silent agreement: *Enough.* They were adults in serious relationships with other people. They didn't have to be the best of friends, but they could grit their teeth and be perfectly pleasant.

"Hello, so nice to see everyone!" Natalie said to them all, and after the necessary introductions, she held out her arms for Christina. "It's the love of my life! Come here." As Natalie took Christina into her arms, bouncing and twirling her around, an image of her as she'd been in that lake house bed with him flashed into Rob's mind, causing an uncomfortable prickle down his spine. He swallowed and squared his shoulders, then felt someone's eyes on him. Gabby was giving him a *look*, different from the distant fondness with which she usually regarded him. Like she knew something. Like if he stepped out of line, she might defenestrate him. Rob made his expression blank, and moved a few inches farther away from the nearest window.

Angus put a hand on Gabby's arm. "I think it's almost time."

"Right, we should go prepare. And, shoot, we have to track down Melinda. Christina needs a godmother." Gabby took Christina back from Natalie. "Not too late for you to convert to Catholicism and take it on instead." Natalie grimaced. "Sorry, was that inappropriate?"

"Yes."

"I'm kidding. Mostly."

As Gabby and Angus headed off, the awkward foursome

turned back to one another. Natalie took a breath, ready to make an excuse and move on, but Jeff leapt in.

"Rob and Zuri! Tell me all about yourselves. Where do you live? What do you do? How did you meet?"

His eyes were bright, full of energy. Not a Boy Scout but a Scout leader, ready to take them through a round of icebreakers.

Zuri gave him the summary—Arizona, academia in linguistics for Rob and postcolonial art for her, they'd sat next to each other at a lecture on the role of the humanities in higher education.

"And did you know right away, when you met each other?" Jeff went on. "Or was it more of a slow burn?"

What kind of a question was that to ask strangers?

"Hm," Zuri said carefully. "Somewhere in between. I was interested in him when we met, but you want to get to know someone and make sure you're compatible, of course. And how about you two? What do you—"

"Oh, love at first sight for me," Jeff said.

"Sorry, no, I was going to ask what you two do?"

Natalie turned to Jeff and lifted her eyebrows, indicating that he should go first. He enthusiastically took the hint. "I work with the New York City Parks Department, helping with their education programming. So there's a lot of coordinating with the public schools around the city, bringing the kids in to explore the parks and learn about nature."

"It's extremely cute," Natalie said.

"That sounds fascinating," Zuri said, and Rob nodded in agreement.

"It is!" Jeff answered. Then he proceeded to talk about it until Rob didn't find it fascinating any longer. Natalie nodded thoughtfully as Jeff went on, adding the occasional supportive comment.

Smiling at his jokes, even though she must have heard this job spiel many, many times. Avoiding Rob's eyes or (and he didn't know why this alternative bothered him) not concerned with his reaction to Jeff at all.

How serious was this relationship? Not that it mattered to Rob if Jeff and Natalie were about to elope or about to break up. He just liked to have all the information.

When Jeff stopped talking, Rob realized he had no idea what the man had been saying for the past thirty seconds and thus had no idea how to respond.

Luckily, Natalie jumped in. "Well, maybe we should go see if—"

"Wait," Zuri said, "but what do *you* do?" Zuri often took it upon herself to make sure that men didn't dominate career conversations while their overlooked girlfriends stood silently by. In normal circumstances, Rob appreciated this. Right now, though, he wished Zuri had let Natalie make her excuses and go to a different corner of the church. Perhaps even another church entirely if she so desired.

Natalie's mouth tightened, as if she were suppressing a sigh. "Currently my main job is as an office manager for a start-up." Her eyes darted to Rob, then away. What had happened to her writing? Had she chucked it entirely? Rob hoped . . . he didn't know what he hoped. He shouldn't particularly care. He didn't. You wanted people to achieve their dreams, though. He opened his mouth to ask, then caught himself, trying to keep his face neutral.

"Oh? And what does that involve?" Zuri asked.

"Fascinating stuff like keeping the fridge stocked. Making sure we don't run out of pens."

"Pens are important," Rob said.

"Are they?" Natalie asked. "Does anyone use pens anymore?"

"I use them all the time," Rob said.

"It's true," Zuri said. "I'm always finding them around the apartment in the oddest places."

"You two live together?" Natalie asked, an almost indiscernible waver in her voice, and Rob nodded.

"Don't sell yourself short," Jeff said to her, then turned to Rob and Zuri. "She also does some amazing freelance writing projects on the side."

"Yes, that's true." Natalie tucked her hair behind her ears. "Anyways—"

"Anyone reading any good books lately?" Jeff asked, seeming to get that Natalie wanted to change the subject. "I, for one, have been loving the new memoir by Tyler Yeo."

Rob let out a half snort. Zuri put a hand on his arm. "Robert read that on the plane ride over."

"I wouldn't have taken you for the target demographic," Natalie said.

"Well, it was front and center at the airport bookstore, and I'd forgotten to pack a novel." Forgetting a book was out of character for Rob nowadays, but he'd been focused on making sure he had more important things safely tucked away in his suitcase. At the airport, he'd wanted something engaging and not too complicated, and *Yeo, It's Tyler!* had seemed like it would do.

Tyler Yeo had been the lead in a comedic action franchise back in the early aughts, about a guy who discovers a portal in his college library. Angus and Rob had gone to see the second one at midnight, along with teenagers across the nation. Tyler hadn't exactly been an amazing actor. He'd been good-natured, serviceable, bolstered by the more interesting performances around him. (And honestly, the idea of him spending time in the college library was . . . well, let's just say he didn't have much going on behind the eyes.) The third installment had never happened, amid rumors of on-set drama, and Tyler's follow-up projects hadn't done well. This memoir had been marketed as a nostalgia trip, perhaps offering some behind-the-scenes secrets as to why *The Portal Makers* had really fallen apart.

"How many stars would you give it?" Natalie's tone was dry. Teasing him? Goading him? Zuri and Jeff smiled politely, oblivious.

Rob straightened his shoulders. "Two and a half. On a sentence level, it was well written. But overall, a disappointment, obviously written more to set himself up for a comeback than because he had anything insightful to say." He turned to Jeff, whose smile was sagging. "No offense if you're enjoying it." He turned back to Natalie, unable to stop himself, for some reason, from bashing Jeff's apparent new favorite book. Natalie listened with a calm expression, one eyebrow slightly raised. "But he was so determined not to offend anyone in the industry who might give him a job that he caveated himself into banality. Where were the interesting stories? The stakes? It was just, 'Oh, this person was awesome on set, and I liked this one too,' and on and on until I nearly fell asleep."

Silence stretched out between them all for a moment as Rob concluded his rant. Jeff's mouth hung open. Perhaps Rob had gone a bit too far in insulting his book recommendation.

Natalie cleared her throat. "Well," she said, "I tried. Tyler didn't give me much to work with."

Rob's stomach fell onto the floor. "No. You . . . ?"

Natalie turned to Zuri, her expression still mild. "One of my freelance writing gigs was ghostwriting."

"Oh," Zuri said. She opened her mouth, then shut it again, at a loss for words.

"As I said," Rob began, feeling inexplicably terrible, "on a sentence level, it was well written." Zuri elbowed him. "But I'm sorry."

"It's fine," Natalie said.

"I think it's a fantastic book," Jeff said. "And Nat worked so hard on it." For just a moment, displeasure flickered in Natalie's eyes, her mouth turning down, before she returned to neutrality. No one besides Rob seemed to register it. To notice, one had to have been looking closely at Natalie's lips and eyes. Why was Rob looking so closely at Natalie's lips and eyes?

"She beat out a ton of other writers for the opportunity," Jeff went on.

"Thanks, love." Natalie kissed him on the cheek. Jeff gazed back at her in adoration. "But, hey, I'm not precious about this one. It was a job, not a passion project. And most readers seem to be enjoying it just fine. Not everyone has Rob's exacting standards."

"'Exacting' is the perfect word," Zuri said. "You should see him try to make a simple cup of coffee. It requires just the right bean, a precise amount of grinding time."

The two women shared a smile, one that seemed genuine. Rob tried not to be too offended that it had come at his expense.

"And can you even taste the difference?" Natalie asked.

Zuri looked at Rob, then said, loyally, "Yes."

"Well," Natalie said, and tucked her hair back behind her ears, "I'm not supposed to be broadcasting my involvement in the book. So please don't put this conversation all over social media."

"Don't worry," Zuri said. "We don't do social media."

"A really cool thing about it is that we got to meet Tyler!" Jeff said. "Well, Natalie spends a lot of time with him, but he took us both out to dinner. And let me tell you, he is fun. Super-nice to everyone."

"Yeah, he's a wonderful guy." Natalie paused. "Definitely required a lot from his ghostwriter, but wonderful."

"So handsome too. I almost felt a little jealous, Natalie hanging out with him every day," Jeff said in the hearty, jokey tone people tended to use when something wasn't quite a joke at all.

"Don't worry," Natalie said. "He's only into supermodels." Jeff blinked, and she quickly went on, "And I'm only into you."

Thankfully, at that moment, the ushers at the church indicated that guests should find their seats.

"Well, goodbye," Rob said, then took Zuri's hand and began to power walk toward the pews, hoping that the crowd would separate them quickly enough from Jeff and Natalie. Still, he couldn't help listening in as, behind them, Jeff nudged Natalie, handing her his phone. "Look at this. This is Drew's place, the one I was telling you about. Exposed brick. And there's enough room for my bike in the hallway!"

"Oh," Natalie said. "It's a little expensive, isn't it?"

"You'd think so, but we can get it without a broker's fee, so that's huge. I ran the numbers, and it saves us hundreds of dollars a month."

"Hm."

"We've just got to let him know by tomorrow, because otherwise his landlord wants to list it."

At that moment, Rob spotted an opening, a pew with only two seats left, and beelined in. Zuri settled beside him as the crowd carried Jeff and Natalie over to a different part of the church. Finally, Rob exhaled.

"Well, that was awkward," Zuri said, opening up her program. "No way for you to know about the book, though."

"Mm." Rob stared up at the front of the church. "That Jeff guy is irritating, isn't he?"

"In what way?"

"He just kept talking. And talking."

"I think he was a man meeting new people, trying to make conversation."

Rob harumphed.

"I love you, but you were not giving him much to work with."

"You shouldn't set traps for people like that. Just *say* that Natalie ghostwrote the book."

"It's fine. I'm sure she doesn't particularly care what you think. Why would she?"

"Authors can be sensitive."

"Well, maybe she's not one of them. Besides, she's not really an author, is she? She's a ghostwriter."

"She *is* an author." Rob's voice came out louder than he'd intended, and Zuri raised her eyebrows in surprise.

"I didn't realize. Good for her."

Rob glanced over at Natalie, a few pews over, as Jeff kept showing her pictures on his phone. Yes, good for her, ghostwriting at such a high level. The book wasn't to his taste, but it was selling, so maybe that would open up some doors. And good for her, moving in with her boyfriend, who seemed competent and devoted, if exhaustingly so. And good for her, wearing dresses that were formfitting but not inappropriate for church, although said dress was getting less appropriate as she crossed one leg over the other and the fabric inched up her thigh, and—

Zuri took his hand in hers and squeezed, and the anxious, unsettled feeling in Rob drained away, replaced by the sensation of her warm palm in his. He squeezed back, grateful, as the christening ceremony began.

After Christina had been sprinkled with water—looking none too pleased about it—and the godparents had done their duties (half-heartedly in Melinda's case, and the godfather was some cousin on Gabby's side that Rob had never seen before. Rob couldn't help feeling that he and Natalie would have done a better job of everything except the religious part), the guests milled around in the receiving line. After, they'd go to Gabby's parents' house for a small reception, a fifteen-minute drive away.

As Rob and Zuri waited their turn to exclaim over an older and wiser Christina, Rob spied Angus's parents. "I should introduce you to the Futon King and Queen," he said to Zuri.

She was worrying at her back tooth with her tongue, face furrowed. "Sorry, I've had something stuck in my teeth ever since the ride over. Let me run out to the car. Then I'll meet the royalty."

"Sure," he said, his attention half on Angus's mother, who had spotted him and was waving him over.

"Be right back." Zuri disappeared as Angus's mom poked her husband, then pointed to Rob, and the two of them came bustling over for a hug.

"Robert! Who was that beautiful creature on your arm?" Angus's mom shouted as she wrapped her leopard-print-clad arms around him. "Is she running away from us?"

"No, I think she just had to grab something from the car—" he began. But a thought struck him. If she had something in her teeth, she'd want the dental floss. Rob always packed the dental floss in his toiletry bag for them to share when they went on trips together. He extricated himself in a panic. "I'm sorry, I also need to run out to the car for a moment!"

Stomach plummeting, he raced into the parking lot after Zuri. She had the trunk open, looking into the mouth of his suitcase, bracing herself with one hand on the car's back bumper. No, no, no.

"I'll find the floss for you!" he called. "It's deep in there, and . . ."

But he was too late. Wordlessly, she turned around, her hand clasped around the ring box he'd hidden next to his toiletry bag. She held it up and slowly raised one eyebrow.

"Huh. What . . . what could that be?" he stammered.

"You tell me."

He hadn't had much doubt about her answer when he'd bought the ring. After all, they'd talked timeline. They would move in together, and then if that went well, they'd get engaged within the year. "I wouldn't mind being surprised," she'd said once when they discussed the issue. "Though certainly not in public. If you propose to me on a Jumbotron, I will have to say no." This was on the earlier side of their year deadline, but there was no denying that the move-in had gone well, right?

Zuri wasn't one to shy from honest conversations. Still, it could be hard to tell what was roiling beneath her placid, slightly cool exterior. Sometimes, he'd catch her staring off into the distance, her expression impenetrable, and he'd worry that he didn't actually know her at all. What if, all this time, she'd been feeling that their move-in hadn't met her expectations? That the twenty-four seven version of Rob was too much? He did grind his teeth at night, and sometimes during the day too without realizing it. A bad habit he was trying to break. Perhaps the noise of it was too loud when she was trying to concentrate on her work, and she could not sign up for a lifetime of that. Or maybe it was that he'd been uninspired in his research lately, had been having trouble mustering up enthusiasm for his lectures, and she was losing respect for him. Perhaps it was simply too soon, or perhaps the idea of *forever* was already unpalatable to her, and her mind was scrambling for the kindest way to let him down.

He looked at her more closely. She was very still, barely blinking as she waited for him to respond. But there. There was a tiny curl at the edge of her mouth, a hint of amusement that he'd seen before, watching her teach classes, when a promising student was so close to giving the right answer and Zuri *knew* they were going to figure it out. It gave Rob hope, even if he was furious with himself for ruining the surprise of it all. He was supposed to present the ring during a stroll on the beach, after dinner at a seaside restaurant with flickering candles that people had rated highly for the romance factor.

"It's not supposed to happen like this. Not in a parking lot—" He cut himself off. "Can you pretend, for another day or two, that you didn't see that?"

"Yes," she said. Her tone was level, but her eyes were shining.

Rob cleared his throat, shifted side to side, and couldn't stop himself from asking, "Yes to what? Pretending you didn't see it or marrying me?"

"Well," she said. She looked down at the ring box again, then back up at him, her mouth turning, finally, into the widest smile he'd ever seen her give. "To both."

His irritation at the ruined surprise disappeared immediately. Overcome, he stepped forward and kissed her then, the two of them holding tight to each other in the parking lot. A gust of wind kicked up around them, pulling some of the blossoms from the trees, and Rob thought that he'd never been happier. Everything that had happened in his life up until this point made sense, had been lighting his way to her. He'd had to go to Arizona, a place he did not love, to find the woman he did.

Momentarily, an image of Natalie floated into his mind. Because he was grateful for how that had turned out too. Thank God he hadn't given in to his momentary impulses with her back on that lake trip. He had protected this relationship when it was delicate so it could grow into the steady, sturdy thing it had become. Now, the life that he and Zuri were going to have together unfurled before them, the future bright and harmonious.

"I'm going to do a very nice proposal overlooking the water," he said. "This doesn't count."

She laughed then. A Zuri laugh was precious, not given out lightly, throaty and beautiful.

"All right. I'll wipe this from my memory." She tucked her head into the crook of his neck while blossoms swirled around them. They stood there together, their hearts beating against each other as the church doors opened and people began to make their way toward the reception. "But first, give me a few more seconds to enjoy it."

18

★☆☆☆☆

Back at Gabby's parents' house, Natalie could feel her pulse spiking each time Jeff told her a new detail about the apartment into which he wanted the two of them to move. "It's only a five-minute walk to an amazing bagel shop," he gushed, and her heart rammed itself against her throat. "One of the top-ten-ranked bagels in the city. I checked. And their smoked salmon cream cheese gets great reviews, so you can get your favorite flavor all the time."

She poured herself a glass of white wine and gulped from it while he found himself a beer, and just as she'd managed to take a deep breath, he returned to her side, enthusing, "And did I mention that it's only a third-floor walk-up? Third floor is perfect in my opinion because you're still far enough above the street that people can't see into your windows, but you're not exhausted each time you try to reach your door."

"That makes sense." Natalie scanned the room. "Oh! I think Gabby's mom is calling me over. Be back in just a second."

She ran over to Gabby's mom, startling her as she laid out a platter of tortillas. "How's the setup going? Can I help in the kitchen?"

"No, no." Gabby's mom waved her hand. "Enjoy the party."

"Please let me help. Please."

Gabby's mother looked a bit taken aback. "If you insist. I could use someone to slice up more avocados."

"I'm on it," she said, then ran back over to Jeff. "I'm being conscripted into helping lay out the food."

"Want an extra set of hands?" he asked.

"You stay here and relax. Look, there's Becks and Shay, you should go talk to them."

Jeff and Natalie had gone on a few double dates with Becks and Shay. (Because, on the dance floor at Gabby and Angus's wedding, in their matching bridesmaid dresses, Becks and Shay had drunkenly declared their feelings for each other. Ever since then, gloomy Becks had walked with a skip in her step. The power of love.)

One thing Natalie admired about Jeff was that he did not lack for conversation. She could leave him alone at a party where he knew no one and find him an hour later with three new best friends. He always had a getting-to-know-you question to throw in. "Which one of you is the Bert, and who's the Ernie?" or "If you could live anywhere in the world for one summer, where would it be?" Sometimes it was fantastic to have someone take charge of the small talk, steering it to unexpected places beyond the usual chitchat about jobs and location. Every once in a while, though, Natalie couldn't stop herself from wincing when he busted out another thought-provoking question that she'd heard before. He'd been a camp counselor for a few years, and sometimes his conversational maneuvering had a tinge of leading games in the woods to distract campers from their rumbling stomachs. There was something effortful about it, a sort of barely suppressed terror of letting a conversation peter out.

"Oh yeah, I've got to ask them how their wedding planning is going." Jeff started over to Shay and Becks before turning back and grabbing Natalie's arm. "Wait, I almost forgot the best part. Drew also told me that the insulation between apartments is so good you can barely hear the neighbors having sex." He grinned and winked at her, and she couldn't help but laugh. Jeff's current upstairs neighbors had a very active bedroom life and would sometimes wake Jeff and Natalie in the middle of the night with their screams. As much as she hated it, she loved those moments too, the way they united her and Jeff, how they made snarky comments to each other until the neighbors quieted and they were able to get back to sleep.

She stepped forward and kissed him briefly, and he tightened his arms around her waist, then gave her a gentle push. "All right, go help Gabby's mom," he said.

Natalie disappeared into the kitchen, resting her head against the refrigerator door in the one empty spot between Christmas cards, magnets, and family pictures.

She didn't understand why she was so anxious. Of course she wanted to live in a lovely apartment near a bagel shop where the neighbors' moans were muffled, even if she was worried about the added expense. And she loved Jeff. She really did! He was an excellent partner who listened to her and adored her uncondi-tionally, believing in her when she didn't believe in herself. Also, as far as she could tell, he was not hiding any secret gambling or sex addictions. But she couldn't stop the slight swirl of panic in her belly when she thought about the prospect of living with him, all the time. Every night, falling asleep locked in his arms. Every morning, listening to him tell her about his dreams. (He had so many of them, and they were always very long and involved.) Sometimes after they'd spent a few days together in a row, Natalie had to go take a long nap. On the other hand, sometimes after they'd spent a few days apart, she'd wake up and wish he was next to her with his cute, soft snore.

Maybe it all felt too quick? But they'd been together almost a year and a half, and she was about to turn thirty. She was very chill about the looming birthday and had zero feelings of terror and anguish! Actually, her relationship with Jeff was the one thing stopping her from completely self-destructing over it. She had no idea what was happening with her career and time was slipping through her fingers, but at least she had a nice man who loved her. A smart and responsible man who paid his rent early and held her with infinite patience and tenderness when she cried over nothing. That was worth so much.

Plenty of her friends were moving in with partners more quickly, starting to panic that time might be running out, eggs withering and single people disappearing from the marketplace. It wasn't like Jeff was springing this on her. He had brought the discussion up months ago. She'd had plenty of time to think about it.

Maybe the problem was that she thought about it too much. Did other people walk around with a constantly shifting mental pros and cons list about spending the rest of their life with their partner?

God, she was defective, missing some small but essential piece required for assembly of a full human. Like an Ikea dresser for which the warehouse had forgotten to include just one screw when packaging everything up. She still looked normal from the outside when she was with Jeff, but give her a little push, and she'd ricket.

No. It was just a big change. Of course it made her nervous! Other people probably felt this way too, they just didn't talk about it.

Someone else walked into the kitchen, and Natalie yanked her forehead away from the fridge, then tried to surreptitiously wipe off the mark she'd left on it (from perspiration? Gross) as she turned to see who had interrupted her existential spiral.

Zuri. Rob's beautiful, serene, slightly imposing girlfriend. She glided in with her high, smooth forehead, her hair pulled back in a series of small braids, her voice low so that you had no choice but to lean in toward her while she was talking. She seemed like the kind of woman Rob would want, one who thought before she spoke, turning the words over in her mind and then presenting them in full sentences with no "ums" or hesitation. A controlled woman, sure to say and do the right thing. The kind of woman you worked hard to impress.

"Hello," she said now. "Angus's father brought Gabby's family a new futon as a present, and Robert is carrying it in, so I came to see if I could be useful."

"Oh. Um, sure. We're supposed to cut up some more avocados, so I was just looking to see where they might be—"

Before Natalie had even finished speaking, Zuri had found the bag of avocados, a knife, and a cutting board. She began slicing and pitting, a model of efficiency.

Sometimes when Natalie read a book written by an incredible writer, she was racked by competing feelings—deep admiration and deep jealousy. Thrilled by the possibilities of what someone could do while feeling like a hunk of useless garbage who'd never achieve anything herself. Zuri made her feel a similar way. Much as it pained her to admit it, Natalie understood completely why Rob had turned her down for this woman.

"Are you having fun so far?" Natalie asked.

"Yes. It has been a wonderful event." A restrained smile played at the corners of Zuri's mouth. "I think I'll remember it for the rest of my life."

"You love watching a screaming baby get dipped in water, huh?"

"Something like that." She gave an avocado pit a light whack with the knife, twisting it out of the green meat. "I do know that Robert feels bad about insulting your book earlier."

"Oh, I'm sure," Natalie said. Was speaking of Rob so formally Zuri's idea of a pet name? "And thank you. But you don't have to apologize on behalf of your boyfriend." A strange look came over Zuri's face. "I'm sorry, did that come off as rude? I didn't mean—"

"No, not rude. You just said 'boyfriend,' and I . . ." Zuri shook her head. "Never mind."

"You prefer the term 'partner'?" Natalie asked, and Zuri shook her head again. She was so restrained that Nat couldn't help becoming almost frantically goofy in reaction. "Ooh! You're in a fake relationship, pretending to be together for some vaguely im- plausible reason, like not distracting Angus at his daughter's christening, despite the fact that you broke up weeks ago."

"That's it," Zuri said, and even though Natalie knew she was kidding, her heart gave a strange little lurch at the prospect.

"Cool, because I was running out of options. Only other idea I could think of was 'secret fiancé,' and—"

At that, Zuri's lips parted fully, her smile showing all of her gleaming white teeth for a brief, uncontrolled moment before she was able to regain her impressive impassive facade.

Natalie gasped. "Holy shit. You guys are engaged?"

Zuri looked around to double-check that they were alone. "Unofficially. He meant to propose tomorrow, but I found the ring today. Please don't tell anyone."

"Wow, that's . . . wow. Congratulations!" Natalie said, even as the ground tilted underneath her feet.

"Thank you," Zuri said, and smiled again, not trying to hide it this time.

Natalie could have this too. Her teeth could also gleam while she accepted congratulations. All she had to do was say yes to Jeff's dream apartment. (And also maybe invest in some tooth-whitening strips.) Then she'd move one square forward on the board game they were all playing right now, one square closer to winning the life everyone was supposed to have.

"You should have seen the look on his face," Zuri continued. "Sheer terror in his eyes as he was waiting to hear what I was going to say. It was quite endearing. He's normally so self-contained."

"Right, Rob doesn't exactly wear his heart on his sleeve." A strange feeling pulsed inside Natalie. A small sense of loss. A door closing. Rob and Natalie would never repeat their overwhelming kiss in the lake, never see what lay beyond it. So she'd never have sex with Rob Kapinsky in this lifetime. So what? The issue wasn't Rob specifically, she told herself, but a more general sense of loss that came with getting older, as the people you knew committed themselves to others and the wide world of possibility began to narrow. At twenty-two, she'd sat in the crook of a fig tree like Sylvia Plath had described in *The Bell Jar*, surrounded by potential partners, potential lives, looking over the shining fruit of all her options. Over time, as she'd dithered and considered, other people had come in and plucked away so many of the potential figs. And now Rob was gone too.

Zuri was studying Natalie. "Sorry, you two have gotten to know each other through Gabby and Angus?"

Natalie became aware that she had no idea what her face was

doing. She plastered on a casual expression. "Yes, we were maid of honor and best man at their wedding. But he's a great guy, and you seem wonderful too, so I'm thrilled for you both! And don't worry, I won't gossip about this with Gabby until you've shared the news."

"I appreciate that," Zuri said, giving her one more flashing smile.

And that smile clinched it. *Screw it*, Natalie thought. She would move in with Jeff. She could dither forever, but it was time to make some choices. Time to grow up. Zuri laid her knife down. Somehow, even newly engaged and buzzing with excitement, she'd sliced up all the avocados while Natalie had not touched a single one.

19

★☆☆☆☆

Natalie had been trying all through the reception to get some time alone with Gabby to catch up. (She'd been trying to do this, rather unsuccessfully, ever since Christina was born.) The list of things they needed to talk about grew longer by the day, plus there was the matter of the favor that Natalie had been turning over in her mind.

Each time Natalie spotted her across the room, another relative swooped in to grab Gabby's attention. That, or an old friend intercepted Natalie, asking when she was going to publish another book (which was Natalie's *favorite* question, thank you so much!) or when she and that nice Jeff guy were going to get married and start having babies themselves (which was Natalie's *second*-favorite question, thank you so much!).

Finally, Gabby stood alone in the corner, Christina fussing and pawing at her shirt. Natalie began to walk over, until a hand on her arm stopped her. Angus.

"Natalie!" he said, and then, in a stage whisper, "I hope it's okay, but Gabby told me about Tyler Yeo."

Of course Gabby had, though Natalie had asked her not to tell anybody. Natalie herself had only told Gabby, Jeff, and her mother. And now Rob and Zuri, which she probably should not have done. But it had been irresistible, unfightable, the urge to let Rob know that she'd had a hand in something you could buy at an airport bookstore.

"I just want to say, wow!" Angus said at his normal volume, then caught himself and returned to the stage whisper. Natalie supposed she should resign herself to the fact that anything she told Gabby, Gabby would tell Angus, and Angus would—inadvertently—tell everyone else. "Sorry. I'll be discreet. But I'm happy for you."

"Well, thanks," Natalie said, her voice tight. "It was a great opportunity." She cast about for an excuse to end the conversation and head to Gabby's side.

Angus squinted at her. "I hope it wasn't too hard, though."

"Tyler isn't always the most eloquent, but he's very nice, so he makes up for it."

"No, I mean . . . watching somebody else get your achievement."

Natalie looked at him, momentarily at a loss for words, and he continued. "Sorry, did that come out wrong? Blabbermouth over here. I just mean that you have what it takes to be a writer, so it must be strange to have somebody else get the big book release instead. I wouldn't be surprised if you felt a little sad about it as well as proud, that's all."

"I . . ."

"Sorry! Forget I said anything besides 'Congratulations!'"

"No, that was . . ." *Strangely perceptive?* "You're right. I do feel mixed-up about it all."

"Yup," he said, and patted her arm in a brotherly way. Then his eyes slid to the side, his father trying to get his attention. "Oh, shoot. Got to keep helping with this futon!"

Natalie stared after him for a moment as he walked away, then shook her head and ran to catch up with Gabby, now ascending the stairs to the second floor with a crying Christina. "Hey! Where are you going?"

"She's getting hungry," Gabby said. "I'm going to go feed her. Nobody here besides Angus needs to see my breasts."

"*I* could see your breasts. Can I come with?"

"Okay, perv," Gabby said, and led the way to her childhood bedroom.

As Gabby sat down on her twin bed with its princessy canopy and unfastened her buttons, Natalie cast a glance around the room, which she'd visited a few times with Gabby in college, sleeping in the trundle bed underneath the one they sat on now. The walls were hung with some of Gabby's original watercolors and old posters from their teenage years. Mostly inspiring women—Venus and Serena Williams, Frida Kahlo, all giving Gabby something to strive toward. But—Natalie opened up the closet to check if her memory was correct—yes, Gabby had plastered the inside of her closet door with pictures of heartthrobs. Natalie bit back a smile as she looked over them all, hidden out of sight of Mr. Alvarez, who would not have approved. Next to Freddie Prinze Jr. and Orlando Bloom, there was a poster of Tyler Yeo from his *Portal Makers* days, holding up a glowing cube and considering it with his shirt slightly unbuttoned. (Natalie knew that Tyler had posed for photos with his shirt fully unbuttoned too, but Gabby had stuck to this one just in case her strict father went into her closet after all.)

Iman had put her in for the ghostwriting job, feeling bad about the failure of her second book. Tyler was repped by someone at the same agency, so a semi-depressed Natalie dutifully submitted a writing sample, assuming nothing would come of it given her recent track record. But then her phone had lit up with Iman's name.

"Good news, Tyler loves your writing," Iman said. "You're on the short list. But he wants to meet all the finalists in person for, and I quote, 'a vibe check.'"

When she walked into what could only be described as a bro pad—the living room of Tyler's huge SoHo loft—Tyler bounded off the couch toward her, arms wide open for a hug. "Hey!" Then he stopped himself. "Wait, would you rather high-five hello instead? No pressure. It will not affect whether or not you get the job."

Natalie was immediately charmed by this gorgeous doofus of a man who still, in his midthirties, thought that a high-five was one of the top ways to say hello. "We can hug," she said, and held her own arms out. He pulled her in. His chest was so rock-hard, it practically bludgeoned her. She deduced that the answer to "Tyler Yeo—where is he now?" was, in general, the gym.

The walls of the living room were hung with framed canvases of neon graffiti, words like "love" and "peace" and "Tyler." A Ping-Pong table sat in a corner. Tyler gestured to it. "I hate just, like, sitting up straight and being all formal. You wanna play while we talk?"

He handed her a paddle. As they took their positions, the whole thing had the surreal quality of a dream. Natalie told herself that it *was* a dream, that some unconscious recess of her brain had conjured up *playing Ping-Pong with has-been movie star Tyler Yeo*, and since she was going to wake up, none of this mattered, so there was no need to be nervous.

He sent over a casual serve, and she sliced it back. "Whoa, you're good!" he said.

"Yeah, after my parents got divorced, my dad got a Ping-Pong table in his new house. Whenever I went to visit him, this was pretty much all we did. I think I channeled all my repressed anger at him into learning how to beat him."

"Family . . . man," he said as they volleyed back and forth. "It can be complicated."

"Yup. Yours too?"

And then he was off and running. As he told her all about his upbringing, *Portal Makers*, and his life now, she casually whupped his ass.

A week later, Iman called with the job offer. "He liked you," she said. "Apparently, you were the only one who didn't let him win at Ping-Pong."

It was still so odd to Natalie that she knew Tyler, an incongruous fact that sat alongside the rest of her life. If she could time-travel back to tell her teenage self that she was working with *the* Tyler Yeo, sweet naive teen Natalie would probably jump up and down in glee, assuming that her older self was set for life. But she wasn't set for life. She wasn't even supposed to talk about it.

Now the job was done, even if Tyler kept calling her every time their book reached some fun new benchmark, wanting to praise her work and also rejoice in their success, assuming she cared just as much about all of it as he did. He probably had no idea that she didn't get any royalties, that his agent had cut a ruthless deal. Still, she was happy for him each time he got another hit for his sweetly ravenous ego, *very* happy to have made in the mid five-figure range for a writing job. Not to flatter herself, but she thought that part of the reason he kept calling was that he missed her. They had spent a lot of time together over the past year. Her job had been to pay rapturous attention to him and ask him questions about himself. No wonder he liked her.

Natalie closed Gabby's closet door and went to join her on the bed. Gabby might have been happy enough to sit there in silence, catching her breath as Christina fed, but Natalie shifted, scratched her ear, then said, "So, Jeff wants to move in together." Interest lit up Gabby's exhausted features. "His friend is leaving his apartment, and we could get it without a broker's fee if we commit by tomorrow."

"Oh yay, do it!" Gabby said, surprising Natalie not one bit. Sometimes Natalie felt that the best way to engage her friend now was to hint that she was joining her in domesticity. If Nat got married and had babies, then they'd have so much to talk about. They no longer knew the day-to-days of each other's lives, but if they could only debate the quality of different strollers, they'd once again be as close as they were at twenty-three. "Living together is great. You can see your favorite person whenever you want."

Natalie bit her tongue. Would she say that Jeff was her favorite person? No, she'd still say Gabby, even if Gabby wouldn't pick her. (Though, she loved Jeff. He was very close to being her favorite person!)

"I really like Jeff," Gabby said.

"Same."

"I should hope so!" They laughed. "And I really like how he treats you. He knows how special you are, you know?"

Natalie nodded. She never had to worry about being enough to Jeff, never had to look into his eyes and hear her mother saying, *He'll get bored with you eventually.* If anything, she wished Jeff would push her a little more, but that seemed like a ridiculous complaint.

"So," Gabby went on, "you're going to say yes?"

"At some point, you've just got to take the plunge, right?" Gabby nodded approvingly. "Besides, the apartment is closer to you and Angus, so that would be nice. Only two subway stops away. We could even walk if we were ambitious."

"Well," Gabby said, "we're considering moving."

"Really? Where? Still Brooklyn, or is Angus jonesing for Manhattan?"

Gabby bit her lip.

"No," Natalie said. "Please don't say the suburbs."

"The apartment is small with a baby, and especially since we want a big family . . ."

"But you guys are rich now!"

"We're comfortable."

"That's what rich people say. You could afford a bigger apartment, right?"

"I don't think you realize how expensive babies are. Any good daycare in the city costs practically as much as college tuition." She shook her head. "Besides, I want a backyard. I want to watch Christina run around and put her hands in the dirt without having to worry that there's broken glass in it."

"Well. Okay," Natalie said, trying not to sound like a sullen teenager. "I guess you've got to do what you've got to do." They sat there silently for a moment. Gabby stroked Christina's hair, and Christina met her mother's eyes, feeding peacefully. Gabby smiled down and Christina smiled up, as much as one could smile with a nipple in one's mouth. A beam of pure love extended between them. Natalie felt a million miles outside of it.

"There was something else I wanted to talk to you about," Natalie said. She took a deep breath, only for Christina to unlatch and let out a gurgle.

Gabby squinted at her child. "You doing okay, sweetie? You done?" Christina scrunched up her face, pawed at Gabby's breast. "More?" Gabby guided Christina's mouth back as Natalie sat there.

Another moment passed, then Gabby sighed. "I'm sorry. What were you saying?"

"Do you know if your company needs copywriters?"

"What?" Gabby asked, processing. "You're asking for yourself? Like, you want a full-time advertising job?"

"If I'm not writing my own stories anyway, I might as well have benefits."

"Your office manager job doesn't have health insurance?"

"Nope, they give me just under the weekly hours for a full-time employee."

"Capitalism," Gabby sighed, shaking her head, even though her husband was a finance bro. "And what about the ghost-writing?"

"Who knows when another job like the Tyler one might come in?" It wasn't as if Tyler was going to write more books. It had been hard enough finding material to fill up the one. Since finishing with him, Natalie had gotten far along in the process for some ghostwriting opportunities, requiring hours of unpaid work writing samples and interviewing. But she hadn't actually landed any of the gigs yet. Did she want to hustle her ass off to write someone else's book?

Natalie noticed that Gabby did *not* ask if she was planning to write another novel. But on that front, well, Sally Rooney had come along and done what Natalie had been attempting with her first novel, done it far better than she could have. The world did not need Natalie to add redundancy. And, as Angus had so surprisingly brought up, she did not need to attend more parties for books she'd helped create but to which she could lay no claim. Coming home from Tyler's launch, she'd cried in her kitchen for twenty-five minutes.

"You said that your work nemesis was thinking about leaving, right?" Natalie went on. "You could recommend your real-life best friend to take her place. Imagine: we could eat lunch together every day."

Gabby blew a puff of air out of her mouth. "I don't know. Are you sure it's the right fit for you?"

At Gabby's unexpected hesitation, Natalie's hackles rose. "What, you don't think I'd be good at it?" she asked, her voice sharp.

"I'm sure you could do the writing part."

"So, what's the problem?"

"I don't know." Gabby pursed her lips. "I'd want to know that you were actually going to care about it."

"Do *you* really care about helping, like, Bud Light sell more beer?"

"Yes! Maybe not Bud Light specifically. But overall, we're helping people who started businesses grow their dreams and connecting the right people with the right products to make their lives better! And fine, even if I sometimes don't care about the clients, I care about being good at what I do." Gabby grew animated, her voice urgent. "This job is my place. It's my passion."

"I'm sorry, since when has *advertising* been your passion? I thought it was art."

Gabby shrugged. "Maybe 'passion' is too strong. But people respect me, and I get paid well to be creative. Besides, it's not like I was going to be a famous painter."

"You don't know that. Have you been painting at all?" Natalie asked, and Gabby pursed her lips again. "You should!"

"In what hours of the day? It takes a lot to keep a human alive. And believe it or not, it takes effort to do good work at the agency too. Which is why I don't want you to come into it half-assing things, being like, 'I guess I'll deign to do this because my actual dream hasn't worked out.'"

"Well, that's harsh."

Gabby sighed. "I just—" Her agitation dislodged Christina, who began to whimper. Gabby stroked her back. "Oh, shh, shh, it's okay, sweetie." Still, Christina mewled, twisting her face away from Gabby's breast, and Gabby's shoulders slumped in despair.

It felt like eons since Natalie and Gabby had been able to have an uninterrupted conversation, since they'd truly been able to pay attention to each other. Natalie reached out and took Christina into her own arms, then stood and began to dance with her, bouncing her gently. The novelty of it all distracted Christina from her cries. On the bed, Gabby rubbed her temples.

Quietly, Nat said, "I didn't mean to make you feel like your workplace is my backup option. I thought it would be a nice way to hang out with you more while doing something at least somewhat creatively stimulating." Christina nuzzled into her, reaching out to grab Natalie's hair, and Nat let her. "I just think it's time for me to get it together, like everybody else."

Gabby gave a slow nod and cleared her throat. "Look, if you're really committed to it, I can't promise anything, but I'll see what I can do."

"Okay. Thank you."

"But I have to warn you. If you come to work with me . . . I'm really earnest. You're going to want to make fun of me."

"Oh, believe me, I got that from the whole 'we're helping people grow their dreams' bit you did."

They both laughed, but half-heartedly, then lapsed into uncomfortable silence. "So," Gabby said, "we should probably get back to the party."

20

★☆☆☆☆

Rob and Angus carried the futon into Melinda's old bedroom, trying not to trip on the clutter. "Let's put it down here," Angus wheezed. "And remember to use your legs, not your back."

"I know," Rob said, and they both grunted as they set the futon against the wall.

"Whew!" Angus mopped his brow. "A heavy sucker, isn't it? But that's good, it means it's sturdy. Julio's been having lumbar issues, but with this big guy?" Angus patted the futon proudly. "He's going to get the support he needs."

Angus's father and Gabby's dad wandered into the room now, Melinda following behind them with a scowl on her face. "What do you think, Julio?" Angus II asked, putting an arm around Mr. Alvarez, proud as if he'd carried the futon himself. "Looks good, right?"

"Looks great."

"And now you can use this room as an office or an exercise room, but there'll still be a place for Melinda to sleep."

"Why aren't you doing this in Gabby's room?" Melinda asked, frowning.

"She comes home more than you do."

"No," Melinda said, her scowl intensifying. "It's because she has a kid, so I'm the lesser daughter—"

"*Mija*," Mr. Alvarez began, but Melinda turned on her heel and stormed out, her father following behind as they continued their argument.

Angus's dad shook his head, then looked expectantly at Rob and Angus. "Well, we might as well load out the mattress while we're here to resell it for them. We can put it in the same truck where the futon was." By "we," he obviously meant Rob and Angus. He turned to go, then shot one final, proud look at the futon. "Melinda will grow to love it. It's a sterling model, isn't it?" Angus nodded eagerly. "Trent has been selling them left and right!"

A storm cloud passed over Angus's face as his father walked out of the room. He and Rob went to opposite ends of the mattress. Rob raised an eyebrow. When Angus caught him looking, Angus fixed a not completely convincing smile to his face. "Let's lift this bad boy up!" He gave another grunt and hoisted his end into the air.

"Who is Trent?" Rob asked, forgetting to lift with his knees instead of his back, then cursing himself as he felt a twinge in his muscles.

"Oh, my father's star employee. Trent is probably going to take over the business when he retires."

"And . . . you don't think he's a good guy?"

"No. What? Oh, no, no, no. Trent is nice. Trent is perfectly nice! And he's a fine salesman."

"But . . . ?"

Angus paused, clearly at war with himself, before bursting out with, "But Trent has no vision!"

"Do you really need vision to run the store?" Rob asked as

they maneuvered the mattress down a hallway to the back door, sounds of the party trickling in from the front of the house.

Angus gaped at him. "Yes! Do you think my father would've expanded up and down the whole turnpike without vision? Futon technology is constantly evolving, and people's needs change, and you've got to be able to stay plugged in. Like with futons for pets—you know that one-third of people in the US own a dog now? That's a whole emerging market, but *Trent* doesn't think it's a good idea—" He cut himself off, his face red with exertion and passion as they carried the mattress outside. "I gotta calm down. If my dad wants to give Trent the business, he'll give Trent the business."

"He could give *you* the business," Rob said mildly.

"No, I am my own man! I'm not some joke who needs his father to hand him a career—" Angus cut himself off, opened the door to the truck, and shoved the mattress in, none too gently.

"Hey," Rob said. "Who's calling you a joke?"

Angus waved his hand through the air, facing away from Rob. "Nobody."

"Angus," Rob said, stepping around to look his friend full-on, grasping his shoulder. "Tell me."

"Oh, sometimes the guys at the office make little remarks, but it's all in good fun." Angus rubbed his hand across his face. "Sorry, I'm tired. It's been a lot, with Christina, and things only getting more intense at work. But intense is good. The boss is giving me more responsibility because he knows I can handle it."

"If you want to talk about it . . ." Rob began, but Angus shook his head firmly and switched on his familiar smile.

"I want to talk about *you*, and why you've been in such a good mood all night!"

Rob could not tell Angus about the engagement just yet.

Angus would immediately tell Gabby, which would be fine—Gabby could keep a secret. But he would also be so obvious about it with Rob during the rest of the party—beaming at him, ruffling his hair, putting an arm around both him and Zuri, and starting to cry—that everyone would figure out something was up. Rob had never been able to tell Angus exciting secrets. (On the other hand, if Rob ever had a truly devastating secret—say, he needed Angus's help in burying a body—he would trust Angus with it, though the effort of holding it in might destroy Angus entirely. Not that Rob would ever secretly bury a body. If, in some unlikely and horrific scenario he accidentally killed someone, he would report himself to the police.)

"It's just nice to see you," Rob said.

"Aw, buddy," Angus replied, "same here. And it's always good to spend time with Zuri too. I want to get to know her even better." He brushed his hair back, sending it sticking up into the air. "Okay, I should go back into the party."

Rob's phone began to buzz. His parents, calling to say hello. (Well, his mother calling and putting it on speaker as she sat next to his dad. Sometimes Rob wondered, if his parents got divorced, would his dad ever take the initiative to call him again?) "I'll see you back inside," Rob said, waving Angus off, then answering the call. "Hello?"

"Hi, sweets," his mother said, while his father called out, "Hello there."

"How are you guys?" he asked, and as his mother began to tell him about a lecture they'd attended the other night, and his father interrupted to talk about the fancy dinner they went to with the guest speaker afterward, Rob thought that maybe he could tell his mom and dad. The exciting news was a battering ram inside his mouth, fighting to burst out into the open.

His parents would be thrilled. His dad and Zuri had gotten along swimmingly when they all got together in the days after Christmas last year, just as Rob had known they would. Professor Kapinsky had come away impressed by her research. Zuri had plenty of questions for him about making a life in academia.

Meeting Zuri, Rob's dad had given his son something so rare: total approval, no notes. Rob could get used to that feeling.

"And how are you?" his mother asked. "How was the christening?"

"The christening was nice," he began as he walked from the driveway into the backyard, pacing on a little stone patio that bordered the house. Sounds of the party hummed in the background. "Angus is very proud. You should see him, he's a natural father. And I'm great, actually. Zuri . . ."

But, no, it wasn't right to tell his parents without Zuri. They would wait to call together when everything was official.

"Zuri got some good news on one of her papers being accepted into a journal," he finished.

"Oh, that's wonderful," his mother said.

"What's going on with your research?" his father asked, and Rob rolled his eyes. "You know you need to publish regularly if you want tenure."

"I am aware," Rob said. God, his dad couldn't even be bothered to say something nice about Zuri's achievements? He'd surely react less dickishly to their engagement. If he didn't, Rob wasn't quite sure what he'd do.

"Please give Zuri our congratulations," Rob's mom cut in.

"Yes, tell her and Angus that they should send us some pictures of the baby," his dad said.

"What?" Rob asked, something catching in his mind.

"No," his mother said in a more muffled voice, "not Gabby.

Zuri, his girlfriend." His mother spoke back into the phone. "Sorry, the reception is a little fuzzy."

"Yes, yes," his father boomed. The reception sounded fine on Rob's end. "That smart girlfriend of yours! Give her our congratulations on the paper."

"I will," Rob said, letting out a breath right as his father continued, "Now, when do we get to meet her?"

The ensuing silence seemed to stretch millennia, though it probably lasted only a second. Rob scrambled to find his footing, opened his mouth to force something out. But then his mom jumped in. "Yes, Rob? When do we get to meet the baby? We'd love to see her sometime."

He swallowed, suddenly unsure whether he was being ridiculous. "I'll ask Angus and Gabby," he said, then couldn't stop himself from continuing, "Mom, can I talk to you privately?"

"All right." The sounds of her walking down the hallway and shutting a door filtered into Rob's ear. "What is it?"

"Mom"—Rob's heart thudded heavily in his chest—"is something going on?"

"What do you mean?" Her voice was strained, as if she was trying for cheerful but couldn't quite get there. He remembered that voice. She'd used it all the time, that one summer when it had been just the two of them trying and failing to prove something.

"With Dad. With his memory."

Rob stepped onto the grass. Dead dry leaves had fallen, scattered around the yard. He crumbled one under his shoe, driving it into the dirt.

His mother sighed. "Oh, goodness. You mean the Gabby and Zuri mix-up? He wouldn't want me to tell you this, but he's having some problems with his hearing. We should go to the doctor and see about hearing aids, but you know him, he's so proud."

"Really? That's all?"

"Well, he's getting older. He's having the little lapses you might expect from someone his age, and I understand how that, combined with his hearing issues, could be disorienting over the phone. But I don't think you need to worry too much. Just call him more often, won't you?" She sounded suddenly energized. "And I'll get him to look into hearing aids. I promise I will."

"If you're sure—"

"Yes. Oh, he's calling for me, I have to go . . . But we love you, sweets, and we'll talk again soon." The call disconnected.

So his father was getting older, becoming more entrenched in his self-centered ways, cracks starting to show in his towering facade. Something that happened to everyone who was lucky enough to live that long. But for the first time, Rob really considered the fact that, someday, Professor Kapinsky would have to retire. What would he do with himself then? Who would he even be? And someday, after that, he wouldn't be there at all.

Well, even better that Rob and Zuri were on the right track, right now. His father could see that Rob was doing better than fine, that his son had everything figured out. At their wedding, Professor Kapinsky would give some toast about how proud he was. He would go on for twenty minutes and receive a standing ovation from the crowd, stealing Rob and Zuri's thunder, and Rob would be angry about it, but it would be so much better than the alternative. And Rob needed to double down on his research, so he could get tenure before . . . well, it would be good to stay on an efficient timeline.

Rob stood there in silence for a moment, then put his head in his hands, unsettled. His eyes stung, and he dug his palms into them to stop the sensation.

A crunching noise sounded behind him. He turned to see Natalie stepping on a dead leaf as she reached for the handle of the back door, trying to sneak back inside unnoticed. She froze with her hand on the doorknob.

"I'm sorry, I didn't mean to interrupt."

"How long have you been out here?"

"Only thirty seconds. I was trying to get a . . . get some fresh air."

"The backyard is all yours," he said brusquely. "I should find Zuri."

"She's manning the food station. Gabby's mom realized how helpful she was and is not letting her go."

"Thanks," he said, and made a move to walk past her, but she reached out and touched his arm, then drew her hand back, as if she'd accidentally put it on a hot stove.

"Wait. Are you okay?" she asked. Her dark eyes X-rayed him.

"Yes." But she wouldn't stop looking at him in that searching way, so he shrugged and continued. "I just had an unsettling conversation with my father. Him getting older, you know?"

"I do," she said. "The other day, I was on the phone with my mom, and in the middle of a conversation about the weather, she just started talking about her will."

"Of course," Rob said, unable to stop a hint of a smile. "Wills and weather, closely related topics."

"Maybe if you live in a flood zone and are trying to figure out the value of your house?" Natalie laughed. "But I am sorry about your dad. I remember meeting him at the wedding. He was . . . a presence. Are you two very close?"

Rob's smile disappeared. "I don't know how to answer that." He didn't like the way she kept watching him, forehead furrowed, like she wanted to ask him to talk more about it, to excavate his feelings, or like maybe she'd offer him a hug. Gritting his teeth, he said, "I'm sorry about insulting Tyler's memoir."

She blinked, her expression clouding. "You don't have to . . . I appreciate the apology, but I was just doing a job."

"The connection could help you, don't you think?"

"What do you mean?"

"When you take your next novel out. It won't hurt that you had a hand in a bestseller." She was silent. So after a moment, he went on. "You are working on another novel?"

"You don't have to pretend that you care. Unless you're worried that I'll eviscerate you in it?"

"No," he said. It had grown dark, the temperature dipping as the sun disappeared. "I just think it would be a shame if you stopped trying."

She looked at him sharply. They stared at each other for a moment, both shivering. Then she blinked and looked away. "I have a lot going on right now. Though not as much as you, I hear."

"What?"

"Aren't congratulations in order? Zuri said not to tell anyone, but I assume you already know."

The warmth he'd felt earlier in the day began to return, a smile cracking through his sadness. Maybe Rob couldn't talk about this with Angus or his parents just yet. But somehow he trusted Natalie to keep this secret. "She told you? Why? No offense."

"She was excited, and I accidentally guessed. It was sweet." Rob liked imagining calm, level Zuri so thrilled that she was confiding in a near stranger. "She seems like a lovely woman."

"She is. I can't believe I get to spend my life with her."

Natalie looked out into the garden, something like wistfulness on her face.

"And you and Jeff," he said. "Congratulations to you too." She whipped her head back toward him. "I didn't mean to eavesdrop. But I overheard him talking about an apartment. You're moving in together?"

"Oh. Yes. We are. I guess I should officially tell *him* that."

"Big step."

They stood there, hugging their jackets closer to themselves in the dark as laughter floated out from the house. "So . . ." Natalie said, elbowing him. Her teeth were chattering. What were they still doing in the yard? They should go back inside, rejoin the warmth of the party. "How did you know that Zuri was the one?" She asked it in an almost jokey tone, like a kid in the schoolyard grilling him about a crush.

But Rob stamped his feet and considered. "Well, beyond loving her and thinking she is smart and beautiful, I trust her. And I don't mean simply trusting her not to lie to me, though that's part of it. I trust her judgment."

The light from the back window illuminated Natalie's face, her jaw set in concentration. "Seems like a good reason. Jeff has good judgment too."

"Good." Rob swallowed. Still, he hadn't captured the enormity of it, the relief and steadiness he felt. "But it's also . . . being with her is easy. When I think about our life together, it makes me calm."

Natalie closed her eyes and took in a slow, deep breath. Her voice, when she spoke, was so soft Rob could hardly hear it. "When I think about moving in with Jeff, it makes me anxious." A low wind caught her hair, lifting the wavy strands of it, but she stayed very still, speaking into the darkness almost as if Rob might disappear if she looked at him directly, and she badly didn't want him to go. "I can't tell if I'm scared because it's a big change or because it's not right. But that's natural, isn't it? I mean, you've felt that with Zuri at some point or other, haven't you?"

He looked down, not saying anything.

She took a step back and tossed her head. "Well, maybe you're a weirdo who got really lucky."

"Maybe."

They lapsed into silence. Still, Rob stayed, and eventually, she began to talk again. "I just want to be settled. To have something to show for myself. To go to a party like this one and, when someone asks what's new, be able to say, 'Oh, Jeff and I moved in together and now we're on the hunt for'—I don't know—'the perfect coffee table.'"

"You're considering moving in with him so you can have something to talk about at parties?" He shoved his hands in his pockets. "That's the stupidest reason I've ever heard."

"Okay, screw you," she said. "I love him! It's not just about party conversation. It's also about growing up, being practical, realizing it's time to stop following my heart and start listening to my head."

"Please stop. You're depressing me."

"Oh my God, you know what I mean." He gave a small nod, and she sighed. "I just . . . I think I'm broken."

"Or maybe you're trying to want something you don't because you think you should."

She looked at him directly then. He stayed right where he was. He did not think he was saying this just because Jeff irked him. Perhaps three years ago he would've enjoyed having the upper hand here. He'd lost their wedding toast battle, but she was lost in a larger way. He didn't enjoy it now, though. Instead, he felt a strange sense of melancholy. Finding the person you were going to spend your life with came down to many factors. Readiness, yes: Rob had wanted a partner when he met Zuri. Good decision-making too: again, thank God he hadn't slept with Natalie when she'd turned to him at the lake, open and wanting and full of need. But also, so much depended on sheer luck. If Rob hadn't gone to that lecture, or if the person walking in before him had sat in the open seat next to the beautiful woman, who knew what his life would look like today?

"But Jeff is wonderful," Natalie said. "I don't have a good reason not to . . . It has to be a problem with me."

Where had all the fire and surety she'd shown at the wedding gone? For a moment, he wanted to put his arms around her. He kept them glued to his sides.

"What if I never want to move in with anyone?" Natalie asked.

"Well"—he swallowed—"how did you feel about living with Gabby? About getting to see her every day?"

"I felt like I could have done it forever," she whispered.

"Then you're not broken. You can feel that way with someone else. And if that person never comes along, you'll live by yourself and be the love of your own life." He dug his hands deeper into his pockets. "Not everyone is lucky enough to love someone as infuriating and interesting and alive as Natalie Shapiro."

They held each other's gazes for a moment. She wiped a tear that had begun to bead in one of her eyes.

"Dammit, Rob. Why did you have to . . ." she began. "I don't know if I want to thank you or punch you." She turned away into the garden, unable to look at him any longer, her voice formal. "You should go inside. Your gorgeous fiancée is probably wondering where you are."

21

★☆☆☆☆

Nat and Jeff got out of the taxi at the train station and walked to the ticket kiosk, the last of their friends returning to the city, having stayed late to help with the cleanup.

You built up routines over a year and a half with someone, all sorts of lovely little patterns. Whenever Natalie was at Jeff's and she got cold (Jeff's roommate refused to turn up the heat, another reason Jeff wanted to move), Jeff would bring her a blanket, then a hat, then gloves, then another blanket, and on and on until she was warm and laughing and nearly drowning in fabric. Natalie poured them both cups of coffee in the mornings when he stayed over at her place and knew exactly how much milk to put in his to make him smile in utter satisfaction. They each had two toothbrushes now, one in the other's apartment. Sometime during the last six months, they'd started buying their train tickets together whenever they went on a day trip, alternating who covered the cost. Natalie had gotten their tickets out to Long Island, so now Jeff sped up ahead of her to start the transaction.

"No, I've got this," Natalie said.

"You do not. You bought last time." He pushed the button to

select the ticket type, and she hurried to the machine next to his, starting her own transaction.

"Yeah, but this was for my friend's event, so I should pay for it."

He looked over, grinning as her fingers flew over the options on the screen. "Oh, is this a race? You know I'm competitive, Shapiro!"

"Not a race. I insist."

Still, laughing, he hustled to remove his credit card from his wallet. Her arm, of its own accord, popped out and whacked the card away from the machine, sending it to the ground.

"Please, let me," she said in a strangled voice, and he held his hands up.

"Whoa. Okay."

Silently, she waited for the machine to spit the tickets out, then led the way to the platform. He stood beside her, shifting from foot to foot as Rob's words echoed in her head. *You can feel that way with someone else.* Rob, with his dark eyes and his hands in his pockets, seeing her to her core. Her fingers had lost circulation as she stood with him in that freezing garden. She hadn't noticed until she got back inside.

It broke her heart that she couldn't feel that way about Jeff.

Beside her, Jeff began to talk about how cold it had gotten, unable to stand the silence for long. Sometimes, when they were quiet together for more than a minute as they walked down the street, he'd say, "Isn't it nice that we've gotten to the stage of our relationship where we don't always have to talk?" and then begin to discuss all the other nice things about the current stage of their relationship. He was so good to her.

"So, what do you think?" he asked now. "You want one more

night to sleep on it, or should we pull the trigger on the apartment?"

Natalie swallowed, dread in her stomach. "I can't say yes to the apartment."

His eyebrows knitted together in concern. "Is it because of the bedbugs? Drew swears that was two years ago, and he hasn't seen one since. But I can look into getting an extra inspection—"

"No, it's not that. The place sounds lovely. I just don't think I'm ready to move in together."

"Oh," he said with such disappointment in his tone. His mouth tightened in determination. "Well, it could be nice to wait one more year. Delayed gratification! Or I could see if I can go month-to-month on my lease."

She hesitated. Maybe things would change in a year. She'd grow into the person she so desperately wished she could be, the person who was right for Jeff. She could keep the one stable thing she had in her life. In the distance, the light of the approaching train appeared, the wind whipping up, a mournful blast of the horn echoing around them. She had sympathy for her mother now, for the fear of loneliness that led her to run headfirst into relationships, to stay even when the joy had expired. She'd always told herself that she'd rather be alone than be in a relationship just to be in one, but she hadn't been acting like it.

Giving this another year—of uncertainty, of the constantly changing pros and cons list in her head—would be unkind to both of them. He'd try even harder to hold her while she pulled farther away. Jeff was not Greg, not her mother's husband by a long shot. And that made it even more important to let him go so that he could find someone who appreciated him as much as he deserved.

She clenched her fists, unclenched them, and forced herself to say, "No. I'm so sorry, but no."

"What do you mean?"

"I don't think I'm ever going to be ready to move in together."

He stepped back, features frozen in hurt. "Then, what are we doing?"

She tried to find the right combination of words, but there was nothing to say to make this better. "I think this is so close to what it should be, but there's just something in me that can't . . . And you're a wonderful person. Some other woman is going to snatch you up—"

"Don't," he said. "Don't try to . . ." The train was growing closer now, the front of it hurtling toward them.

"I'm so sorry."

"You said that already." He turned away from her. "I need to . . . I can't sit with you. I'm going to a different car."

"Okay."

He took a couple of steps, then ran back and gathered her in his arms, holding her one last time against his broad, solid chest. She breathed him in, knowing that she might never see him again or that when she did, they'd be strangers to each other, all the important and vital things they'd shared gone hazy, if they remembered them at all. Then he pulled himself away and strode down the platform, shoulders shaking, not looking back.

When the doors opened, she found an empty row in a sparsely populated car. The train lurched, then began to glide back toward the city.

Trying to fight off tears, she reached for her phone to call Gabby. But Gabby was exhausted. And also, maybe Gabby wouldn't understand.

Instead, she dialed her mother. Ellen answered on the second ring. "Natalie?"

"Hey, Mom," Nat said, her voice breaking.

"Honey, what's wrong?" her mom asked, and Natalie's shoulders slumped at the familiar, comforting sound. She could go home to Philly for a few days, sleep in her childhood bed, start to recover. Yes, that would help.

"Jeff and I broke up," she began.

"Oh no. Are you all right? What happened?"

"I . . . I don't really know how to explain."

Ellen made a sympathetic noise. "I had no idea you two weren't happy. He always seemed so smitten. I thought he just doted on you."

"He did."

"Ah," Ellen said, and Natalie could hear how valiantly her mom was struggling to hide her disappointment.

"I know you think I'm making a mistake," Natalie said. "But I tried. I really tried. And I think I deserve to be smitten too."

"Of course you do," her mom began with such surprise and tenderness in her voice that for the first time, a possibility struck Natalie. Maybe, just maybe, Ellen didn't even remember saying the things that had burned themselves into Natalie's brain the night before her wedding. Maybe Ellen had simply been expressing a loose collection of thoughts rather than some unshakable, unchangeable truth about her daughter's core.

Just when Natalie was about to ask, a voice in the background interrupted. "What's going on?"

"Natalie and Jeff broke up," her mother said quietly.

"Here," the voice went on, and then the sound quality turned grainier as Natalie was yanked onto speakerphone. "Do you need me to talk some sense into him?" Greg asked, his booming voice grating against her ears. "If he needs a little mano a mano—"

"No, thank you," Natalie said, her chest tightening. "He didn't do anything wrong."

"So, you broke up with *him*? That sounds like our little perfectionist," Greg said, and Natalie swallowed the urge to tell him that she was not his little anything.

"Greg," her mother said, frustration creeping into her tone. "Let's not—"

"I'm just saying that the clock is ticking."

"Really?" Nat said. "No one's ever told me that before."

On the other end of the line, things went muffled, as if her mother was holding a hand over the speaker, saying something that sounded like "You are not being helpful" as Greg protested.

Natalie needed to get off this call immediately. "Sorry, I'm on the train, and . . . service . . ."

"Wait," her mother began. "Do you want to come visit?"

"I can't," Nat said. "And you're going in and out . . . I'll try you later."

Then she hung up, sat back on the hard seat, and let the tears come.

She had to start over, and loneliness lay ahead, and she wept at the prospect with racking, muffled sobs. But there was relief in her tears too, relief from finally having made a choice, hard as it may have been.

Maybe five years from now, she'd look back at this moment and wish she'd chosen differently. But somehow she didn't think so. Talking to her mother and Greg had helped after all, even if not in the way Natalie had expected. There were so many elements of a life with Jeff that could have been wonderful. She trusted him. She admired him. But she just didn't love him enough.

Maybe one person in a relationship was always going to be the one to commit more, give more, love more. Maybe someday, despite how much it scared her, she could let that person be her. And if not, well, she'd commit to loving herself as hard as she could, starting now.

Her phone began to vibrate. Her mother, having snuck away from Greg to talk further? But instead, Tyler Yeo's name appeared on the screen. Probably calling to talk about some new exciting article pinned to the memoir: **Tyler Yeo Is Now a Bestselling Author. What's Next?** or **5 Facts You Won't Believe About Early 2000s Heartthrob Tyler Yeo! #1: He's Lactose Intolerant!** She was not in the mood, so she sent it to voicemail and looked back out the window, the outlines of trees and houses blurring together in the dark.

Another buzz, a text from Tyler. Dude! I just finished Apartment 2F!

She stared down, then immediately called him back. "You read my book? What?"

"Yes! It took me forever to get a copy. It's too popular, it's sold out everywhere!"

"I think it's just been remaindered."

"Cool!"

"No, that's when they take your book out of stores because no one is buying—" She cut herself off. "Never mind. Thank you for reading, that was really nice."

"I loved it. That Dennis guy? He had me cracking up! And I had the best idea. You want to hear it?"

"Um, I think so?"

"Oh, come on. I need some enthusiasm here. You're gonna like it. So tell me you want to hear it, Natalie Shapiro."

"I want to hear it," she said. She leaned forward as Tyler kept talking and the train gathered speed, hurtling into her future.

"I think we should make a TV show."

Part Five

HAPPY HOLIDAYS FROM THE ALVAREZ-STOATS!

What a year it has been! Angus continues to thrive at Insight Capital. Gabby got a promotion at her ad agency, heading up all sorts of new and exciting accounts. (Perhaps you saw a certain Super Bowl commercial this year that was her brainchild?) And of course Christina keeps getting promotions in our hearts. We love her more every day, even as her energy levels present us with new and exhausting challenges. Forget the gym—we're getting more exercise than we ever have before by simply running after her. But the biggest change of all is that we moved to a house in beautiful Westfield, New Jersey! We have a guest room! We have a staircase (and a childproof gate at the top and bottom of it).

Yet, there is one problem with our house that we can't solve on our own. It's too cold. We've tried turning up the heat, but nothing except a housewarming party will do the trick. Please come join us Saturday, December 14, for food, drink, and friendship.

22

★☆☆☆☆

Sweet Natalie Shapiro, with a network TV show. I never would have seen this coming back when we were together, but I'm so impressed," said Conor of the inscrutable short stories, sitting across a wobbly table from Natalie in a crowded West Village coffee shop.

"Thank you," Natalie said, taking a sip of her cappuccino. Men always called her sweet when they didn't actually know her. Before a couple weeks ago, her last communication with Conor had been a poem he'd sent her a month after their breakup back in 2013, something he'd written about her that was actually about him. Conor had viewed Natalie as a manic pixie dream girl sent to fill his life with sex and adoration, and she, craving his approval, had played the part he asked of her until she outgrew it.

But recently an email from him had landed in her inbox, asking for a "pick your brain" coffee the next time she was back in New York. She hadn't yet learned how to say no to those requests. Besides, it was nice being in a position where she could help others.

And, okay, fine, she liked the idea of Conor craving *her* approval for a change.

"You're not running the whole thing yourself, are you?" he asked.

"Oh, no. They hired an experienced showrunner for that, thankfully." She straightened her shoulders, strove to appear entirely calm about the turn her life had taken even though sometimes she still couldn't believe her luck. "But I'm second-in-command in the writers' room, and an executive producer on it as well."

"Man, it's inspiring that you get to do this work. How did you make it all happen?" he asked, scratching the gray at his temples.

She pictured herself from his point of view, her hair shiny and blown out. (She could afford nice hair care products now!) Sophisticated. She'd become the kind of person who wore blouses tucked into tight leather pants. Satisfaction burned in her.

"Would you say it was mostly connections?" he continued as she opened her mouth to speak.

"Well," she said, and cleared her throat, "connections certainly played a part. And so much of the industry is luck. But you also have to do the work on your craft so that when you're in the right place at the right time, you're ready to step up." Apparently she'd also become the kind of person who very seriously said "your craft."

"Are your connections solely on the network side?" Conor asked, scratching his chin. "Because I think my work lends itself more naturally to streaming. It has an auteur, complex, almost filmic tone, if you know what I mean."

"Mm. Wow. Yes, we took ours out to networks first since Tyler wanted to go big and broad with the comedy. I don't know how much you've watched of it—"

He nodded in an evasive way. "I don't have regular TV anymore."

"Right," she said, then sat through another interminable half hour, during which Conor rerouted the conversation to talk in depth about the script *he* was working on, clearly hoping that she'd be so blown away by the brilliance of "it's a Kafkaesque look at working in a big-box store, revealing the rot at the heart of the American experiment" that she'd have no choice but to connect him with her agent. Why had she ever been so desperate to keep this insufferable man entertained? Finally, blessedly, her phone dinged.

"And it would be incredibly punk rock having this show about the evil of big corporations on Amazon Prime, you know? Tricking the biggest corporation of all into spreading the message."

Natalie held her phone up. "I'm sorry, but I have to go to a housewarming party, and my ride's here."

"Sure. But first, what do you think of the concept?"

She rose to standing. "I know it's only network TV, but *Superstore* has been doing smart, interesting commentary on the big-box store for a while now. And as for the rest of your vision, I'm afraid I don't quite get it." She grabbed her coat and gave him a blinding smile. "But best of luck."

Then she walked outside and over to the black car idling at the curb, opening the door and sliding onto the seat. "Thank God that's over."

"Damn, no fun?" Tyler asked, sprawled out next to her. "Then it's a good thing we get to party!"

On the turnpike, Natalie looked out the window as they passed a billboard for Stoat & Sons and then, behind it, a newer, shinier billboard advertising *Meant 2B*, Tuesday nights on CBS. In the foreground of the picture, Tyler mugged, a himbo unintentionally leaving destruction in his wake. In the background of the shot, two women watched—one with adoration, another rolling her eyes.

"I think we should make a TV show," Tyler had said on the phone last year, the night that Natalie had been crying on the train.

"Of your memoir?"

"No, *Apartment 2F*! Don't you think it could make a great sitcom? Two roommates, the kooky boyfriend who comes in and screws things up? We make Dennis a lead. I play Dennis. You help adapt it."

It was all so completely strange, Natalie couldn't stop herself from laughing. "I never pictured it as a sitcom."

"Really? I think it's perfect for multicam! Anyway, my agent says that because *Yeo, It's Tyler!* is doing so well right now, we've got to act fast to capitalize on the Tyler-ssance."

"I'm sorry, the Tyler-ssance? Like the Renaissance?"

"Oh." Tyler paused. "Yeah. That's what he meant."

"I'm just trying to wrap my head around this. I'm so flattered, but are you sure about *Apartment 2F*? We could come up with something different, something original."

"Nah, it's gotta be intellectual property. Everyone's into IP now! So, what do you say? Can I set up a time for you to talk with my agent?"

Strangely, in that moment, Natalie pictured Rob, the way he'd called her out at the wedding over her cruel portrayal of Angus. Could she really put that on television? (Assuming the show made it through the development process. Even with stars attached, plenty of projects failed. This whole moral dilemma was probably moot.)

But she could change the character of Dennis. Change the circumstances, the details, make him unrecognizable. Tyler didn't have Angus's energy, not in the slightest.

And how could she look this gift horse in the mouth? This

was everything she'd ever dreamt about. Angus hadn't proven to be as bad for Gabby as Natalie had feared, but that didn't mean she had to kill her own ambitions just on the off chance this might upset him.

"Of course," Natalie said, feeling like she was about to faint. "I'm in."

The development process had been a fast-tracked whirlwind. Despite the dominance of streaming, it turned out there was still a market for network sitcoms in the mold of *The Big Bang Theory*, and Tyler had been right. If you took the most basic scaffolding of *Apartment 2F*—two roommates who are best friends, one falls in love with an annoying fop who the other one hates, annoying fop unofficially moves in—and added in "shenanigans ensue," it *did* work as a laugh-tracked multicam.

Their unofficial mandate was "Dumb it down," starting with the stupid, punny title. ("They live in apartment 2B, and the girl-friend thinks they're *meant* 2B!") Natalie stayed true to her vow to herself, leaning into the dopily attractive interpretation of Dennis. Surely nobody would connect Tyler's version—always walking around the apartment shirtless—with Angus. Plus, given the title change, people wouldn't associate the show with the book unless Natalie pushed for it, and she wouldn't.

Somehow, each time they reached a new step where she thought the project would die, it just kept going, like some mon-ster with regenerative powers. Maybe it had something to do with Tyler's chill confidence. He was manifesting, he'd explained to her, and had acquired a crystal meant to guarantee success.

So, here she was, less than two years after she'd begged Gabby for a job in advertising, one of the head writers on a tele-vision show that was pulling in numbers, respectable numbers, enough that they felt secure in starting to talk about what they might do in a second season. She got to sit in a room full of other writers every day and come up with dumb jokes and ridiculous situations. What if Dennis decides he's going to fix their clogged sink and ends up flooding the whole apartment building? What if Dennis starts a dog-walking business with apartment 2B as his home base?

Occasionally, in quiet moments, she could admit to herself that the work wasn't the most creatively fulfilling. The Sisyphean structure of each episode where nothing changed and nobody grew might eventually bring her to a breaking point. Her pitches to have the characters deal with more complicated feelings or break out of their rigid roles were mostly shot down by the show-runner. She was inundated with well-wishes from people who knew her, but it was less that they respected her work, more that they respected that she'd gotten the chance to do it. Also, she'd had to move to the West Coast, and every time she drove herself to the writers' room, she worried she might die on the freeway.

But holy shit, who cared? In almost all the ways, she was living the dream.

It was a delicious irony that she'd spent so much of her twenties thinking that she had to figure out her life before turning thirty or she'd be doomed. And then, at thirty, an opportunity she'd never even let herself imagine dropped into her lap.

No, she shouldn't say *dropped*, as if she'd had nothing to do with it. The opportunity had come about because of groundwork she'd laid without realizing. That was the strange part about success—there was no predicting it. The things you thought would pan out didn't, while the random job you took to pay your bills might reward you beyond your wildest dreams. It was enough to drive you insane, the unpredictable not-knowing of it all.

Now, she was back in NYC for a few days before the holidays, seeing Iman, taking some meetings alongside Tyler, who had also come back to the East Coast.

Then she'd bring her mother on a trip, just the two of them, to Italy, which Natalie was proudly paying for. And look, Greg was welcome to come if he wanted to pay his own way! A notorious cheapskate, he did not, and Ellen did not seem too upset about that. Natalie had finally figured out a way to get alone time with her mother. Maybe some night in a cozy trattoria over a bottle of wine, she'd bring up that devastating conversation they'd had all those years ago the night before her mom's wedding. She'd tell her mom what she'd begun to learn over the past year and a half—that she'd become so much less afraid of men getting bored with her once she'd learned how not to get bored of herself.

But before all that, Gabby and Angus's housewarming party. She'd mentioned it to Tyler at lunch that day, as they were walking out of an overpriced steakhouse where they'd met with a New York–based exec. "Ooh, can I come?" Tyler had asked.

"Really? It's just going to be hanging out in the suburbs."

"Yes. I love going to normal people parties! Sometimes it's nice to be around, like, less people doing cocaine, more people eating chips and salsa."

Natalie grimaced. "Unfortunately, Gabby and Angus are huge cokeheads."

"Oh." He thought hard. "Well, that's okay too."

"I'm joking," she said, laughing.

"Always writing jokes, even on vacation!"

"That's me."

"You write the jokes, I tell them, it makes us a perfect pair," he went on, and she shot him a look. "Pair of friends. Unless we ever decide to be something more. Which we could, but we don't have to."

"Okay," she said. "I don't know if you going to this party is a great idea."

"It is!" He'd pulled a puppy dog face until she agreed.

Now their car pulled into Gabby and Angus's driveway. Gabby had sent Natalie pictures of the place, but it was prettier in person, with white trim and a dark slate roof. Electric candles flickered in the windows. The front door, painted a cheery red, beckoned.

Tyler followed Nat as she strode up the walkway and tried the door handle. Unlocked. They walked into the party, which was already in full swing. The crowd spilled out of the living room, and throughout the first floor, a mix of people Natalie recognized who had come in from the city and those who she assumed were Gabby and Angus's new neighbor friends. Gabby had decked the halls and then some. Combine Gabby's Catholic upbringing with her stifled artistic talents, and this was what you got: garlands and lights competed for space, a Christmas tree stretched almost to the ceiling, and there were plenty of Santas ranging from stuffed dolls to an animatronic Kriss Kringle near the door whose belly shook with laughter whenever someone passed by him.

Nat had walked into rooms alongside Tyler plenty of times in LA. She'd felt the current of excitement that began to buzz when people realized a celebrity had entered the building. People's conversations would grow more animated, as if they might draw Tyler's attention to them, might make him think that they were *fun*. They'd throw their heads back in laughter, their eyes flitting Tyler's way. But that was LA. Celebrities entered buildings all the time.

In suburban New Jersey, Natalie and Tyler walked in, and people's conversations stopped. Not all conversations. It wasn't like in the movies, where a hush descended over the room. But the people who noticed them poked one another and whispered. Not just about Tyler, she realized. About her too, their friend who had made good after they'd all spent years worrying to one another: *Does Natalie have a backup plan? Such a shame, she had potential, the world is just so tough for creative types.* She flashed them all a wide smile.

And then Gabby swept toward them. "Natalie!" Gabby yelped and hugged her. As Tyler examined the animatronic Santa, entranced, Gabby whispered shakily in Nat's ear, "You brought Tyler Yeo? Is this my Christmas present? Am I allowed to talk to him?"

"Yes, he's very nice," Nat whispered back.

Gabby smoothed her hair, then smoothed it again, and attempted a calm smile as she turned to Tyler. "Welcome to our party. And house. This is, um, my house." She let out a loud laugh for no apparent reason, her cheeks flaming red.

"Sweet place. And these decorations? We're in a winter wonderland!" Tyler said, holding his arms out wide and coming in for a hug.

"Thank you," Gabby squeaked as he enfolded her.

Angus came over with Christina on his back. "Natalie! And, oh wow, *the* Tyler Yeo? Huge fan! Welcome to our humble abode." Angus shook Tyler's hand heartily, then gave Nat a bear hug. "Your TV show! It's hilarious. Appointment viewing for me, every Tuesday!"

"Thanks so much," she said, exhaling, even as she noticed Gabby's dreamy expression clearing, turning sour for a brief moment. But here was proof: Natalie had done her job disguising

Dennis enough that Angus could watch the show and have no idea.

Angus gave Tyler a hearty handshake, then leaned forward so that Christina, on his back, could respond to Tyler's proffered high five. "What can I get you? I have a bottle of Scotch I've been saving for a special occasion. Or . . . steak! Want me to grill you a steak?"

Angus, Tyler, and Christina headed off toward the kitchen, chatting happily. Gabby squeezed Nat's hand quite hard. "You guys walked in here like a couple. Are you?"

"No. We're coworkers."

"But he came to a party in the suburbs with you. You don't do that for a normal coworker."

Natalie had heard that ghostwriters often fell half in love with their clients, having spent so much time thinking about them. Strangely enough, in their case, the opposite seemed to have happened. Tyler had fallen half in love with her.

She didn't flatter herself—she knew it had started because of how eagerly she listened to him talk about himself. But now he actually seemed to respect her mind for what it could do outside of making him look good, though that was still a central feature.

"Please tell me you've at least . . ." Gabby waggled her eyebrows.

"No. Well, we went on one date. The night we found out the pilot had been picked up. We were drunk and hopped up on adrenaline, and he took me out to this fancy dinner."

"And did you smooch?" Gabby asked, with all the seriousness of a policewoman interrogating a murder suspect.

"Yes."

Gabby emitted a small shriek. "Why did you not call me immediately?"

"Maybe because right afterward, he said, and I quote, 'It's so refreshing how you're pretty in a normal person way and not like a supermodel.'"

"Okay," Gabby said. "But still. You kissed Tyler Yeo! I can't believe you haven't told me every detail."

"I thought it might be more fun to tell you in person and see your face, but—" Nat cut herself off, and Gabby awkwardly fiddled with her hair.

"Yeah. I'm sorry again about missing the premiere. I just figured that Angus needed more emotional support for his work retreat than you did at a fancy Hollywood party where everyone wanted to suck up to you."

"Right," Natalie said. Sure, the *Meant 2B* premiere had been wildly exciting, but it had been destabilizing too, the kind of night where she could've used Gabby's grounding force. Instead, Gabby had bailed a few days earlier for some last-minute, high-pressure invitation from Angus's boss, a retreat for Insight Capital's top employees and their spouses. Yet another example of one of Natalie's proudest achievements passing by without Gabby's support.

"After going with Angus," Gabby continued now, talking fast in an almost anxious tone, watching Natalie's face, "I've got to say, it's good I was there. Those guys are such competitive, status-obsessed assholes. No wonder Angus is always on the verge of developing a stress ulcer. Did you know that they call him 'Sofa Stoat'? As in 'Can Sofa Stoat handle taking on more hours, or is he preoccupied thinking about recliners?' Which is ridiculous because futons and sofas aren't the same, and he's actually preoccupied being an equal partner in raising his *child*. I keep telling him that if he wants to quit, it's fine by me, but—" She shook her head and pressed a hand on Natalie's arm. "Anyways! I would have had much more fun walking the red carpet with you. Dibs on being your date to the next show you create." She waggled her eyebrows. "Unless *Tyler* wants that position instead."

"You aren't letting this go, huh?" Nat asked.

"Nope! Now back to discussing Tyler's mouth," Gabby went on. "It must have been the best kiss of your life, right?"

Natalie started to confirm, then stopped. Because although making out with a movie star had been plenty exciting, the best kiss of her life had been with Rob Kapinsky in a cold, clear lake.

Where was Rob? Nat scanned the room for him, hoping he would and wouldn't be here in equal measure. If he'd seen the show, he'd probably treat her with an icy superiority, Zuri on his arm. Last Gabby had told her, Rob and Zuri had sent out the save-the-dates for their wedding, to be held in April of next year, and Angus had been running himself ragged trying to be the best best man the world had ever seen (despite the fact that Rob had barely asked anything of him).

No sign of Rob. Well, of course not. Why would he fly out across the country for a housewarming party, especially while in the midst of wedding planning?

"Hello?" Gabby asked, bringing Nat back to earth. "Lost in reveries of Tyler? Sorry, but I still don't understand why you're not trying to make something happen with him."

"Because we work together! That's messy. I don't want people thinking I got this show just because Tyler wants to get into my pants."

It wasn't just that, though. Five years ago, Natalie would have dated him anyway, gossip be damned. An actual movie star wanting to be in a relationship with her? How could she say no? But now, she didn't want to date someone for status. She wanted to date someone who was right. And even though their date had been exciting, adrenaline-filled, and Tyler was clearly a practiced kisser, she couldn't stop the nagging feeling that she was like a *Bachelor* contestant, there for the wrong reasons.

Still, the "being professional for work" excuse was an easier one. And that was what Natalie had said to him when she pulled back from their drunken kiss. Well, first he'd said the shit about the supermodels, and then she'd told him that she didn't think going any further was a good idea.

"Cool," he'd said. "Like, I obviously would love to get in your pants. But no presh. The show comes first. And if you ever change your mind, I'm here."

He had been a real gem about it throughout the process. He was happy enough to wait for her to change her mind—he could get plenty of action in the meantime. She couldn't seriously imagine making a life with Tyler. But she had to admire his persistence. He was growing on her.

"Shoot, I've got to go say hi to some parents from Christina's daycare. Get yourself a drink, and we will continue this later," Gabby said.

Natalie wound her way through the room to pour herself a glass of sauvignon blanc, making her way through the gauntlet of couples, everyone at this party in a pair besides her. Sometimes Nat felt like an ark had come by calling for the people to line up two by two just when she'd happened to be in the restroom.

But maybe that was okay. She had a lot of joy in her life, and she'd keep finding joy even if she never had a partner to experience it with her. She could discover moments of absolute ecstasy in taking herself to dinner alone, savoring the cold brine of a martini, exchanging life stories with the bartender if she was in a social mood or sitting silently with her own thoughts if she wasn't. People said that joy was sweeter when you shared it, and maybe that was true. Perhaps she'd always have a pang of regret.

But when she stretched out in her big soft bed as the morning light filtered in through her window, her joy tasted sweet enough to satisfy her.

This party too was full of joy. The last time she'd seen most of these people, she was treading water. Now she was a star and had brought an even bigger star along. She whirled from conversation to conversation, basking in praise and admiration, ready to soak it up all night long.

Halfway through her glass of wine, Natalie was talking with Becks and Shay as a man in a corduroy jacket stumbled out of the kitchen, knocking over yet another one of Gabby's Santa figures with a clatter.

"Uh-oh, someone's been hitting the eggnog a little too hard," Shay said, her hand resting on her pregnant belly.

The man straightened up, then squatted down to righten the Santa. In doing so, he turned in their direction, and Natalie had to do a double take. What was Rob Kapinsky—a man who kept a tight leash on himself in almost every way—doing drunkenly wreaking havoc with Gabby's Christmas decorations? She'd never seen him so loose-limbed, so floppy and careless, like a Muppet instead of a man.

Nearby, Gabby was looking over too. Rob regarded the Santa with a foggy mask of woe on his face.

Nat grabbed Gabby's arm. "Um, what is happening over there? And where's Zuri? I can't imagine her approving of him getting that drunk."

Gabby blinked at her slowly, then brought a hand to her mouth. "Oh my God," she said. "I can't believe I didn't tell you."

23

★☆☆☆☆

Zuri Balewa had given herself a ten-minute break from work to do some wedding planning, entering RSVP information into the spreadsheet she shared with Rob, secure in the knowledge that her life was going to plan.

And then the head of her program, Dr. Levitt, knocked on the door of her office. "Zuri? Got a second?"

When Zuri nodded, Dr. Levitt walked into the room with an apologetic smile on her face, leading in a man in tight pants. "Meet Michael Garrido. He'll be joining us for the semester as a guest lecturer." The pants on this guy were flashily tight, impractically so. "We're all very excited to have him here! He was at the Phoenix Art Museum for a while and now runs a successful gallery there focusing on contemporary art. But the pipes burst in the room we were going to give him, so he'll be sharing with you for the time being."

Immediately, Zuri was annoyed. Her office was her oasis. She had three succulents placed at nice intervals and some scented candles burning. Tasteful scents, of course. (She couldn't burn the candles at home because Rob was sensitive to smells.) She was junior, yes, but not the most junior.

"Why not with Boris?" she asked.

Michael and the department head exchanged a glance. "It became clear that Boris's office was . . . inhospitable," Dr. Levitt said. "We'll hopefully get the pipes fixed soon. And in the meantime, I'm sure you two will have lots to talk about!" She walked out of the room, leaving the two of them alone.

"Thank you, you've saved me." Michael grinned at Zuri, an impish kind of smile, while she gave her interloper a cool, appraising stare. His whole body had a loose ease to it, as if he danced happily through life thanks to his moderate good looks and charm and, she supposed if he were here as a visiting lecturer, some amount of intelligence. People like that irked her. She found them unreliable and lazy, giving up on whatever didn't come at the snap of their fingers.

"Well, I didn't have much choice," she said. "But it's not your fault." She pointed to a table in the corner. "You can sit there."

He began to unpack his bag, laying out his computer and notebooks while she turned back to her laptop, trying to block out the distraction.

"I know I should let you work," he said, breaking their silence and her concentration. "And I will. But I really want to tell you the real reason I'm not staying in Boris's office. If you'd like to hear it."

She considered leaving him hanging. But, actually, she did want to know. Because if it was something sexist, Boris claiming his work was more important than hers, she could lodge a complaint, and then perhaps her oasis would be hers alone again. "Fine, what's the real reason?"

He perched on the table and leaned forward confidentially. "It smells like something died in there."

"Do you think something did?" she asked as she continued typing, pretending not to care, curious despite herself.

"It could be a mouse behind the wall," he said, then flashed her a sideways grin. "Or maybe Boris needs to start taking more showers."

"Rude. Boris is my best friend."

"Shit, I'm so sorry," he said. "Please forget I said—"

"I'm kidding. Boris is a jerk." Boris regularly made demeaning comments about her work in comparison to his, and when she called him on it, he pretended that she was overreacting. "So I'll allow it." She tossed her head. "Now, I have work to do. You're welcome to use the office as you'd like until the pipes in your room are fixed. But don't distract me, or I'll stop taking showers too."

He guffawed at that. She didn't make people guffaw often. "I'll be a perfect office mate, I promise." She looked at him. He had a rather nice laugh. He probably deployed it all the time to win people over. "So, what are you waiting for?" he went on, and she realized she was still watching him. "Get back to work."

She did, biting down on her own smile.

That was a Friday. On Monday, she walked into her office to find Michael already there, working diligently on his computer to plan a lesson. He gave her a silent nod, and so she beelined to her desk, hopeful that he'd be a nondisruptive force after all.

A framed drawing sat next to her pile of books. "What's this?" she asked, picking it up to examine. She recognized the style. "Is this a Nia North?"

"I wanted to say thank you for letting me invade your space," he said.

"She's one of my favorites."

"I know. I read your article." Zuri had published a piece recently about up-and-coming artists who were working in a postcolonial framework. Nia had gotten a whole page to herself. Michael went on. "We've worked with Nia at the gallery, and I bought this piece after the show. I drove back to Phoenix this weekend to get it. Figured as long as you have to put up with me, you might as well get to look at this to make up for it."

Zuri looked at the messy lines of the drawing, something welling up in her. This was why she loved to study art. Sometimes she felt herself on the outside of the world, an observer of her own feelings, or rather the feelings she was supposed to have. But a beautiful, interesting piece of art could poke a hole in the border between her and her emotions.

A tear came to her eye, and she brushed it away.

"Oh no," he said. "I didn't think my presence was *that* bad."

"It's not you. I just love the way she puts her whole soul on the page."

"I know. During the run of her show, every time a potential buyer asked me about this piece, I kept steering them to something else, until I finally realized it was because I didn't want them to take it away. So I bought it for myself."

They kept geeking out over Nia, then about other artists his gallery had featured. He told her about why he'd wanted to open the gallery in the first place, how so many galleries were run for wealthy people, helping them collect art for the purpose of enriching themselves even further rather than for the sake of enjoyment or real love. He wanted to change that, to make things accessible while still helping artists thrive, to feature people who maybe weren't at the top of everyone else's list. He made her crack up with the way he imitated some of the blowhards he'd met in the art collecting world. And she made him laugh too with her academic perspective, which was an odd feeling, because she'd never thought of herself as funny. Perhaps sharing an office for however long it took to get the pipes fixed—it couldn't be more than a couple weeks—would not only be peaceful but actively pleasant.

At home that night, as she and Rob ate dinner, Rob asked her, "Are you all right? You keep touching your face."

"Oh," she said. "It's odd. The tops of my cheeks hurt."

"Too much sun, maybe?"

But that wasn't it, she realized. Her muscles were sore from smiling.

As the semester passed, she and Michael began to get to their office earlier and earlier, staying later and later. Whenever she hit a dead end, she'd groan, and he'd shut his computer and spin around. "Talk it out," he'd say, and she would, with him challenging every weak spot in her argument, forcing her to defend and rethink.

One day, a few weeks in, they'd both eaten big lunches and were starting to get sleepy in the midafternoon despite having a lot of work to complete. "We need to wake up," Michael said. He clicked a button on his computer, and the iconic opening to Biggie's "Hypnotize" began to blast. She turned around, and he was rising to his feet, shrugging his shoulders in time.

"Oh no," she said.

"It's happening."

"It doesn't have to."

In response, he leapt into rapping the first verse. He did it with the infectious enthusiasm of someone who had worn out this CD as a teenager. When it came time for the woman's part, Michael pointed at Zuri. She demurred at first, covering her face, but he danced closer.

So as the second *Biggie Biggie Biggie, can't you see* began, she broke into a grin and began to sing along too, getting to her feet, her body moving of its own accord. And when Biggie started the next verse, she kept going. Because she'd *also* worn out this CD as a teen, though she hadn't thought about it in forever. Somehow, she'd stopped listening to music over the past few years. During commutes or chores, she put on podcasts instead, not wanting to waste time on songs she already knew when she could be enriching her mind. When had she become so rigid?

"Oh! Okay!" Michael yelled, as Zuri rapped the second verse, and then they did the rest of the song together, a couple of minutes of unbridled joy, finishing it breathless and alert, their former sleepiness totally gone.

After that, whenever they needed a midafternoon pick-me-up, he'd blast a song from his computer and make her dance around with him in order to wake themselves up. (Not *with* him, exactly— he would not swing her around the room. They would simply dance at the same time for the length of one glorious song, spitting the lyrics at each other.)

She ignored it for as long as she could, this strange tension between them. But over Thanksgiving break, when she took Rob home to feast with her family and they pumped them for details about the wedding, she couldn't stop herself from checking her phone to see if Michael had texted. And when they all went around the table to say what they were thankful for, Rob squeezed her hand tight before turning to the rest of her family and saying, "I'm thankful I get to spend the rest of my life with your daughter," and Zuri felt a tiny curl of dread begin to grow in her stomach.

This thing with Michael was simply a crush. Cold feet. A side effect of forced proximity. She was a sensible woman, not the kind to spin out fantasies of throwing away everything good in her life to do long-distance to Phoenix with him. (Although the drive was under two hours. Plenty of people commuted for longer than that every day.) Besides, he was a charmer. Owning a gallery required one to be a salesman, and he was selling her on himself. Perhaps he left a trail of swooning office mates everywhere he went. Yes, she could tell he was attracted to her from the way he looked at her lips sometimes when she talked. But that didn't mean she was special. If anything, he wanted a quick secret fling for the semester before he went back to his real life.

And she would never do that. She was not a woman made for lies and late-night texting and frenzied, clandestine couplings in a car parked down a back road.

And Rob. Rob was so good and loved her with a steady commitment and was all she'd dreamt she wanted in a man. Not flashy and smooth and a little too confident like Michael, which meant she could trust Rob, could trust that their life together would be safe.

So she said nothing. Did nothing. And the days flew by, each one bringing her closer and closer to the end of his time at the university. The last day of classes arrived. Students still had their exams and their papers to turn in, but Michael was heading back to the gallery, which needed his attention.

He packed up his papers and books, then turned to her. She tried to hand him the Nia North drawing, but he shook his head. "You keep it. She belongs with you."

"That's too generous," Zuri said. "And I haven't given you anything."

"You gave me a place to stay for three months," he said, "and a wonderful semester."

She swallowed hard. "Well."

"Well," he said, and held out his hand to shake hers. "Goodbye."

They didn't let go when the handshake was done. Outside, students trudged along the campus, lost in thought, or shrieked with laughter with their friends.

"Nobody ever ended up fixing those pipes," Zuri said, and finally withdrew her hand, waving it dismissively through the air as if she could brush her own feelings away. "Academia, it's always slow."

"I bribed him," he said.

"What? Who?"

"A repairman came two weeks into my time here. I gave him four hundred dollars to tell the department that he wouldn't be able to fix them until next semester."

"Why did you do that?"

He gave her a sad smile, no touch of his usual impish grin. "You know why."

A breath escaped her.

"I've never felt . . ." he began, his voice choked, then cut himself off. "I'm sorry. You're engaged. This is inappropriate. Please forget—"

She kissed him then. In the split second before their lips met, Zuri wished for the kiss to be disappointing, a pale imitation of whatever she'd built up in her head. Then she'd go home to Rob and confess it to him. He'd be able to forgive her a single kiss, even if it might take some counseling. It would be the one thing she'd needed to get out of her system, her one moment of dubious morality, of impulsivity in a life that had been so rigidly disciplined.

But the kiss was not disappointing. It knocked them both sideways. That border between Zuri and her emotions, through which she could occasionally make a small hole? This kiss ripped the border down entirely. On the other side of the wall lay a rippling sea of possibility. Who she could be, what she could feel, if only she was brave or foolish enough to take the plunge.

That night, she went home to Rob, who was typing diligently in their wedding spreadsheet, entering the allergies and food restrictions of the guests who had responded in the affirmative so far. He'd been so good about the planning, taking exactly half of it, offering to do more. He'd gotten a little obsessive, actually, spending far more time price-comparing DJs than anyone else might have done, reading every single online review of their venue before they booked it. It all seemed to take up more space in his brain than his academic work did, a pattern he'd need to break if he was hoping to make tenure.

"Do you think Celia is gluten-free, as in she'll be sick for days if she eats a crumb," he asked by way of a greeting, "or as in 'gluten-free is trendy'?"

How could she be the kind of woman who called off a wedding? Especially when the groom-to-be had done nothing wrong? Her family would be ashamed, her friends would whisper, worried that she must be losing her mind. It was so entirely out of character. And yet, knowing what she knew, feeling what she felt, how could she not?

"Robert," she said, and he whipped his head up at the tone of her voice, penitent.

"I didn't mean to make fun of Celia. I just want to tell the caterers exactly how careful to be."

"That's not it. Can we talk?"

He looked handsome and vulnerable in the black-frame

glasses he wore when he was working, a wrinkle of concern in his forehead, his hair mussed from his habit of running a hand through it while concentrating. He had become her best friend, and if she said the words hammering in her throat, she would lose him forever.

"I kissed someone else," she said.

He sat up straight, blinking a few times. "What?"

"I'm so sorry."

His shock was written all over his face, that she could be capable of such a thing. Rob saw her as she'd always presented herself. Everything she told him and herself about who she was, about what she wanted, he took it at face value. Perhaps because they were so outwardly similar, they never pushed each other to dig for their own sharp corners, the mess inside, the parts that made them interesting.

"One kiss?" he asked, and she nodded. "When? And who was— No, I don't want to know. We can go talk to someone about why it happened, what I should be doing differently." She'd thought he'd react this way. It was how she might have reacted too, the same way as when an obstacle came up at work. "We can fix this."

"No," she said. "I love you." She forced herself to keep going. She considered herself a brave person, but this was the most terrifying thing she'd ever done. "But I don't think we're *in* love the way we're supposed to be."

"I don't understand what you mean."

"It's not just the kiss; it's the feelings that went along with it. I've tried to push them away." She thought of Michael dancing and grinning in their office. "But these are the kinds of feelings people write songs about." She was not normally a woman who trafficked in clichés. Love—axis-spinning, all-consuming, eye-opening love—had stunted her intellectual agility. All her blood was flowing to her heart, none left for her brain.

"But I am in love with you like that," Rob said, a plaintive note in his voice as he reached for her hand.

She squeezed his palm and shook her head. "You're not. One day you'll understand that you're not."

He withdrew his hand, stiff, his eyes dark. "I don't need you to tell me how I'm going to feel."

They sat silently for a moment. "The wedding," Rob finally said, his voice raw. She put an arm around him. He was shaking, even as he stared resolutely ahead into the middle distance.

Alongside her deep sadness, she couldn't help the flare of anticipation that rose in her, for the unknown that came next. "We need to call it off."

24

★☆☆☆☆

There were too many fucking Santas in this house. Rob liked Gabby, but this was obscene. How was a person supposed to walk through a party when inflatable snowmen and reindeer kept springing up in one's path, a holiday spirit—themed obstacle course? And they were all grinning grotesquely, as if they didn't know that at any moment, a person you loved could throw a bomb at you and ruin your entire life.

He'd knocked over the Santa just now accidentally, but as it lay on the ground, he was tempted to give it a good kick. The world was not all cookies and milk, buster!

No, this Santa had done nothing wrong. This Santa had not seduced his fiancée. In fact, Rob saw that this Santa's smile had a dazed, dead-eyed quality to it. Much like Rob's face had looked over the past weeks, when he was somehow expected to continue on doing his job and appearing in public as if he didn't have a pile of broken glass where his heart used to be.

Rob lifted Santa back up to his feet. They both wobbled. Then Rob took a step back and looked around the room. Were people sneaking glances at him? He would not give them more to laugh at or sympathetically cluck about. He gave Santa a little pat on his head, as if he'd been assessing his sturdiness. For all anyone else knew, Angus had sent him out here to see how childproof the living room was before letting Christina loose in it. Reliable Rob.

"That one's stable, all right," he muttered under his breath, then looked up defiantly to find—oh Christ—Natalie Shapiro studying him. Well, this was a situation straight out of his nightmares—Natalie looking more self-possessed and radiant than he'd ever seen her, while he was falling apart.

He hadn't even wanted to come to this goddamn party. But Angus had insisted that Rob stay with him and Gabby for at least a long weekend on his way home for Christmas with his family. Angus had gone so far as to move Rob's plane ticket for him. "You shouldn't be alone right now, buddy!" he'd said. "We can do whatever you want for the weekend." Then he'd bitten his lip. "Shoot, we have this housewarming party. But a party could be good, don't you think? A little nog, maybe some light flirting under the mistletoe?"

After the holidays, Rob would return to Arizona for the next semester, a prospect that was more unappetizing than regurgitated tuna fish. In the weeks since Zuri had called things off, he'd had bad days and worse days. If he wanted to get tenure, he couldn't just up and disappear at the end of the semester. He still had to hold office hours. But when students came in asking for advice on linguistics PhD programs, he had to stop himself from shouting, *Don't do it! There are no jobs!* Each time he started to plan for the following semester, he wanted to bellow into the abyss: *What is the point?* What was the point of standing in the ivory tower of academia, burying oneself in research, oblivious to the important things happening in one's real life? He'd built his career on the idea that there was an order to everything. He wasn't sure he believed that anymore.

His daily routine involved telling himself he needed to grade papers, then proceeding to Google-stalk Michael Garrido instead. Michael's online presence was show-offy, like the man himself. He had not yet posted a straightforward picture of him and Zuri together on social media, perhaps out of some sense of respect for Rob. (Where had that respect been when he shamelessly flirted with an engaged woman?) But evidence of Zuri was everywhere in the snapshots of his life. Her shoes on his floor. Her hand around a sweating bottle of beer, even though Zuri didn't drink beer! She only liked wine! Most egregiously of all, Zuri from the back, standing on a balcony, just starting to turn toward the camera. She was silhouetted by the setting sun in front of her, the sky alight with color. Most beautiful sunset I've ever seen, Michael had captioned the image. How corny and unoriginal of him.

Zuri had offered to handle the wedding's dissolution, which was decent of her. The worst part was how decent she'd been about it all. Well, the decency plus the way she looked at Rob as if she were a guru who felt vaguely sorry for his level of unenlightenment. She'd emerged from her love nest long enough to try to get back some of their deposits and to send their guest list a brief note: We are sorry to announce that we've made the difficult decision to cancel our wedding. We appreciate your love and support during this time and always. (The decision hadn't seemed particularly difficult to her. And "we" hadn't made the decision, Rob wanted to shout when she sent the draft over to him for approval. But he didn't have the energy to send back anything more than a This is fine.)

But there were still people who hadn't gotten the memo, and that was how the trouble today had started. One of these acquaintances, another groomsman from Angus's wedding, clapped Rob on the back five minutes into the party. "My man, long time! I hear congratulations are in order." Rob stared at him, so he continued, "Angus said you're getting married. When's the big day?"

Heartbreak on its own was bad enough. Mixing it with humiliation took things to a whole other level. "It's been called off," Rob said stiffly.

The man made a shocked face. "Holy shit, what happened?"

"She simply fell in love with her soulmate, a man who is not me." Rob proceeded to choke down the entire glass of eggnog in his hand. The man awkwardly backed away.

Eggnog was too thick, too cloying to get the job done. For his next drink, Rob poured himself a glass of Angus's whiskey.

Now, as Natalie began to weave through the guests toward him, Rob tried to remember if he'd had two glasses of whiskey or three. The details were fuzzy.

Perhaps she was simply heading toward the kitchen, and he could duck into a nearby broom closet before she passed by him. Then she'd forget about him, and he wouldn't have to—

No. She'd somehow gotten much closer as he'd been deliberating the broom closet plan. Close enough that he could see her looking at him with a new kind of gentleness in her eyes. He would not be pitied. He did not need to be treated like a small child. He was a strong grown man. A strong grown man for whom his former fiancée could apparently not feel the kinds of feelings that people wrote songs about. Had Natalie heard about the wedding? Or was she simply concerned that he'd had too much to drink? (Now that he thought about it, the three glasses might have been four.)

"You doing all right there?" she asked, placing a hand on his arm. "Want to go get some fresh air?"

He flashed back to the last time they'd seen each other in the fresh air, standing out in the backyard after Christina's christening. How idiotic he'd been, waxing poetic about how he knew that Zuri was The One, thanking his own lucky stars that he wasn't still flailing about in the muck like Natalie was.

She didn't seem to be flailing now. He had a stain on his shirt while she was all dewy and fresh. Her leather pants hugged her lower half like she'd been sewn into them. Had she done something to her hair? Some special cream, or whatever people did when they wanted to look nicer?

It felt imperative that he keep Natalie Shapiro from pitying him. Her pity would be the final nail in his coffin, the one thing that could make his humiliation even more complete. "I'm perfectly fine," he said, yanking his arm away, banging his elbow into the banister behind him in the process.

A grunt of pain escaped him. If he had to put it into letters, the sound would look something like "*mraghhh.*" He rubbed his elbow, squeezing his eyes shut. He could fix this.

Somehow the grunt was still coming out of him. He turned it into more of an "*ahhh*" sound, then reopened his eyes and looked at Natalie as if he'd forgotten she was there. "Oh. Excuse me. Just marveling at the house."

"With your eyes shut?" she asked.

"It has good strong bones," he said, patting the banister. "Solid wood. Not the flimsy stuff you often find in new construction."

She held her hand up over her mouth, trying to stifle a laugh.

"I don't see what's so funny about wanting to make sure that our friends live in a well-built house," he said stiffly.

"You're right," she said. "Nothing amusing about this at all."

As if things couldn't get worse, a familiar-looking man slid toward them smoothly, like he was on a moving walkway. Rob shook his head to clear it. Was he hallucinating the presence of Tyler Yeo?

"Nat! This party is lit!"

Nope, it was the man himself. Was she *with* him? Perfect, now she could stand there and compare him to a literal movie star.

"Hey, man, you a friend of Nat's?" Tyler held out his hand for a shake, and Rob reluctantly took it. God, Tyler's grip. He might accidentally crush Rob's fingers. Rob would not let him. He gripped back, squeezing as hard as he could, until Tyler looked down at their handshake, confused, and extricated himself from it.

"Are *you* a friend of Nat's?" Rob asked back.

Tyler furrowed his brow, as if surprised Rob didn't already know all about him. "Not just friends. Coworkers too." He slung a casual arm around Natalie. "We've got a TV show together."

"Ah, right," Rob said. "I think I've seen some billboards."

He'd watched most of one episode, actually, sprawled catatonic on the couch that he'd until recently shared with Zuri, empty beer bottles on the coffee table in front of him, thinking it might be the kind of mind-numbing entertainment he needed. Then he'd had to turn it off. Why had he thought that anything to do with Natalie could be mind-numbing? At least the character of Dennis was different now. If Rob hadn't read the book, he would never have connected him to Angus. But would this show drive more people to pick up the source material? He couldn't stop worrying about how it might hurt Angus, if he ever put two and two together. And more than that, Rob couldn't stop thinking about Natalie jabbing her finger into his chest in the hallway outside the wedding reception, how cruel he'd been to her that night.

Rob's phone began ringing with an unfamiliar number. Spam,

most likely. Still, it offered an excuse to get away from Natalie's raised eyebrows. "I'm getting an important call," he said loudly, and began to walk down the hallway, ready to fake a meaningful conversation with whatever random telemarketer had dialed him up. "Hello?"

"Robert?"

"Yes. Who is this?"

"This is Bill Flanagan, your parents' neighbor."

"Right." Bow Tie Bill, a man in his fifties who was always dressed formally even while mowing his lawn. Why the hell was Bill calling him? For a moment, Rob wondered if his parents had shared the news of his ruined wedding with the whole neighborhood, knocking on every door with Rob's tale of humiliation, and Bill was calling to express his condolences. But of course not, Rob's father was probably too ashamed of him to tell anyone.

The phone call where he'd had to tell his parents about Zuri had been one of the worst moments of Rob's life. He'd made it as brief as possible, saying goodbye into their stunned silence. His mother called him so frequently now, he had to occasionally pick up so that she didn't send the police to his apartment to check on him. But he hadn't spoken to his father since. He couldn't bear to hear a lecture or disappointment or, worst of all, a hint of triumph in his father's voice.

He caught Natalie watching him out of the corner of her eye and gave her a nod. *Everything is fine. I am an in-demand person.* She did not seem convinced, so Rob forced out something adjacent to a chuckle and said, "Nice to hear from you, Bill. Happy holidays."

"I'm sorry to bother you. I tried your mother, but she wasn't answering her phone, and I had your number from a list of emergency contacts she gave me a while ago."

"Ah yes," Rob said, nodding as if Bill was saying something of extreme fascination.

"Your father is standing on my porch yelling about how I've stolen his wallet."

"What?" The sentence was not computing in Rob's head. All that whiskey making him slow. "Why . . . why did you take his wallet? A mistake?"

"No—"

"Whatever your reasons, it's all right. You can just give it back to him."

"I haven't taken anything from him," Bill said. "I think he's confused again, but your mother isn't around this time. So I don't know what to do."

A buzzing started up in Rob's ears. Suddenly, he was stone-cold sober. He looked around for the nearest doorway and opened it, ducking into Angus and Gabby's laundry room, bracing himself on the washing machine. His mouth had gone dry, and he forced himself to swallow before saying, "What do you mean 'again'?"

"It's been a couple of times now. Your mother usually comes and takes him home, talks him down."

And with that, Rob did understand, fully and irrevocably, what he'd been convincing himself not to see for over a year now. The moments of confusion that his father had covered with bombast, the way he missed details of Rob's life, it went beyond normal aging. His father was a lion, a star, the man who sucked up all the oxygen in the room. Rob had found it so much easier to believe that he was becoming more of an asshole rather than less of himself.

"Hello?" Bill asked.

"Yes, I'm here. Sorry," Rob said.

"I've tried to convince him to go back inside, but I don't think he's pleased with me."

"Right. Um. Let me try to call my mother. I'm sure she's close by."

"Gotcha," Bill said. "I'll keep an eye on him in the meantime."

"Thank you."

Rob hung up and dialed his mother's number, waited as it rang to voicemail, then dialed again, over and over. No answer. He sent her a text. Where are you? Dad's in trouble.

Nothing. He tried his father, but no answer on his phone either. Rob stood there, resting his head against the wall, a sick sensation in his stomach. Where was his mom? And what the hell had she been thinking, hiding this? A nagging ache in his head told him that he had made it easy for her, in the way he'd found it increasingly unpleasant to talk to his dad, hurrying off the phone when he could, throwing himself into wedding planning and letting weeks go by without contact.

Then he pulled himself upright and snapped into action, stepping back out into the party, powering through the guests toward the front door as he wrote Bill a text: Not sure where my mother is but I'm on my way. There in 50. Someone followed him outside into the crisp night air. Natalie.

"Are you abandoning ship?" she asked. "I'm sorry, I didn't mean to make fun—" Her words cut off at the devastation on his face.

"What happened?" she asked in a low voice. "Are you okay?"

"I have to go. My father needs help." He headed toward his rental car, pulling the keys out of his pocket. In his haste, the key ring fell onto the ground.

Natalie stepped forward and scooped the keys up before he could get to them. "You are not allowed to drive right now. Ten minutes ago, you were nearly weeping over an inflatable Santa."

"I was not," he grumbled. She shot him a disbelieving look, and he knew she was right, no matter how sober he felt at the moment. "Fine. I'll see what the taxi situation is." He reached in his pocket for his phone, scanning the various apps for available cars. They were all at least twenty minutes away, and the cost would be astronomical. But better than nothing.

Natalie was still standing there, shooting a look back at the party, shifting from side to side. She let out a sigh and muttered something like *Fuck it* under her breath. Then she pressed the unlock button on his keys and headed toward the rental car.

"Well, come on," she said.

25

★☆☆☆☆

The forty-minute car ride was a mostly silent one, Rob's face turned toward the window, Natalie keeping to the speed limit, putting her Los Angeles driving training to good use.

She could tell herself a lot of stories about why she was here with Rob right now. She was trying to be a good citizen of the world. Rob had been kind enough to her a couple of times, so this was a quid pro quo. Alternatively, Rob had been a real dick to her a couple of times, and she was showing him how far above it all she was. Still, she clenched the steering wheel tight, anxiety thrumming in her over the feeling that she was transporting precious cargo.

When they were a few minutes away from their destination, Rob's phone rang, and he snapped out of his catatonia to answer faster than Natalie had ever seen him move. "Mom? Where are you? Are you okay?"

Natalie could hear a woman's voice, low and panicked, on the other end of the line. "New York? What are you doing there?" Rob asked. Another pause from Rob as his mother spoke. "Right." His voice was bitter. "Well, Dad's wandering around in the cold." He shook his head. "How could you leave him? How could you not tell me—" He cut himself off with a glance at Natalie, suddenly brusque. "Never mind. I'll be there soon, and we'll talk when you get home."

He hung up and dropped the phone into his lap. After a moment of dazed silence, he said, "She decided to go see a show. Didn't check her phone until intermission."

"And your dad is . . . ?" Natalie began, turning on to Rob's street.

He leaned toward her and spoke urgently. "It's dementia, I think. I don't know what he'll be like. I only just realized that he even . . . Well, I've thought maybe, a few times, but I'd written it off, and my mom didn't tell me anything." He took a deep breath. "This isn't important to you. Sorry. You can wait in the car if you want. Or go back to the party. I don't want to ruin your night."

He seemed so at loose ends, so unlike his usual self, that she couldn't help herself. She placed a hand gently on top of his. "I'll stay. I'm here for whatever you need."

He blinked quickly, his eyes shining in the dim light, and she realized that she needed to pay more attention to the final stretch of road.

As she turned into the driveway and parked the car, they spotted Rob's father, agitated and pacing on the front porch, his breath making puffs of white in the chilly evening. An imposing man, wearing a blazer as if on his way to teach a course. He must have been freezing. Had he locked himself out, or was he staying in the cold out of stubbornness?

Rob peeled out of the car, taking the porch steps two at a time with his long legs as Natalie followed.

"Robert!" Professor Kapinsky said, as soon as he spotted his son. "This is an outrage!"

"Why don't we go inside, Dad?" Rob said as he located his old house key on his key ring. "I bet we can find your wallet in there."

"No, I *know* where it is. It's with Bow Tie Bill!" He gestured across the street to where a round-faced man was peeking out his front door, a red plaid bow tie tight around his neck. The neighbor gave Rob a relieved wave, then disappeared back into his home.

"He doesn't have it, Dad," Rob said, unlocking the door and attempting to shepherd his father indoors.

"He told you that? He's probably lying," Rob's father went on, still not having registered Natalie's presence. Hesitant, she followed the two of them inside. The house was nice, historic-feeling, with dark wood walls and more bookshelves than Natalie had ever seen in one place outside of a library.

"Well," Rob said, "why don't we have a cup of tea to warm up, and then we can figure it out." Rob turned the kettle on and his father continued to pace, shivering, his hands shaking and drained of color. Thank God they'd gotten there when they did, before he stayed outside longer and the temperature grew colder. Thank God he hadn't wandered farther afield. "And here, let's find you a blanket."

"I don't need a blanket. I need my damn wallet!"

As Rob grabbed a throw blanket from a nearby couch, Natalie hung back, an interloper. The expression on Rob's face as he stared at his father was so vulnerable, so private, that Natalie looked away and around the kitchen instead. Cheery tiled walls, a six-burner stovetop. Everything was neat in the way that suggested it was cleaned fairly often—no layers of grime or built-up clutter. Yet at the same time, little splatters of sauce on the counter and a smell of rotting bananas suggested neglect over the past day or two.

Rob breathed in and then in a calm voice said, "Take a seat, Dad. You should relax."

Professor Kapinsky curled his hands into fists. "I can't, when Bill is probably gloating—"

Still unnoticed, Natalie scanned the room for the overripe banana. There it was in the fruit bowl. Right next to a brown leather wallet.

She stood frozen for a moment, considering, then quietly grabbed the wallet. She walked back outside, then reentered the house, closing the door with a clatter. "Found it!" she called.

In the kitchen, the two men froze in a strange tableau, Rob holding out a blanket, his father pushing it away as they both turned their heads toward her entrance. Rob's father peered at her, startled, then looked back and forth between her and Rob. He was trying to figure out if he was supposed to know her, she realized. If he needed to pretend. "I'm Rob's friend Natalie," she said, and handed the wallet to him. "So nice to see you. And here's your wallet back."

"Thank you," Professor Kapinsky said, and then, "How did you find it? It was with Bill, wasn't it?" He worried at the leather of the wallet with his fingers, turning it over in his hands, his shoulders hunched defensively.

Natalie glanced at Rob and then said, "Yes." Rob furrowed his eyebrows at her, and she soldiered on, hoping she was doing the right thing. "I just talked to him and it was a misunderstanding."

At that, Rob's father came alive, straightening up to his full height, a vindicated smile spreading over his face. "I knew it."

"He's so sorry. He didn't mean to take it, he just thought it was *his*."

Professor Kapinsky shook his head and finally sat down in the chair Rob had pulled out for him, taking the proffered blanket and throwing it across his shoulders, almost rakishly. "Of course. Not the brightest bulb, that Bill."

Natalie sat across from him. "So, what is the story with this bow tie?" she asked, leaning in confidentially. "He's just hanging out at home!"

Rob's father chuckled. He was still shivering a bit, but the blanket and the warmth of the kitchen seemed to be helping. "Let me tell you something about Bill. That old idiom about dressing for the job you want? He's been trying that for years, yet he still hasn't gotten tenure."

"Time for a new tactic, it seems," Natalie said. She glanced over at Rob, who was standing at the stovetop watching her, seemingly at a loss for words. Like he wasn't sure how she had gotten here or, just maybe, how to keep her from going away.

"He's never liked me," Professor Kapinsky said, and Natalie managed to pull her gaze away from Rob's. "Jealousy. I bet that's why he keeps bothering . . ." He trailed off. "Well, my boy is on track, isn't he? Rob won't have any problems getting tenure, I can tell you that."

Rob gave him a weak smile. "Thanks, Dad. Would you like tea too, Natalie?"

"Sure," she said. "Thank you."

As he put her mug down on the table, his arm brushed against hers. He swallowed hard, then straightened back up. "Dad, do you want some dinner?"

Professor Kapinsky gave a cursory nod, then sat back, continuing to talk to Natalie. "Of course, much of it comes down to the examples you have set for you. Rob grew up in academia, so he's lucky in that way. I don't mean to be uncharitable to Bill. I remember how disorienting it was to enter the Ivory Tower when I was first starting out." He was in his element now, all traces of his earlier agitation gone, speaking with enough authority to hypnotize a lecture hall. "You know, my father was an immigrant who had never even graduated high school, and I had to make my own way."

Rob began to boil water for pasta on the stovetop, raising an eyebrow at Natalie as he indicated the pot. She nodded, then continued to let his father regale her while Rob made them all spaghetti.

And regale her he did, unceasingly, with the confidence of a man who felt he was giving her a gift. After all, people paid good money to listen to his opinions, and here she was, getting them for free. How strange, how impossible, it must have been to grow up under this all-consuming presence. Natalie made the appropriate expressions of awe and interest (and it *was* interesting, hearing him speak). Over at the stove, Rob poked at the pasta, then served it to his father with a tenderness she wouldn't have expected from him.

They all sat around the table and dug in, and as his father paused his talking to chew, Rob said, "You know, Dad, Natalie is a writer."

"Ah. What MFA program did you attend?"

Rob and Natalie caught each other's eyes. Without thinking it through, she winked at him. Rob seemed startled, momentarily lost for words, then said to his father, "She didn't attend an MFA program, but she's very successful."

"Hmph," Rob's father said. "Well, I always think it's good to have the educational underpinnings, but good for you. Nonfiction?"

"No, fiction, mostly," Natalie said.

"When's your next novel coming? I'll buy it for Rob's mother."

"I'm actually in TV now. I think I'm done with novels." Writing a novel took so much from a person. You had to pour your heart out for hundreds of pages, and she didn't know if she could ever bear the vulnerability of that again, not after how badly it had gone before.

"Really? Done forever?" Rob asked, with a strange expression on his face. If she hadn't known better, she'd think it was disappointment.

She swallowed, a confusing swirl of feelings inside her. Making her tone bright, she continued, "Rob here is one of my most regular readers, even if he doesn't always enjoy the work."

Rob cleared his throat. "I do always find it . . . interesting."

Rob's father had been looking back and forth between them. Now, he put his fork down. "The maid of honor!" he said, pounding the table. "That's how I know you!" He chortled, then indicated Rob. "Oh, you smoked him with your toast, didn't you?"

Rob raised his eyebrows in outrage.

"Hey now," Natalie said, "Rob's toast was nice too."

"Thank you," Rob said.

"But, yes, I did smoke him."

Rob shook his head, but a small smile tugged at the corners of his mouth. "I'm not the professional writer. You had an unfair advantage."

"Well, not a competition," Natalie said, then grinned. "So what if people are still talking about your defeat all these years later?"

Rob's father laughed, and Rob sighed. "You two. I go to all this trouble of making you dinner, and this is how you repay me."

"You're right," Natalie said. "We should be grateful. You boiled water."

"I am nourishing you," Rob said.

"Thank you," Natalie said, and the two of them held each other's gaze. Somewhere in the recesses of her mind lay the ghost of the night she was supposed to be having: sparkling and mingling at a party, accepting well-deserved praise for all her success, friends pulling her aside to ask what was *really* going on with her and Tyler. Despite the circumstances, it seemed more right, more natural, to be here at Rob's old kitchen table.

After dinner was done, Natalie cleared their plates as Rob helped his father up to bed. The dish soap had run out, so after looking in the nearby cabinets, Natalie walked upstairs to ask Rob if he knew where the extra was.

The primary bedroom was at the top of the stairwell, the door open a crack. Natalie peered in silently, not wanting to interrupt. Rob was flipping through channels on the TV as his dad settled into bed.

"And remind me when the wedding is?" Rob's father was saying. "She's a good match for you."

"The wedding. You mean with Zuri?"

"No, you and the maid of honor." He paused for a moment at Rob's expression, rubbed his forehead. "I'm sorry. Something . . . something is wrong, Robert." His voice was leached free of bravado, of anger, of charm.

"I know, Dad," Rob said, his own voice so gentle. So full of grace for a man who had given him so little of it.

At that, Natalie walked farther down the hall out of earshot, swallowing a lump in her throat. She looked through another open doorway, then couldn't stop herself from going inside. Because this must have been Rob's childhood bedroom, unless he had a sibling she didn't know about who also hated fun. She turned the switch on a lamp, revealing dark green walls and a twin bed. A big framed poster of Einstein dominated one wall, a display shelf of fancy dictionaries on another. As if Rob hadn't been allowed to be a fan of anything that didn't further his education. There didn't seem to have been any updates to the room since high school, except for some framed diplomas hanging on the walls, heralding Rob's impressive degrees.

His footsteps sounded in the doorway and she turned.

"Ah. You found the most important and most embarrassing room in the house," he said quietly, not wanting to disturb his father's rest.

"Where are the sports posters? The movie stars?" she asked, indicating his walls.

"I didn't really go in for all that."

"I bet that made you very popular in high school. 'No, I won't be watching the game this weekend, I've got a fascinating biography of Kierkegaard on my nightstand instead.'"

"You're forgetting the Ken Burns documentaries," he said. "Strange how people never wanted to come over for movie nights of those."

They smiled, then circled each other warily.

"Thank you for helping," Rob said, cocking his head in the direction of his father's bedroom. "He loves you."

"I think he probably loves anyone who listens to him," she said, then cringed. "I'm sorry, I didn't mean to—"

"No, you're right. My father has always needed admirers to come alive."

"I understand that. Admiration can be intoxicating. Now that

I've finally got some . . . well, I can see how it changes you. How you could start needing the adulation."

"From the TV show, you mean?"

"Yeah," she said. "The one you think you've seen on the billboards."

"I know it from more than the billboards."

She'd thought he might have been bluffing earlier with Tyler, when he'd pretended not to know about the show. Although, why would he have felt such a need to one-up Tyler, unless . . .

Her heart was pounding. "What would you rate it?" she asked, though she didn't know if she could handle hearing the answer. She didn't look at him, studying the dictionaries instead, his silhouette in the corner of her eye.

"I don't know," he said. "I'm sorry, I've only watched one episode. It's been an eventful fall. It's not you." He ran a hand through his hair. "Well, it is you."

"What do you mean?"

"I was worried about Angus, and then I was watching the show and I couldn't concentrate on it." His voice grew quiet, and she turned toward him right as he said, "I kept thinking about you. The way I handled things at the wedding . . ."

The lamp Natalie had turned on cast the room in a low light. In the shadows, the scruff on his face darkened his cheeks. Since when had Rob been a man who allowed the existence of scruff? It suited him, this hint of wildness. She stared at his cheeks. Then she was staring at his lips, slightly parted. Then she was moving toward him.

Downstairs, the front door creaked open. Rob stepped back. "My mother." He turned and quickly walked out of the room. Natalie stood frozen for a moment, then followed him.

In the front hallway, a woman in her late fifties wearily

brushed off the flakes of snow that had started to fall outside. Natalie glanced at Rob, halfway down the stairs. His mouth was set in a hard line. He'd said his mother had been keeping his father's condition from him. Was he furious? How unforgiving would he be? She pictured him at the wedding, his moral outrage and complete certainty that he was correct.

"He's all right?" Rob's mother asked.

Rob nodded.

"I'm sorry," she said, her voice breaking on the second word. Her eyes were red, her nose swollen, as if she'd spent the whole journey home crying.

The step creaked under Natalie's foot, and Rob's mother registered her presence. "Oh goodness, hello."

"My friend Natalie," Rob said, with a barely imperceptible pause between "my" and "friend."

"Hi," Natalie said.

Rob's mom touched her chest. "Carol. I'm so sorry for interrupting your night. You two should go back to your party."

"Natalie, I'll meet you in the car," Rob said, voice tight. "My mom and I need a few minutes to talk."

26

★☆☆☆☆

Rob shut the door behind Natalie and turned to his mother.

"Honey," she said, holding her hands up as if to ward off his anger, "please let me apologize—"

"What happened?" he asked. He found it hard to summon the fury he'd felt earlier that night in the car, when she'd finally called him back, full of panic and vowing to get on the next train home. Mostly, he felt sad, drained, and daunted by what lay ahead. "You went into the city to see a play? I don't get it."

She sighed and sunk into the nearest chair. "No. To attend a lecture on dementia. About caring for a loved one with it and the progression of the disease. Your father seemed to be having a good day. I had a friend swing by and check on him at one point. I thought it would be all right. And when I called him afterward, he sounded fine too. He was all set up in front of the TV, acting like his normal self, and said he'd be turning in early. So on my way back to the train station, I just . . . ." She rubbed her eyes, exhausted. "My mind was full of everything from the lecture, about how hard it was all going to become, and then the subway stopped at Times Square."

"And, what?" he asked, pacing the room. "You got an uncontrollable urge to see *Phantom of the Opera?*"

"Robert." She gave him the mildly stern look she'd summoned whenever he got a little too smart as a child. "It wasn't *Phantom*, not that it matters. I know I made a mistake. Believe me, I've been beating myself up this whole train ride." She tugged at the sleeve of her shirt and hesitated before continuing, "But I felt, in that moment, that maybe I could take one night, before things got really bad, to do something for myself. Something where I wasn't just an extension of your father."

"An extension? You're not . . ." he began. But then he caught sight of her face, and the rawness of her expression knocked him sideways, even as she tried to smile.

Rob had always known that his father didn't particularly care if he ruined other people's careers. But Rob had never stopped to think that one of those ruined careers might have been his mother's.

His mother shrugged. "The student, the mistress, the wife. And now I'll be the caretaker. Tonight, I just needed to be something else too."

Twenty-six. She'd only been twenty-six when she got pregnant with her married adviser's baby, in an insular academic community where people talked. Rob looked at her more closely in her button-down shirt and dark slacks. She could have fit in seamlessly with the middle-aged female professors he saw around his own campus if she'd had a different adviser all those years ago, if things had gone a different way. She was only in her late fifties now, staying healthy with her twice-a-week Zumba classes. Soon, if not already, she'd be the one in charge around here, even if his father didn't realize it. Yet that wasn't the kind of control anybody wanted, the kind where one person could only gain because another lost so much. And she'd be tied to him even more tightly, losing what little independence she'd managed to eke out.

"Mom." He sat down on the arm of the sofa near her. "I'm so sorry."

"No, stop. I'm supposed to be the one apologizing here. And I don't want you to think . . ." She took a long breath, her voice faltering. "You know, that summer when I took you to New York, I was trying—"

"It's all right, we don't have to talk about that," he said quickly, standing up again. "We should figure out Dad—"

She looked sharply at him then, concern in her eyes. "Oh," she said. "Oh no."

"What?"

She reached out to clasp his hand, anchoring him in place. "I would hate if the only thing that came out of that time was me making you afraid to fail. Afraid to try something outside of what you'd known—"

"That's not . . . I'm fine," Rob said, his pulse starting to race. "I just think we need to—"

"Listen, please. Despite everything, I love the life your father and I have. He's the most interesting man I've ever met. I hate that I'm losing him." She sounded entirely drained. "But I've lost myself too. And I hope, more than anything, that *you* don't feel like an extension. You're his son, yes, but you're also mine, and you're so much more besides."

Rob couldn't articulate words for a moment, everything from the night all mixed-up inside of him. "Well, thank you," he finally said, then extricated his hand and went back to his pacing, the comforting rhythm of back and forth on old familiar floors. "But you don't have to handle the situation with Dad all alone. I just

need you to tell me things. How long has this even been going on?"

She sighed, then sat up straighter. "Years, I think. But he's so
smart that he was able to cover it for a while, and I didn't want
to see. Things were deteriorating slowly, and it's only in recent
months that everything started happening all at once." She shot
him a sympathetic glance. "I was going to tell you soon, but it's
been such a rough time for you recently."

"You could say that."

"I really can't believe Zuri would do such a thing—"

"Let's not, please."

"All right." Her face was gentle. "He did read your dissertation, you know. When he couldn't talk about it after reading it so
thoroughly, that was the first time I thought maybe something
was really wrong."

Rob swallowed the lump in his throat. "Well, we'll figure this
out somehow. Jamie and Sarah will help too, I'm sure of it." His
half siblings had a complicated relationship with their father, but
they'd come through. "But I'm here. For him and for you."

She gave him a nod, a sad smile. "I know." He stood up then,
moving over to her and hugging her tightly, and they stayed
like that, breathing quietly, for a long time. Then she cleared her
throat and pulled away. "But in this particular moment, you have
that nice girl sitting outside in the car." She drew her shoulders
back, rearranging herself into the woman who was ready to take
care of them all as she always had. "Don't make her wait too long."

27

★☆☆☆☆

When Natalie had driven a few minutes away from the house, before they reached the highway, Rob sat forward in the passenger seat.

"Can we turn off here for a moment?" he asked, and she followed his directions to a grassy field.

"The Princeton Battlefield," he explained. "I liked to come here when I was a teenager, when I needed to think. It's pretty. Peaceful." He paused, looking out into the inky blackness before them. "The effect is ruined somewhat in the dark."

"Yeah, it feels more like you've brought us here to murder me," Nat said.

"Sorry," he said. "We should go back to the party. I've already taken you away from it long enough."

But Natalie didn't restart the car, and after a moment, Rob folded his arms on the dashboard, then leaned over them. Head down, he took in deep breaths. Natalie couldn't tell if he was crying or trying hard not to. She put a tentative hand on his back, and at that, the tears did come, fast and quiet, his back hot under her palm even through his shirt.

The car smelled of whiskey and pine. Natalie didn't say

anything as Rob cried, only kept her hand steadily on him, realizing just how much trouble she was in.

After a while, he shuddered and then sat up, wiping his nose on his sleeve, then looking at said sleeve with faint disdain, as if upbraiding himself for not having the foresight to pack a handkerchief. "I feel like an idiot, not knowing," he said. Outside, the wind blew the clouds across the sky, revealing a moon so bright it filled the car with a faint, ghostly light.

"You're not an idiot. I think it's easy to make excuses with something like this."

"Yeah," he said wearily. "And my mom didn't want to admit to herself how bad it was. Plus, she thought, 'Poor Rob, his life has already imploded, he doesn't need this on top of everything else.'" He finally turned in his seat to face Nat. "Gabby told you about the wedding, I assume. Is that why you're here, being so kind to me?"

"Yes," she said. "All that's going on right now is good old-fashioned pity."

He huffed out a laugh. "You should pity me. Everything has fallen apart. Zuri, of course, but also . . ." He hesitated, searching her face, then burst out, as if he had to say it quickly or else he'd lose his nerve, "I hate my job. And I think it might not be just the job but academia more broadly."

"Really?"

"I don't know, I have nothing else to compare it to. You were right, back when we first met. I came out of the womb, and academia was stamped on me, and I never considered any other options." A spark of hope, of possibility, kindled in Natalie's chest, that Rob remembered something she'd said offhand almost seven years ago. Strange, how she remembered too, how all their interactions over the years stood out in Technicolor in her mind, though she couldn't even recall what she'd eaten for breakfast that morning.

"What do you love about academia?" she asked carefully.

He held his hands in the air. "Every time I'm teaching, I feel like I should be doing research, and every time I do research, I feel like I'm just trying to impress the tenure committee instead of doing something that matters. There are so many practical applications of what I learn in my research, but I'm not *using* any of them—" He looked at her. "Yes, I realize that you asked me what I loved, and I told you what I hated."

Natalie waited, and Rob caught himself, shaking his head. "Enough. This is embarrassing. I will get myself under control."

"Don't do that for my sake. This is the best I've ever liked you."

"No, it's not."

"Yes! Maybe not the part where you were brawling with a Santa at the party, but the rest of it."

He gave her a sideways glance, then shook his head. "I don't understand. I did everything I was supposed to do. I followed all the rules and met the expectations, and I'm so unhappy." He leaned toward her. "But do I just . . . give up?"

"Well, it's not like I have everything figured out," Nat began.

"You seem like you do," Rob said.

She looked down at herself, at a body that finally felt rooted. She no longer woke each morning to a ticking clock in her ears. All that time she'd spent in the muck, making lists of her goals and failing to meet them, trying things and falling flat on her face as the years slipped by . . . How could she have known then that the time she thought she was wasting was actually time she'd spent growing?

"I think some flailing is good for everyone," she said. "I mean, flailing sucks. But it might be necessary." He was staring at her, at her mouth, as if she held the key to something. She felt suddenly like the next sentence she said would be more important than any line she'd ever written for TV, any phrase in one of her books. It was difficult to take a full breath as she continued, "Maybe you should try doing some things you're not supposed to do."

"You think so?" he asked, his voice ragged. Slowly, he reached out his hand and traced the line of her cheek. Every nerve in her body woke up, alert and tingling.

"I do," she said.

Rob reached his other hand up, tangling his fingers in her hair. Then he pulled her forward and kissed her.

He tasted faintly of salt. From crying, she knew, but it made her think of an ocean, the overwhelming shock of walking into something so much larger than herself. That awe-inspiring, destabilizing feeling she felt with an ocean swirling around her, that was how she felt now as Rob kissed her.

As his stubble prickled her cheek and he ran his hands through her hair, she pressed herself even deeper into him. This was different from their kiss in the lake all those years ago. Just as full of feeling but gentler too. Well, gentler at first. Then he unbuckled her seat belt and pulled her toward his lap.

She almost got stuck on the gear shift, her limbs an awkward tangle, and she had to stop kissing him for a moment to laugh.

"What?" he asked, out of breath and disheveled.

"She is beauty, she is grace," she said, indicating herself, and a smile broke over his face as he registered her position.

"I don't care how graceful you are." The two of them grinned. No, "grin" was too small a word. They were both beaming. Then his voice turned lower, almost a growl. "Just come here."

She catapulted herself the rest of the way across the car,

straddling him, their mouths meeting again. He ran his hands down her back, gripping her hips, his fingers making indents in the leather of her pants.

She rocked against him. At the feeling of him growing beneath her, a thrill ran up and down her spine. Urgently, he pulled her shirt out from where she'd tucked it, his hands finding her bare skin beneath. She wanted to gasp in wonder. All this time, it had been Rob she wanted. Rob, whom she'd loathed. Rob, whom she could love.

He pulled back to catch his breath, shaking his head in disbelief. He muttered something to himself, so softly that at first Natalie didn't register what he'd said. But then the words hit her. He'd said, "Dammit, Zuri."

And that broke the spell.

What was she doing, letting herself fall for a man who was so vulnerable and recently single? Anybody with half a brain knew that you didn't hook up with someone you genuinely liked two weeks after they'd called off their wedding. For Rob, the major attraction she offered right now was being anyone but the woman whose name he'd just uttered.

He leaned forward again, but she extricated herself, climbing back into the driver's seat. "No. We should stop."

"What?" he asked, alarm in his voice. "Are you okay?"

When she was younger, she might have ignored the warning signs in favor of her immediate want, giving in to something that would leave her feeling used and mixed-up in the morning. But now, she'd learned how to be kinder to herself. "I can't be your rebound hookup. I'm not here to be a distraction or a bad decision. Not with you."

"You're not a rebound," he protested, and it was so tempting to believe it.

"Your fiancée ended things less than a month ago. You literally just detached your lips from mine so you could say her name."

"I'm an idiot. I shouldn't have said that." He rubbed his eyes, his words coming out choppy, his voice rough with desire. "It's just . . . she'd told me that we could feel more for other people, and, kissing you, I realized she was right. I've been so angry at her, but she was right."

Her heart swelled. She longed to jump right back into his lap. But instead, she reached out and took his hand. "Still, when we do this, I want to be the only person on your mind."

"Natalie," he said helplessly. "I like you."

She tucked her shirt back in, brushing her hair away from her face. "And I like *you*. Too much for this, I think." She kept her voice steady, though part of her wanted to cry. "You're not ready, and I have to protect myself."

"If that's what you want." He sat back in his seat as if realizing that it was useless to fight her on this. Which was probably good, because if he'd said one more beautiful thing to her, she might have immediately taken off all her clothes. Even now, her body was screaming at her mind to stop being so fucking sensible. But this was the right thing to do.

"We should go back to the party." Dimly, as she put the key in the ignition, she registered that they'd fogged up the windows.

28

★☆☆☆☆

An awkward car ride later, back at Gabby and Angus's place, Rob cursed himself and his lack of filter. *Dammit, Zuri, how dare you be correct about everything?* he'd thought as he'd held Natalie, awestruck by how kind she'd been with his father, how beautiful she was in the hint of moonlight, how much he wanted every part of her. How much she had failed but how much she had kept trying, and God, how she glowed, how *content* she seemed with herself now. She'd done the work to be ready for success, so when it finally came around, it fit her perfectly.

But he didn't just like her now that she was successful, he'd realized as he gripped her even more tightly. He'd liked her all along, this woman bursting with life who made him more alive. Even when he'd hated her, she'd made him feel more than anyone else ever had.

Overwhelmed with hope and joy, he'd gone ahead and ruined everything.

But only for now, right? How much time did Natalie require for him to prove that he was ready? In this moment, his body aching to go back to touching her, he would do whatever she directed him to. Overly expensive psychoanalysis? He'd let an old man interpret his dreams. Hiking the Appalachian Trail alone with his thoughts? He'd brave the bears. (Were you supposed to yell or play dead? He would research.)

Perhaps he could start by being kind to Tyler Yeo, who was currently standing in front of the snack table studying a tortilla chip as if fascinated by its various ridges. In the time Rob and Nat had been gone, many of the guests had cleared out, leaving only the most committed (and drunkest). One of Angus's finance bro coworkers had sprawled out on the living room couch, snoring, while in the little space he'd left, those two bridesmaids from the wedding were stroking each other's faces, murmuring how much they loved each other.

Rob cleared his throat, then walked up next to Tyler, forcing himself to engage.

"Excuse me? I'm sorry if I was rude earlier. I had a little too much to drink."

Tyler looked over in surprise. "Oh, hey! Nah, man, you're good. It's kinda nice when people don't just kiss my ass, you know?"

"Happy to help keep you grounded. But seriously, congratulations on the show. You made Dennis your own."

Tyler finally made the decision to eat the chip in his hand. As he chewed, he said, "You think that's all right, yeah? Nat's book is so good, but TV is a different medium."

"Right." Even while doing something as strange as talking with a movie star, Rob couldn't help looking for Natalie. Scanning the room, he found her standing with Gabby and Angus, nodding intently at some story Angus was telling. She tucked a strand of hair behind her ear, and Rob was hit by a wave of re-membering what it had felt like to run his fingers through that hair, the soft warmth of Natalie's bare skin. He wanted to catch her attention, shout, *Look over here! I am being civil! Don't you think I am emotionally mature and therefore ready to recommence taking off your clothes?* All this was running through his head as he went on, "I think it's good that you didn't just play Angus."

"Angus?" Tyler asked, pulling him back to their conversation.

"Dennis!" Rob said quickly. "Dennis from the book, I mean. Sorry, slip of the tongue. I'm still sobering up, apparently."

"Right, right, all good," Tyler said. But he was squinting, computing something in slow motion in a way that made Rob uneasy.

He seemed like the kind of man who could be easily misdirected, so Rob went on, "How has it been working with Natalie?"

That did the trick. Tyler lit up. "Oh, awesome! We really vibe, you know? Like, she *gets* me, which means the stuff she writes for the show always makes sense. Sometimes I've been on sets, and the script is like, *Now your character feels this way or does this thing*, and I'm like . . . *What?* But Nat, she's different." Tyler glanced over at Natalie then, admiringly, so Rob felt it safe to look too.

Natalie had never had a problem capturing people with words. She'd used the power thoughtlessly in her novel. But now she was using it to help Tyler play the part that most perfectly showed what he could do. A generous use of her strengths. Sure, she was keeping her meal ticket happy. But it seemed to fit with this new version of her too, the version who could sit quietly touching his back while he cried, not needing to make a joke or observation out of his weakness.

As if she could feel the force of their gaze, Natalie looked their way, raising a questioning eyebrow. She gave them a little wave, and as Tyler waved back with enthusiasm, Rob identified the same ailment afflicting both him and Tyler. They each wanted it to be *him* that she was looking at.

When Nat went back to her conversation with Gabby and Angus, Tyler gave Rob a swift pat on the back. "Well, hey, great talking to you." He sauntered over toward Natalie. Rob would not be jealous. He turned away to the snack table himself, pretending to be fascinated by the bowls of processed foods, willing himself not to watch. (Was *Tyler* ready for a relationship?) Rob lasted a good minute or two, spooning M&M's onto a paper plate before turning around, steeling himself to see Tyler flashing his gleaming smile at Natalie, casually flexing his biceps.

But Tyler wasn't talking to Nat at all. He was talking to Angus.

29

★☆☆☆☆

Gabby was telling Natalie some long and involved story about the preschool application process, so although Natalie could hear Tyler talking next to her, it took her far too long to register the meaning of his words.

"I *knew* there was something familiar about you," Tyler said, slinging his arm around Angus's shoulder. "I kept feeling like I hadn't just met you tonight, and it was sending me on this whole spiral of, like, is my guru right, and past lives really *are* a thing, and you and I fought in a war together or something? But, nah, our girl here just captured you good."

"And they have to interview the *parents*," Gabby was saying at the same time. Natalie forced herself to pay attention to her words. It was tough with Tyler talking so loudly and the persistent buzzing memory of Rob's mouth on hers sending aftershocks through her body. "I have to write a two-thousand-word essay about Christina's good qualities. It's like applying to college all over again."

"What?" Angus asked Tyler.

"In *Apartment 2F*." Tyler squeezed Angus's shoulder, concern on his face. "Hey, listen. I hope you're not offended by what I did with Dennis, given that it's so different from the book. I want to take your opinion into account. So, how are you feeling about the portrayal?"

At the mention of *Dennis*, Natalie's split focus zeroed in entirely on Tyler. She turned away from Gabby, only half catching sight of her look of offense.

"Tyler—" she started.

"Just a sec!" he said.

"Oh wow," Angus said, not quite understanding. "That's so kind of you to ask me for my thoughts about your character."

"Of course. It's yours too! Having a version of yourself out in the world for public consumption can be a sensitive thing. Believe me, I know, especially after the memoir." Natalie grabbed Tyler's arm to try to make him stop, but he just put a hand over hers affectionately and kept going. "Part of the acting process is finding your own way into a character, but I also want to honor the source material, especially now that I know what it really is. So, truly, if you want, I can make some changes going into season two." Angus put a hand on his hip, cocking his head in confusion, and Tyler pointed, a smile breaking over his face. "That mannerism? Sure! I can totally incorporate." He mirrored Angus as Natalie's stomach threatened to come up her throat.

"I'm sorry," Angus said, as Gabby threw a *What have you done?* look at Natalie. "I'm just computing a moment. You're not saying . . . Is Dennis in the book modeled after me?"

Shit.

"Uh," Tyler began, his eyes beginning to widen in concern.

"No!" Natalie jumped in. "That was not my intent. Some of the scenarios in the book were rooted a little bit in real life, but I didn't mean to make him you."

"I am so sorry," Tyler said, looking back and forth between

them all. "I thought it was like an in-joke with you all. An homage. But I must have misunderstood."

Every Tuesday night, Angus sat down and watched *Meant 2B* full of pride over Natalie's achievement. He'd probably spent hours laughing at the buffoonery of the Dennis character, never realizing he was the source of it.

Natalie opened her mouth to offer more excuses, but Angus cut in.

"You said he was different in the book than the TV version, though. How?" His voice was hopeful, but his eyes filled with worry.

Nearby, a few of the other houseguests turned toward them, the tension ringing like alarm bells. Natalie felt a sinking sensation, her past sins finally, finally catching up to her. The Christmas lights strung up around the house blinked merrily on, undisturbed. Rob came power walking up toward them, then stopped short, alarm on his face.

"He's . . ." Natalie began.

"You haven't read the book?" Tyler asked. "Well, he's way different. He wears a shirt all the time. And now that I think about it, I totally jumped to the wrong conclusion here, because Dennis from the book isn't similar to you at all! Like, the main character really *hates* him. Plus, he and the best friend are probably going to get divorced."

"Tyler—" Nat began. Gabby's eyes were shooting out a glare of death. But Tyler carried on, determined to fix things.

"Oh! And you're, like, killing it in finance, yeah? Dennis in the book isn't that good at anything he tries, so he's just gonna fail upward into running his family's business!" He held his hands open triumphantly.

"Please stop talking," Natalie said.

"Sure," Tyler said, and snapped his mouth shut.

Natalie stepped closer to Angus. "I'm sorry. I did a stupid, selfish thing when I was twenty-six, but I truly didn't mean any harm by it. And I barely knew you at that point—"

"Right," Angus said. He nodded, then kept nodding, giving himself the appearance of a sad bobblehead. "Well, we all make mistakes."

For some reason Natalie couldn't comprehend, Rob decided to step in. "I think anyone who knows you recognizes that the book version is not the full picture of who you are."

Angus looked around at the group of them. "Does everyone but me know about this, then?" he asked. For such a naturally buoyant man, he seemed deflated, all the air let out of him. "Has everyone known the whole time?"

"No," Natalie said weakly, as Rob looked down at his feet and Gabby reached out a sympathetic arm.

"I guess it *is* an in-joke," Angus said to Tyler. "I just wasn't part of it." Angus's face, previously flushed with the joy of the party, had gone pale, even as he tried to keep his mouth fixed in a smile. "Serves me right, I should've read the book, huh?" His attempt at cheer was the worst part. Suddenly, Natalie could see him as a little boy, keeping his chin up as bullies taunted him. No wonder Rob had flown so fully to his defense. Watching Angus like this was hell.

"Excuse me." Angus swallowed a few times. "I need to . . . I should go check on Christina." Giving them all an awkward goodbye salute, he turned, then power walked away as they stared after him.

"I'll go see if he's okay," Rob said after a moment of silence.

"No, let me," Gabby said, her voice flinty.

"Gabby, wait," Natalie said, grabbing her arm, and Gabby turned with fury in her eyes.

"I have to go check on my husband."

"I know. But please . . ."

"I've got it," Rob said, and disappeared up the stairs after Angus.

"Fine, you want to talk?" Gabby spat at Natalie. "Come here."

She stalked over to a nearby door and threw it open, leading Natalie down into a finished basement. Wall-to-wall carpet, on which lay scattered mounds of Christina's toys, a pretend kitchen here, a ukulele there. The muffled clomping of the guests upstairs sounded above them, faint compared to the ringing in Natalie's ears.

Gabby folded her arms across her chest. "Well, what do you want to say to me?"

"I'm sorry, I can't believe that Tyler would say all that." Nat held her hands up. "But at least maybe this has cured you of your crush?"

She'd been trying to make Gabby laugh. And Gabby *did* laugh, but it was hollow, disbelieving. "Really, that's it? You're just going to blame it on him."

"No." Natalie breathed out. "Obviously this happened because of me. And I'm sorry, and I wish I could go back and re-write the book, which is actually why I made Dennis so different in the TV show—"

"A TV show that is probably bringing a whole new audience to the novel," Gabby said, her tone flat.

"Not really. You might be shocked to learn that the people who love the show aren't that interested in reading semi-masturbatory literary fiction about girls and their feelings. And

I told the team that I didn't want any of the show's publicity or press releases to mention *Apartment 2F*."

"How noble of you. Now, if you're done, I'm going up to Angus," Gabby said, starting to turn away.

"Wait," Natalie said, and Gabby turned back. Natalie felt like she and her best friend hadn't really *looked* at each other in years. Now, the two of them standing across from each other like cowboys getting ready for a duel, Nat noticed all the new details that she hadn't been privy to as they were happening—the threads of gray at Gabby's temples, the way her round cheeks had grown thinner. She used to be able to read her friend's expressions as easily as her favorite book. Now, she barely recognized her. "Please stay, and let's talk this out just a little longer."

Gabby rubbed her eyes and said quietly, "You're always trying to make me choose between him and you."

"That's not true."

"It is! Don't you see? You've humiliated the man I love for your own benefit, not just once, but for years. You wanted me to fawn over your book when it dragged my husband through the mud, and now you want me to make you feel better about this too. But I won't. If you're going to force me to pick sides, I choose him."

A breath escaped Natalie like she'd been punched in the stomach. "Oh, believe me, I know," she said, unable to keep the bitterness from her voice. "You've been choosing him ever since you met him."

Gabby thrust her chin up. "You're my friend. He's my family."

"I get that. And it's not like I'm asking you to leave him and run away with me. But you're still my first priority, and I feel sometimes like you could take me or leave me."

"I shouldn't still be your first priority! That's not healthy!"

Gabby shook her head, pacing the basement. "And besides, it's not even true. *You* are your own first priority, as you've made very clear with this TV show."

"Okay, so you want me to turn down the opportunity to write for television, finally be financially stable, just because your husband might be a little bit hurt?"

"Of course not. But you could have at least talked to me about it before you made the decision!"

Natalie's voice was rising, and she didn't know how to stop it. She felt out of control, skidding down a dangerous path, no choice but to plunge forward. "Are you kidding? I've tried to talk to you about so many things over the years, and you have shut me down over and over again. It feels like you've never cared about me the way I care about you. I can't open up to you about my writing, you've never even read a full book of mine, and you make it very clear that all you really want me to do is get married and have children like you."

"You're one to talk! Every time I try to tell you some detail about the parenting shit I'm dealing with on a daily basis, your eyes glaze over. No wonder I'd rather talk to other people instead. They don't make me feel like I'm boring because I care about raising my child or wanting a big family."

Gabby and Natalie had snapped at each other before, had arguments over meaningless things like Natalie leaving the window open when they used to live together. But they'd always turned away when it came to confronting the deeper issues.

Perhaps they'd been saving up all their vitriol for this, every time they'd swallowed down resentment or failed to understand each other. They had reserves of anger from all the times they didn't let it out before, and now it was coming to drown them.

"I don't know when it got so difficult to connect with you—"

Gabby was saying, and Natalie couldn't just stand there and let Gabby dump her, couldn't let the woman she'd loved most say something irrevocable, so she said it herself instead.

"Maybe we've outgrown each other." At Nat's words, Gabby stopped her pacing. Natalie straightened her spine, heart breaking as she went on, "We love the memory of each other instead of each other now."

"Maybe you're right," Gabby whispered, eyes shining. "So, why are we wasting our time?"

Natalie realized that she'd been memorizing the new details of Gabby to store them up. Unless it wasn't too late, unless she could take it all back, throw herself at Gabby's feet, and promise to keep trying to grow together instead of apart.

But Gabby turned on her heel and headed to the stairs. Before the first step, she said, over her shoulder, "I'm going to talk to Angus. I think it's time for you to leave."

And then she was gone. The girl who had made Natalie feel at home the moment she met her. The woman who had held Nat's hair back and made her laugh so hard she peed herself, and rubbed her back while she wept. Her plus-one, her confidant, her soulmate. A part of Natalie's past. Now, inconceivably, not a part of her future.

She wanted to sink onto the carpet and wail. But if she let herself start crying, she'd never stop. She'd melt onto the basement floor, a pile of defenseless, quivering guts, and eventually Gabby would come downstairs and say, *Didn't I ask you to leave?*

So Natalie forced herself to walk back upstairs into the pathetic remainders of the party. She spied Tyler sitting on a chair in the corner, looking at his phone. He'd ruined so much, but she couldn't blame him. He hadn't known.

Rob, who'd been pacing by the snack table, locked eyes with

her and came her way. He, on the other hand, had known every-thing, had told her way back from the beginning how cruel and careless she was. And Rob had been talking to Tyler right before everything went to shit.

"I think Angus just needs some time," he started, but Natalie cut him off.

"Did you say something to Tyler? What did you do?"

He sighed, running a hand through his rumpled hair. "I'm sorry. I misspoke."

A dry, disbelieving laugh escaped her. "Misspeaking all over the place tonight, huh?" He'd misspoken, and now her best friend didn't want to see her again. The hard line of Gabby's mouth as she told her to go flooded Natalie's mind. The pain she felt was so strong and sharp, unbearable. She spat at Rob, "Your life is so screwed up that you have to blow up mine too?"

Rob stepped back. "Natalie," he said, the sound of his voice matching the hurt inside her.

She began to turn away from him.

"Stop," he said, reaching out a hand for her. She couldn't let him touch her, couldn't bear to feel the hands that had made her shiver earlier that evening. She pulled back.

And suddenly she wasn't in Gabby's living room anymore. The other party guests disappeared, and she stood in the hallway outside the wedding reception, facing off with a man who con-fronted her with the parts of herself she didn't want to see. She was supposed to be grounded and successful, but Rob had plum-meted her back into all the shame and confusion she used to feel. And if he was going to drag her back there, she could act like her younger self, someone who got hurt, and hurt in turn.

"What happened with Gabby?" he asked, concern in his eyes, and her fury gathered strength in her chest.

"It's over."

"What?" He shook his head. "No, she'll come around. It can't be that bad—"

"It is, actually." She threw her shoulders back, formal and cold. "You've ensured that I won't get invited to any more of Gabby and Angus's events. So, goodbye. I guess this is the end of us meeting like this."

"No. What? Stop, it doesn't have to be—"

"I think it does." Tonight, he'd cost Natalie her best friend. So how could she ever fall back into his arms? "I hope you have a nice life and figure your shit out."

"Come on," he said, his voice rough with frustration. "You can't blame me for everything here. I messed up, but at the end of the day, you're the one who wrote the book."

"You're right. I did something cruel, and I've finally gotten what I deserve," she said. "Congratulations. You've won, once and for all. I hope that this victory can keep you company, because I'd rather not."

He stepped back, his face closing off, but she couldn't let herself feel guilty about this too. There was simply no more room inside her.

Instead, she turned around. "Tyler? It's time to go." Tyler rose from his seat with a chastened nod. She was supposed to be a grown woman, and all she wanted to do was cry like a little girl. Natalie held her head high and, not letting herself look at Rob, she walked out the door.

SELECTED TEXT MESSAGES BETWEEN NATALIE
AND GABBY, DECEMBER 2019 TO DECEMBER 2020

MARCH 15, 2020
7:32 PM
From: Natalie Shapiro
To: Gabby Alvarez

Hey you. I know it's been a long time, but everything
is absolutely topsy-turvy so I wanted to check in and
make sure you all were safe and doing okay.

[Message unsent/deleted]

APRIL 19, 2020
1:15 PM
From: Natalie Shapiro
To: Gabby Alvarez

I just made the decision to stop wiping down my
groceries. Living dangerously, I know. You're still
disinfecting yours thoroughly, aren't you? I bet
you're going stir-crazy, being cooped up with a
toddler, but thank God you got that backyard you
wanted. And I bet you and Angus are making this all
seem like a grand adventure for Christina, and I bet—

[Message unsent/deleted]

MAY 12, 2020
11:49 PM
From: Natalie Shapiro
To: Gabby Alvarez

I adopted a cat back in February and named her
Dolly (after Dolly Parton, obviously) and it's proving
to be one of the best decisions I made. I would be
going nuts without her. She's cute and scruffy, and
regarded me suspiciously for about a week, but
now she'll climb up my body and sit on my shoulder
like a pirate's parrot, purring into my ear so loud and
close that it can't be good for my hearing. You
would be obsessed with her, and I wish I could
introduce you. Then again, she'd probably fall in
love with you and want to live at your home instead,
so maybe it's good we're not speaking? I don't
know, I try to find the upsides of this situation
wherever I can.

[Message unsent/deleted]

DECEMBER 2020
One Year Later

FROM: AngusStoatTheThird@gmail.com
TO: NatalieShapiro5@gmail.com
SUBJECT: Some News

Hello,

Long time no talk. I hope you've been staying safe and healthy in these trying times. On our end, I hate to be the bearer of bad news, but Gabby has gotten a scary health diagnosis. The doctors think it's uterine cancer, and she will have to undergo major surgery in the next few weeks so they can go in and see just how bad the situation is. (Rob's going to come help out with Christina since it turns out it's especially difficult to do this when we're still in the midst of a pandemic and can't get reliable childcare.) Gabby has been in shock since finding out, or I'm sure she would have called you. Well, maybe that's not true. She's a stubborn woman, my lovely wife. But, pardon my French, I think it's stupid (sorry!) that you two aren't talking, especially now, so I wanted to let you know about this so you'd give her a call.

Best,
Angus

30

★☆☆☆☆

Rob had never babysat before. His part-time jobs as a teen had involved shelving dusty books in campus libraries or otherwise building his academic résumé. Somehow his teaching skills from the university did not translate particularly well to keeping three-year-olds entertained, as evidenced by the fact that Christina was currently running around the living room of Angus and Gabby's house screaming.

But Rob was trying new things nowadays. He had started eating breakfast instead of just drinking two cups of coffee. Perhaps more importantly, he'd given Arizona his notice in the beginning of 2020, telling his bosses that he'd finish out the semester, but then he'd be leaving academia. He didn't have another job lined up. How reckless, how unlike him. In his evenings, when he otherwise might have been watching a documentary with Zuri or working on new research to win himself tenure, he spent hours on job websites, trying to figure out what the rest of his life might look like, applying for positions whose descriptions gave his heart a little pulse of excitement. He imagined himself doing good at a nonprofit or teaching high school or, in a more fanciful moment, being a lumberjack. (He'd read a study that lumberjacks reported very high levels of job satisfaction.)

Of course the onset of the pandemic had thrown a wrench into everything. Rob had moved home to live with his parents then. Nothing made a person feel like they were succeeding at life like moving back into one's childhood bedroom at age thirty-two. He was able to help his mother with his dad's care, though, and that was important. Sometimes his father remembered that Rob had left academia and seemed to be okay with it. Other times, he'd ask how the tenure process was going, and Rob would have to remind him, then endure a lecture about how he was making a huge mistake. His father could still be as unforgiving as ever. But Rob was learning how to forgive him for it.

And over the summer, after rejection upon rejection, an offer had finally come through from a start-up working on increasing literacy in children. Turned out that Rob's linguistics background was helpful. He'd never thought of himself as a start-up guy. (He'd been surrounded by them when he was doing his PhD in the Bay Area, and they wore too many hoodies for his taste.) But the job had given him enough disposable income to, with proper notice to his mother, move into a studio apartment in New York. More than that, it gave him a sense of purpose. Kids were falling behind in their reading now more than ever, and Rob was at least trying to do something about it.

Speaking of, maybe he could use this time to teach Christina how to read early. When this period of intense stress and uncertainty was over, when Gabby was healthy again, Rob would sit Christina down in front of her parents and hand her a chapter book, and she'd pull a Matilda, flawlessly intoning the words. And then Gabby and Angus would think, *Well, this was an awful*

*time in our lives, but look what good came out of it! We are the
parents of a child reading prodigy!*

So, as Christina ran in circles around the living room, Rob
pulled Angus's well-worn copy of *Dune* from the nearby book-
shelf. "Excuse me, Christina?" he asked, opening the book up to
the first page. She paused momentarily, looking at him. "Should
we try to sound out some words?"

Slowly, as though Rob might be tricking her, Christina lum-
bered over. She took the book from his outstretched hand. "All
right," he began. "Now——"

"No, thank you!" she yelped in a bloodcurdling tone. She
threw the book on the ground and jumped on it, then fell off-
balance onto her bottom. She let out a wail, then pushed herself
back to her feet and began to run around again. Her emotions
passed as easily and clearly over her face as Angus's did, but she
had Gabby's steely determination.

On second thought, perhaps it would be enough to keep
Christina fed and alive. It would be enough for everyone to stay
alive, more than enough.

Christina headed for the stairs. Gabby had given Rob a long
lecture about how Christina still needed stair supervision, so he
pushed himself after her, right as the doorbell rang.

"Christina, can you stop?"

"No!"

Rob groaned, then picked her up, and she squirmed against
this unjust restriction on her freedom. As she pounded her fists
on his back, Rob carried her to the front door and looked through
the peephole. His heart suddenly skipping out a strange rhythm,
he unlocked the door and swung it open to reveal Natalie on the
front step, a rolling suitcase beside her.

"Hello," he said, hesitant.

"Hi," she croaked. She had driven across the country after isolating since they'd all agreed that the last thing Gabby needed right now was to get COVID on top of everything else. Nearly three thousand miles later, she was disheveled, her sweatpants and shirt rumpled, purple bags under her eyes, like she'd been sleeping in her car to be extra safe. Was that . . . yes, Cheeto dust on her chin. And still, Rob couldn't take his eyes off her.

"You have something there," he said, pointing at the orange powder.

She narrowed her eyes in confusion. "What?" She swiped at her cheek, missing the dust completely.

"No, it's . . . here." He reached out and slowly brushed it from her chin, their eyes locked on each other's, neither speaking. She did not breathe until he dropped his hand. Rob hadn't previously realized that Cheeto dust could be erotic. He had spent the last year of his life trying to figure out what he actually wanted instead of what he'd been told to want. And right now, despite all the circumstances, despite how badly things had gone the last time they'd seen each other, his body hummed with a certainty that he wanted Natalie.

But Natalie pulled her gaze away and focused on Christina.

"Christina! Do you remember me?" Natalie held her arms out, and Rob handed a curious Christina over.

The toddler pulled at Natalie's greasy hair as Natalie hugged her tight. Then she twisted her face away. "Yuck," Christina said.

Natalie burst out laughing. "I think she can tell that I need a shower." The laugh died quickly in her throat, as if she'd remembered her reason for being here all at once. And Rob remembered it too, with an extra rush of guilt over his erotic Cheeto dust thought.

"Yes, come in," Rob said. "Gabby and Angus should be home from their appointment any minute."

"Thank you." Her voice had gone formal. Did she still blame him for his mistake with Tyler, still want nothing to do with him? Angus had told Rob that Gabby and Nat hadn't spoken for nearly a year. All those wasted months that, now, could be some of the last that vibrant, busy, full-of-life Gabby would have.

The surgery itself was scary enough, carrying with it a not-insignificant risk of things going wrong on the operating table. Rob had done thorough research on the process and learned that the doctors had to do something called "debulking," where they removed the parts of the body that had been affected. The whole thing just sounded so unnatural that Rob was surprised the body could withstand it. But the more worrisome part was what the doctors would find when they went in. Testing had been inconclusive. There was a cancerous mass, but no one knew how far it had spread. The doctors might be able to get most of it out and then pursue a course of treatment, and slowly but surely, Gabby would get better. But the scenario keeping Rob up at night was equally likely, if not more—the doctors might find the cancer everywhere, woven inextricably into Gabby's organs, and then there would be nothing to do but wait.

"The last time we saw each other . . ." Rob began.

She didn't look directly into his eyes as she said, "The important thing is that we're here now." Then her glance skittered back to him. "Oh, but wait, how is your dad?"

"He's up and down. We're figuring it out. Thank you for asking."

"Of course." She lifted her hand as if to touch his arm, then pulled it back to her side. They lapsed into silence.

And then a key jangled in the lock of the front door, and

Natalie swept around. Angus opened the door, on the phone with work, attempting to deal with another emergency. They'd agreed to give him a week off but kept calling him anyway and keeping him on the line while he was trying to do other things. Right now, that other thing was holding the door open for Gabby, who was coming in heavily beside him. Gabby had been moving heavily since Rob had gotten here yesterday, though Angus had said it was due less to physical issues (she was having some pain, yes, but it was nothing compared to what recovery would look like) and more the dread of the upcoming surgery.

"Oh," Natalie said in a strangled voice, and Gabby looked up.

"Oh," she said back, her own voice going high.

Natalie ran across the entryway and threw her arms around Gabby as gently as one could do such a thing. Gabby wrapped her arms around Natalie right back, and they stood there breathing each other in, Natalie sniffling, until Gabby said, "I'm sorry, but you smell awful."

Natalie stroked Gabby's hair. "I know. Are you okay to deal with it for a few moments longer? I don't want to let you go yet."

"I'll breathe through my mouth," Gabby said.

31

★☆☆☆☆

Finally clean, no longer smelling like an unholy combination of her car, sweat, and drive-through cheeseburgers, Natalie changed into fresh clothes in the small back bedroom that Gabby and Angus clearly intended to use as a nursery at some point. The walls were painted pale blue, and in the corner sat Natalie's bed for the next week or so, a—what else?—futon topped with decorative pillows. Natalie dropped on it and attempted to breathe through the knot of anxiety in her throat. It was useless. She hadn't been able to take a full, deep breath since she'd gotten Angus's email.

It seemed unreal that she was here after almost a year of no contact with Gabby. She kept thinking, in the early days of the pandemic, that one of them would break the silence to check in. But the longer Gabby went without reaching out, the more Natalie felt that *she* couldn't either, and their estrangement grew more and more solid, a tray of ice hardening in the freezer. She coped with her loneliness by taking long walks with her neighbor friends in the Los Angeles sunshine or talking out loud to her cat, Dolly (whom she'd left temporarily in Tyler's care). Now, it didn't feel right to say that she was grateful to be sitting on a futon in

Gabby's home, because the reason for it was so utterly fucked. But, God, it had been good to hold her best friend again.

Her fingers had been trembling so badly after getting Angus's email that while trying to call Gabby, she'd nearly dropped her phone.

"I'm so sorry and I love you so much," Natalie had blurted the moment that Gabby answered.

"Natalie?" Gabby had said, sounding slightly confused.

"Angus told me about the surgery."

Gabby had sighed. "That sneaky bastard."

"He is a sneaky bastard and thank God for it."

"I love you too. I should have called you right away," Gabby said. "I just . . . the last time I saw you, I said awful things about how we shouldn't be in each other's lives. And then I was going to reverse course the moment I needed help? I didn't want to make myself your problem—"

"You're not making yourself my problem. My problem would be sitting here in blissful ignorance while you were going through something hard."

"Yeah," Gabby said quietly. "It is hard." She let out a rueful laugh. Natalie could imagine her shaking her head on the other end of the line. "I'd thought I was pregnant again. I was feeling a similar way, tired and achy, and we'd been trying. So, for a little while, I was *happy*. Walking around with a stupid grin on my face, thinking that something good might be growing inside of me instead of this."

"Oh, Gabs. It must have been so disorienting. How's your family doing?"

"Terrible. My parents offered to come help out, but I think they'd just create more stress. Every time I talk to my mom on the phone, she weeps and then goes through a list of everyone at her church who is praying for me. It's so well-intentioned but also emotionally exhausting, you know? And Melinda . . . well, she has basically fallen off the face of the earth. When I told her the news, she said she was sorry and then spent the rest of the call asking for advertising advice on how to grow her business. Like she figured she'd better get it all out of me now just in case. So, not exactly a pillar of strength. I thought a sister's job was to drive you crazy but to show up when shit hits the fan."

"I'll show up," Natalie said.

"Thank you."

"I mean it, literally. I want to come help."

"But you're all the way across the country."

"Well thankfully it's the twenty-first century, and we have transportation options beyond horse and buggy."

"What about the show? Don't you have a writers' room?"

"We're doing it over Zoom anyway. And I'll take time off. Someone else can think of scrapes for Dennis to get into." She didn't say that she had a final-round interview to write for a different show that week, a show with much more prestige, that needed someone to join the writers' room ASAP. Hearing Gabby's voice again, that interview didn't seem to matter. "I'll isolate, I'll drive, I'll pee in the woods instead of going into rest stops, whatever you need me to do. But I'm showing up. Screw Melinda. I'm your sister-friend."

"Sister-friend?" Gabby asked, amusement creeping into her voice. "Does that have anything to do with sister-wives?"

"Yes, surprise, I'm also marrying Angus."

"After everything, I cannot imagine a universe in which that would happen."

"What I mean is that you and I, we're more than friends. So what if we go a long time without talking, or if sometimes we hate each other? I'll be here for you when it counts, just like I know you would be for me."

Gabby was silent for a moment before she said quietly, "Even when I thought I was pregnant, I wasn't one hundred percent happy because I couldn't tell you. I think that's why I didn't take a test right away. Because the last time I took a test, we were together, and . . . well, you know."

"I do."

"I love you, Natalie."

"I love you too. I'll see you soon."

Now Natalie could hear someone moving around in the room next to hers. Rob, staying on the other side of a thin wall.

As soon as she'd seen his face again, framed in the doorway, a host of complicated feelings had risen up in her. Anger at him, still, for making the mistake that had denied her Gabby all these months. But anger at herself as well for reacting the way she had, plus an inconvenient lingering desire to push herself up against his chest. It all made for an incredibly awkward soup of emotions. The best course of action was not to look too hard at him, not to stand too close. Because the last thing Gabby needed right now was a bunch of extra stress and angst flying around her house. And Natalie couldn't exactly handle extra angst either. Already, her feelings threatened to spill over and drown her each time Gabby's prognosis entered her mind.

Three days from now, her best friend would be on the operating table. Whenever Natalie thought about that, the ground grew slippery beneath her feet, the world playing by all sorts of new rules that didn't make sense.

"Knock knock," Angus said, poking his head through the crack in the door. "Is now a good time for me to help you set up the futon?"

"Oh." Natalie jumped to her feet. "Sure, thank you."

He came into the room, smiling awkwardly. Her betrayal of him sat between them. "Hey, I've been thinking, and in case I haven't said this enough, I'm sorry again," she began, her voice faint. "About Dennis."

"I did finally read the book. It was, uh, pretty brutal."

"I know. It was more about me dealing with my own fear and resentment at the time than anything about you."

"But you weren't wrong about me entirely." Angus shrugged. "I've always worried, a little bit, that I wasn't good enough for Gabby."

Natalie searched for any sense of vindication but couldn't find it. Instead, her heart cracked. "Please, don't say that."

"I know it's silly. But if I'm just a guy who fails upward, who gets things handed to him, when she's so amazing and works so hard—"

"Stop that. Look at this life you've built together. Look at the child you made. Gabby loves you so much. And if you don't believe me, ask Rob! You should know that he was such a fierce defender of you. He hated me for what I wrote."

"He's a good person to have in your life," Angus said, and for a moment, he seemed like he was going to say more. But then his phone dinged in his pocket. He took it out, eyeing it with a furrowed expression, then quickly typed out a text back and put the phone down on a shelf by the door. "Sorry, work stuff. Let's get you settled."

Letting out a grunt, he sank to his knees and crawled beneath the futon. By the sound of it, he was unhooking and unsnapping various straps. "Wow," Nat said. "This is some advanced futon technology."

"Don't even get me started," Angus said. He paused for a

moment, another strap pinging, then went on in a rush, "My father's number two ordered a bunch of these for the store because they were the latest model and, well, they are just the biggest pain in the butt to set up."

"Yikes."

"Don't worry, it's very comfortable for sleeping, I give you my word on that. But you've got to think about the big picture when you're deciding what to sell, you know? What good is a comfy futon if the average furniture owner can't get it open? Anyways, I decided to take one off their hands since I don't mind doing this stuff personally, but—"

Over on the shelf, his phone began to ring. Angus's feet, sticking out from the edge of the futon, wriggled. "Mind checking that to make sure it's not the doctor?"

Natalie looked at the screen. "It just says, 'Lord of Darkness.'"

"My boss. You can ignore."

"Okay," Nat said. "Can I help with this? I'm supposed to create less work for you, not more."

"No, no, I enjoy it. It's like meditation."

The phone began to trill again. "Lord of Darkness really wants to get a hold of you," Nat said.

Angus sighed. "Can you put it on speaker? I can't stop this in the middle, or the whole thing will collapse, which Trent should have looked into before ordering so many of these." He caught himself. "Not to be mean to Trent. He's trying."

Natalie did as requested. "Hello?" Angus called, his voice slightly muffled.

"Angus? I need your thoughts on the Quartz investment." Just from the sound of his boss's voice, Natalie would bet anything that the man had spent far too much money on hair plugs.

"Right," Angus called. "I can email them over tonight. But as I've said, I'm mostly out of the office for a little while."

"What is it again? Family?"

"Yes, my wife is having surgery."

"Oh, of course, that's right. Take all the time you need."

"Thank you—"

"But you will be back in by Wednesday, yes? Because we'll have a big client coming in, and we could really use you."

At this, Angus wriggled partway out from underneath the futon, frustration all over his face. He took a deep breath, then said, "Well, my wife will only be two days out of surgery then, best-case scenario, so I was hoping to stay home with her. And you know I don't feel comfortable coming into the office when she's so vulnerable, healthwise, but I can hop on Zoom—"

"That's going to be difficult. Why don't you just come in, and you don't have to go to the luncheon afterward. Face time is important if you're hoping for that promotion we discussed."

Natalie waved to catch Angus's attention, then mouthed, "Rob and I can handle it."

Angus shook his head, his jaw set, his curls wild around his head, a smudge of dust on his cheek. "But I want to be here," he whispered.

"Sorry, Stoat, what was that?" his boss asked.

Still looking at Natalie, Angus asked, under his breath, "What am I trying to prove?"

Natalie shrugged her shoulders, gave her head the smallest shake. And from his undignified position on the floor, Angus glanced at the phone for a moment as if mystified. Then he blinked, his expression clearing. "I quit."

"Excuse me, what?" his boss began.

Angus hauled himself to his feet with a grunt. "I said I quit."

"Very funny, Stoat. Don't be unreasonable—"

"I can't keep working for a place that doesn't respect my family. Goodbye." Angus gestured to Natalie to hang up the phone and, her mouth hanging open, she did, plunging the room into sudden silence. This was a noble gesture, quitting for Gabby. But impulsive too, a far more serious version of the wedding zip line. What about their health insurance in the midst of this emergency? And how was Angus supposed to job hunt while caring for Gabby? And—

Angus caught Natalie's eye and shrugged as if he'd read her mind. "Don't worry, we're all on Gabby's health insurance plan. She's raised the idea of me quitting before. And I want to run my dad's futon store anyway. Trent is a disaster." Then he turned and gave the futon a firm tug, and it flopped itself open into her bed.

Nat stepped forward and hugged him. This bumbling boy, now a man she trusted to take care of someone as precious as Gabby. This whole time, almost ten years now, he'd never wavered in the way he'd loved and treated her. She'd been so skeptical that Angus deserved Gabby. Now she realized not only that he did, but that Gabby deserved him too. *God*, Natalie thought, *may we all be so lucky as to have an Angus Stoat the Third.*

"I really misjudged you," she said into his shoulder.

"Well"—Angus extricated himself; his face had turned pink—"people often do."

32

★☆☆☆☆

Sometime over the last two days, Christina had decided that she liked Rob well enough to stop running away from him. Instead, she led him by the hand around the house to show him where she'd hidden away her various treasures. In the basement behind the TV, a pile of rocks. "Wow," Rob said, as she carefully handed them to him one by one. In her bedroom under a teddy bear, a sparkly barrette, which she demanded Rob fasten in her hair. And in the living room, she pulled a piece of paper from under a couch cushion to show him the stickers she'd put on it.

"Beautiful," Rob said, then looked closer at the paper. To-Do Before Surgery, it read at the top, followed by a long list of items. The handwriting was far too neat for Angus. "Let's go show this to your mom."

Slowly, he and Christina walked up the stairs. (Sometimes she liked to walk up a few steps, sit, and scoot back down on her bottom, then do it again. It was cute, if inefficient.) At long last, they made it to the door of the primary bedroom. Rob knocked.

"Come in," Gabby called. She sat on the bed, efficiently packing herself a hospital bag, forehead furrowed in concentration.

"I think Christina may have something that belongs to you." Rob held up the list.

Gabby let out a sigh. "I wondered where that had gone. Was starting to feel like I was losing my mind." She held out her hands for Christina, who ran over. Gabby lifted her daughter onto her lap and kissed her cheek. "You little stinker."

Christina wriggled away and climbed over to Gabby's jewelry box, lifting the lid to make it tinkle a merry tune, humming along.

Rob handed the list over to Gabby. "I tried not to read it, but I did see the title. And if you have a long to-do list, I can take some of it on."

"Oh." She stared at the sheet of paper, the corners of her mouth turning down. "Thank you. But this is more . . ." Gabby looked over to Christina. She was playing around in the jewelry box, lost to the world. "Most of this is the stuff I want to do with Christina just in case I . . ."

"You're not going to," Rob said.

"You never know these things." She stood up briskly and began to rifle through her closet. "I'm just trying to be practical here. Besides, if the doctors find it everywhere, who knows what my remaining time will look like? I'll be trying to recover from major surgery and maybe doing treatments, and everything will be a mess, so I wanted to do as much of this as I could now." She folded a sweater into neat fourths and placed it in her hospital bag.

This was the most personal conversation Rob and Gabby had ever had, just the two of them. Whenever they'd been left alone over the years, they were polite and fond for three to five minutes, and then Angus would return from the bathroom, or one of them would make an excuse. Now it would be easy enough for Rob to nod, take Christina out of the room, and let Gabby get back to her tasks. But instead, he asked, "So, what's on the list?"

Gabby looked up from her packing in surprise. Then, after a moment, she picked the list up and studied it. "Well, I did manage to get some of this done before Christina spirited it away. 'Write letters to loved ones.' Check. 'Make my mom's special soup together.' My mom always made it for us when we were growing up, whenever we needed to feel better. Christina and I did it the other day, but of course she won't remember it, so I taught the special tricks to Angus too, so he can teach her again when she's older." She smiled. "He was good at it, actually. What he might lack in natural cooking ability, he makes up for in effort."

"Nobody can fault Angus for not trying," Rob said.

"At least if I . . . Christina will have a father who tries." Gabby's gaze grew faraway. "Natalie's that way too. She doesn't always get it right at first, but she doesn't give up." She cleared her throat. "So I feel lucky, despite everything. Because that's a good kind of person to have in your life, and Christina will have both of them."

"She'll have me too," Rob said.

"Thank you," Gabby said, touching him briefly on the arm. "I really, really appreciate that."

"And she's going to keep having you."

"Well," Gabby said, "I hope so." She shook her head and looked back at the list. "I got a little overambitious here. 'Take her to see *The Nutcracker* at the New York City Ballet.' Nope, not in the year of our Lord 2020."

"My mother took me to that once."

"Didn't you just love it?"

"I thought it was . . . fine."

Gabby's mouth opened in outrage. "You are wrong. It's perfect. We went every year when Melinda and I were little, up until Melinda decided we had outgrown it. You know, we'd take the train into the city, make a day of it. It was like magic. I thought it would be nice to watch Christina experience the wonder of it all." Her eyes had grown wistful, almost glassy. To Rob's knowledge, she hadn't cried since he'd arrived. Angus, meanwhile, kept coming out of the pantry swallowing sniffles, honking his nose into a tissue. This was the closest Rob had seen to Gabby letting go of her control.

Then she snapped out of it. "But the show's not even happening this year. They're streaming it, but that's not quite the same, and besides, it doesn't start until after the surgery. Oh well." She put the list down and began to bustle around again, her face betraying nothing, the conversation clearly over. "Thank you for returning this to me."

Later that night, after they'd all distractedly shoved some takeout down their throats and gone their separate ways, Gabby putting Christina to bed and then going to sleep early herself, Rob stood up straight outside Natalie's door. His thoughts had been pinging, insistently, over the past few hours. They all had one more day here together before Gabby went into surgery. He paced back and forth, anxiety in his chest. "Just do it," he muttered to himself, then returned to the door and knocked quietly.

Natalie opened the door, wearing an oversized T-shirt that skimmed her legs at midthigh, her hair up in a messy bun. Her face turned guarded at the sight of him. "Yes?"

"This is a bit of an odd question," he said. "But how much do you know about *The Nutcracker*?"

33

★☆☆☆☆

n the late afternoon the day before Gabby's surgery, Natalie found her standing in the upstairs hallway staring into space, shoulders creeping up toward her ears. She touched her back lightly, and Gabby jumped.

"Sorry! Didn't mean to give you a heart attack."

"Yeah, am I not already dealing with enough health issues?" Gabby gave a half-hearted smile. "What's up?"

"Have you finished everything you need to do for tomorrow?"

"I think so. I'm packed, I sent all the work and personal emails I had to get out. I want to spend some time with everyone, and then I guess I just . . . wait? Try to sleep?"

"Well, if you want to come downstairs, we have something for you."

Gabby narrowed her eyes suspiciously. "What?"

"You'll see! Come on."

Natalie led Gabby down the steps and into the living room, where Angus was sitting on the couch waiting for them. Gabby's gaze turned to the corner where a Christmas tree now stood. Angus had run out to buy it that morning, and they'd done a speed round of decorating once Gabby had gone upstairs,

Natalie waving Angus and Rob into the living room like she was directing a military raid, the two of them running in, each clutching one end of the fir. They'd haphazardly thrown on as many ornaments as they could in the time they had. It wasn't quite aesthetically pleasing, but it was something.

"Oh, you all got a tree," Gabby said, distracted but trying to be appreciative. "That's very sweet."

"The tree is only part of it," Natalie said. "Sit on the couch, please, and make yourself comfortable for the show."

"Um, okay," Gabby said, and sat next to Angus, who tucked a blanket over them both.

Natalie cleared her throat. "Presenting a one-night-only, not-at-all-official production of . . . *The Nutcracker.*" She hit play on Tchaikovsky's gorgeous, merry soundtrack.

"Oh my God, you did not," Gabby said, her hands flying up to her mouth. "What?"

"Ahem, we ask the audience to be quiet and respectful," Natalie said in a lofty tone, and Gabby made a zipping shut motion with her mouth, the skin around her eyes starting to crinkle.

Last night, when Rob had knocked on her door, he'd explained all about Gabby's to-do list. "It sounds like she's done most of the stuff on it," he said, shy, his hands fiddling with the empty air at his sides. "Taught Christina how to make soup. Wrote letters to her loved ones."

"Oh," Natalie had said, "that explains the matching envelopes I saw on Christina's and Angus's dressers."

Rob's eyes flitted to the top of Natalie's dresser—empty—and then he quickly went on, "But she can't bring Christina to *The Nutcracker.* So I wondered if there was any way we could bring *The Nutcracker* to her."

"I haven't seen it in forever," Natalie said. "I'm not sure if I even remember what it's about." She turned away from him and walked deeper into her room.

"Right," he said, nodding. "Probably a silly idea. I'll let you get some rest—"

"Come on," she said. Having Rob in her room was messy and confusing, but they were doing this for Gabby.

"What?"

"Let's see if . . ." She sat on her futon bed and typed a search term into YouTube. "Okay, I found at least part of an old recording."

Tentatively, he sat down a few inches away from her. His body seemed to radiate heat, or maybe there was some other reason she felt warm.

"Ready?" she asked, trying not to look directly at him, and he nodded, so she pressed play.

An hour and a half later, they'd made it all the way through, charmed by this blurry bootleg, smiles on both of their faces. Natalie put on her creative writing hat, ready to problem-solve. "Okay, obviously we're not ballet dancers. Unless you have a secret talent?"

"Certainly not ballet."

"But we could still tell the story. It'll be corny, but Gabby likes corn. And they have a shitload of Christmas decorations in the closet. I mean, you remember that housewarming party."

He looked at her then, his gaze steady and intense. "I do, very well."

They'd somehow scooted closer during the video, their bare knees nearly touching, the space between them buzzing. Almost as close as they'd been in his car a year ago before they'd both blown everything up.

Natalie sprang to her feet. "All right then. So we're doing this.

The big question is do we have one of us play Clara? You want to pretend to be an excited little girl?"

"I think we've got the perfect casting right under our noses," Rob said.

They discussed their plan, hashing out a rough script, Natalie typing it up on her computer. She would have expected that collaborating with Rob would mostly involve fighting against his rigid opinions, his eviscerations of her ideas. But there was none of that. He listened and built on her suggestions. In another world where he hadn't gone into academia, he could have made a good editor. By the time Natalie typed, "The end," it was one a.m., and they were both fighting yawns. For a moment, she thought Rob might fall asleep right there on her futon bed, and she pictured letting herself curl up next to him. Though she hadn't gotten a good night of sleep since learning of Gabby's diagnosis, maybe tonight could be different. But Rob roused himself and power walked to her door. "Well. Thank you," he said, before disappearing into the hall. She lay awake for the next two hours, tossing and turning.

Now, with Gabby and Angus waiting on the couch, Natalie cleared her throat. "Our story begins with a little girl named Clara, the night before Christmas."

The door to the coat closet swung open, and Rob ushered out Christina, dressed up in a pink, poofy dress. (There had been many *Nutcracker*-esque costume options in Christina's closet— Gabby's style for her daughter was plenty girly.) Christina wore an expression of delighted mischief, thrilled to be the center of attention.

Gabby drew a sharp intake of breath at the sight of her daughter, and Christina looked over to her. As Gabby gave an encouraging nod, Christina twirled around. "Look at my costume," she said.

"It's beautiful," Gabby said, her voice catching.

"Clara was so excited for Christmas and loved to look at the tree," Natalie said, pointing Christina in the right direction, and Christina went and stood by the Christmas tree as they'd practiced earlier. "And their family had lots of guests come over to celebrate."

Rob swung open the coat closet door again and came marching out wearing one of Angus's ill-fitting work blazers, only the slightest hint of self-consciousness on his face. He went over to Christina and swept into a deep bow, holding out his hand. Laughing, she placed her hand in his, and he swung her around the room. Never in a million years would someone mistake him for a professional dancer, Natalie thought, covering her smile, but he threw himself into the task at hand. He had a look of concentration on his face, even as a lock of his hair fell forward into his eye, and something in Nat's chest swelled at the sight of him. He'd be a good father, she thought suddenly, if he ever wanted that for himself. And then for the briefest, strangest moment, an image flashed into her mind of the two of them taking a child to a pumpkin patch. *What the hell?* The last time Natalie had done anything remotely autumnal, it had involved going to a pop-up "pumpkin patch experience" in LA with some friends from the show. They'd spent the whole time directing her to take photos of them holding up various gourds in a carefree way.

Rob looked over at her and raised an eyebrow. Right, because she had another line to deliver. She blurted, "And then the creepy toymaker slash magician slash random old man who was somehow friends with Clara's family had a special gift to give her."

"Herr Drosselmeyer is not creepy," Gabby said. "He's her god-father!"

Natalie shot her a look.

"Okay, he's a little creepy," Gabby admitted.

Rob reached into the pocket of his jacket and pulled out a small toy nutcracker, because of course Gabby and Angus had a toy nutcracker among their pile of Christmas decorations.

"Clara was so happy with her gift, she just had to dance," Natalie said, jumping and doing a little twirl as she indicated Christina should follow, and Christina began to hop in a kind of mad glee, clutching the toy so hard Natalie thought she might break it. On the couch, Gabby watched her daughter, rapt, as Angus sat next to her, holding her hand, looking back and forth between his two girls. From the expression on Gabby's face, the New York City Ballet had nothing on this thrown-together pan-tomime. And they hadn't even gotten to the good stuff yet.

"And then it was time for the guests to go, and Clara fell asleep," Natalie said.

Christina hesitated, putting her fingers in her mouth.

"Right over here by the Christmas tree, she fell asleep," Rob said, pointing to a cushion on the floor, trying to get her to move.

Christina stood stock-still, working something out in her mind. "I want to watch *Blippi*," she said.

"Honey," Angus said. "Let's do this fun performance first!"

Christina began to toddle over toward the basement, where Gabby and Angus kept their biggest TV. Angus jumped off the couch and made to go scoop her up, but she swatted him away. "*Blippi!*" she wailed.

"But—"

"Now!"

Angus looked at the others helplessly, then back at his daughter, who had taken off in the direction of the steps. "Wait," he yelped. "Okay, maybe just one video, and then we'll come back."

The door slammed behind them, leaving Rob and Natalie standing in front of Gabby, flat-footed. In the silence that followed, the music reached a useless crescendo. Natalie reached over to pause it, cutting off the strings and bells as they blared.

"Sorry," Natalie said. "We practiced a lot more . . ." She trailed off. In the ensuing silence, the faint sounds of some godforsaken children's program rose from the basement.

Gabby folded her hands in her lap and looked down at them. "It's like she doesn't even realize that I might be dying," she said. Then she lifted her head back up and fixed them both with an almost mischievous look. "What a little idiot."

They all began, slowly, to laugh. A laugh that gathered momentum like a train speeding down a hill until they were shaking with it. Natalie had to brace herself on the stair railing. Even Rob was overcome in a way she'd never seen before, and the sight of him doubled up made her laugh even harder.

"We spent hours practicing the rest of it," she wheezed. "Rob even learned a little bit of the choreography. It was going to be very moving."

"No," Rob said. "It's better for everyone that Gabby doesn't have to see that."

"Christina's screwing me out of a chance to watch Rob humiliate himself? That's the real tragedy here!" Gabby managed to force out amid peals of laughter. "I guess we can forgive her since she's only three." And then she froze, like she'd just registered her own words. Almost in slow motion, her face crumpled. "She's only three," she repeated, and began to weep. "I don't want to . . ." But she couldn't get the rest of the sentence out. Her body shook with great, racking sobs.

Natalie and Rob looked at each other. Then, in unison, they ran to the couch, one of them on each side of Gabby. "I know," Natalie said, taking Gabby in her arms, unable to stop her own tears from beginning to fall as her best friend cried into her chest. "I know."

Rob tentatively patted Gabby's shoulder, and she reached out a hand to meet his, pulling him in too, so that the three of them were smushed into a Gabby sandwich on the couch. They stayed like that for a long time, not speaking. As stupid fucking *Blippi* blared in the basement, they held one another tight, facing down a terrifying tomorrow.

34

★☆☆☆☆

That night, Rob lay in bed in the guest room unable to sleep. An hour had passed since he turned off his light, and all he'd been able to do was toss and turn and worry. Just like last night and the night before. With a sigh, he flicked the light back on and attempted to read one of the novels he'd brought. It was too complicated, the author too impressed with his own intellect. Rob let out a groan and tossed it aside.

A knock sounded at his door, quiet enough that he would've missed it if he were asleep. He hesitated, unsure if he'd imagined it, then threw the covers back.

When he opened the door, Natalie was turning away, about to walk back to her own room. She wore that oversized T-shirt again, plus pajama shorts, her face scrubbed clean. "I didn't wake you, did I?" she whispered.

"No, I can't sleep."

"Me neither. Too sad and anxious." She rubbed her eyes, seemed to be summoning her courage. "Look, I wanted to say thank you for having the *Nutcracker* idea. And . . . I know it's not your fault, me and Gabby not talking for so long, despite what I said last year at the party. You're a good person. Really, all the reasons I hated you seem very trivial now, which is obvious and trite to say. But I'm sorry. And I'm glad we're both here for this."

"I'm sorry too. And *you're* a good person."

"I hope so." She gave him a sad smile. "Okay, I'll let you get back to not sleeping." She began to turn away, then paused, one foot extended in the direction of her room.

"Do you want to stay in here?" Rob asked right as Natalie turned around and blurted, "Can I stay with you?"

They both let out a breath. "It's hard to be alone right now," she said.

"I know. I feel that way too." He indicated the room. "Come in."

Tentatively, she walked over to his bed. How much distraction was she looking for? He had wanted her for a long time. But a weight lay on his chest tonight.

"Maybe we could just hold each other," she said, slipping beneath the covers.

"That sounds like exactly what I need right now."

She gave him a grateful smile. As he began to climb into bed next to her, she turned over, looking at his bedside table. "How is that book?"

"Incredibly pretentious. Why did I think that now was the time for a five-hundred-page experimental novel?"

"I know what you mean," she said. "I brought *Anna Karenina*. It's very good, but I am not in the mood to read eight hundred pages about the struggles of nineteenth-century landowners."

"You don't think it's worth hanging in there for the upbeat ending about how being an independent-thinking woman is so hard, she might as well throw herself in front of a train?"

"Fair point, maybe I should stick it out." She rubbed her eyes. "No, I just need something comforting and warm."

"I'm not a book, but I can try to be those things," he said, and she managed a laugh.

"I hope that wasn't a pickup line, because it was very lame. But, yes, please, let's just . . ." She scooted closer to him. He wondered if she could feel his heart beating as she pressed her back into his chest. Slowly, he reached his hand up and stroked the soft waves of her hair. She let out a sigh, then lifted his arm and wrapped it around her.

"You know when you're in that horrible limbo of being so tired and yet unable to fall asleep?" she asked.

"Oh, that's been me the past few nights. Too many anxious thoughts."

"Same. I keep wondering if there's something more we can do or trying to bargain with a God I don't necessarily believe in." She laughed softly. "And then around two a.m., I move over to the truly ridiculous thoughts, like being jealous of a three-year-old that she got one of Gabby's letters to the people she loves most when I didn't."

"From Gabby's to-do list, you mean?"

"Yup."

"That is a bit ridiculous," he said gently, and she laughed, giving his arm an almost playful hit.

"I know. I'm telling you, I'm going loopy. I'm not upset in the light of day. Obviously, a daughter and a husband are on a different level than a best female friend. And I'm just grateful to be here. If Gabby always matters a little more to me than I do to her, I'm okay with that."

He tightened his arms around her. "You and I both, we're maybe more devoted to our best friends than the average person. Do you know what I mean?"

"I do," she said.

"I wouldn't change it. Even if, in moments like this, loving people that deeply can break your fucking heart."

"Yeah," she said, her voice quiet, moving her hand up and down his forearm in a gentle, soothing rhythm.

They nestled in, their breath starting to sync, their chests rising and falling in tandem. As her eyes closed and she seemed to teeter on the edge of sleep, he wondered how much time had passed. For a moment he felt both that she'd been in his arms forever and not nearly long enough. And then, somehow, he fell into a grateful, dreamless sleep himself.

35

★☆☆☆☆

They woke in the gray early-morning light to say goodbye. As Angus loaded up the car, Natalie gripped Gabby's trembling arms. She imagined that, with every press of her fingers, she was sending bits of her own strength and health into her friend, then wanted to cry because she knew it didn't work that way. "You're going to be okay," she said, wishing she could make herself believe it.

Gabby tried to say something, then pressed her lips together as if to stop herself from weeping. Instead, she just nodded, rested her head on Nat's shoulder for a moment, and walked out the door.

After their car disappeared down the street, Natalie realized that she'd buttoned her shirt all wrong, one button off.

A layer of dread clung to the surfaces around them like dust, stirred up into the air whenever they moved. Natalie's anxiety was a hand clamped around her throat. She managed to put it somewhat to the side when Christina was awake, since Christina ran around with her usual energy and there was no choice but to follow her lead. Rob and Natalie played with her, their ears alert to any dings from their phones that might change the course of their futures.

Natalie almost wanted to laugh, remembering her twenty-something self relentlessly checking her email in hopes of a book deal. She'd thought waiting for that news was the most agonizing form of torture. What a lucky, naive girl she'd been.

Each time a text came in, Nat and Rob pulled their phones out with fumbling fingers. But it never told them what they wanted to know. It was always only Angus with the update that they were waiting to go into surgery, Angus checking in to say that the doctors had wheeled Gabby in and put her under, Angus letting them know that he didn't know anything at all.

When bedtime came, Natalie and Rob both tucked Christina in, and Rob sat by her side, reading Christina multiple stories with all the patience in the world. He tried to do character voices, though he wasn't very good at it, which was charming in its own way—a bunny speaking in a dry tone, a dump truck speaking in the same dry tone, just louder. Thank God he was here, a sturdy, steady anchor despite the anxiety that must be thrumming in him too.

"Another story," Christina said, then frowned at Natalie. "Just Rob stays."

Natalie raised her eyebrows at Rob, and he shrugged. "I see who wins the popularity contest here," she said.

"Can't help it that I'm immensely and universally likable," he replied, and she actually managed the ghost of a laugh.

"I'll leave you to it." She slipped downstairs and stood in the kitchen, useless, unmoored.

Maybe she could tidy something to keep her hands busy. She turned around all the spices in the spice cabinet so that they were facing the exact same way, then went into the front hallway. The day's mail had spilled onto the carpet from where the mailman had pushed it through the slot, and Natalie bent down to pick it up, sorting it into a neat pile to place on a nearby table. Mostly catalogs and junk.

But her hands stilled as she registered a small envelope, one that looked like it had been through the wringer, marked RETURN TO SENDER. An envelope with her name on it, in Gabby's neat handwriting, along with an outdated LA address, the place she'd been living the last time she and Gabby had been on speaking terms.

Shaking, she slid the seal open, pulled out a letter, and began to read.

Dear Natalie,

I have cancer. I'm going to work up the courage to tell you before this letter makes its way to you, so I don't need to go into details here. But I scheduled my surgery and mangled an entire box of tissues, and now I'm sitting in my bedroom writing letters to the people who are most important to me. Despite everything that's happened between us recently, that list could never be complete without you.

I keep thinking about something you said during our fight—that you never mattered to me as much as I mattered to you. I hate that I made you feel that way. Please don't think that you were someone with whom I was just killing time while I waited for "my person" to come along. You are my person too.

Sometimes I think about the alternate universe in which I met Angus later, and you and I had more time to live together in that crappy apartment. (I can say that now that we've both moved out of it, right? That place was a hellhole. And yet I remember it with immense love because you were there.) I'm very happy with my life. Well, except for the cancer of it all. But there would have been so much joy in that alternate universe too. So many more long talks about everything and nothing that went deep into the night, without either one of us having to worry about catching the subway home. So much more laughing until our stomachs hurt and exploring the city and trying new things, figuring out who we were together. I wish that, somehow, I could have had that and everything I have now (again, except for the cancer) or that ours was a world where it was normal to live in a commune with all the people you wanted to see every day.

I know that commune living probably isn't for us. But if I make it through this, I hope that we can be in each other's lives again in a more honest way than we've been in the past few years. I don't want to keep shying away from difficult topics because they make us uncomfortable or because talking about them might be unpleasant. Our relationship is about so much more than pleasantness. Things will never be the same as they were when we were twenty-three. But maybe, in some ways, they can be better.

And if I don't make it through, I hope that Christina can know you. I don't want to put pressure on anyone or anything. But it would mean a lot to me if she could have a role model like you in her life—a woman who loves deeply and fights for herself, who puts herself out there and holds out for what she deserves. You have more courage in your pinky than most people have in their whole lives.

I love you,
Gabby

When Natalie reached the end of the letter, she went back and read it again, then a third time, tears streaming down her face. At some point, without realizing it, she'd sat down on the couch, her legs giving way beneath her. As she memorized Gabby's words, wanting to tattoo them onto her soul, she startled at a hand on her shoulder.

Rob, looking down at her in concern. "What happened?"

"Gabby wrote me a letter after all," she managed to squeak out. Rob sat down next to her and pulled her into him, and she cried into his chest until she managed to get a hold of herself.

When she finally pulled back, she wiped her eyes and said, "It's been so long since she went in. Shouldn't we have heard something by now? Is the radio silence a good thing or a bad thing?"

"I don't know," Rob said.

"I can't help worrying—" Natalie began, then cut herself off.

"What?" he asked, a wrinkle in his forehead.

Looking at Rob, talking to Rob, felt like standing on the only stable ground in a disintegrating world. "I worry that Gabby and Angus moved so fast, did things so much quicker than the rest of us, because somehow Gabby knew, subconsciously, that she wouldn't get as much time as everyone else."

"I know what you mean," Rob said. He cleared his throat. "Or perhaps they moved fast because Gabby is a goal-oriented person. And if her goal is to beat this cancer, then she's going to send it packing."

"Yeah," Nat said, another tear springing up in the corner of her eye. She knew it didn't work that way, that cancer didn't take only those who weren't willing to fight it. It was an indiscriminate monster. Rob knew that too, but sometimes you had to say things you didn't fully believe. He moved forward and gently brushed her tear away with his thumb.

And then, on the arm of the couch, Natalie's phone began to ring. Angus's picture flashed on her screen. Her stomach dropped. She wasn't sure if she'd be able to move. Because on the other end of that phone call lay a different world, one that potentially included a future without Gabby. And if that was the future Angus was calling to share, she wanted no part of it. She'd rather stay in this moment of agonizing ignorance forever than face a life without her best friend.

Rob squeezed her hand. "Do you want me to answer it?"

"No," Natalie said. "I will." She swiped the phone open and put it on speaker. "Hi, we're here." Her voice sounded faint, but maybe that was because of the roaring in her ears drowning everything else out.

No, not everything else. She could hear Angus on the other end of the line. He was crying. "Oh, guys," he said. "She's . . . she's . . ." Natalie and Rob locked eyes, their expressions hollowing into sorrow. A sob caught in Natalie's throat, her heart beginning to plummet through her chest down into the basement, burrowing into the center of the earth. Rob's hand shot out and found hers, holding on tight.

But Angus was forcing out more words. "She's going . . . they think she's going to be okay."

Natalie blinked, unsure if she was hallucinating. "What?"

"It hadn't spread too much," Angus went on, "so they managed to get it all out. She's resting now."

"I thought . . ." Natalie said, unable to fully believe it. "You were crying so much . . ."

"I'm having a lot of feelings right now," Angus blubbered.

"So, wait," Rob said, his voice so calm it seemed he might be in shock, "everything's okay?"

"Not everything. We'll have to monitor and possibly discuss

treatment, and it could always come back, and they had to take out her uterus. But the doctors told me this was the best case they were hoping for."

"Oh my God," Natalie said, jumping to her feet and pacing, the energy bursting out of her. "Oh my God!" She stared at Rob as tears of relief began to spill from his eyes, the two of them beginning to beam matching unrestrained grins.

"I love you, buddies," Angus said. "I gotta go kiss my wife."

"Go," Rob said.

"We love you too, Angus," Natalie said. "We love you guys so much."

Natalie hung up the phone and dropped it onto the couch, her whole body humming. It was going to be okay, or at least as okay as it could be. Gabby would get better and come home to them all and swing Christina up in her arms and kiss Angus good morning and gossip on the phone with Natalie and so much more. The road ahead wouldn't be easy. But it existed.

Without thinking, she screamed, a guttural sound of relief she didn't even know she was capable of making. On instinct, Rob stepped forward and covered her mouth. "You're going to wake Christina," he said, laughing and crying all at once.

The awareness hit her: without seeming to realize it, Rob had looped his other arm around her back. The two of them were standing an inch away from each other. Their eyes locked as Natalie took a shaky breath in, Rob's warm, strong palm on her lips.

With what seemed like great effort, he started to take his hand away from her mouth. She reached her own hand up and placed it over his, then moved his palm to her cheek. Still, they could not look away from each other.

Over the past few days, her fear had hung over the rest of her emotions like a heavy curtain. But now, relief swept that curtain away, revealing all the longing that had built up behind it. The intensity of it made her knees go weak. Here he was, this infuriating, wonderful man who had been by her side through these terrible days. His eyes were glued to hers, his dark lashes casting shadows on his face. All she had to do was step forward and press her mouth against his.

So she did.

At the touch of her lips, his whole body seemed to loosen. Then he drew her closer to him and kissed her back, hard. She lost herself in the feel of his mouth, of his hands running up and down her back. He let out a groan as she pushed herself into him, and she wished she could play that sound on loop for the rest of her life. (Though it wouldn't be practical for her to go through the rest of her life being as turned on as that groan made her. She'd never get anything useful done again.) He ran a hand under her shirt to cup her breast, and one imperative ran through her mind: she had to touch every part of him. But as she reached to unbutton his shirt, another thought intruded.

"Wait," she said, scrambling backward. "We're not just doing this because we're so relieved about Gabby, right?"

His breathing was ragged. When he spoke, his voice had gone hoarse. "I am very relieved. But I don't know about you . . . I've wanted to do this since the night I met you."

"I have too," she said.

"Good." In a quick motion, he stepped forward and picked her up, as if to carry her over a threshold. She stifled a yelp.

"What are you doing?"

"Taking you upstairs."

Those lean, sneaky muscles of his, stronger than they looked, made her feel weightless as he walked them over to the stairs. Or maybe the reason he could pick her up like she was nothing was that he was running on adrenaline. Nothing got one's strength going like the prospect of finally getting to take someone's clothes off after nearly a decade of waiting. She couldn't stop laughing a giddy laugh, shaking in his arms, and he glanced at her as he took the first step up. "You moving around like that makes this seem dangerous and inefficient."

"I'm sorry. Put me down, and we'll get to a bed much faster."

He smiled at her and placed her on the second step. She started kissing him again right there, then forced herself to pull back, and they raced up the remainder of the staircase. Natalie's room was closer, so they ran in there, breathless. She shut the door, then turned to find him right behind her. He backed her up against the wood, his hands in her hair, and kissed her again, then lifted her shirt over her head, staring at her breasts in the light filtering in from the streetlamp outside with an expression of awe on his face.

"No fair," she said, and he blinked as if coming back from some faraway place.

"What?"

"That you get to see me when I don't get to see you." She unbuttoned his shirt with shaking fingers, easing it off his shoulders, revealing his bare chest. The sight of it made her head spin with desire, but it wasn't enough. She needed more, so she reached out again for his belt buckle, tugging his jeans and boxers down.

"Who's being unfair now?" he asked with an almost competitive glint in his eyes, and reached for the button on her pants. In contrast to her impatience, he moved slowly—How did he have such restraint in a time like this?—his hands skimming her hips, her thighs, as he stripped off all her remaining clothes too.

When they were both completely naked, they stood in silence, trying to catch their breath.

There he was, all of him, the parts she had already known and the parts that people didn't get to see, looking right back at the tender, precious parts of her. She traced the ridges of muscle in his arms, the soft trail of hair on his stomach, everything new and unfamiliar yet also making complete and total sense.

He made a sound as she touched him, a low rumble in the back of his throat. Her blood whooshed in her veins, a whole symphony happening inside her. How was it that she walked through the world every day barely aware of what her body was doing when it was capable of all this feeling?

She was supposed to have a way with words. If he didn't make her feel so giddy and off-balance, she could pen odes to Rob's body, to the electric current running between them. But in this moment, all she could manage to whisper was "Holy shit."

"I know," Rob said, a shaky smile breaking over his face. "How are you even better than I imagined?"

"Oh, you've imagined this?" she asked, raising her eyebrows innocently.

"You know I have," he replied. He backed her against the wall again and kissed the tender skin of her neck. "And I know you have too." Moving to her earlobe, he bit down gently and said, in a low voice that wasn't gentle at all, "So go lie down."

Unsteady with anticipation, she walked to the futon and did as he'd told her. Rob began kissing his way down her stomach. The press of his mouth on her bare skin made her shiver. He studied her as if she was the most fascinating rare text he'd ever seen, then bent his head to the tops of her thighs. "Is this okay?" he asked.

"Yes," she breathed.

"And this?" he asked again, making his way up, his mouth more insistent.

"More than okay. It's perfect."

And then he stopped asking her. But that was fine, because she stopped being able to articulate words anyway.

It took her a while to catch her breath after falling apart. "Robert Kapinsky," she said when she finally managed to speak again, her voice full of wonder, her limbs full of warmth. "How are you so good at that?"

He lifted his head from between her legs, a sheepish grin on his face. "I am in my thirties, so I'd better be by now," he said. "Also, the sounds you were making were not subtle, and I'm a quick study."

She grinned back at him. "Academia, I guess."

He propped himself up on his elbow. "Oh, I didn't tell you. I quit the university."

"You did?" she asked, sitting bolt upright. "I'm so excited for you! How has it been? What are you doing now?"

"I want to tell you the details," he said, his face turning serious. "But first I'd really like to have sex with you."

"Oh, yes," she said, pulling him into her. "Yes, we'll come back to all that."

Afterward, Natalie rested her head on Rob's chest, his heart thumping under her ear. She ran her hand up and down his stomach, tangled her fingers lazily in his chest hair, both of them spent, content. Credit where credit was due, Angus's futon had proved remarkably sturdy. Whenever it had gotten a little awkward, as first times always did, Rob had simply laughed. She'd never seen him laugh so readily, so happily.

And she saw everything, because unlike with other people, she didn't want to look away from him. She refused to close her eyes for one moment despite the rush of feeling overtaking her. His discipline, his rigor, his control, they'd all added up to something richer than she'd had with anyone else. But when she'd made him lose that discipline and control entirely? That had been the best part. What they'd just done together had felt sweet and passionate and more intimate than she'd realized was possible. But that wasn't all, she thought as he kissed her forehead.

It had also felt like a beginning.

36

★☆☆☆☆

abby returned home from the hospital a few days later, dazed and in pain but full of relief. They treated her like a queen, as she deserved. (Well, except Christina, who thought she was a queen herself. She kept insisting that her mother get out of bed to play with her and didn't understand why Gabby wouldn't obey.)

There was so much going on that Rob and Natalie agreed that they wouldn't broadcast the fact that they'd started sleeping together. At least not yet.

After dinner, when Christina had gone to sleep, the four of them would watch a movie in the living room, Angus, Rob, and Natalie piled onto the couch while Gabby stretched out in the recliner beside them. They made their way through old comfort movies and buzzy new ones that had gone straight to streaming because of the pandemic. The night they watched the new movie written by that former teen starlet who had spent so long as a cautionary tale, they all ended up crying, even if it was far from perfect.

As the movies played in the dark, Rob was always hyperaware

of Natalie's body on the couch, inches away from him. Some-times, they'd sit under a blanket, and she'd slowly move her leg over until it pressed against his, and whole plot developments of the movie would pass by without Rob's awareness, because the only thing he could concentrate on was the woman beside him. One night, she brushed her hand against his thigh, moving it slowly higher and higher. He looked over. She regarded the screen as if in deep contemplation, but the corner of her mouth quirked up ever so slightly. He ended up having to go to the bathroom for a moment to cool down, and texted her: You are extremely cruel. Also extremely sexy.

One day, up in his room alone for a moment, he felt an irre-sistible urge to listen to Frank Sinatra. For the entire length of "It Had to Be You," he simply stood next to his bed and nodded along, a silly little grin coming over his face. The moment the song ended, he shut his computer and shook his head, because he was being ridiculous. He should not let himself get carried away, even if he'd never felt this way before.

Each night, after everyone else went to bed, he'd knock on her door or she on his, and they'd try to be as quiet as possible. Rob had never thought of himself as a cuddly person. He was very particular about his sleeping position—flat on his back—and how silent he liked the room to be—as the grave—but he found himself not wanting to let go of Natalie after they were done. He lay awake as she drifted off, listening to the softening of her breath, inhaling the scent of jasmine and sex on her skin, and half the time he ended up falling asleep too before he'd made himself let go of her.

It was all stolen kisses in the pantry and secret glances until one morning, when Rob ran into Angus in the hallway as he was creeping back to his own room.

"Well, well, well, what is happening here?" Angus had said, the biggest grin spreading over his face.

"Erm," Rob said, scratching his chin, unable to keep his cool.

Angus ran forward, grabbed Rob's hands, and jumped up and down. "Finally!"

37

★☆☆☆☆

Natalie and Rob were lying in bed, their legs tangled together, as Rob told Natalie about his new job at the literacy start-up. She propped herself on her elbow and watched him as he grew increasingly animated, describing some of the data they were getting back about their program's usefulness. She bit down on a smile, but not quickly enough.

"What?" he asked, cheeks going a bit pink. "Oh, am I going on too much?"

"No! I just remember when I used to try to get you to tell me about academia, and you were practically monosyllabic."

"I think, to my utter surprise, this is a better direction for me." He ran a finger up and down her arm, and she shivered. "But what about you? When are you going to write another novel?"

She shook her head and flopped back onto the pillow. "Never."

"Don't say that."

"It's true! Why would I want to give the world another chance to break my heart? With *Meant 2B*, I get to be creative without having to bare my soul. Besides, so many people would kill to write for TV. I'm incredibly lucky."

"That's true," he said.

She poked him. "But?"

"I know you've said you don't want to be selfish about your writing. But I just hope you don't go too far in the other direction."

"I'm not! I love collaboration."

"Sure." He rolled over on top of her, bracing his hands on either side of her body so he could look her right in the eyes. "But you also want to make something that's fully yours."

"How do you know that?"

"To write a book that captured her heart on a page, and then captured others' hearts as they read, seemed the most magical thing a person could do," he recited.

"What . . . what did you say?" she asked, her belly fluttering.

He gave her a half smile. "I think you heard me."

"That's a quote from *Apartment 2F.*"

"Is it?" he said mildly. "I just know that it's stuck with me over the years."

"You hated *Apartment 2F.*" She pushed his chest, and he collapsed over her with a laugh, taking her in his arms and rolling over so they lay on their sides, faces turned to each other.

"Sure. But I also thought I'd never read a writer with more promise," he said before leaning in to kiss her.

The next night, Natalie sat beside Gabby's bed, a slim paperback in her hand. She'd started reading to Gabby for half an hour or so each day as Gabby dozed. But today, Gabby was restless, pulling her blanket from side to side. Natalie put the book down just in time to see a tear beginning to trickle down Gabby's cheek.

Nat reached out and wiped it aside, and Gabby met her eyes. "Sorry."

"Don't you dare apologize. What's going on? Just . . . all of it?"

"Yeah." Gabby spoke slowly, her voice dull. "I want to feel better now. I want to be who I was before. Am I going to spend the rest of my life with this anxiety hanging over my head, worried that it'll come back and I won't be so lucky? And it seems silly to even be upset about this, given how well things went, but . . ." Her eyes scrunched up, and she put her hands over them. "I wanted more biological children."

"That's not silly. You're having to reorient, which is really tough."

"It is. Christina would be such a great big sister."

"Would she? Or would she try to murder the baby for taking attention away from her?"

Gabby huffed out a laugh. "Excuse me, that's my daughter you're talking about. But you're right. Still, I want so badly to give her siblings. More of a team to get through life with, you know?"

Natalie nodded.

"Oh," Gabby continued, "speaking of, I didn't tell you. Melinda sent me a gift. I guess she has been thinking about me after all."

"What is it?"

"A piece of jewelry from her line. You know how she makes those pendants and carves the name of your enemy into them?" Gabby paused. "She sent me a pendant engraved with the word 'Cancer.'"

Natalie tried, unsuccessfully, to stifle a laugh. "Just what you need."

"Still, at least she's trying. Anyway, I know there are other ways to have a bigger family. And I guess it could be nice to have another child without feeling so sick that I have to stick my head in a toilet for two months straight."

Natalie reached out for Gabby's hand. "No matter what you decide to do, I'll be here."

"Thank God. Remember how we didn't talk to each other for a year?"

"What the hell were we thinking?"

Gabby shook her head and took a slow breath in and out. "On another note, Angus told me he found Rob coming out of your room yesterday morning." Natalie sputtered, and Gabby gave her a thin smile. "What's going on there? A hookup of convenience or something more?"

Natalie's neck flushed red. "I don't know. It's, um, amazing. But it'll go from convenient to inconvenient real fast once we both go home. And it's not like I'm going to drop everything in my life and move across the country for a man after a week and a half of bliss."

"Bliss?" Gabby asked, raising an eyebrow.

"No, I didn't mean . . . obviously this time period has not been *blissful*—"

"It's fine. I'm happy if something good can come out of all this, especially if it involves you getting your world rocked."

"Look. It's been unreal. But throwing yourself into something so impractical is what you do when you're twenty-three years old, not thirty-two." At twenty-three, your body was resilient and your heart was too. Now, if Natalie slept at the wrong angle, she couldn't move her neck for days. So if she threw everything into taking a shot with Rob and it didn't work out, how the hell was her heart supposed to recover?

"Unless," Gabby said slowly, "after years of dating and experience, you feel in your bones that this one is different."

Natalie swallowed against a lump in her throat.

"But I don't want to pressure you to do anything. I love you and am interested in your life even if you decide to never pursue a romantic relationship again." Gabby's tone was so sincere she had to be teasing a little bit, and Natalie's heart lifted. Because here was a spark of Gabby's old mischief. And a spark meant that things were getting better, starting to heal.

"I would swat you if you weren't recovering from surgery," Natalie said. "Now, shall I keep reading to you?"

"Sorry, this book is not holding my attention. Not its fault. Nothing I'm trying to read has been grabbing me." She flashed Natalie a look, a slyness in her eyes, another spark. "Maybe I should finally finish *Apartment 2F.*"

"Oh Lord, don't," Natalie said. Words came to her mind as if they'd been there for a long time, so she just opened her mouth and said them. "I'll write you something better."

Gabby leaned back into her pillow. "Really?"

No. Even considering trying to write a novel again filled Natalie with anxiety. But Gabby was looking at her with hope. Sincere hope. "Well, maybe."

Maybe she could. Open up a new, terrifyingly blank Word document and write something that tried not to impress people but to comfort them. Not in the mindless comforting way of *Meant 2B*, though, where a viewer never risked *feeling* anything. A story that was honest about life but approached it with warmth and hope instead of a cynical eye. The kind of thing they all wanted to read, needed to read, in such strange and uncertain times. Something to show Gabby that the narrative dominating her life right now didn't have to be her story forever. The impulse solidified in Natalie's mind, sending her imagination racing, her heart thumping with adrenaline.

She could start by writing this one just for Gabby. And if it turned into something more . . . well, she would see what happened.

Dammit, Rob was right. She wasn't done trying after all.

"Not maybe," Natalie said. "Yes."

38

★☆☆☆☆

And then, somehow, it was time to go. She'd been at Gabby's for two weeks, but her mother expected her back in Philly for Christmas, and then she had to return to Los Angeles. She could only trust Tyler to catsit Dolly for so long. Even now, she checked in with him every day to make sure he hadn't accidentally left his door open, allowing Dolly to vanish into the night.

Her car all packed up, she hugged Christina and Angus, then held on to Gabby extra-tight. "We'll see each other soon," Gabby whispered. Then she gave Natalie a little push. "I think someone wants to walk you out to your car."

Rob stood at the door, looking at her as if to memorize every detail. She linked her hand in his, and they stepped into the bracing December air. His palm was the one spot of warmth in the world. He drew her in closer as they approached the car, wrapping his arms around her in the driveway. She didn't want to put an entire country between them. For one wild moment, she thought about saying, *What if I didn't go back to Los Angeles?* or *What if I got my cat and came right back?* But you couldn't put that much pressure on something new and expect it not to break. So instead, she said into his chest, "Thank you for bringing me a lot of happiness during what was otherwise an incredibly stressful time."

He drew back and held her by her shoulders. His forehead was furrowed. "I think we should be in a long-distance relationship."

The serious, no-nonsense way he said it startled a laugh out of her. "You want to be boyfriend and girlfriend all the way across the country, during a pandemic, when traveling is especially tough?"

"Yes."

"After we've only had two weeks together?"

"Well, two weeks. But also, in a way, eight years."

She felt light-headed. His hands still clasped her shoulders, comforting and solid. She blinked and stepped back, trying to gather her thoughts. "We've been in this strange bubble—"

"Yes."

"And who knows how this will translate outside of it—"

"Sure."

"And do you know how difficult and annoying all the logistics would be?"

"I do. On the other hand, we would be idiots not to try."

Her eyes began to sting. She couldn't tell if it was from the cold or from the pain of saying goodbye to him or because his certainty made her whole body fizz. After so many years of them fighting each other, now he was fighting *for* her. She was utterly moved and utterly terrified.

"I didn't realize you'd become such a hopeless romantic."

"And I didn't realize you'd become such a cynical realist."

"Excuse me!" she said, laughing. "I'm not a cynic!"

"Look at the evidence," he said, deadpan. "Here you have your dream man—"

"Dream man, huh?"

"Yes. And you're not going to even see where it goes?" He was still deadpan, teasing, but at his sides, his hands shook a little with nerves. Her heart swelled at the evidence of what this meant to him, the effort it was taking to put himself in this position. Rob had spent so much time afraid of failure, and now here he was, insisting that they try something that could very well be doomed.

"Here's what I've been thinking, as a counterproposal," she said. "No pressure, no labels. We simply call and talk when we want to hear each other's voices. And we'll see where it goes. How about that?"

He stared at her for a moment, his dark eyebrows knitted together. "Fine. Deal."

She held out her hand for a shake. He took it, then pulled her in, startling her into laughter again. "Please stop laughing so I can kiss you."

She cut her laughter off quickly, and he tilted her mouth to his. This kiss was bittersweet. It could very well be their last one. But it could also be the beginning of many more to come.

When he released her, she gasped, having forgotten entirely about the cold while his arms were around her.

"Goodbye," he said, and his own eyes were growing shiny too. She reached out and touched his cheek.

"Goodbye for now."

She got into the car, settling in for a long journey, sneaking glances at Rob in the driveway. He was standing resolute in the cold to wave her off.

At the end of the driveway, as she readied herself to turn onto the road, her phone began to buzz. Rob. She answered on the car's speakers.

"Hi, did I forget something?"

"No," he said. "You said I should call when I wanted to hear your voice. I'm simply doing as directed."

Part Seven

APRIL 2021

Three and a Half Months Later

FROM: AngusTheThird@StoatAndSonsFurniture.com
TO: GabriellaAlvarez88@gmail.com
BCC: NatalieShapiro5@gmail.com, RobertKapinsky
@gmail.com, and many others

Hello all!

It has been a long hard winter (well, really a long hard entire year), but spring has sprung! Gabby has recovered beautifully from her surgery, which is not a surprise because she does all things beautifully. We thank you for all the home-cooked meals, the babysitting offers, and the rides to and from the hospital, and are pleased to say that Gabby's doctors are very hopeful. And I've been learning the ropes at the flagship Stoat and Sons. That's why I'm writing today. Hold on to your hats, but my father and I will be unveiling our first billboard together, and you're invited! We'll gather right near Exit 14 on the Turnpike to watch the unveiling (my picture is going to be ten feet tall! And the doctors said I'd never grow beyond 5′6″), then head over to the store's patio for drinks and food. Perhaps we will even get to hug again! How I've missed hugging. Can't wait to see you there.

39

★☆☆☆☆

We should get to the billboard unveiling," Natalie said. "If we're late, this is not my fault."

"There will be more billboards," Rob said, kissing her neck, a neck he'd seen in Zooms and photos over the past few months, a neck he'd imagined kissing countless times on hours-long phone calls, a neck that smelled like sex, a neck that was even better in person than in his memory of it, much like the rest of the person attached to it. "I have a feeling Angus will have a long, illustrious career in the furniture world."

Natalie cackled as he rolled back on top of her, pinning her to his bed, and for a while they stopped talking entirely as they refamiliarized themselves with each other for the third time that afternoon.

Over the past few months, Rob had tried to convince himself that it was romantic, being so far away from each other. By not being able to touch, they were getting to know each other's minds, like correspondents falling for each other via letters in olden times. But he was a good multitasker, and this visit was proving to him that he was perfectly capable of getting to know both her mind and body simultaneously.

"So, I talked to my agent," Natalie said, when they finally emerged from bed to get a snack from Rob's kitchen. Her hair was mussed, her bare legs sticking out from one of Rob's button-down shirts. "She read the rough draft of the book."

"Yeah?" Rob asked, eating a spoonful of peanut butter.

Natalie had been sending Gabby chapters of her new project, Dickens-style installments, to help keep her entertained through her recovery. After some convincing, she'd agreed to send them to Rob too, telling him to be kind. This new novel was a love story, though not just about romantic love. The chapters he'd read were suffused with warmth and humor, all the best, goofiest, most sincere parts of Natalie on the page. No overt facsimiles of real life, though he flattered himself sometimes that he could see hints of himself in the male lead if he squinted hard.

He'd rate it six stars if he could. Though he was far from impartial at this point.

Gabby and Rob finally had their own text thread now, devoted mostly to talking about the plot developments or lines in Natalie's book that particularly delighted them. And slowly, over the past month or so, Gabby had started sending Rob and Natalie illustrations of her favorite scenes, watercolors of how she imagined the characters. *Fan art*, she called them, *for your eyes only*.

Natalie took a breath. "Iman thinks that, on the strength of the manuscript, plus the TV writing credit of *Meant 2B* and the promise of a blurb from Tyler, she can get me a book deal, and a good one at that."

Rob stepped forward and picked her up. "Hey!"

She squealed and held on to him, then said, "I don't want to get ahead of myself. She could be overconfident."

"She's not. It's incredible."

Natalie blushed as Rob set her back down on the ground. "It got me thinking . . . our writers' room is going back in-person for the show. But I have some savings, and I might want to take a step back. Focus on the novel-writing for a little while. And"— she laced her fingers in his, looking down at their hands, the blush on her cheeks deepening—"I can really do that from anywhere."

"Are you thinking of coming back to NYC?" Rob asked, his heart starting to pound.

"I wouldn't be moving just for you!" she said, her eyes wide. "So I don't want you to feel that pressure! There are lots of other reasons to come back. I still hate driving, plus I want to be closer to Gabby and Angus. I know moving just for you would be ridiculous at this stage—"

"I'm in final-round interviews for a job in LA," Rob said.

Natalie blinked. "What?"

He nodded. "It would involve a pay cut, and the work would be less interesting than what I'm doing now. I don't like LA, and I love my job here." He steeled himself, then looked straight at her. "But I love you more."

"You love me?" Natalie whispered, a radiant grin coming over her face. "Funny, I was just thinking that I love you too."

Warmth flooded his cheeks. He drew her in and kissed her, then pulled back, eyes crinkling from the strength of his smile. "You don't know how hard I had to work not to blurt it out back in Angus and Gabby's driveway. But you were being so cautious—"

"I liked you too much! I had to protect my fragile heart. And, yes, in hindsight, it seems ridiculous—" He pulled her back into him, and they were kissing again, happy and hungry for each other, until she disentangled herself. "Also, obviously you should not take this LA job, and I should move here instead!"

"Yeah, if you're amenable to that, I would probably prefer—"

But he didn't get to finish his sentence before they were touching again. And as he lifted her onto the kitchen counter and she wrapped her legs around him, he decided they could figure out the details later.

EPILOGUE

★★★★★

Y ou're so calm right now. How are you not a ball of stress?"
Gabby asked, as she zipped up Natalie's dress.

"Oh, I had my 'screw it' moment when I woke up this morning with a huge pimple on my face," Natalie said. "Aren't you supposed to be done with acne by your midthirties?"

"Life. You never know what it'll throw at you."

"Zits on your wedding day," Natalie said, beaming.

"Well," Gabby said, stepping back, "concealer is a magical thing. You look beautiful. So let's get you out there."

Natalie took a last peek out the bedroom window, out into the yard of the small upstate farmhouse she and Rob had rented for the weekend. On the lawn, fifty or so guests chatted in their seats, waiting for the main event. Some of them craned their heads to look at Tyler, there with his serious girlfriend (a physicist!), as he talked to Natalie's mom, there alone. She and Greg were trying out a separation, a decision her mother had come to shortly after Natalie and Rob had told her about their engagement. Her mom had seemed lighter since then, hopeful. Natalie's dad, there with his second wife, kept glancing over at Ellen, chatting so easily with a celebrity, but Ellen didn't seem to notice or care.

Perhaps unexpectedly, Natalie's mom and Rob's mom had become extremely good friends, both women moving into new phases in their lives. After talking it all through with Rob, his mother had made the difficult decision to move Rob's father into a care facility, where trained professionals could manage his care while she visited regularly. He'd been having more bad days than good ones recently. But today was one of the beautiful good ones, and he chatted up the nearby guests with gusto. It helped that Rob's half siblings had come too, to watch out for their dad but also to celebrate their little brother.

Natalie smiled down at the assembly, then followed Gabby out into the hallway.

By the front door, Angus stood on tiptoe to straighten Rob's tie, already blubbering happy tears.

"Sorry," Natalie said as she and Gabby began to descend the stairs. "I know we took our time!"

Rob turned, then did a double take, his eyes widening at the sight of her. He looked so handsome in his navy suit that it made her heart ache. An ache at how lucky she was, how much she wished she could go back to Natalie five years ago and whisper to her, *It might not feel like it now, but good things are coming. The best stuff takes time, so keep the faith.*

Rob cleared his throat. "No need to apologize. You are completely worth the wait."

When they'd talked about how they wanted their wedding to go, they realized that they didn't feel particularly wedded (ha!) to tradition. They wanted to keep things small, somewhat casual.

No big wedding parties, just a maid of honor and a best man. No tossing of a bouquet or expensive wedding cakes.

"And I don't think I want my dad to walk me down the aisle," Natalie said, feet in Rob's lap, as they sat on their couch discussing how the ceremony might go.

"Really?"

"Obviously he's invited. But he's barely been around in my life. I'm not going to attain some special sentimental significance having him by my side."

Rob tapped a pen against his lips. "Maybe we walk down together? After all, you're not being presented to me. We're two people entering into this commitment side by side."

Natalie bit her lip, thinking it over.

"Unless you want a moment to shine alone, of course," Rob went on.

"It's not that," Natalie said. "Just that I was kind of hoping you'd make your entrance via zip line?"

So now, here they were, just the two of them and the friends who had made this possible, who had hung on through life's ups and downs, and would be there as the years yet to come unfurled their inevitable surprises, their triumphs and heartaches. Natalie knew enough now to realize that nothing lasted forever—no bliss, but no sadness either. Happiness followed pain and pain followed happiness, and all you could do was hang on and feel every bit of it for as long as this world would let you.

For today, though, everything was all joy. And, looking at her fiancé, she couldn't help feeling that, yes, their relationship would change with time, but she'd never stop knowing how lucky she was. Rob offered Natalie his arm, and she threaded hers through it. Struck by a thought, she laughed.

"What is it?" he asked.

"I just can't believe that I have to walk down the aisle, twice, with a man who gave my book one star on Goodreads."

"I'll have you know that I deleted that rating years ago," Rob said.

"You did? I haven't been on that website in forever. Not even to check the advance reviews for *Friend of the Family*."

"My fiancée. A woman of great restraint."

"Yes, that's what people have always said about me."

"Are you lovebirds ready to stop flirting and start moving?" Gabby asked, and they nodded. So Gabby looked out the door and gave a signal, and the small band they'd hired began to play.

Rob leaned over to Natalie and whispered in her ear, sending a shiver down her spine. "I hope you brought your A game when you were writing your vows. Because I've been practicing."

"Please. I brought my A-*plus* game. Prepare to be blown away." She made her expression innocent, batting her eyes sweetly at him. "But it's not a competition."

"Right," he said with a smirk. "Not a competition."

Angus pulled the door open. The people they loved turned to look as Gabby and Angus began to walk. Nat and Rob smiled at each other. Then, together, they stepped into the sun.

ACKNOWLEDGMENTS

★★★★★

I don't know why it took me so long to write a romantic comedy, given that I've been obsessed with love stories ever since I wore out my VHS of *Beauty and the Beast* as a little girl. (Does *Beauty and the Beast* count as a rom-com, or is there too much Stockholm syndrome for that?)

But I'm extremely grateful to my editor, Jen Monroe, for encouraging me to try something new. Jen, you're a master of both the ego-boosting text and the brilliant, necessary critique, and I feel so lucky to work with you.

Speaking of lucky, I've got a dream agent team at Janklow & Nesbit. Stefanie Lieberman, Molly Steinblatt, and Adam Hobbins are all-stars: creative yet detail oriented, kind yet willing to fight hard for their authors.

The wonderful people at Berkley have taken such good care of me and my books. Undying gratitude goes to my marketing and publicity team—Tara O'Connor, Danielle Keir, Jessica Mangicaro, and Elise Tesco—for helping this book get into the hands of readers; to Emily Osborne and Suzanne Dias for making sure that said book is so freaking PRETTY; to my copyeditor, Will Tyler, and production editor, Liz Gluck, for their eagle eyes; and to Candice Coote, Craig Burke, Claire Zion, Ivan Held, Christine Ball, Jeanne-Marie Hudson, Pat Stango, Kate Whitman, and everyone else at Penguin Random House who has supported my books. Similarly, many thanks to the rest of the Janklow & Nesbit team, Olivia Blaustein and the others at CAA, and Brittani Hilles.

The members of my writing group read this novel right from its very messy beginning, giving me incredible feedback the whole way through. Sash Bischoff, Lovell Holder, Blair Hurley, and Daria Lavelle, I am fascinated by your minds and love reading your words.

While I might understand the struggles of the writing life in great detail, I'm grateful to the experts who talked me through some areas I knew less well. Alexandra Satty's medical advice was invaluable, Sophie Taylor gave me great insight on academia generally, and Toni Cook did a wonderful job spreading the gospel of linguistics (while helping me come up with the perfect title for Rob's dissertation).

For anyone who is trying to plan a wedding without entirely losing it, I recommend reading *A Practical Wedding* by Meg Keene. From her, I took the spirit of the "screw it" advice that Gabby has such trouble following. Credit also goes to Tom Malinowski for inspiring another important part of the wedding section.

I have to thank the members of the book community, without whom I couldn't do what I love. The fellow authors I've gotten to know inspire me endlessly with their talent and their generosity. The passion showed by the booksellers and librarians I've met never ceases to amaze me. Book bloggers and Bookstagrammers: How are you so creative and wonderful? And a special shout-out to BookTok: I made a random video telling an anecdote from my real life, and you all told me that it needed to be a book. Here it is!

Thank you to Sam Fox Krauss for the ginger chews, to Liz Dengel for writing me a beautiful letter about courage, and to Hannah Barudin for the inspiration. And thank you to the female friends I've had for almost two (!) decades (!!), if not more, who helped me be able to write the relationship between Gabby and Natalie. We may move through life at different speeds sometimes, but I hope we always come back to one another.

Speaking of lifelong friends, I want to mention my mother and her best friend, Carol. Years after they met in college, Carol came to stay and help out when my mom needed her most. Thinking about them inspired part six of this novel.

I wish that my mother could be here to read my books and for everything else. But I'm so grateful to the rest of my family for all their support and love   the Hankins and the Creightons, and now the Christies and the Handelsmans too.

Dave, I love talking out every detail of these books with you, even if I won't let you read them until later. I'll never write a romantic lead as good as the real you.

Rosie, you didn't yet exist when I wrote the first words of this book. Now you're snoozing on me as I write the last. All the stars for you, my love.

Laura Hankin is the author of *Happy & You Know It*, *A Special Place for Women*, and *The Daydreams*. Her musical comedy has been featured in publications like the *New York Times* and the *Washington Post*, and she is developing projects for film and TV. She lives in Washington, DC, where she once fell off a treadmill twice in one day.

VISIT LAURA HANKIN ONLINE

LauraHankin.com
 LauraHankin
 LauraHankin
 LauraHankin
 Laura_Hankin

Ready to find
your next great read?

Let us help.

Visit prh.com/nextread